WHAT IF YOU STOOD IN FOR SOMEONE ELSE
IN THE TRIAL OF THE CENTURY?

WHAT IF YOU WERE THE ONLY ONE WHO
KNEW THE TRUTH?

WHAT IF YOU WERE THE . . .

JURY DOUBLE

HIGH PRAISE FOR EDWARD STEWART AND HIS BESTSELLING PREVIOUS NOVELS

MORTAL GRACE

"One of the best serial-killer stories of this year."
—*The Plain Dealer* (Cleveland)

"GRIPPING . . . the suspenseful plot hurtles to its startling and satisfying conclusion."
—*Kirkus Reviews*

"A gritty tale."—*Orlando Sentinel*

"PROVOCATIVE . . . CLEVERLY PLOTTED . . . PSYCHOLOGICALLY COMPLEX."
—*Booklist*

"Absorbing . . . keeps the reader enthralled."
—*Library Journal*

"Stewart grabs the reader and doesn't let go."
—*St. Petersburg Times*

Please turn the page for more extraordinary acclaim. . . .

DEADLY RICH

"STUNNING NEW SUSPENSE . . . thoroughly venal, frightening, and then some."
—New York *Daily News*

"A compulsive page-turner . . . keeps the reader gasping and guessing."
—*The Flint Journal* (Mich.)

"AN ELECTRIFYING SERIAL-KILLER THRILLER . . . RIVETING ENTERTAINMENT."
—*San Antonio Express-News*

"TASTY, GOSSIPY, SUSPENSEFUL!"
—*Publishers Weekly*

"A roller-coaster ride of adventure and excitement."
—*The Chattanooga Times*

PRIVILEGED LIVES

"READABLE AND PROVOCATIVE . . . the place names, familiar events and hints of real people . . . give Edward Stewart's [*Privileged Lives*] an immediacy that is irresistible."

—*The New York Times Book Review*

"AN EDGE-OF-THE-CHAIR THRILLER."

—*Cincinnati Enquirer*

"A shocking, compelling slice of decadent late-20th-century life . . . a satisfying, intricate web . . . the reader . . . is hooked."

—*The Plain Dealer* (Cleveland)

"COMPELLING!"

—*US Magazine*

"GLAMOROUS, GLITZY FARE."

—*Kirkus Reviews*

"I couldn't put it down!"

—*The Houston Chronicle*

Also by Edward Stewart

ORPHEUS ON TOP
HEADS
ROCK RUDE
THEY'VE SHOT THE PRESIDENT'S DAUGHTER
LAUNCH!
THE GREAT LOS ANGELES FIRE
BALLERINA
FOR RICHER, FOR POORER
ARIANA
PRIVILEGED LIVES
DEADLY RICH
MORTAL GRACE

EDWARD STEWART

JURY DOUBLE

ISLAND BOOKS
Published by
Dell Publishing
a division of
Bantam Doubleday Dell Publishing Group, Inc.
1540 Broadway
New York, New York 10036

ISBN: 0-440-22278-8

Printed in the United States of America

Published simultaneously in Canada

January 1997

10 9 8 7 6 5 4
OPM

For Lois Wallace,
because once in thirty-two years isn't enough

ONE

Five years ago
April 15, tax day

"We're into countdown, boys and girls." Walter Egan, a red-faced man with curly brown hair and an oddly sweet voice, slapped three white plastic belts down onto the kitchen table. Scottie Egan, the greatest five-year-old who ever tumbled out of a crab-apple tree and laughed at his skinned shins, made a face. "Why are they so lumpy?"

Walter patted the boy's copper-blond head. "Because they won't work without the lumps."

Marla Egan lifted up Scottie's blue-striped polo shirt. "Now just hold still a minute, Mr. Flibbertigibbet." She placed the smallest belt around his little tummy and fastened the Velcro-tipped ends together.

"Ouch!" he groaned. "Too tight!"

"It has to be tight, honey, or it won't stay up." Marla picked up the middle-size belt. "Look the other way, guys."

Walter faced the wall. His heart gave a jump when he saw that the hands on the kitchen clock were tiptoeing around to 8:30.

Marla unzipped her skirt and fastened the belt around her waist. Scottie jammed two fingers into his mouth and let out an ear-fracturing wolf whistle.

Marla turned around with that I'm-going-to-be-mad-at-somebody face, and Scottie put on his nobody-here-but-us-mice look, eyes all sky-blue innocence, staring up at the ceiling.

"And Daddy gets the biggest." Walter opened his shirt and slipped the third belt around his stomach. "Anything showing?"

Marla examined him. Boss shirt, Calvin Klein necktie, hair slicked down from the shower—he looked good, he smelled good. "You look great, hon. What about me?" She held her hands out in a fashion-model pose and slowly twirled. She had a body to stop time and not even a floppy cardigan could hide it.

"Perfect."

Marla smiled, but the smile died when she saw the kitchen clock. "Oh, my. Twenty-seven to nine. Shake the lead out, fellas, or we're going to be late!"

Scottie took a leap over the kitchen chair, startling the dog, and the kitchen was full of running and laughing and barking. Any other day Walter would have told Scottie to cut it out, but today was special; ordinary rules didn't apply. He felt his hip pocket for the small white plastic box that had come with the belts in the Fellowship carton. He snapped the box open to check that the four AA batteries were aligned correctly, positive to negative. Everything looked copacetic. "We're all set, boys and girls."

Marla checked details. Window curtains were closed.

Formica tabletop was wiped clean. Dishwasher was clackety-clacking. After she was gone, she didn't want anyone saying she'd been a poor housekeeper.

Walter saw tears beginning. "Come on, hon." He gave her a cheer-up squeeze and steered her toward the back door. Scottie and Robespierre ran ahead, shrieking and yapping.

Wham. The screen door banged open. Walter Egan stuck his head out into the morning. The day had a brand-new smell. Sunlight rocked the trees and the houses like the oompah of a brass band.

The Egan family piled into the Ford pickup.

"Robespierre stays behind," Walter commanded. "Today's a people day. Dogs aren't included."

"Shoot." Scottie tipped Robespierre over the window and the dog landed light on his front paws and scampered across the lawn.

Walter drove down to the center of town, savoring the rush-hour traffic and the tangerine haze that hung over the streets like a sweet pout of Mother Nature. Scottie kept tugging under his shirt.

"Don't pull at it," Walter warned. "It won't work right if you keep fiddling with it."

"It itches," Scottie whined.

"Now, just sit straight," Marla said, "and think about something that *doesn't* itch."

Walter pulled up at the garage entrance of the White Plains Post Office Building. People called it the P.O. Building, but it also housed the offices of twelve separate U.S. government agencies and bureaus. Over four hundred federal employees worked there. Smoky windows climbed twelve stories of shimmering black granite facade.

Walter kissed his wife and son good-bye. He could

feel Marla wanting to cling. She looked into his eyes, but he let her see only calmness behind his sunglasses.

"Are you sure?" she whispered.

He nodded. "See you in seven minutes."

"Seven minutes," Marla echoed.

He tousled Scottie's hair and patted Marla's butt. Those seven minutes were going to be an eternity.

Today, instead of pulling away, Walter sat with the motor idling and watched his wife and son go into the building, Scottie tugging his mom forward, Marla with her diagonally slung little purse bouncing on her hip. You'd never have guessed they were each wearing seven pounds of explosives. They joined the scurrying stream of government employees that crowded through the door.

The metal detectors didn't even notice them. That was the beauty of plastic explosives.

In the fourth-floor day care center for employees' children, a tidal wave of kids was leaping and galloping and shrieking. Marla Egan checked to make sure nothing was showing under Scottie's shirt. "Now, don't touch it," she reminded him.

The teacher came to greet them. "Good morning, Marla—and my oh my, aren't we wearing a handsome shirt today, Scottie. What's the big occasion?"

"I'm going to heaven in seven minutes," Scottie boasted.

The teacher's smile was sly as a jack-o'-lantern. "Well well well."

"Now, Scottie," Marla chided, "don't tell stories." She stopped and brushed the hair out of his eyes and kissed him. "I could murder you! Behave yourself. I love you, honey."

Marla Egan didn't look back. Her eyes were tearing and the hallway became a carousel blur as she hurried to the elevator and pressed 12. The Medicaid office was buzzing with prework chatter. She wasn't in the mood. Not today.

She put on an all-purpose smile and sat down at her console and fired up the computer. She tried to forget the press of the plastic belt around her middle. *There's still time. I could pick up that phone and dial 911 and call the whole thing off.*

But she knew Walter would never forgive her. God would never forgive her. Corey Lyle, founder and leader of the Fellowship, would never forgive her. She forced her hands to stay on the keyboard. Her fingers flew. Glowing amber symbols cascaded across the monitor screen.

Oh, Lord, she prayed, *please don't let my little boy suffer, give the suffering to me!*

A coworker looked over from the neighboring console. "You're going like a house afire, Marla."

"Lots to get done."

"Relax a minute and tell me how your evening went."

"Real nice—Walter and I took Scottie to the Fellowship meeting."

"You sure love those meetings."

"Corey Lyle was there and he personally received Scottie into the Fellowship."

"You folks certainly seem to worship that man."

"Corey Lyle is a saint."

"I hear the government's investigating him. Tax fraud."

"The government burned Joan of Arc."

"The government pays your salary, toots. By the way, I love your cardigan. Is it Penney?"

"What?" Marla tapped a wrong key and had to back up and delete. "Oh, thanks. It's Sears."

Down in the pickup truck, Walter Egan stared at the second hand of his watch as it crawled around toward twelve. On one knee he had placed a Polaroid of Marla and Scottie; on the other knee, the little white plastic box.

He tried to remember what Corey Lyle had said at the Fellowship meeting last night. *Fear is the enemy of perception. When you embark on the last and greatest adventure of your life—keep your senses open!*

His senses were open, and terror was sluicing through them.

Dear Lord, he prayed, *I'm a scared-shitless sinner and I'm never going to get through this without your help.*

At that moment a red-breasted cardinal sailed down from a tree and lighted on the pickup hood. Walter's jaw dropped. He realized that little bird was a sign from the Almighty.

I hope you mean it, Lord, because I'm taking that for a go-ahead.

He raised the Polaroid to his lips and kissed it. He moved the switch on the little white box ninety degrees clockwise, closing the circuit with a faint click.

The second hand of his watch touched twelve.

"Hello, God." Walter Egan pressed the detonator button.

At 9:07 A.M., simultaneous explosions with the combined force of nine hundred tons of TNT ripped through the Medicaid office, the day care center, and the garage of the White Plains Post Office Building. Eighty-nine government employees and children were killed and over two hundred were injured. It was the worst peace-time disaster in the United States in eighty-five years.

TWO

Three years ago
Tuesday after Labor Day

Lieutenant Vincent Cardozo stood in the doorway of the Park Avenue bedroom, seeing the crime scene with his own eyes before technicians and photographers could stomp all over it.

The dead woman lay on the canopied bed beneath a comforter, her head propped on two pillows. Her skin was yellow. Her gray hair fanned out on the lace-fringed pillowcase. She'd never shown the gray publicly. A third pillow, curiously hollowed, had been placed beside her left arm.

Cardozo stepped across the doorsill into a whispering light that had the texture of fine rain. One foot fell with a click on polished oak parquet. The next fell silently on a deep-blue Persian rug. Slipping his hands into a pair of thin plastic gloves, he stepped around a bentwood rocker with a knitted afghan neatly hung over its back. He stopped three feet from the bed.

The woman's eyes were shut. Her lips were parted, the line of the mouth relaxed, almost smiling. A speck of orange clung to the lower lip.

A half-filled tumbler sat on the nightstand. Cardozo bent and sniffed. Orange-colored, but not orange juice. Carrot. Pungent, sweet, just a shade short of repulsive.

The telephone had been knocked from the tabletop. The receiver lay on the floor, and periodically it gurgled like a strangling duck. Cardozo did not pick it up.

He scanned the room. The walls were painted soft violet, hung with richly framed landscapes and flowers and sunsets. The moss-velvet curtains were drawn, except for a window overlooking a dark courtyard. Even for four thousand dollars a month maintenance, even if you were a former Secretary of the United States Treasury, you couldn't buy sun in a Manhattan courtyard.

Bottles of perfumes and lotions were neatly organized and displayed on a triptych-mirrored dressing table. A carved standing lamp cast a glowing circle of light on a faceless, curly-topped wig stand. He smiled. *That* was the woman whom newsmen had loved to photograph.

A tiny ormolu clock ticked softly on a small leather-topped desk. Cut flowers drooped from a narrow porcelain vase. An engraved crystal paperweight rested on a stack of unopened mail. A folio-size silk-bound engagement book lay open to the preceding week. The pages were blank.

He turned to the present week. There was only one entry, and it was for today: *Tuesday, September 8. Lunch, 1 P.M.—Jack.*

He searched past and future weeks. All blank.

He glanced up at the sound of a footstep. A very young-looking woman in the uniform of a New York City cop stood in the shadow of the doorway. She had tried to butch up her appearance by cutting her hair short, using no makeup, and clenching her jaw. He recognized Sergeant Britta Bailey from his precinct.

"Lieutenant—this is Jack Briar." Her voice trembled, and Cardozo suspected that this might be her first homicide. "Mr. Briar found the bodies."

A tall, ponytailed man in his thirties held out a hand. The hand was shaking badly and he had swollen, shell-shocked eyes.

"I'm very sorry," Cardozo said.

Jack Briar nodded. "Thank you."

"We'll need a statement. Would you wait for me in the living room?"

Cardozo waited till Briar was gone. "There's another body?"

Officer Britta Bailey nodded. She led him down a carpeted corridor through a high-ceilinged sitting room filled with antique needlepoint furniture and beaded lamps and age-spotted mirrors. With tasseled velvet curtains shutting out the bright September day, it had the clutter of an antique shop. Cardozo had heard rumors that former Treasury Secretary John Briar and his wife had profited from the bailout of a dozen Midwestern savings and loans. The sounds of traffic surging by down on Park Avenue seemed light-years away.

They went down a long hallway, the walls covered with framed photos of John Briar grinning at long-forgotten dignitaries. A uniformed cop stood outside a door. His face looked as though he'd just been force-fed a plateful of rat gizzards. Cardozo felt a trickle of foreboding. He pushed the door open.

He wrinkled his nose. A rancid odor floated in the dank, warm air.

He reached for the wall switch and flicked.

On the oriental carpet by the bed, crumpled between the lion's paw of a black marble table and the silk seat of a toppled lyre-back chair, John Briar lay faceup in a scattering of books and magazines, shattered lamps and feathers. A goose-down pillow had burst and he had pulled it and the bedsheets with him.

His face was the color of yellow chalk. Beneath an unbelted satin robe, his body was appallingly skinny; ribs showed like white welts. His lips and nipples had drained of pigment. Thinning jet-black hair was slicked back from a high, amazed forehead. The roots were silver. A lump of hair-weave had matted halfway up the tangled strands. Mouth and eyes gaped in a scream of silent terror.

Cardozo felt his nerves clench. He wasn't the block of ice he used to be. Reality was landing punches that he'd have blocked five years before.

He took his notebook from his jacket pocket and began jotting.

Sergeant Britta Bailey rapped on the open door. "Lieutenant, the crime scene team is here."

Six dark-suited men and a woman hurried into the room. They snapped open their black carrying cases and went to work, collecting stain samples, dusting for latent fingerprints, searching with infrared light for suspicious fibers and oils and dirt and stains. With their silent purposefulness they reminded Cardozo of starlings gathering in a dead apple tree. Two men from the medical examiner's office dragged a black plastic body bag into the room, straps trailing on the rug.

Cardozo stepped out of their way and crossed to the door. "You said you have a suspect in custody?"

Sergeant Bailey nodded. "If you're a football fan, get ready for a jolt."

She took him down another hallway and through a dining room, where the table was laid for six with linen and silver and china and crystal. Two uniformed officers stepped aside.

"I used to worship this guy," she said. "Seriously."

She pushed open a swinging door. They stepped into a dining room–size kitchen.

A heavyset man sat at the butcher-block table sucking spaghetti from a five-gallon pot. His fork and spoon made hungry scraping sounds on the stainless steel. His dirty blond hair needed a cut badly. He wore a loose khaki shirt, cotton trousers, and Top-Siders. Underneath all that loose cloth a lot of muscle moved and a lot more was held in reserve.

"Hello, Mickey." Cardozo had never met Mickey Williams before, but he knew the face from photos and TV ten years back, when Williams had been a star running back for the Houston Oilers. Cardozo opened his wallet and flashed his ID. "Vince Cardozo, Twenty-second Precinct. I'd like to talk to you."

Williams's eyes came up and swung around, death-trance brown with icy black dots. He grinned. "Have a seat." The voice was soft. A thick hand went out and pushed back a chair.

Cardozo sat. "How long have you been in this apartment, Mickey?"

Williams shifted. "Three, four days."

Cardozo sensed something seriously out of whack. The voice was pitched like a child's. The words were toneless, the affect flat.

"Are you aware that there are two dead people on the premises?"

Williams nodded. "Yes, sir, I'm aware of that. Johnny and Amalia."

"Friends of yours?"

"Good friends. He was."

"How many hours have you known of their deaths?"

"Since they died. I killed them."

Cardozo angled his green Honda Civic into the alley. Britta Bailey held open the passenger door.

Mickey Williams, shading his eyes against the afternoon sun, stumbled into a stack of A-frame crowd-control barriers. His face colored. "Sorry about that." He crouched and began restacking.

Funny guy, Cardozo thought. *Doesn't blink an eye at murdering two defenseless old people but goes to pieces when he makes a mess in an alley.* "Don't worry about it now." He steered Williams up the steps of the century-old East 63rd Street precinct building. One of the green glass globes was busted and the ironwork was rusting and the painted bricks were peeling.

Sergeant Bailey followed, a hand on her holstered service revolver.

The inside of the precinct was every bit as dingy as the exterior. Cardozo waved to the lieutenant working the complaint desk. Cops prided themselves on their cool, but not even ten-year men were immune to celebrity worship, and the lieutenant did a double take at the sight of the Houston Oilers' former star.

"Come on." Cardozo hurried Williams up the steel-banistered staircase. "Before they start asking for your autograph."

"You kidding?" Williams had a wistful, "if only" look. "Nobody remembers me."

"They're going to remember you now."

The marble steps leading to the third floor smelled of

their weekly ammonia bath, but the cracks were grit-caked and filthy. On a bench in the hall a detective was taking a statement from a bag lady with Park Avenue diction.

"What's this city coming to?" she wailed. "Twelve-year-old children carrying automatics on the Lexington Avenue *local*?"

Cardozo nodded. "You're absolutely right, darling." He opened a door and gestured Williams into the detective unit squad room. Mickey Williams's legs and butt so stretched his seersucker trousers that the pocket linings showed as white half-moons.

Cardozo pointed. "You can make yourself comfortable in that little room over there. How do you like your coffee?"

"I dunno. Sugar and cream."

"Optimist." Cardozo threaded his way between old metal desks. An antique coffeemaker sat gurgling on the padlocked cabinet where detectives stored their revolvers. He poured two plastic cups of tarlike liquid, then added to each a plastic spoonful of nondairy creamer and an envelope of sweetener.

It was late in the shift and the squad room was deserted except for Detective Greg Monteleone.

"What's happening?" Cardozo asked.

Monteleone shrugged. "A ten-thirty came in five minutes ago." Ten-thirty was cop-code for reported stickup, and they'd been on the rise throughout the Upper East Side. "A male Caucasian with a box cutter held up a Mr. Softee ice-cream truck on Madison."

"What kind of moron is this town breeding?" Cardozo shook his head. "Criminals used to have brains."

"Hey." Monteleone lowered his voice. "Is that Mickey Williams in your office?"

"Yeah, but keep it under your hat."

"What kind of trouble is he in?"

"The worst." Cardozo crossed to his cubicle and nudged the door shut behind him.

Mickey Williams stood by the window, watching a pigeon pinwheel in the amber light of the alley. "Pigeons are funny creatures. I could watch them all day."

"Parrots are better comedians." Cardozo set the two cups down on the desk. He opened the middle drawer of his file cabinet, found the camcorder, and checked to make sure it was loaded and working. "You're not camera-shy, are you, Mickey?"

"Hell no, nothing bothers me."

"Unless you've got guts of steel, that coffee might."

Mickey sipped. "I've been served worse in the White House."

Cardozo angled the desk lamp. "Why don't you sit right there in that chair." He placed the camcorder on the desk and sighted Williams through the viewfinder. "Is it Mickey or Michael?"

"It's always been Mickey."

Cardozo pressed *record* and enunciated into the microphone. "Mickey Williams, interviewed by Lieutenant Vincent Cardozo, four forty-five P.M., September eighth." He clicked on the power in his desktop computer, a Model-T Macintosh that you couldn't have sold for scrap. "Mickey, before we review the events that happened this weekend, do you want to have a lawyer present?"

"Is that required?"

"No, but you're entitled to one."

Mickey shrugged. "Why bother?"

Cardozo had an itching sense that this was all falling into his lap a little too easily: the killer waits at the crime scene to give himself up; comes voluntarily to the precinct; gives up the right to a lawyer as though he were saying "no thanks" to a second helping of french fries.

"Would you do me a favor? Speak slowly and clearly."

Mickey obliged. It was almost a verbatim repeat of the statement he'd given at the crime scene, only this time every monotone syllable was on tape. He described murdering two defenseless senior citizens with all the emotion of a weatherman reading the forecast off a TelePrompTer.

When he'd finished, he shifted back in his seat, sighing as though it had been a long, tiring day. The chair beneath him creaked ominously but held. "How'd I do?"

"Just fine."

There was a knock at the door.

"Come in," Cardozo shouted.

Detective Ellie Siegel, dark-haired and brown-eyed, stepped into the cubicle. A cool, fresh breeze seemed to pass through the room.

"Would either of you guys like some apricot juice?" She held a thermos and two paper cups. Over the past several years she had insinuated herself into the position of chief nudge in Cardozo's life. Since he was a widower, she made it a point to worry about his nutrition, and she was always offering to share homemade yogurts and juices. Cardozo found her mothering sort of sweet—so long as there were no witnesses.

"It'll zing your blood sugar," she said.

"Sure." Mickey Williams stretched out a hand.

"I'll pass," Cardozo said. "Ellie, Mickey Williams. Mickey, Detective Siegel."

Mickey Williams raised his eyes shyly. Liquid, dark brown eyes floated in a suddenly sheepish face.

Ellie leaned over the computer keyboard, cleared Cardozo's file, and entered the code for the FBI's national crime stats. She angled the monitor away from Mickey, but he was sipping juice and watching his pigeon and he didn't seem to notice.

The computer bubbled and hiccuped, and in a moment the twenty-year criminal record of Williams, Michael Armitage, Jr., glowed from the screen.

Cardozo scanned eight charges of sexual misconduct, mostly with young girls; two confinements to prison, and one to a mental hospital. The rape and attempted mutilation of a twelve-year-old Korean orphan had resulted in a judge's paroling Mickey to a "fellowship community" directed by a man named Corey Lyle. There were several drunk-driving charges.

Cardozo frowned. "Mickey, would you excuse us just a moment?"

"Sure thing."

Cardozo cleared the screen and motioned Ellie into the squad room. He closed the door. "Corey Lyle—that's the cult leader who supposedly ordered the White Plains bombing because Internal Revenue was harassing him?"

She nodded. "And the government's been trying to indict him for seven years."

He took a small morocco-leather address book from an evidence bag in his jacket. "I found this in Amalia Briar's bedroom." He turned to the page where the name *Corey L.* and a phone number had been block-printed and underlined.

"Be careful, Vince. This case could turn out to be a carton of firecrackers."

Cardozo's phone rang. "Cardozo."

"Vince? Dan."

He recognized the easygoing baritone of Manhattan's deputy assistant chief medical examiner.

"I've completed the preliminary examination on the Briars. Something surprising turned up and I'd rather not discuss it over the phone."

"John and Amalia Briar both suffocated." Standing at the sink in his office two stories below East 30th Street, Dan Hippolito quartered four apples with a pair of autopsy scissors and fed them down the screaming chute of a Juicematic machine. "Luckily for us, their two pillows had begun to leak goose down." He tipped the juice into two coffee mugs. His jogging shoes padded across the concrete floor and he set a mug on the table beside Cardozo's elbow.

Cardozo scowled. "What's this?"

"It's good for you."

"When did you join the health fascists? Ellie's on my case all the time."

"Ellie's a smart girl. Drink it while it's potent. Exposed to light, Vitamin C has a half-life of eight minutes."

Cardozo lifted his cup of juice and took a testing swallow. It was unbelievably sweet, unbelievably good.

Dan strolled back to his desk. He turned a page of a laser-printed draft report. "There were feather particles on John Briar's face and lips. There were feather particles inside his mouth and esophagus. But there were no feather particles in Amalia Briar's mouth or esophagus. None on her lips or even on her face."

Cardozo studied Dan's brown eyes, large and luminous beneath his receding hairline. "And what does that suggest to you?"

Dan moved his mug in a circular motion, stirring up waves in the apple juice. "Small veins at the back of John Briar's eyes had hemorrhaged—we call them 'petechiae'—they're a pretty reliable sign of forcible asphyxiation."

"What about Amalia's eyes?"

"That's the odd thing. The veins were unruptured."

Cardozo sat forward in his chair. Something had shifted and he wanted to understand it.

"In my opinion," Dan said, "John Briar was murdered and Amalia suffocated on her own phlegm. She died a natural death."

Ellie Siegel turned the final page of the preliminary autopsy report. She exhaled a long, sighing breath.

"Explain it to me," Cardozo said. "Mickey admits committing two murders and one of them's not a murder."

"This is only a preliminary report." Ellie's finger tapped her coffee cup. The clear polished nails caught glints of light from the fluorescent desk lamp. "Dan could have overlooked something."

"No." Cardozo shook his head vehemently. "Not Dan."

Ellie didn't answer. She pushed up from her desk and walked to the squad room window and stared out. Above the western skyline, pink welts stretched across the darkening heavens.

"There are a lot of unanswered questions," Cardozo

said. "Why was Mickey waiting in the apartment? Why didn't he get the hell out of there and save his ass?"

"Maybe he wants to be punished."

"Then why doesn't he show remorse?"

"Some men don't like to show their feelings. You don't."

Cardozo had trained himself to ignore Ellie's jibes. Her aim was laudable: the improvement and sensitizing of Vince Cardozo. But her tactics could be a pain. "How did Mickey get into the apartment? He didn't have a key; the building staff were on strike; the Briars were bedridden. So who let him in? And why the hell did he even *want* to kill John Briar?"

Down on 63rd Street, two ambulances raced by, sirens screeching a fierce duet.

Ellie turned. "It's only been six hours, Vince. Give yourself a break. You may not have all the answers yet, but at least you have the killer."

"Then why's he lying about killing Amalia Briar?"

"Maybe he doesn't know he's lying. Maybe Amalia was already dead when he suffocated her."

Cardozo studied the crime scene photo of Amalia: a dear old grandma who seemed to have dozed off contentedly in bed, smiling as if in recognition of an amusing irony. Mounds of pillows, percale cases. The way to go.

He compared it to the photo of John Briar, sprawled on a green-bordered oriental rug—his silk robe open, exposing malnourished nakedness and an adult diaper. The eyes, gaping in terror and shock, were the horrible detail.

"Even if Amalia *was* dead," he said, "there'd be pressure marks on the face; postmortem bruises; feathers; *something.*"

"At this point, I frankly don't see that you've got a beef." Ellie's gaze rested on Cardozo, thoughtful and quietly concerned. "Maybe Mickey's mistaken about Amalia. Or maybe he's lying. But he's not lying about John Briar."

"I want him to take a lie detector test."

Ellie's eyes were suddenly shrewd and alert. "Be careful, Vince. You don't know who's going to be watching over your shoulder."

Cardozo nodded. "First thing tomorrow, before the polygraph, we'll get Mickey a lawyer from Legal Aid."

THREE

Wednesday after Labor Day
10:30 A.M.

Today was supposed to be Cardozo's RDO, his regular day off, and he'd already wasted an hour of it waiting in a windowless room beneath Criminal Court. It was almost ten-thirty when the Legal Aid lawyer finally showed up. Keys rattled and two figures stood silhouetted in the doorway.

"Vince Cardozo?" The woman held out a hand. "Tess diAngeli." She was short and slender with lively dark eyes. "I'm the assistant D.A. assigned to the case, and I've been hunting all over for you."

"I'm sorry. Didn't they tell you we were here?"

"They said you were in Mr. Williams's cell. We've had a tour of the whole damned jail." She turned to Mickey Williams, hand extended. "Hi. Tess diAngeli."

Mickey Williams, seated at the conference table, looked up from the *New York Post* horoscope. He smiled bashfully. "Are you going to be prosecuting me?"

"At this point it's too early to say. But the court's appointed David Moriarty here to represent you."

Moriarty stepped into the conference room and thunked an overstuffed briefcase onto the table. "Hi there, Mickey." He was a young man with thick eyeglasses and a grating voice. "You're a Texas man, aren't you?"

"Texarkana-born."

"I thought so."

"Vince," Tess diAngeli said. "You don't mind if I call you Vince, do you?"

"Ask Ellie," Cardozo said. "She handles my social life. Detective Siegel, Counselor diAngeli."

Ellie rose from the table. "Good to meet you."

Perplexity clouded diAngeli's face. "I don't recall seeing you on the list of detectives assigned to the case."

"Vince assigned me."

DiAngeli glanced over at Cardozo. She opened a notepad and made a quick notation. "David and I have both read Mr. Williams's statement. I'm satisfied and so's David."

"Is that true, Dave?" Cardozo said. "Are you satisfied?"

David Moriarty flashed a grin that ought to have been taken to the orthodontist twenty years ago. "Absolutely." He pulled a skimpy manila folder from his briefcase. "And if Mickey will just initial each page at the bottom and sign the last one, we're in business."

The lawyer turned the sheets of the transcribed confession, and Mickey bent over the table and signed without bothering to read. Moriarty and diAngeli witnessed his signature.

"Then I have one request," Cardozo said.

Moriarty's eyes shot up. "Which is?"

"I'd like your client to take a lie detector test."

It was Tess diAngeli who broke the silence. "Vince, let's talk." She rapped for the guard to open the door and motioned Cardozo into the dimly lit corridor. "A skillful defense could use a polygraph to get the case thrown out."

"Are you calling your man Moriarty skillful?"

"He crosses his *t*'s, and that's why he was chosen."

"Then why doesn't it trouble him or you that Amalia Briar's autopsy contradicts Mickey's confession? Or am I the only one in this city who'd like to know what really happened in that apartment?"

Anger flashed through diAngeli's eyes. "Look—that autopsy was only a preliminary. And the clock's ticking. If we don't hurry up and get Mickey arraigned, we'll have to release him, and this whole discussion—pleasant as it is—will be water under the bridge."

Cardozo settled himself next to Ellie on a bench in State Criminal Court part 312. A harried-looking judge slapped one manila file shut and opened the next. "Mickey Armitage Williams, Jr.?"

Mickey Williams rose. He struck Cardozo as unusually relaxed for a man facing arraignment on murder charges. Unshaven and smiling, he seemed casual, almost cheerful.

"Mr. Williams, you are charged with two counts of second-degree homicide. How do you plead?"

David Moriarty bounded to his feet. "Your Honor, my client pleads guilty."

A door slammed and a voice shouted, "Just a moment!"

Cardozo turned his head. The benches held the usual midday sprinkling of lawyers, criminals, cops, and reporters. Those who weren't asleep were clearly nodding off. At the rear of the court an elderly man with a wild crown of white hair pushed through the doorway.

A jolt of surprise caught Cardozo. He recognized the face from front pages of supermarket tabloids: Dotson Elihu—antigovernment gadfly and successful defender of murderous billionaires, international terrorists, and homegrown serial killers.

"Attorney Dotson Elihu, Your Honor. Mr. Williams's sister has retained me to represent him."

The judge peered dubiously over half-moon lenses. "Mr. Williams, which of these attorneys is defending you?"

"Your Honor," Moriarty called out, "the court has appointed me to Mr. Williams's defense. At no time has he expressed the slightest dissatisfaction with me."

Elihu threw back his head and burst out laughing, as though he could savor a good legal tall tale as well as the next lawyer. "Mr. Moriarty has done nothing for my client except hold him incommunicado while the state lays the tracks to railroad him. If that sort of malfeasance is advocacy, then someone has rewritten the canons of the New York Bar Association."

The judge's gaze rested patiently on the prisoner. "Mr. Williams, have you chosen *either* of these attorneys to represent you? Or do you wish to do so now?"

"Your Honor." Tess diAngeli rose. "I must protest."

"Save it for trial. This is arraignment. Well, Mr. Williams? The court hasn't got all day."

Mickey Williams blinked painfully, as though embarrassed to be the center of controversy. "Well, Your

Honor, if my little sister really hired the gentleman with gray hair—"

"Indeed she did, Mickey." Elihu waved a piece of paper. "I hold in my hand Rilda-Mae Turnbull's fax retaining me."

Williams shrugged. "Then I guess he's my lawyer."

"My client," Elihu said, "pleads not guilty on all counts."

Tess diAngeli strode angrily to the bench. "Your Honor, in view of Mickey Williams's appalling record of past offenses and the savagery of the Briar murders, we request that he be held without bail pending trial."

"Ms. diAngeli . . . as we are both well aware, criminal court has an overflowing calendar." The judge sat tapping his fingers on the open file. "How much time are we realistically talking—two, three years?"

"I hope not. The state will do all it can to reasonably expedite trial."

Dotson Elihu ambled toward the bench. "Your Honor, since my client has no previous record in New York State, and since the police coerced his so-called confession *in the absence of counsel*—"

"Mr. Elihu," the judge cut in, "none of that's relevant here today."

"Then I ask Your Honor to release Mr. Williams on nominal bail on his own recognizance."

"Your Honor," Tess diAngeli cried, "Mickey Williams's continued freedom constitutes a clear danger to the community."

For a long, deliberating moment, the judge was silent. "The court understands your concern, Ms. diAngeli, but it must balance that concern against the prisoner's rights. We therefore set bail at five hundred thousand dollars."

"Mickey's people are dirt farmers. I don't believe for one minute his sister could afford to hire a big-ticket defender like Elihu." Cardozo thumped his mug on the desktop. Coffee sloshed across a stack of unsolved crime reports awaiting their semiannual update. "So who's paying? Where did Elihu get the money to put up bail?"

"Give the coffee a rest, Vince." Ellie reached down with a Kleenex and daubed the papers dry. "That's your third cup in ten minutes. You should switch to ginseng tea."

Cardozo relied on coffee to stoke his brain. Like all addicts, he didn't want to discuss or defend his habit; and like all addictions, it had begun to deliver diminishing returns. Today his synapses weren't getting the jump start they needed; the chemical switch in his head refused to click. "How the hell does a showboater like Elihu get in on the act?"

The linoleum floor deadened the slow, careful tap-tap of Ellie's heels. "You want an educated guess? Elihu represented Corey Lyle in the White Plains hearings. So the cult hired him to help Mickey."

Cardozo ran it through his mind. "Where do they get their money?"

She shrugged. "Rich supporters."

"I wonder. They've got enough troubles with law enforcement. Why would they go out of their way to identify themselves with a wacko like Mickey? He's a known rapist and child molester, and now he's a killer."

"It could be the cult's loyal to their members."

"There's got to be more to it than that." Outside the shut door of Cardozo's cubicle, the squad room kept up its steady bubbling—footsteps hurrying, voices chattering, cop radios giving off bursts of static. "And I'll be damned if I'm going to sit on my duff and wait for Mickey to rape another little girl."

"What makes you so sure he will?"

"Look at his rap sheet. He's a compulsive sociopath. He can't control his actions and I doubt he even wants to." Cardozo's gaze came up, angry and grim. "If the court's not going to deal with him, then it's up to us."

"Hold on a minute." Misgiving was written in capital letters on Ellie's face. "What are you planning to do?"

"Whatever it takes." Cardozo searched the cluttered desktop and found the transcript of Mickey's confession. He reread it. He reread Dan Hippolito's preliminary autopsy and his own report on yesterday's crime scene. He couldn't get past a nagging sense that the picture was incomplete—some vital element was still missing.

On his computer, he called up Sergeant Britta Bailey's crime-scene report. According to Bailey, a man named Jack Briar came to the precinct at 1:10 P.M. yesterday and reported trouble in his parents' apartment. Bailey then checked with the telephone operator. Learning there was a receiver off the hook, she broke into the Briars' apartment and found John and Amalia's bodies.

That much Cardozo already knew. Now came the part he hadn't known. "Well, how about that?"

Ellie leaned to read over his shoulder. "What have you found?"

"It turns out Jack Briar wasn't the first person to report trouble in the Briar apartment. According to Bailey, a woman named Yolanda Lopez made an identical report three days ago."

The door to the female officers' changing room was partway ajar. Cardozo rapped loudly. "Is Britta in there?"

"Who's asking?"

"Cardozo."

She came to the door tucking her plaid work shirt into faded jeans. "What's this I hear about Mickey Williams making bail?"

"You heard right."

Her eyes brimmed with open disgust. "It makes me sick."

The Muzak was playing "Goody-Goody." Cardozo hated Muzak. He didn't see why a police force that was still 20 percent undermanned was wasting any part of its budget on canned music. "Let's go somewhere we can talk. I'll buy you a cup of coffee."

"Make that a beer and you've got a date."

The waitress leaned into the booth and set down a Heineken and a ginger ale.

"Could I ask you something?" Britta lifted her mug.

Cardozo lifted his and clinked.

"Are you on a diet or in AA or something?"

He smiled. It wasn't the first time a cop had asked him that question. Nowadays, diets and alcohol were two subjects that made a lot of cops insecure. "No, I'm not on a diet and so far I'm not in AA, knock wood."

"So why the ginger ale?"

"With ginger ale there's no collateral damage. Gotta keep the old brain clear."

Britta sighed. "I wish you'd talk to my husband sometime. He's a cop in the twelfth precinct, and lately he could use a little less booze and a little more clarity."

This could have been Britta's roundabout way of saying she trusted Cardozo. His ego enjoyed the stroke, but he knew better than to play marriage therapist or alcohol counselor. "Tell me about Yolanda Lopez," he said.

Britta shrugged. "Came into the precinct Sunday. Dark-haired, petite Latina—barely five feet tall. She was hysterical. She said John Briar and his wife were very sick and needed help."

"What kind of help?"

"I couldn't tell you. Her mouth was going ten miles a minute and half of it was in Spanish. Frankly, she was acting like a crazy."

"Did you check on it?"

"I phoned the Briar apartment and a guy answered and said the Briars were just fine. He also said he didn't know any Yolanda Lopez."

Cardozo ran it through his mind. "Did you get her phone number and address?"

"I always go by the book, Lieutenant."

Cardozo dropped a quarter into the pay phone, dialed the number, and put a finger to his ear to shut out the fifties retro-rock thudding from the jukebox. There were four rings, a click, and then a female voice weirdly stitched together from sound bites: "I'm sorry, but the number you dialed is no longer in service."

The coin clanked into the change-return slot. Cardozo dialed zero and identified himself to the operator. "I need some information." He gave her the number. "When was that line disconnected?"

There was a long, silent wait with ghosts of other

phone calls crowding the circuit. And then another click. A district manager asked if she could help.

Cardozo explained who he was and what he needed to know.

"That number was disconnected two hours ago."

"Why?"

"The subscriber requested it."

As Cardozo hung up, reality seemed to shift. The light in the bar seemed yellower than a moment ago, as though it had to fight its way through darker impurities. Shadows of customers hunched over their drinks seemed to run at a steeper angle and stretch further.

He returned to the booth and counted out five singles from his wallet. Britta looked up at him curiously.

"I have to run," he said. "Catch you later."

FOUR

1:30 P.M.

Yolanda Lopez's address, 828 West End Avenue, turned out to be a melancholy old apartment house with cornices and pilasters and oculus windows peering from the sloping, green-copper mansard roof. Cardozo parked beside a busted hydrant, propped his NYPD placard in the windshield, and crossed to the front entrance.

The door had been tied open with a length of wire, and moving men were carrying furniture out into the street. Cardozo peered at the rank of buzzers and pressed the button for *Lopez, Y.* There was no answering buzz. He pressed the super's button.

At the far end of the poorly lit lobby, a door opened. A woman with a red wig stuck her head out.

Cardozo approached, ID extended in his right hand. "I'm looking for Yolanda Lopez."

Wariness rippled off the woman like heat. "You just missed her. She moved out an hour ago."

"Where'd she move to?"

The woman shrugged. Cardozo was getting an odd vibration from her—an edgy kind of secretiveness.

"Come on," he said. "She must have left a forwarding address."

"Not with me she didn't." The woman's eyes followed a quilted sofa leaving on the shoulders of two sweating men. "But those are her movers. They should know."

Cardozo went out to the moving van. The license plates were from Virginia and the company's name was XYZ. The driver had rolled up the arms of his red Coke Classic muscle T-shirt to display his biceps, and he was using the steering wheel as a serving tray for his baloney sandwich.

"Excuse me." Cardozo showed his shield.

The driver's eyes came around with a bored look. They were gunmetal blue—eyes of an android.

"Where are you taking Yolanda Lopez's furniture?"

The driver shook his head. The movement was slow and boulderlike. "We can't give out client information."

"In that case, could I see your manifest?"

"Can I see your search warrant?"

Okay—it was going to be that kind of conversation. "I don't need a warrant. You're suspected of transporting narcotics."

"I don't care if you suspect plutonium." The driver dredged a wallet out of his hip pocket and flipped open to a Treasury Department ID. "We're Secret Service, Lieutenant. Outside of your jurisdiction."

DiAngeli answered on the second ring. "Tess diAngeli."

"Tess, it's Vince. Something weird's going on. I tried to contact a witness by the name of Yolanda Lopez. She's disconnected her phone. She's given up her apartment, no forwarding address. The Secret Service is moving her furniture and they won't say where."

"That's understandable. She's in the federal witness relocation program."

"Why? Are the Briar murders suddenly a federal offense?"

"The argument could be made. John Briar *was* Secretary of the Treasury."

The moment felt weirdly off-center. "Tess, who's prosecuting this case? You or the feds?"

"We're prosecuting and the feds are helping."

"Helping how?"

"We can't give a frightened witness the kind of protection they can."

"Protection from who? Mickey Williams?"

"It's only a courtesy. She requested it."

"Fine, and meantime, who's protecting the children of New York City? Because according to the record, Mickey's a compulsive sociopath with multiple convictions for preying on little kids."

"Where'd you get that information?"

"The FBI's national crime stats. I don't suppose you ever bother to look at them?"

"Vince, I'm not saying I like the direction this case is taking any more than you do. But with the Corey Lyle connection, federal interest in the killings is a given. We've got to accept it. And if you don't believe me, take another look at those stats. You may be surprised."

The line went dead in his hand, and at first Cardozo thought his phone had died: it was a rickety, early Touch-Tone model that had been discontinued a quarter century ago. And then there was a dial tone and he realized diAngeli had hung up on him. He laid the receiver back in the cradle and called up the national crime stats on his computer.

He cursored quickly to the *W*'s. There were hundreds of Williamses, but today the only violation listed for Mickey Armitage Williams, Jr., was a two-year-old drunk-driving charge.

Cardozo's mouth tasted like a tablespoonful of copper pennies. He cleared the screen and opened the door to the squad room. Detective Greg Monteleone was taking a statement from a woman who'd witnessed a shooting in a shop on Madison.

Cardozo waited till he'd finished.

"Hey, Greg, how would you feel if a murderer and child molester was remanded to the custody of Dotson Elihu?"

"Scared." Greg was wearing snakeskin boots with clicking metal toes that jittered on the linoleum. "For my money, Elihu's an incompetent, foaming-at-the-mouth sixties liberal. He sees government conspiracies as the root of all crime."

"Don't you believe the government ever conspires?"

"This government? They couldn't conspire to deliver a first-class letter."

"But they could screw up the Briar murders," Cardozo said. "Which is why I need your help."

A Chelsea church ran a grade school three blocks from Dotson Elihu's home, and Cardozo had a hunch it was only a matter of days before Elihu's client and houseguest would begin checking out morning recess in the school playground. So weekday mornings at eleven, Detectives Greg Monteleone and Rob MacPherson took turns—scrunched down in the front seat of a blue Toyota—watching Elihu's filigreed granite town house.

It was Tuesday in the second week of the vigil and the crisp air was ringing with children's yells, when Greg Monteleone saw Elihu's oak door swing inward.

Mickey Williams stepped onto the sidewalk and spread his arms like a man embracing the bright blue of a perfect morning. He turned in the direction of the shrieking voices.

Monteleone got out of the car and followed on the opposite sidewalk.

Mickey ambled ten steps past the playground, slowed, and looked furtively backward along the sidewalk.

Monteleone pretended to be unlocking the door of a maroon Camaro with a Jersey license plate.

Mickey strolled back to the playground and stopped at the chain-link fence. He watched the children, his attention taut and stretched and scanning.

After a moment his hand slid to his pocket and sneaked something out. Metal glinted in sunlight.

For one disbelieving instant Greg Monteleone felt he had been dropped headfirst into a vat of ice water. And then Mickey raised the object to his eye, and Monteleone saw it was not a gun, but a camera.

In her eighth-floor office in the state court building on Thomas Street, Tess diAngeli's melancholy dark gaze fixed on each of the photos in turn. They showed Mickey Williams watching children, photographing children, talking to children through the playground fence. She made no physical show of emotion except for the way her mouth tightened.

"Jesus, Vince—these are in broad daylight. Mickey

knows your face. If he recognized you, it could blow the whole case."

"I didn't take them," Cardozo said.

Her eyes registered puzzlement. "Who did?"

"One of my best detectives—Greg Monteleone. I'll introduce you sometime."

"Did he have a court order?"

"Why? He was acting as a private citizen. Same as Mickey."

Tess fixed him with a waxen stare. "The last thing we need now is for Mickey to file a charge of police harassment."

"Harassment? How do you figure that? The stats may have been erased, but Mickey Williams has been convicted of three aggravated assaults against children. And these photos show he's building up to another. He can't be left running loose."

DiAngeli glanced uneasily toward the closed door. Sounds of indistinct voices and footsteps and ringing phones pressed in from the corridor.

"Do you have any idea how long the government's been trying to link Corey Lyle to some kind of indictable felony? He's sent mail bombs, he's trafficked in drugs and porn, he's blown up buildings, he's been responsible for upwards of eighty deaths, and so far no one's even been able to indict him for littering."

"And what does any of that have to do with Mickey Williams?"

"Everything—because we're indicting Mickey Williams and Corey Lyle as coconspirators."

Cardozo's eyebrows shot up. "I hope you're basing that indictment on something more than the name *Corey* and the initial *L* in an address book. Especially when Mickey's already confessed to doing it alone."

DiAngeli gave him a long, silent look. "How much do you know about Corey Lyle?"

"I know what the media tells me."

"It's much more than that, Vince. And much worse. Corey Lyle is a charismatic fanatic with enormous control over his followers. He recruits them from among ex-cons, the mentally ill, the terminally ill, and the filthy rich—and they think he's God's spokesman. They're willing to die for him. Unfortunately, over the years, he's had tax problems and he's come to the notion that the government must be destroyed. By any means possible."

She yanked a drawer open and slammed a manila folder down onto the desktop. It was stamped COREY LYLE—CONFIDENTIAL.

"Remember the post office bombing in White Plains two years ago? Go ahead, look."

Cardozo opened the folder. The photos showed twisted girders and toppled concrete and exploded bodies. His eyes flinched. He wondered what these human beings had done to deserve such deaths. Why had they become punching bags for all the malevolent karma in the universe?

"Okay," he said. "Prosecute Lyle for blowing up eighty-five men, women, and children. And leave him out of the Briar case."

"Don't you think we would if we could? But Corey Lyle's M.O. is to use his followers as human bombs—even the children." She threw another folder down. FINDINGS OF THE WHITE PLAINS SELECT COMMITTEE. CONFIDENTIAL. And another. SENATE WHITE PLAINS HEARINGS: TESTIMONY. "The accomplices die with the victims, and there's never enough evidence to prosecute. Till now."

Cardozo pushed the folders away. "It's a lousy idea. I

don't think I've ever heard a lousier idea. You haven't got the evidence to tie Lyle into the Briar killings. And Mickey could wind up walking."

Tess sat regarding him with quiet, steady eyes. She swiveled to the P.C. Her fingers tapped faintly on the keyboard. A file came up on the monitor. "I see our friend Gregory Emmanuel Monteleone has a little drinking problem."

"He's over that now."

"Does his wife know about his girlfriends?"

Cardozo leapt up. "What the hell are you reading?" He squinted at the screen and recognized an Internal Affairs report from three years ago. "That's privileged. How did you get it?"

Tess's face was suddenly blank, closed like a desk drawer. She lifted the phone and tapped in a number. "Pete Corigliano, please. Tess diAngeli calling."

Corigliano was the new district attorney for Manhattan, and Cardozo had read editorials calling him a one-man Spanish Inquisition when it came to weeding out corruption.

"Pete? Tess. We're in trouble. The Briar case. A cop over in the Twenty-second Precinct has been running unauthorized surveillance on Mickey Williams." Her eyes came around to Cardozo. "His name is—"

Cardozo chopped his hand down against the phone cradle, breaking the connection. "What are you trying to pull?"

Tess smiled and replaced the receiver. "Just trying to save my career—and yours."

"Pick on me if you want to play dirty—but don't use one of my men as a pawn."

"I'd never pick on you, Vince. I've read your record. But if you don't stick to catching the bad guys, and leave the prosecuting to us—your friend Greg will be off the force without a pension. How are his three kids going to feel about that?"

The phone rang. She snatched it up. "Tess diAngeli. Oh, hi, Pete, we got cut off. Look, forget that problem I mentioned. A detective in the twenty-second is taking care of it. Lieutenant Vince Cardozo. A great guy. I'll introduce you sometime."

She hung up and gathered the photos of Mickey at the school playground. "We'll have to burn these. You'd better give me the negatives."

"Tess—this is wrong."

"You're right, Vince—and welcome to the real world."

FIVE

Last year
Monday, September 16
7:15 P.M.

It was a rush job, to score a TV movie, and Anne Bingham had less than a week to finish it. Her fingertips grazed the black and white keys of her synthesizer. Electric leads ran from the keyboard and the VCR to the P.C., waiting for her to tap in instructions.

On the twenty-four-inch TV screen, a beautiful, impossibly well-groomed woman sat in hushed discussion with an impossibly well-groomed, gray-haired man. The actors' pink-and-tan skin tones glowed against gray walls.

Ten seconds of rat-a-tat dialogue established that the woman was a top corporate lawyer; the man was a client who had just walked in off the street. They were already falling in love.

If only life were like that, Anne thought.

She replayed the scene. She listened with her mind,

trying to pick up the hidden vibration. Gone were the days when love at first sight got swooning strings for background music. Her inner ear told her the right accompaniment would be an oboe—moody, faintly Byzantine, plangent, with a puckish sting of klezmer.

The phone rang. "Hello?"

"Something awful has happened." It was her sister, Kyra.

"Sweetie—what on earth's the matter?"

According to family legend, Anne had been born twelve minutes before her sister. Which made Anne the older sister. The take-charge sister. The here-let-me-bandage-your-broken-doll sister. They had identical genes and they'd had identical nurture, and they were identical in every way except outlook, temperament, taste, lifestyle, and just about every other human variable you could name.

"I'm on jury duty," Kyra groaned. She had a gift for overdramatizing.

"Is that all? For a moment I thought someone had died. What trial?"

"Corey Lyle. The cult leader." Stress had pushed Kyra's voice high and tight in her throat. "They say he blew up that post office in White Plains and murdered that ex-secretary of the Treasury."

Anne shuddered. "Horrible business." No more horrible, actually, than half the TV movies she earned her bread and butter scoring. But TV movies at least were make-believe.

"Please please please—I've got to talk to you. But not on the phone. Could you possibly come down and we'll have something to eat, nothing fancy, just some deli from Balducci's?"

Anne surveyed a worktable laden with problems. Cue

sheets of scenes still to be scored. Bills. A dunning demand from the New York City Department of Finance for twenty-six thousand dollars commercial rent tax, payable immediately. She knew the notice was a mistake, another case where some fumbling bureaucrat had asserted control over a perfectly able and customarily well-mannered computer. But it was more money than she had in the bank. It was probably more money than New York City had in the bank.

"Annie," the voice in the receiver begged. "Are you there?"

Anne sighed. "I'm here. It'll have to be late-ish."

"It was the stupidest thing," Kyra Talbot was saying. "They sent me a jury summons a month ago, and I forgot to write in for an exemption. So when I went down last week to get excused—they told me it was too late. And now they want me for the Corey Lyle jury!"

Anne still hadn't the faintest idea how she was expected to help Kyra out of this fix. They were sitting at the circular oak table in Kyra's kitchen, finishing a late, light dinner of cold stuffed veal from Balducci's. They were five: besides Anne and her sister, there was Toby, Kyra's eleven-year-old son; Juliana, her au pair; and Mark Wells—her lawyer.

"That's the trial of the year—most jurors would kill to get on it." Mark jabbed his fork into the last stalk of asparagus on the serving plate. "Anyone else want it?"

The others shook their heads. He lifted the asparagus from fork to fingers and downed it in two hungry chomps.

"I know it's my responsibility as a citizen. But I'm swamped with work." Kyra gathered the plates and took them to the sink. They were hand-painted Provençal birds and flowers, glowing and cheerful. "It's not as though they needed me *personally.* And now is the worst possible time—with Norton Stanley Publications reorganizing, and Toby's c-u-s-t-o-d-y hearing next week. . . ."

"I like it when Toby's dad has c-u-s-t-o-d-y," Juliana said. She spoke with a slight Dutch accent and she was wearing a Diet Slice T-shirt and chartreuse exercise leotards. They did not go well with luminescent cobalt eye shadow. "I've never met him, but in my book he's a good guy—I get two weeks off."

"News flash." Toby scowled with towheaded, prepubescent toughness. He had too many freckles to bring it off. "The kid can spell *custody.*"

"That's it for you, smartass," Kyra said. "Time to go to bed."

"Come on, Mom. It's not even ten-thirty. You're always treating me like a baby. You make me go to bed early and Juliana has to leave me at school and pick me up—the other kids laugh at me! I'm not an eight-year-old!"

"And you're not a twelve-year-old—yet." Juliana took his hand and dragged him toward the door. "Say good night to everyone."

"Good night," he said sulkily. The sound of shuffling and pushing faded down the hallway.

"Is that true?" Mark said. "He still gets dropped off at school and picked up?"

"It's easier than risking a kidnapping." Kyra passed a hand through her hair. She'd done it in a different style today. *My style,* Anne realized. "After all, he's a very rich young man."

"Is that why you're upset about the custody hearing?" Mark said. "You're worried about the trust your mother left him?"

As Anne recollected the terms of her mother's will, Toby's parents shared an income from his trust. The divorce court had decided that when Toby reached his twelfth birthday he would choose which parent he wanted to live with, and that parent—as sole guardian—would have the income.

"He'll be twelve next week," Kyra said.

"What's the problem? You know Toby will choose you."

"Do I?"

Mark stared at her in astonishment. "You don't seriously think he'll choose his father."

"If I'm on a jury and don't show up at the hearing, who knows? Toby may decide to punish me. Or the court may decide I don't care enough to deserve custody. Besides, Toby misses his father. What boy wouldn't? Catch is capable of horrible behavior, but Toby's never seen it—thank God. And when money's at stake, Catch can be charming. Don't forget, I've seen him in action."

"But you haven't seen him in four years. He never shows up at the September custody hearing."

"Believe me, he'll show up this year. And he'll have armloads of presents for Toby—even though he can't afford them."

Mark frowned. "How do you know he can't?"

"He's having money troubles. A client has accused him of embezzling."

"Who told you that?"

"Catch told me—last week."

Mark groaned. "Haven't I told you never to communicate directly with him?"

"He phoned me. He sounded desperate. What could I do, hang up on him? Like it or not, he *is* the father of my son."

"Explain to the judge about the trust and the guardianship. That will get you excused."

"But it's all so technical. I know I'll garble it."

Mark looked at his wine thoughtfully. "Well—maybe I could explain."

"Mark—you've always been wonderful to me. You got me a great divorce and you listen to my complaints and you hardly ever bill me. I feel like a louse asking you to come all the way down to the courthouse just to get me out of a silly jam."

It seemed to Anne that her sister had just maneuvered Mark into pleading her case.

"The courthouse is still on my way," he said. "Some of us still work on Wall Street, remember?"

Anne took a long look at this gentle, friendly man sitting at her twin sister's kitchen table, this man determined to solve the whole world's problems. This man she had once loved. The moment seemed framed in stillness.

"Besides," he said, "I have an ace in the hole. I'm an old friend of your prosecutor. Tess diAngeli and I graduated in the same class at Yale Law. She owes me one."

Anne had a fleeting mental image of two law students grappling under a quilt in a New Haven dormitory. She felt a kick of vestigial jealousy.

Mark pushed up from the table. "See you at nine-thirty in court, okay?"

"Leaving?" Kyra said.

"Big day tomorrow. Thanks for feeding me. Good night, Anne. Good seeing you."

Kyra walked him to the front door.

As Anne sat staring at her almost-empty wineglass, Juliana padded to the sink and rinsed out an empty Häagen-Dazs container.

"Lucky Kyra. She has a lawyer who makes house calls. And in a weird way, he's not bad-looking." Juliana shook the excess water from the cardboard container and placed it upside down on a piece of paper towel. She observed recycling laws and it seemed to Anne she added a few of her own. "Kyra said you and Mark used to be lovers?"

"We were engaged," Anne said quietly.

"What happened?"

"Kyra happened. It wasn't her fault."

"Really? Are they still—?"

"They're just friends now."

"Alone at last!" Kyra floated back into the kitchen.

"Toby wants you to kiss him good night," Juliana said.

"Come on. We'll both kiss him good night." Kyra took Anne's hand and led the way to her bedroom. With its coordinated colors and fabrics, the room looked like a fantasy from a magazine centerfold: king-size canopied bed with carved wooden headboard, heaped with silk pillows; beautiful old peachwood armoire and chest of drawers; walls decorated with signed, antique-framed photos of Kyra caught in intimate yet posed moments with the greats of the decade—the president, Liz Taylor, Mother Teresa.

"Sorry about the mess." Kyra shut the door. "My glorious career."

For three years Kyra had been photography editor at *Savoir,* one of a group of glossy magazines put out by the Norton Stanley Publishing empire. The tables were stacked with Stanley products: sports and celebrity weeklies, show-biz and antique and fashion and cooking monthlies.

Kyra dropped onto the edge of the bed and began crying softly.

Anne felt the first panicky stirrings of responsibility. "Sweetie—what's the matter?"

"I never told you everything about Catch—the way he used to shout and threaten—the brutal things he'd say. . . ."

Anne sat on the bed beside her twin and smoothed the reddish-brown hair away from the trembling forehead. "Now, just take a deep breath and tell Annie all about it."

Kyra sniffled and reached for a Kleenex. "You can't imagine what it was like, living that way."

"It's over, sweetie—why dwell on it?"

"Because he might get custody. I couldn't bear for Toby to go through what I had to."

"That's not going to happen," Anne said softly, firmly, allowing automatic pilot to guide her. She was musing on the combination of annoyance and protectiveness that her sister's problems had inspired in her since childhood; and wondering why protectiveness always won. It was odd, considering that Kyra had had the best life could offer—the storybook career, the storybook marriage, the storybook divorce; the beautiful son, the talented lovers, the famous friends; and money—and all Anne had was a failed marriage, a stalled concert career, and a modest reputation in a more-than-modest field.

"But what if I get stuck on this jury thing tomorrow?

The judge will give Toby to his father and I'll never see him again."

"Come on. You heard Mark. He's going to get you off."

"Oh, Annie—Annie-Pannie—there's a rumor that Nort's going to fold one of the magazines. What if he folds *Savoir*?"

"Now, stop catastrophizing."

"Our ad inches are way down. Newsstand sales have plateaued." Kyra's eyes came up, slow and moist. "Oh, Annie, I'm so scared—I've put three years into this job. I've done everything I could to give Toby a home and send him to a good school."

"You're doing a wonderful job. He's a great kid."

"But now this damned jury thing is going to wreck it all." Kyra's teeth pressed down into her lower lip. "Could you save my life, Annie? And Toby's? Could you please please please take a half hour off and go down to the court and sit in for me?"

"Sit in for you?"

"Pretend to be me. It's only a formality. It'll only take a minute or two."

"How could I do that? It's illegal."

"But Mark's going to get me off, so what difference does it make?" Kyra's eyes beseeched. "Please, Annie—please?"

That tone and that look did it. They always had. Anne felt herself softening like candle wax. "But no one will think I'm you."

Kyra pushed Anne down in front of the dressing table glittering with silver and tortoiseshell. "All you have to do is brush your hair like this. . . ."

Anne looked at their reflections in the mirror. She

saw Kyra—groomed and fashionable even in her distress, silken colors coordinated to bring out her strong points: the hazel-green eyes; the hair with its auburn highlights; the pale, milk-smooth skin with jeweled accents twinkling at her ears and throat.

And then she saw herself—the colorless sister, too practical to bother with froufrou, simple and sensible in a gray blouse and jeans from the Gap and a necklace of amber beads from a vendor on 63rd Street who she'd felt sorry for.

Kyra removed Anne's barrette and jumbled the hair and patted it down loosely. "See?"

Now they looked like an actress playing identical twins in one of Anne's TV movies, a dual high-contrast role. "But what about our clothes?"

"I've taken care of that." A little needlepoint-and-pigskin Vuitton suitcase sat on the easy chair, as though Kyra had been preparing an overnight getaway. "I packed a few of my things." She laid the suitcase on the bed and snapped it open. The sleek, simply cut clothes screamed style and taste and money.

"And a little present." Kyra pulled a Lady Seiko watch out of a pocket in the suitcase lining. "You get to keep it."

"Kyra, I couldn't—"

"And some perfume. Because Mark would know the difference. You don't mind wearing Joy." Kyra spritzed her with the tiny beaded atomizer.

A perfumed dew settled. *Besides scoring, I'm not doing anything tomorrow,* Anne thought. *Nothing that I can't put off a few hours . . . It would be killing two birds with one stone. Kyra pulls out of this tailspin; and Anne gets to be queen for a day.*

"All right," Anne said. "But just for tomorrow."

"Hey," Toby called. "Somebody forgot something."

"His good night kiss." Kyra pulled Anne into Toby's half-darkened bedroom.

Toby sat in bed with a laptop computer, tapping instructions into the keyboard. "Look, Mom, I figured out a way to access the Internet without paying."

"That's not legal," Kyra chided.

"Sure it is. All you do is dial the eight-hundred number of your software provider, enter your user code, and—"

"That's enough net-surfing for today." Kyra set the laptop on the bedside table. "Now say good night to your aunt."

Toby turned and scowled at Anne. "You're not going away, are you?"

The suitcase, she realized. "No such luck. Just borrowing some things from your mom."

"Good. I don't want you to ever go away." He threw his arms around her neck and tugged her into an embrace. She kissed him on the forehead.

"I love you, Aunt Anne."

She winced at the sound of the words *Aunt Anne.* They seemed to put her somewhere between unmarriageable and buried. "I love you, too, Toby. Sleep tight."

"Hey, Mom. It's too dark. Turn the TV on?"

Kyra flicked it on but lowered the sound. "Now get some sleep." Thin lines of light and shadow pulsed across the life-size poster of Joe Montana of the Kansas City Chiefs, which kept guard above the bed.

"Mom?"

"Yes, honey?"

"I wish we were all together again—you and me and Dad."

"I do too. But sometimes things just don't work out the way we'd like them to. Sleep tight."

Kyra walked Anne to the front door.

"Isn't he a little old to be afraid of the dark?" Anne said.

"It's only started lately. His shrink says it's because he's looking for a father figure."

"Is there a connection?"

"Absolutely." Kyra pulled the apartment door open. "This custody hearing has got him as much on edge as it has me."

"It'll work out." Anne kissed her on the cheek. "Good night, sweetie. Thanks for dinner."

"And thanks for saving my life. I mean it."

SIX

Tuesday, September 17
Last day of voir dire
9:20 A.M.

Pickets surged around the 60 Centre Street entrance of New York State Supreme Court, which despite its name was not the highest court in the state system. Voices and placards screamed, *Free Corey Lyle!*

Freedom of religion!

Stop the government-sponsored witchhunt!

Anne threaded her way up the steps, through the mob, past the pillars. The picketers were a satanic, druggy-looking lot. Many of them, male and female alike, had shaved their heads.

As she approached the brass-framed door, a young woman jumped in front of her. "Juror! Juror!" she screamed.

Anne recoiled from eyes of hatred and madness. "You're mistaken—I'm not on any jury."

"Liar! Bitch!" The girl swung her picket.

A tall, dark-haired man stepped forward and caught the blow on his outstretched arm. Seizing the picket, he snapped it in half and flung the pieces to the ground.

"Fascist!" the girl screeched. "Racist!"

The man held the door and shot Anne a grin. "Pretty nerve-racking around here today."

"I'll say. Thanks." Anne stepped into a two-story marble rotunda lined with plaster friezes and carved inscriptions. Scores of people with scores of purposes hurried through. Echoing voices and footsteps rained down from the vaulted ceiling.

She went through the upstretched arms of a metal detector. Her Good Samaritan bypassed the detector and showed the guard his wallet. Anne caught the flash of a detective's gold shield.

"So you're a detective," she said in her most chirping Kyra manner.

He looked at her oddly.

"I'm Kyra Talbot. Good to meet you."

"Lieutenant Vince Cardozo. We've had this conversation before."

"Have we?"

"We met yesterday."

"Of course. I'm sorry, I—"

"Don't worry. Happens to me all the time."

They walked to the elevator. A wave of chattering secretaries swept past. He stepped aside for her to go in first and pushed a button. "You're five, same as me, right?"

She had no idea. "Right."

The door shut and the elevator lifted with a lurch.

"Know what I hate?" he said. "Waiting. I've been

here since nine-thirty yesterday, waiting for the prosecutor, waiting for your jury."

"Sorry about my jury."

"It's not your fault. It's the lawyers."

The elevator stopped. He walked her down the corridor to room 506. "Have a good one," he called.

Cardozo knocked at room 509. The door opened and Tess diAngeli extended a hand in greeting.

"Thanks for coming by. Sorry I couldn't see you yesterday. Excuse this broom closet. We're a little short of space. And time." She motioned to one of the folding metal chairs. "You took notes on the crime scene, right? Will you be testifying from them?"

He sat. "If I need to refresh my recollection."

"Could I see them?"

He reached into his pocket and handed her the notebook.

She leafed through the pages. "You have nice handwriting—for a cop." She smiled and it softened her face, and for an instant she looked like the young woman she was. "I know some cops who scribble so no one else can read the notes if they're subpoenaed."

Cardozo had a feeling that was a suggestion.

She flattened out a page. "You certainly were thorough." *Too thorough,* her tone said. "Actually, we're not going to be using all of this." She took a small roll of Scotch tape from the desk drawer. "We're going to soft-pedal the physical details of the killings."

At first he thought she was patching a tear in one of the pages, but then he realized it was masking tape and she was covering several lines of his writing.

"We've rethought our strategy. If the Briars' suffering

is made too vivid, the jury may have trouble seeing Mickey as a victim."

"Victim?" Cardozo's eyes jerked up. "What are you talking about? That bastard's no victim—he was *responsible!"*

"We're not interested in Mickey Williams's responsibility. Forget it. That's not what this trial is about."

"Then what *is* it about?"

"*Corey Lyle's* responsibility. Because Mickey was carrying out Lyle's instructions."

"Tess, will you please skip the commercial?" Cardozo pushed out a weary exhalation. "Just tell me in plain English what the hell you're up to now."

"Mickey is no longer under indictment." Her glance flicked up. "He's testifying for the prosecution against Corey Lyle. Do you have a problem with that?"

"Excuse me, but yes, I have a big problem. It stinks." Cardozo had to wonder: If the deal had been worked out recently, why had the feds erased Mickey's stats two years ago?

"Sometimes you have to make a deal with a demon in order to catch the devil. The Briar murders are the first case where we can *prove* Corey Lyle programmed a man and sent him out to kill. Corey Lyle is a monster. He's responsible for close to a hundred deaths that we know of. And hundreds of millions of dollars in property damage. Compared to Corey Lyle, Mickey Williams is *insignificant."*

"Fine, but Mickey Williams happens to be a murderer too, and a sociopath, and a child molester. And it sounds like you're letting him walk."

"Mickey Williams is not legally responsible." DiAngeli slid a manila folder across the desk: PAYNE-WHITNEY. PSYCHIATRIC EVALUATION OF MICHAEL WIL-

LIAMS. CONFIDENTIAL. "He's no more a murderer than your gun is. He's a weapon. And Corey Lyle loaded him, aimed him, and pulled the trigger."

"That's a load of bull guano and you know it."

"Damn it, Vince. I don't impugn your professionalism and I wish you'd respect mine."

"Then give me something to respect."

Her color darkened. "Now, just hold on a minute. I've worked twenty-hour days for almost two years, researching every angle of this case. I've interviewed I don't know how many potential witnesses. I've consulted with the country's top psychologists and criminologists and forensic experts. And one fact emerged time and time again: In and of himself, Mickey Williams is no more dangerous than a cup of water."

"Tess, I *saw* John Briar's body. No cup of water did that. I also saw Mickey's record before the feds shredded it. The man's a threat to any community he sets his foot in. Including wolf packs and alligator colonies. For the public good, he has to be kept under twenty-four-hour lock and key."

"Stop worrying about that. He's under guard."

"Where?"

"All right—if you must know, he's in the federal witness relocation program."

"Christ. That program's about as secure as a paper bag."

"Vince, I understand the new strategy may come as a shock. I understand you may feel hurt we didn't call you in at the planning stage. You may even feel we've thrown your work out. But we haven't. You did terrific work, and without it we'd never have had this chance to nail Corey Lyle."

"So I get a gold medal, you get your chance, the government gets Corey Lyle, and what does the public get? *Shafted.*"

"There are considerations and ramifications here that you're not aware of."

"Then make me aware of them."

"You know I can't do that."

"What a shame."

"Would you please stop seeing this thing in black and white?"

"Believe me, I'm seeing it in full color."

DiAngeli drew in a long, deep breath and slowly let it out. "I hope you're not planning to take that attitude onto the witness stand with you."

"Depends."

"Vince . . . be reasonable. You and I are on the same side. We both want the same thing. We want justice. We want the bad guys locked up and the good guys safe. That's why I'm prosecuting this case, and that's why you're testifying. And your testimony could make the difference between winning and losing."

"That's beautiful. I'm supposed to fine-tune my attitude and edit my testimony to win your case, and Mickey Williams goes scot-free to rampage anytime his hormones sound the hunting horn."

There was a silence that reminded Cardozo of that speak-or-forever-hold-your-peace moment in wedding ceremonies.

"Believe me," Tess said, "Mickey's not going to go free. That is absolutely not going to happen."

"How can I be sure of that?"

Tess rose and walked to the window. After a moment she turned. "Because you have my word of honor."

Anne saw wooden benches. No cushions. No armrests. There must have been two hundred long-faced jurors and potential jurors trying to get comfortable on those benches. Half of them—obviously veterans—had slipped earphones over their heads. Their Walkmans made mysterious squeaking sounds, like a rain forest of insects at nightfall.

A middle-aged man with dyed red hair sat at a desk clipping his nails. The desktop held a microphone, three telephones, and jumbled stacks of paper.

Anne fixed a smile on her face. "Excuse me."

The man's eyes flicked up. "You wish." Barely a glance.

"I'm Kyra Talbot."

"What do you expect me to do about it, Kyra—dress up as a snow leopard and sing Turandot?"

"I'm expecting my lawyer—I thought he might have asked for me?"

"He hasn't been asking *me* for you, honey. And when he does, you'll be the first to know. Now, why don't you go park your tush."

She found an empty seat. She sat down and glanced at the *New York Post* that someone had left behind.

"Day two at the twiddle-your-thumbs club." A woman dropped into the seat beside her. "How are you holding up?"

Anne looked at the stranger blankly.

"You Kyra, me Donna? Remember? Donna Scomoda? Hey, you look great. Is your hair different?"

"A little."

"Changes you." The stranger's dark eyes scanned her face without embarrassment, as though she were a photograph. "Don't mind me, it's my medical training: always eyeball the patient."

"You're a doctor?"

"Used to be a nurse. Nowadays I freelance. TV commercials."

In all her nights of channel-surfing, Anne couldn't remember ever seeing anything like Ms. Scomoda's sixties-throwback bouffant.

"You haven't *seen* me. But you've heard me. I record voice-overs."

They chatted the better part of an hour. Donna did most of the talking; Anne threw in the occasional "uh-huh" and smiled her best Kyra smile. She kept looking around the benches for Mark. *Damn. Has something gone wrong?*

Up at the front of the room, a phone rang. Somehow, the man with red hair knew instantly which of the three to answer. He bent toward the mike. "Sandro—Sandrovitch. Please present your summons to the clerk in the courtroom, right through those doors."

A man in a denim shirt pushed up from his seat and lumbered toward the next room. Mark Wells bumped into him in the doorway, eyes searching and anxious.

Anne jumped up. "Mark!"

He came and embraced her. There wasn't even a hint that he recognized her. "I've been waiting an hour in there. Didn't they page you? Come on. I've fixed it with the prosecutor."

He took her arm and steered her into the courtroom.

"If it please Your Honor," he called out. "Could we approach the bench?"

The judge was a middle-aged woman with close-cropped silver-blond hair and an extraordinarily erect carriage. She fixed Mark with a quizzical stare.

He introduced himself. "I apologize for the interruption, Your Honor, but I represent Kyra Talbot, one of the jurors in your pool." He explained that Mrs. Talbot and her ex-husband were having custody problems. "Next week, her son turns twelve. The court will decide custody and appoint a guardian. If Mrs. Talbot is on this jury, she won't be able to make that hearing."

The judge studied Anne with dubious eyes. "Mrs. Talbot, you should have mentioned this before you were accepted for the jury. Last week, you said jury service posed no difficulty for you. If this wasn't a problem then, I fail to see why it's a problem now."

Mark's jaw dropped. He turned to Anne, voice lowered. "Why on earth didn't you tell me you were already impaneled?"

A chair squeaked across linoleum. A petite, wiry, dark-haired woman rose from a document-strewn table and came with brisk-clicking heels to the bench. "Your Honor, the People have reviewed this juror's voir dire. We strongly object to having Mrs. Talbot on this jury."

"Ms. diAngeli," the judge reminded her, "the juror has already been impaneled."

"We challenge for cause." The prosecutor's brown-eyed gaze met Anne's straight-on, a mano-a-mano sizing up with no attempt at amiability. "Mrs. Talbot's employer published an article in the *Manhattanite* magazine eighteen months ago." DiAngeli slapped a back issue of the *Manhattanite* onto the bench. "The 'Town Crier' column. As you can see, it prejudged the case."

The judge opened the magazine and scanned. "Mrs. Talbot, did you write any part of this article?"

"Actually, Your Honor, I'm photography editor for *Savoir* magazine. We share a publisher with the *Manhattanite.*"

The judge stared at the prosecutor. "Ms. diAngeli, let's get real. I for one am sick of this slipshod, nit-picking voir dire. We've reached the point where a little accommodation is in order." She turned. "Mrs. Talbot, please take a seat over there."

Anne crossed to the spectator section and sat next to a bald-headed man whose pencil was flying across the *New York* magazine crossword puzzle. He glanced at her. "Egyptian god of the Nile, three letters?"

She shook her head. "Sorry."

Voices eddied over from the bench, low but urgent. Mark was pleading. Prosecutor diAngeli was pleading. Finally the judge interrupted, curt and angry.

"Mr. Elihu." She beckoned.

A gray-haired, stoop-shouldered man rose from the near table. Anne estimated his age as mid-seventies. He approached the bench. Four heads bent together.

Mark crossed the courtroom, grim-lipped. "Kyra. We have to talk. Not here. Outside."

They went into the corridor and found a quiet alcove of nonfunctioning candy and snack machines.

"The problem's Gina Bernheim. The judge." Mark gave Anne a look of whimsical, charming helplessness. "She says there's no legal basis to re–voir dire you."

"What does that mean?"

"It means she won't excuse you."

It came at Anne like a tennis ball slammed across the net. "You said this was a formality—nothing to it."

"You didn't tell me you'd already been impaneled."

"Isn't there *anything* you can do?"

"Under other circumstances, we might have a little wiggle room to work it out. But Bernheim's aiming for a

Supreme Court nomination, and till she gets it, she's observing every rule in the book—no exceptions." Mark hauled a cellular phone from his attaché case. "There's not much reason for Catch to come in next week to discuss custody. Not if you're going to be stuck in court."

She watched him tap a number into the keypad. She couldn't believe his nonchalance.

"Catch Talbot, please—Mark Wells calling from New York." He strolled to the window, braced a foot on a bench, stared down into the street. "Catch, that you? . . . Just fine, thanks. Look, I'm sorry for the late notice. But Kyra is on jury duty. The Corey Lyle trial, can you believe it? Looks like we're going to have to change a few plans."

Anne turned on her heel. Finding the bank of phones was easy. Finding a phone that worked was not. She dropped her last quarter into the last slot and dialed Kyra's number at home. The call clicked through a shunt and she realized Kyra must be forwarding calls to her office.

A voice answered on the third ring. "Hello?"

Anne recognized her sister pretending to be a secretary.

"Mark couldn't get me off. I mean, you off. So you're still on."

"But, sweetie, I can't possibly—"

"We'll discuss it later, as soon as I can get out of here."

But there was no way of getting out before the entire jury had been impaneled, and that wasn't until a quarter of five.

"Before I dismiss the jurors and alternates for the day," Judge Bernheim announced, "it's come to my attention that members of the Corey Lyle cult have threatened and even assaulted some of you. To guard against any such disturbances in the future, this jury will be sequestered."

There were groans from the jury box.

"So when you come to court tomorrow, bring a suitcase with everything you'll need for the next week."

Anne hurried to the bank of pay phones in the corridor and dialed Kyra's work number. An assistant said Kyra was on jury duty. She dialed the apartment and Juliana said Kyra was out of town.

"How long will she be gone?"

"Who can say? You know Kyra."

"Would you tell her the jury's sequestered and there's no way I can do it?"

"Do what?"

"She'll understand."

As Anne broke the connection, another juror—a slender, African-American woman—came clattering down the corridor. She was wearing high spike heels that a pigeon would have had trouble squeezing into, and her hair hung in gleaming coils that looked hand-dipped in honey.

"Hey, Kyra—I have your betting sheets."

"*My* betting sheets?" Anne wondered what on earth Kyra had been telling people.

The woman thrust several leaflets into Anne's hand. They had a line drawing of a charging running back, football cradled to his chest. Heavy print warned: *This publication for reading matter only. Not to be used in violation of any law.*

“Fill them out and give them back to me before the weekend. Let me know if you need more.”

“Thanks. I’ll look at them later.” Anne dropped a quarter into the phone slot and called her apartment, tapping in the code for the machine to replay messages.

“Anne,” an urgent male voice said, “are you there? It’s Tim Alvarez.” She had a sudden premonition of trouble. Tim was her father’s male nurse and live-in companion. Her father had reached that age where any news tended to be bad. “Could you give me a ring as soon as possible?”

She dropped another quarter into the slot and placed a collect call to Connecticut.

“A problem has come up.” Tim Alvarez sounded tense and pressured. “It’s your dad. We’ve got to talk in person. Today.”

“Couldn’t Kyra make it?” Kyra was their father’s favorite, and as a rule she handled his problems.

“Your sister’s on jury duty.”

SEVEN

6:40 P.M.

Anne pulled her green Toyota into the driveway and cut the motor. She delayed a moment, gazing out from behind the windshield at her father's little corner of Connecticut.

Across the lawn, the woods were beginning to dim with twilight. In the pond, a frog was already crooning a love song.

The old house had aged well. The white wood siding had been recently repainted. The ivy was thick on the brick chimneys but neatly trimmed. The boxwood were clipped. Lights glowed in the downstairs windows.

She wished she could love the old place.

Her heels crunched across gravel. She lifted the brass knocker and thumped.

Through bubble-glass panes she could see a shadow hurrying toward her. The door opened and Tim Alvarez stood smiling the practiced smile he always bestowed on visitors.

"Sorry if I'm late. Traffic was awful."

"Tell me about it." A tall, thin young man, Tim Alvarez wore oversize steel-rimmed spectacles and a moppish brown hairdo. "I wish this could have been one of your father's good days."

She stepped into the front hall. The old half-forgotten silence rose up around her like a familiar smell.

"Some days he's actually very alert. In fact he's been alert enough to do a little pro bono legal work."

"Really?" she said. "What cases?"

"Invasion of privacy stuff—*amicus curiae* briefs."

She peeked into the library. Stacks of books and magazines and files wriggled up from the floor. Her mother would never have allowed it. An unwatched television set was quietly laughing to itself. "What's so urgent?"

"Let's save that till we're all here," Tim suggested. "We're waiting for your father's old law partner."

The old Yankee floorboards groaned louder under his weight than hers. At the end of the corridor he stood aside. She stepped into the living room.

Her father was stretched out in a leather recliner by the window, tilting in a wedge of dying daylight. He had a woolen afghan spread over his legs and he was wearing a canvas harness on his chest. He was hanging up the telephone.

She raised her voice to a singsong. "Hello, Leon."

At the sound of his name he turned, his expression part curious, part hopeful. With his gray hair wisping in a crown around his head, he looked like a dandelion gone to seed.

She crossed the Tibetan rug, stepping over worn figures of phoenixes and dragons.

His pale gray eyes finally recognized her. He frowned. "I was expecting your sister—the prodigal career girl."

"Sorry to disappoint you. Kyra's on jury duty." She leaned down to kiss his cheek. Her lips touched stubble. Tim hadn't shaved him today. "What's all this?" She touched the harness.

"I dial the hospital in Stamford and put the receiver over my heart. The telephone relays my heartbeat. My pacemaker talks things over with the computer. If I'm beating too slow or too fast, the computer dispatches an ambulance."

He lifted the harness from his chest and hooked it over the back of the recliner. The elbow of his left arm was almost rigid, with barely ten degrees of flexibility.

"I hope the computer says you're doing okay today."

"It made the usual satisfied noises." He pushed himself up from the recliner, got his legs steady under him, and moved toward the sofa.

She remembered him as a tall man, but nowadays he wasn't. It pained her to see the difficulty he had walking. His right leg dragged. She wondered if he'd had another ministroke.

"Tim, the eternal girl-student looks tired and thirsty." Years ago Leon had decided that Kyra was the achiever, the career girl, and Anne was the laggard, the bookworm. "I'd say she's earned a drink, coming all this way."

"Scotch and water," Anne said.

"The computer says I can have the same," Leon said.

"Are you sure?" Tim Alvarez's tone was doubtful.

"Sure I'm sure." The furniture had been arranged so that Leon always had the edge of a table or the back of a chair to grasp. He lowered himself carefully onto the sofa and spread a small quilt over his legs.

She took the chair facing him.

He handed her a small wrapped package from the

coffee table. "This is for Toby. Would you see that he gets it?"

It felt like a book. "I'll be glad to."

A kind of formality descended. Leon looked up at her. "How's your beau?"

"I don't have a beau."

"You got rid of your stockbroker friend?"

"Larry and I divorced just before mother died."

Leon shook his head. "My daughters sure married lulus—Kyra hitched herself to a neurotic and you wound up with a bum. I don't suppose your lawyer friend is still in the picture?"

Anne bit back annoyance. She could never tell how much of her father's tactlessness was old age and how much was intentional goading. "That was two years ago."

"You got rid of him too?"

"It didn't work out."

"I liked him."

"I did too." Anne didn't like the way the discussion was headed. She saw a game of solitaire half completed on the coffee table. "Are you playing cards by yourself?"

"I enjoy it if I win. In that regard it's like arguing a case in court." Leon turned over a ten of clubs from the pack and laid it on the jack of diamonds. "Speaking of which, which jury is Kyra on?"

"Corey Lyle. The Briar murders."

"Conspiracy." For a moment there was no sound except the clicking of Leon's false teeth. "That's a real life-or-death case for the government pork barrel."

"Why do you say that?"

"We haven't got a Cold War, so they have to cut the

fat out of the security budget—or show the public a real cavalcade of domestic conspiracies. Can't say I'm impressed with the evidence so far. Are you?"

"I haven't heard any."

"Conspiracy to murder two politically antediluvian twits." He shook his head, eyes sparkling like two Boy Scout flints. "Corey Lyle's a social visionary. And he has the guts to stand up to government bureaucracy. And that's why the government's railroading him."

"Why do you say they're railroading him?"

"I've got an acquaintance pretty well placed in the court system. She says the way they put that jury pool together is just a rat's whisker short of jury-fixing."

"They'll have a hard time fixing any jury that Kyra's on."

"Just wait till the government drags in that boo-hoo about children."

"Children?" She'd read about the case in the papers, heard it discussed on TV—but she didn't recall any charges involving children.

"Next thing you know, we'll have preverbal infants giving testimony in capital cases—and after that, chicken entrails will be admissible."

Tim Alvarez moved the playing cards aside and set drinks and cheeses and crackers on the coffee table. He handed Anne a glass and sat on the sofa beside Leon.

"This isn't Scotch and water." Leon held his glass up to the light. He made a face. "It's water and food color."

Outside the window, automobile tires crunched gravel.

Tim Alvarez hopped to his feet. "There's our other guest."

Tim Alvarez came back into the living room escorting a tall, gray-haired man. "Anne, meet Bob MacLeod. Bob, this is Anne Bingham, Leon's daughter."

"Well, well, little Annie." MacLeod strode forward, hand extended. "You used to sit on my knee when I was your father's partner—remember?"

Anne tried to pull a match out of her memories. He had a strong jaw, piercing metallic eyes, and he looked ten or fifteen years younger than her father. She couldn't remember him. "Are you sure that wasn't my twin sister? Kyra used to love sitting on men's laps."

"Kyra was always flirting," Leon said. "She still flirts. You'd like her."

"That's a pleasure for another day." Bob MacLeod settled himself in the easy chair. "What I'm here about, Anne, is your father."

A silence passed. Bob MacLeod tapped his fingers together. Anne realized he was wearing a toupee.

"Leon is one of the brightest lights in the history of American jurisprudence—and, of course, we'd like to keep it that way."

Anne shifted. The tone disturbed her. MacLeod was talking as though something had ended. He was also talking as though Leon wasn't there in the room with them.

"Over the past two years," MacLeod said, "young female relatives of some of the most distinguished lawyers in America have been receiving anonymous obscene phone calls." He paused, biting his lower lip. "The father of one of the recipients put a trace on the line . . . and the trace led here—to this address."

Anne's first instinct was that her mind had tricked

her; she had missed something in MacLeod's explanation.

"Tim phoned me to handle damage containment. I naturally contacted the other numbers Leon had phoned. I discovered four other recipients of similar calls."

"Who were they?" Anne said softly.

"They were all daughters of lawyers with whom or against whom Leon has argued in United States Supreme Court."

She looked over at her father, cozy under his afghan. He nodded at her as though to say: *Yes, it's true. Your old dad has still got the stuff.*

"You're sure these were obscene calls?" she said.

"There's no doubt about that."

"And you're sure Leon made them?"

MacLeod turned to Leon, giving him the floor.

"The calls are protected speech." A benign, wise, half-smile floated on Leon's lips. "In fact they're part of a test case I'm working on."

Has he gone crazy? Anne asked herself.

Tim Alvarez laid a stack of bills on the coffee table.

Anne's hand hesitated and then she leaned forward in her chair and nudged the bills into the circle of lamplight.

Four dozen statements, stretching back twenty-four months. The name and address computer-printed at the top were Leon's. Half the bills covered calls made from the house phone and half covered calls from the cabin up in the woods, where Leon used to go for privacy. Toll charges to out-of-state numbers had been highlighted in a glowing nail-polish pink. They'd been placed to a variety of area codes. She recognized Connecticut and California. The other codes were unfamiliar.

"The families are willing to forgo a trial," MacLeod said. "Provided Leon signs a consent form, promising to make no more such calls. And makes a substantial financial contribution to a rape hotline."

Anne fanned the bills together, tapping them on the edge of her wrist. "Are you willing, Leon?"

"I'm giving it some thought."

Crazy or not, she thought with exasperation, *you're still sly. Still exasperating.* She rose and stalked into the kitchen.

Tim and MacLeod followed, footsteps creaking swiftly behind her.

"Just tell me one thing." She placed both hands on the butcher-block table and faced Tim, barely managing to control her voice. "We pay you to keep an eye on Leon. How is it you didn't know he was making these calls?"

A tiny drop of sweat crawled down Tim's cheek, glistening in the lamplight. "Leon made the calls from the phone in his cabin."

"And for your father to limp all the way up there, with that bad leg of his . . ." MacLeod glanced toward the hall and lowered his voice. "I'd say that shows a pretty clear conscience of wrongdoing."

Anne reexamined the bills. Without exception, the highlighted calls had been direct-dialed from the cabin phone. A second oddity leaped out at her: the calls had all been placed after one in the morning. "If Leon was limping all the way up to that cabin—two hours past the time you're supposed to have him in bed—I don't see how you could have not noticed."

"You know your dad. He got me to lower my guard." Apology danced a hesitation waltz across Tim's eyes. "I goofed."

Anne wondered why Leon had chosen this moment to out himself as a dirty old man. Her hands balled into fists. "I don't believe any of this. I don't believe that old phone up in the cabin even *works.*"

It had begun to rain. Drops made slapping sounds on the rhododendron leaves. Half-groping in the dark, Anne made out the vine-tangled path that led up the hill into the woods.

Lightning ripped a neon crack in the sky, showing her the weathered pine cabin.

The door was unlocked. Thunder growled as she stepped inside. Her hand scrabbled along a plank wall and struck a switch.

On the desk a lamp went on, throwing a circle of raw 100-watt light over strewn newspapers and books.

She searched beneath the papers but couldn't find the phone. Couldn't even find the cord.

She tilted the lampshade. Light tipped out over rickety porch chairs and tables. The cabin gave an impression of dust and clutter and emptiness, of time overflowing like an ashtray.

The light caught a group of framed photos hanging on the wall above the camp bed. She crossed the room for a closer look. In all, there were thirteen glossy black-and-white portraits.

One was a group portrait of Leon and Kyra and Toby, posed in her father's rose garden. Toby couldn't have been older than six. Toby's father, who had taken the picture, was present only as a shadow falling along the flagstone path.

Another was a family Christmas portrait, taken when

she and Kyra had been six, and their mother had still been alive.

Her eye traveled across the eleven others. They were lawyers who had argued with or against Leon before the Supreme Court of the United States. Several had posed with their families. All were signed, but only one—a photo of Earl Warren in full regalia—was dated.

The other ten had been photographed with their families. The homes of five had received obscene phone calls.

What was it about the five—*these* five? Why had they been chosen?

She went to the desk and lifted the gray plastic cover from the little Rolodex. Her fingers riffled through the cards. The five were listed—business and home phones.

The screen door squeaked. Bob MacLeod stood in the doorway, shaking off raindrops. "I know it's hard to believe a thing like this about your father. Believe me, it's hard to believe it about my ex-partner."

"Why would Leon do it?"

"He's old. He's breaking down. Losing his inhibitions. Old people sometimes develop sexual manias."

"Could there be a different explanation? What if someone wanted to hurt Leon? Destroy his reputation? He has enemies."

"But he as much as admitted he made the calls."

"He doesn't remember things. Tim showed him the bills, Leon assumed he made the calls."

"I frankly find that hard to believe."

She stood frowning. "There isn't even a phone here."

"Well, there certainly used to be."

"And even if there was, anyone could have walked in and made those phone calls. That door's not secure."

Bob MacLeod examined the door latch. He swung the door back and forth. The hinges meowed. "Hardly."

She lifted a corner of the army blanket from the bed. "And look at this. Someone's been using the bed. Leon wouldn't sleep here—he has a bed of his own. With a mattress and inner springs."

"Solving the mystery is step two," Bob MacLeod said. "Step one is making sure there's no publicity." He nudged back the cuff of his suit jacket and scowled at his watch. "I have to be going." He darted a kiss on her forehead. "I'll be in touch."

The door slammed.

She sat down on the edge of the camp bed. Her foot struck something. She looked down and saw a black plastic lump hiding under the bed. She crouched and pulled out the phone.

She lifted the receiver. A dial tone stung her ear.

She saw that the phone had an automatic redial button. Which meant the last outgoing call would still be registered.

Curious, she pressed the button. The phone blipped. There was lag, and then a phone rang. Once. Twice.

"Hi there." The woman's voice was recorded. "I welcome your call. No one is home at present—please leave your name, your number, the date and time of your call, and I will get back to you as soon as possible."

There was a beep.

"I'm sorry. I must have dialed a wrong number." Anne disconnected.

She studied the cabin phone bill and saw that one number in Manhattan—a 427 exchange—had been dialed the same dates as the obscene calls. She tapped it into the keypad.

Two rings. "Hi there." It was the answering machine that she had just spoken to. She hung up.

Now she studied the house phone bill. Calls to two New York City numbers—an 831 and a 929—had been made from the house on the same dates that the obscene calls had been made from the cabin. The 929 number always followed the 831.

She dialed the 831 number. "Hello." A man's voice, genially gruff. "You have reached the answering machine of Judge Robert MacLeod. Please leave a message at the sound of the—"

Anne pressed the disconnect bar and dialed the 929 number.

At the fourth ring a machine clicked on. "Hello, you have reached the residence of Gina Bernheim. If you have a message for the judge, please—"

A woman's voice cut in live: "Hello? Hello?"

Anne's finger came down sharply and broke the connection.

"So Bob MacLeod's a judge," Anne said. "State or federal?"

Leon's thumb tapped lightly across a dark stripe in the afghan. "Federal. Southern district of New York."

"Have you represented any clients before him?"

"I don't have clients anymore."

"Then what's your business with Gina Bernheim?"

A startled look flashed across his face and then he covered it. "Gina and I are old chums."

She knew there had to be more to it than that. "You phoned MacLeod and Bernheim the same nights those obscene calls were made. But you phoned from the house, not the cabin."

Leon shrugged. "It's a free country. I'll use whichever damned phone I want and I'll say whatever I want." He thumbed his nose.

"I suppose the calls have something to do with your pro bono work?"

"What pro bono?"

"You said you're doing some pro bono."

"No, I didn't." He drew the afghan up to his waist and patted it smooth over the sofa. "Though from the looks of things I may have to consider representing myself. Which would be extremely pro bono."

Anne felt a shaming surge of jealousy. For as long as she could recall, her father had been involved with one client or another who took precedence over his family's needs—an atomic spy, a Hollywood black-listee, a Weathergirl protesting Vietnam with an Uzi and killing two Chicano bank guards.

"And you've engineered the perfect free-speech case. Dirty phone calls to the homes of five of the most distinguished lawyers in the nation." She shook a handful of phone bills at his face. "With all the trouble you have walking, you still managed to drag yourself up to that cabin just—"

"It's not a crime, you know, telling a pretty girl she's pretty. Brandeis decided that issue once and for all."

"Leon, this isn't the forties—this is the nineties—society has changed." She felt anger now, compounded with an instinctive desire to protect this irresponsible old genius who happened to be her father. "There's a thing called sexual harassment. There are laws against it."

He shrugged. "I'd like to argue against a few of those laws in the Supreme Court. The telephone is still protected speech. The government can't listen in, and they can't censor it."

"Then you admit you called those girls?"

"I'm under no legal obligation to give out that information to any government. Or to any daughter."

"For God's sake, you're not in court. I'm trying to help."

"It's a little late for help." He stared past her, out the window into the darkness. "None of this would have happened if you'd taken the time to come see me a little more often."

She flinched at the old familiar attempt to arouse guilt. "If you want a daughter's company, why don't you ask Kyra to visit?"

Leon shot her a tight, judgmental look. "Kyra does visit. But she has a child to look after, and a career. You don't have a career. You don't have children."

He was as good as saying that her work didn't matter; didn't stack up to her sister's. It wasn't the first time he'd made the comparison. She turned and walked to the door.

"Anne."

She stopped but did not turn.

"I'm redrawing my will. Leaving the bulk to a foundation to fund worthy legal defenses. And setting up an annuity for Tim. He's a good young man. He keeps me company, which is more than some people do. Would you be interested in acting as executor?"

She couldn't remember the number of times Leon had redrawn his will. The drafts all had a common denominator: a fortune to this foundation or that, pittances to the daughters just large enough to ward off disinheritance suits. She suspected he'd already offered the executor position to Kyra and she'd turned it down.

"It's sweet of you to think of me, Leon."

"You'd get expenses and you could bill the estate for your time—on a reasonable basis. Does a hundred an hour seem equitable? Up to thirty hours' work a year? Above that pro bono?"

"I really don't have a legal mind. You'd better get someone who does."

Tim Alvarez intercepted her at the front door. He was wearing an apron and his face was shaken. "Aren't you staying for dinner? I just put in a third lobster. Your dad so rarely has company."

"No, I'm not staying to dinner—if that selfish old fraud wants company he can advertise for it."

"Please don't leave angry. Leon's old, he doesn't always know what he's saying."

"He knows exactly what he's saying and he's been saying it all his life. *Legal Genius at Work. Do Not Disturb.* Well, I have no intention of disturbing him."

EIGHT

9:10 P.M.

Anne pushed the buzzer. Juliana opened the door in bare feet, a spatula in one hand.

"Hi. Want some fish fingers?"

"No, thanks. I want to speak to Kyra."

Juliana turned and shouted. "Kyra—your sister's here!"

Anne followed her into the kitchen. Juliana flipped a spatulaful of battered fish fillets into a hissing skillet.

"Hey, Aunt Anne, do you think Max is sick?" Toby sauntered into the kitchen with the cat draped over one forearm. The animal's nonjudgmental eyes observed Anne with a watery shimmer.

"He doesn't look any too happy."

Toby reached into a box of breakfast cereal and pulled out a fistful of flakes. He let the cat nibble from his hand.

"What are you feeding him?" Juliana said.

"Organic almond-date breakfast oats."

"That stuff's no good for a cat."

"Why not? It's good for me."

"Says who?"

"Says the back of the box."

A piece of fish was belching black emission. Juliana pried it quickly away from the skillet. "You're the ideal capitalist consumer, Einstein—a complete dupe."

Anne handed Toby his grandfather's package. "Leon sent you this."

Toby set the cat down and pulled off the tissue paper. He had a look of caution unmistakably edged with suspicion. "It's *A Boy's Life of Justice Louis Brandeis.*"

Kyra floated into the kitchen wearing a bathrobe and eye shadow. She trailed a scent of lilac bath oil. "Hi, Sis. How was jury?"

"Tim Alvarez said you were too busy to see Leon today."

Kyra shrugged. "What was the problem?"

Anne glanced at Toby. It wasn't the sort of thing she felt comfortable discussing in front of a child. "Apparently Leon's been making annoying phone calls."

Kyra crossed to the refrigerator and poured herself a tumbler of white wine. "Who to, besides you and me?"

"Daughters of lawyers he's pleaded with in Supreme Court. Young women. These were—you know, dirty phone calls."

Kyra brought her glass to the table. "And are Leon's little victims going to prosecute?"

"Not if he signs a consent order and promises to stop."

"Will he?"

"You've always had more influence with him than I have."

"You expect me to persuade him?"

"I just thought you'd want to know."

"Oh, sure, I want every dreary detail."

Anne stared at her sister. "They say that extreme changes in behavior can be a sign of Alzheimer's."

"He's been goofy ever since Mom went." Kyra sighed. "I was hoping his work would pull him out of it."

"He hasn't got any work. All he has is you and me."

"He has that case," Toby said. "The amicus brief."

Anne glanced at her nephew. "What brief is that, Toby?"

"The case he won. *Mathis* v. *Doe.*"

"He never mentioned any amicus brief to me. And he certainly never mentioned winning any case."

"It was pro bono." Kyra's tone was dismissive. "No big deal."

"A parolee in some redneck state broke parole and moved to New York." Toby stuffed a forkload of fish into his mouth. "The home state wanted him back. But if he went back, he faced punishment that Leon said was against the New York constitution. So the issue was, did New York have to return him? Leon said no."

"And what was Doe's original crime?" Anne said.

"The usual tabloid merde." Kyra had a calm little smile. "Something to do with child molestation."

Anne frowned. "That doesn't sound like anything Leon would defend."

Juliana poured herself a glass of iced tea and wine. "Sounds to me as though your father's had his mind on this stuff for so long, he's started mixing work and recreation."

"It's not a joke," Anne snapped, surprising herself with the fierceness in her own voice.

"Lighten up," Kyra said. "It's all very sad, but it's water under the bridge."

"Maybe if Leon had more visits," Anne said, "and didn't feel so isolated, he'd have an incentive to keep out of trouble."

Kyra looked wounded. "I do my best—but I do have a job, and a family." She glanced at the wall clock. "Could we have this talk in private?"

Anne followed her sister to her bedroom. "You certainly made a hit with a lot of people in court."

"Oh, really?" Kyra cocked her head to the side. "Like who?"

"That pretty girl who runs the football betting. She seems to think you've got the makings of a good customer."

"Lara. She's a kook, isn't she?"

"And you obviously did something to make Donna Scomoda adore you."

"Oh, God. That hair." She handed Anne a small prescription bottle.

"What are these?" Anne studied the label. *Phendomenzapan tartrate.*

"For you. They're not habit-forming and you work straight through the night and get wonderful ideas. I use them every time I've got a deadline. The whole office swears by them. Great for weight control, too."

"Why would I need pills?"

"For jury duty."

"But, Kyra—didn't you get my message?"

"Message?"

"The jury's sequestered and I've got work to do. I'm not going back."

"We had an agreement, Annie. You can't back out now."

"I agreed to substitute for you for one day. Today. Period."

Kyra's face seemed to say, *Is there anyone in the world who does desperation as well as I do?* "But I haven't got anyone else to help me. Who'll take care of Toby?"

"Juliana."

Kyra lowered her voice. "She takes drugs—and it's getting worse."

Anne could hear the *bonk* of Toby's bouncing a tennis ball off one of the apartment walls.

"Toby, cut it out!" Kyra screamed. She dropped onto the edge of the bed. After a moment her eyes came up, wounded and reproachful. "Of all the times you could possibly choose to let me down, this is the absolute worst. With Toby's custody hearing and this shake-up at work . . . What if I lose my job? What if I lose Toby? Catch was an abusive husband and he'll be just as abusive a father."

"Sweetie, sweetie." Anne had a sensation of arrows going into her lungs. "Mark phoned Catch and postponed the hearing. Why can't you be realistic? Why do you have to project worst-case scenarios?"

"You haven't got anything urgent that needs doing, have you? I mean *really* urgent? I'll pay you a hundred a day for as long as the trial takes."

"Stop it. Please. Money isn't the point. It's illegal and we could both wind up in jail."

"Mark says they're only jailing violent offenders. And you need money and why shouldn't I help you—you've always helped me. Please, Annie?"

Anne considered the options. She was desperately low on cash. And her adjustable mortgage had gone up again. And New York City wanted twenty-six thousand dollars. With Kyra's pills, she might be able to finish that TV movie tonight. She hated to take her sister's money, but the fact was, Kyra was rich and Anne was flat broke.

"Please, Annie." Kyra began crying softly. "I need you."

Anne felt the old familiar knives twisting inside her. She realized it wasn't a question of deciding. It was a question of accepting what had to be done. "Don't be a silly baby. Of course I'll help you. On one condition: Could you feed the goldfish and water my plants?"

"I'll water them with champagne."

Oh, God. She probably will. "Plain water—please."

Anne's mailbox was stuffed with junk mail. Riding up in the elevator, she glanced through the return addresses. She recognized appeals for contributions from spokesmen for orphans, for the homeless, for Channel Thirteen; a half dozen offers of unwanted charge cards; and a slender envelope from the New York City Department of Finance, stamped THIRD AND FINAL NOTICE. *Notice* was spelled "notce."

She let herself into the apartment, hung up her raincoat over the bathtub, and fed the goldfish. One seemed to be trying to swim upside down.

There was a message on the answering machine—a hurry-up call from her producer. "Where's the tape? The sponsors want to see the finished reels ASAP."

She put the last of the vegetarian lasagne in the microwave and sat down at her worktable. A message on the computer monitor indicated she had e-mail. She called up the file.

Tuesday Sept 17:
Hi Aunt Anne!
It was fun seeing you.
Mom says you're saving her life. I have a

question though: why does Mom's life always need saving? Yours never needs saving. Not criticizing, just wondering.
Let's see a movie soon. Just you and me.
love you
XXX
Toby

She entered Toby's electronic mail address and typed a reply.

Hi Toby—
It was fun seeing you too. "Saving life" is a figure of speech. Your mom has helped me out of some very close scrapes.
I'd love to see a movie with you—I'll be pretty busy for the next few weeks. How about next month? But please, no more kick-boxing! Hope Max feels better soon.
lots of love
A.

She entered the command to send. While her modem quietly clicked and buzzed, she loaded her *Scoremaestro* program.

The biggest scene still to be scored was the final sequence—the lovers' decision to part and return to their respective spouses. Renunciation seemed to be a big theme in TV movies this season, like cancer two seasons back. Anne tried different keyboard stops, looking for a sound that suggested faith without being churchy or pompous. Finally she opted for a series of floating hymnlike chords played on an alto harmonica. She edged them in echo and laid a subliminal pulse underneath, like a heartbeat.

A bell in the kitchen summoned her. She stopped the VCR and took her lasagne out of the microwave. While she ate, she studied Leon's AT&T bills. The calls highlighted in pink had come out gray on the photocopies.

She got the phone directory and consulted the map of area codes and time zones. The 203 number was Connecticut, the 912 Georgia. The hands of the electric clock on the wall pointed to eleven-thirty—too late to phone East Coast numbers.

The 214 number was Texas, probably Dallas. Texas was central time; it was only ten-thirty there. She lifted the phone and dialed.

Ten rings. No pickup.

The 312 number was Chicago. Central time again.

Four rings. An answering machine picked up. The woman's voice in the recorded message had a young quality. "And please remember to wait for that signal."

There was a beep.

"I'm sorry to trouble you." Anne's throat was suddenly very dry. "My name is Anne Bingham. I'm Leon Brandsetter's daughter. I need to speak with the person who received a nuisance call from my father. It's urgent." She left her number. "Thank you."

The fifth number—213—was Los Angeles. It was only 8:30 out on the West Coast. She dialed.

"Hello?" A man with broad, Brahmin vowels.

"Hello—I'm sorry to trouble you. My name is Anne Bingham."

"Yes?"

"I'm Leon Brandsetter's daughter."

The voice froze. "What do you want?"

She felt a quick skid into shame. "My father apparently made nuisance calls to your home?"

"Apparently?"

"I'd like to discuss those calls with the person who received them."

"Mrs. Bingham—your father has done trailblazing work in American jurisprudence. I have great respect for his accomplishments. But he's obviously become a very sick, twisted person. If you or any of your family call my home again I give you my word I shall prosecute him to the full extent of the law and see him jailed for what he did to my daughter." The phone slammed down.

She sat blinking as though she'd been slapped.

No sense brooding, she told herself. *There's work to be done.*

It was past three in the morning. Anne had reached the last unscored scene, when the phone rang. "Hello?"

"Yes, hello." It was a woman's voice, young and nervous. "I'm sorry to bother you. This is Candace Loffler. Returning your call."

Loffler. It took Anne a moment to recognize the name and to place the apologetic, babyish voice that she'd heard on an answering machine. Leon's alleged telephone victim in Chicago.

"I got your message. And I don't like what they're trying to do to your father. The phone company traced the call, but what does that prove? I mean really? Anyone can pick up someone else's phone and dial. Even if they say they're your father, it doesn't mean they are, does it?"

"Did the person who phoned you actually say he was my father?"

"No. They didn't give a name. But I had a feeling"—for a moment Candace Loffler was silent—"the person who called me . . . was pretending to be a man."

"Wait a minute." Anne felt slow—as though she had only the slumbering brain of a lizard to process her thoughts. "The person who phoned you *wasn't* a man?"

"She was forcing her voice down—trying to sound like a man. She was saying things that I guess she thought a man would say. It wasn't very convincing. In fact it was pathetic."

"You're *sure* it was a woman? Would you be willing to make a sworn affidavit?"

A hesitation. "If I had to."

NINE

Wednesday, September 18
First day of trial
6:55 A.M.

Anne finished the tape of the score a little after six in the morning. Outside her window, the water tower on the building across the way was just beginning to catch the early rays of dawn.

She lay down and to her astonishment felt not the least need to sleep. At seven she left a message on her producer's answering machine: "The tape of the score will be with the doorman."

She waited till eight before phoning Connecticut. Tim Alvarez answered.

"Sorry to phone so early. Did I wake you?"

"That's okay." He sounded groggy. "I was up."

"What do you know about *Mathis* v. *Doe*?"

"Leon was pretty secretive about that case, and once it was decided he destroyed his records."

That seemed odd. Anne had never known her father

to destroy a piece of paper in his life. "Who was his client?"

Tim hesitated. "Your father never told me the name."

"Did the client ever come to the house?"

"Once or twice."

"Do you recall the dates?"

"A while ago." He sounded apologetic. "Is it important?"

"It could be."

"I can look the dates up and call you back."

"Could you look them up now? I'll hold." She lifted a steaming mug of herb-and-clove tea from the kitchen counter. The warm aroma reached soothingly into her sinuses.

"Okay." Tim was back. "I have the log of household expenses. Every time the client stayed over, Leon had me lay in hot dogs and diet Dr Pepper. The client's first visit was a year ago, the weekend right after Labor Day. The second visit was December fourth and fifth, same year. A weekend again."

Anne jotted down the dates. She compared them to the dates of the obscene calls on the cabin phone. They matched.

"The third visit was six months later—June seventh and eighth. Another weekend."

And another match.

"Did Leon's client stay in the cabin?"

"I couldn't say. Does it matter?"

It struck her as an odd thing for Tim not to know. "Yes, it does, because the visits coincide with the dates of those obscene calls. Doe was accused of sex offenses. I think he made those calls. And I think Leon's protecting his client."

"But Doe won the case."

"That doesn't mean Doe wasn't guilty. All the court decided was a constitutional issue. Was Leon's client a man or a woman?"

"I don't know."

"You don't *know*? How were they dressed? Was their hair long or short?"

"I never saw the client. Leon always sent me away before they arrived."

Anger flashed through Anne. "But you're never supposed to leave Leon alone."

"I know, I know, but he was adamant. His client's identity had to be secret."

"You never spoke with them on the phone?"

"I never got the chance. The client phoned at prearranged times and Leon always got to the phone first."

"That's incredible, even for Leon."

"Wait a minute. Once I did pick up the extension and Leon was talking to someone. And he was furious at me afterward."

"Was it a man's voice or a woman's?"

"It was a unisex voice. Never heard it before in my life. Or since."

Anne glanced over the bills for the house phone. "The same weekends that the client visited, Leon was placing phone calls to two judges: Gina Bernheim and Bob MacLeod. Was either of them involved in *Mathis* v. *Doe*?"

"I have no idea. Look, I have to go—Leon just buzzed. We'll talk later, okay?"

Anne studied the home phone bills. The sequence of calls to 831 and 929 struck her as curious. They were always in the same order: 929 immediately followed 831 and was always dialed three or four minutes later.

Except for September thirteenth, one year ago: on that day a 929 call was dialed at exactly the same time as the 831 call. On December fourth the same thing happened. On December fifth, it happened a third time.

She scanned the rest of the bills, then dialed the telephone business office. "I have a question about my AT&T invoice. There seems to be a mistake. You've billed me for eight calls to a 929 number in Manhattan, but they were made at the same time as calls to an 831 number."

"Could I have the number you were calling from and the dates?" A moment later the operator was back. "There's no mistake, ma'am. You were speaking to both parties. Those were conference calls."

"Anne!" a voice yelled. Heels tapped rapidly on the sidewalk. "Annie!"

She turned around and there was Kyra, running down the sloping pavement. "Your phone's been busy for *hours.*" She was wearing a silk jacket and dungarees, as if she'd dressed to be photographed from the waist up. "Thank God I caught you. Let's get a cup of coffee. You've got time."

Anne set down her suitcase and glanced at her gift wristwatch. "No, I don't, not if I'm going to make your trial."

"They never start on time." Kyra took her by the elbow, steered her past the cash machine on the corner and through the little knots of pedestrians on Lexington. The coffee shop was brightly lit and crowded, but they found a corner booth with sponged Formica glistening.

Kyra pushed a Bloomingdale's bag across the table. "This is for you."

Anne peered inside. Four pairs of nylon panties. "What in the world . . . ?"

"They say sequestered jury duty is worse than Europe on five dollars a day. Chances are, you'll wind up doing your own washing. These dry fast." Kyra placed a small powder-blue box on the table. "This is for you too."

"Tiffany's?"

"Only the box."

Anne opened the box and picked through a layer of cotton that seemed to have been saved from pill bottles. She found a carved jade locket and lifted it by its gold chain. "Mother's old cameo." She had always loved it. "But why?"

"You've been awfully kind to me over the years. And I'm not very good at saying thank-you."

Anne snapped the locket open. Inside was a woman's profile carved in ivory. "Mother always said it was Great-grandma. Sweetie, you can't give this away. She left it to you."

"And I'm leaving it to you."

"Fine. I'll accept it when you die."

"That's too long to wait. Besides, we won't be seeing each other for a while. I want you to have it now."

"Sweetie, it's only a trial."

"You never know what's going to happen in this world." Kyra gave the word *what* an odd inflection.

"Kyra, what's the matter?"

"Nothing. It's just that . . ." She seemed to have to force herself to exhale. "I had a dream. It was about you and me and . . ." She broke off.

"Sweetie—something *is* the matter. Tell me. Tell Annie."

"I just wanted you to know—you're my best friend. That's all I wanted to say."

"And you're mine."

"But I'm not good like you or strong. Time and time again you've helped me out of scrapes and you've never asked for anything in return."

"Because my life is simple. You have to worry about a child and a crazy job."

"And Catch." Suddenly Kyra's eyes had no gift for pretending. "Annie, I'm scared."

An aching empathy slid through Anne, a sense that all her life her sister had been walking a high, thin wire with nothing below, dreaming that someday a pair of godly arms would lift her to safety—and then discovering that those arms belonged not to a god but to a fallible human being.

"What if he gets custody?" Kyra gazed at her with naked, uncomplicated fear. "What'll I do?"

"Sweetie, that's not going to happen."

"How can I be sure?"

Anne slipped the locket chain around her neck. "Because I promise you."

Ignoring picketers, Anne hurried up the steps and into the lobby of the federal courthouse.

The guard at the metal detector grinned at her. "Late today, Kyra." He had a Russian accent and the overbred profile of a prizewinning Afghan.

She stepped through the metal detector. The alarm didn't challenge her.

"Nice locket." His dark eyes were like tiny suction cups. "The jade brings out your eyes."

There was a smell in the jury room like a refrigerator that needed cleaning. Anne took a chair beside Donna Scomoda. "Didn't you say you used to be a nurse?"

Donna smiled. "Four of the weirdest years of my life."

"Did you ever take care of men in their late seventies?"

"A few hundred, I suppose. Alzheimer's mostly."

"Did any of them still have an interest in sex?"

"Tell the truth, it was about the only interest they had left." Donna folded her crossword puzzle. "I had this one case, every time I was alone with him, he'd offer me money. Ninety-three years old and he wanted me to strip."

"Did any of these men use the phone?"

"Phone sex services?" Donna sipped a plastic cup of deli coffee. "You should see the bills these old goats ran up."

"Did they ever make anonymous calls?"

"If there's a law against it, they tried it. One time the FBI came down on me, like I should've known my patient was an interstate phone flasher. He was sneaking a cellular phone into the john. When they get to that age, they're kids. Some doctors say you can control them with medication. Personally, the only medication I'd trust is handcuffs."

The bailiff rapped on the door. "Ladies and gentlemen, the judge is ready."

In the courtroom, a genial babble floated above the benches, like the chatter of an opening-night audience eager for the curtain to rise.

Most of the players were ready at their places. Corey Lyle, the defendant, was speaking quietly with his attorney. Anne had never seen him in person before. He had the same wavy, graying hair as in his pictures, but photos couldn't catch the animated eyes, the broad, relaxed movements. In his dark-blue pin-striped suit he looked like a businessman cheerfully resigned to sitting through a tiresome meeting.

The court stenographer began setting up her machine. There was a wave of applause. She ignored it.

A door swung open at the front of the courtroom.

"All rise," the bailiff commanded. "The Supreme Court of the Southern District of New York, Judge Gina Bernheim presiding, is in session."

Judge Bernheim, black-robed, glided to the bench. "Be seated." She allowed her gaze to sweep the room. Not an empty seat in the house. She seemed satisfied. "We are here today to hear the case of the People of the State of New York versus Corey Lyle. Will the clerk read the indictment?"

The clerk stood. "It is charged that Corey Lyle did unlawfully conspire with others to murder John Briar and Amalia Briar."

Judge Bernheim explained the conspiracy law. "Is any juror unclear on the meaning of the statute?"

Silence.

The defense attorney rose. "Your Honor, we move for dismissal on grounds that the conspiracy statute is vague and punishes thought and is therefore unconstitutional."

"The United States Supreme Court is going to have to rule on that," Bernheim said. "In the meantime, we'll hear the evidence and make our decision on the basis of the present statute."

Tess diAngeli rose from the prosecution table and cut a direct line to the jury box. "Gentlemen and ladies of the jury—we are here to exact justice for as evil and cowardly an act as I, in all my years as assistant district attorney, have ever prosecuted."

Tess diAngeli's unlined brow suggested that for several of those years she must have been prosecuting dolls.

"When I show you how Corey Lyle, unwilling to expose his own hand or risk his own neck, compelled an innocent man to suffocate the life from John and Amalia Briar—two distinguished and trusting senior citizens who had dedicated their lives and their resources to public service and to helping others—you will begin to grasp the depths of moral savagery to which the defendant has sunk—and to which he has dragged the cult that bears his name."

Corey Lyle sat quietly, patiently erect at the defense table—watching his beautiful accuser with undisguised fascination.

"Today we are confronting an act of pure governmental terrorism." Dotson Elihu faced the jury, enunciating with concentrated fury. "This is the persecution of an innocent man for a murder that the State of New York admits—yes, *admits*!—was abetted not by Dr. Corey Lyle but by the federal government's own hired agent. And why has the State of New York brought this charge? Because of pressure from the federal government, which is using this trial to justify the obscene bloat of the domestic security budget and bureaucracy"—*B* consonants shot from Elihu's lips like bullets—"and to silence its critics. Make no mistake, ladies and gentlemen of the jury: it is not Corey Lyle who is on trial here today, it is the United States government."

TEN

10:50 A.M.

Tess diAngeli was on her feet again. "The People call Jack Briar."

"Objection!" Dotson Elihu bolted up from his chair. "The People have never turned over the police tape of Jack Briar's interview; the defense has a right to see it before Mr. Briar is examined."

Smoke came into Judge Bernheim's gaze. "Ms. diAngeli, does such a tape exist?"

"Yes." Tess diAngeli spoke the word grudgingly, giving it the emotional force of *no.* "And it contains precisely the same statements that Mr. Briar made in his depositions. Mr. Elihu has had those documents for six months. If he really needed to see this videotape, why didn't he request it months ago?"

"Your Honor . . ." Elihu's face was doing astonishment; and he angled himself so the jury couldn't miss it. "I didn't even *know* of the tape's existence till last night when I came across a page of footnotes that the People had omitted to show me."

"This tactic is pure, calculated obstruction." DiAngeli pushed out a sigh. "Mr. Briar is our most important witness, and his testimony is absolutely vital to our case."

Judge Bernheim studied the prosecutor, eyelids low. "The People will furnish the defense with a copy of the tape. After Mr. Elihu has had twenty-four hours to review it, the People may call Jack Briar."

"Yes, Your Honor." DiAngeli did not hide a flicker of annoyance. "In that case, the People call Britta Bailey."

It was four minutes before a door opened and a short, stocky woman in a navy blue dress crossed to the witness stand.

"Place your hand on the Bible." The bailiff held out a small book bound in black leatherette. "Do you solemnly swear that the testimony you give shall be the truth, the whole truth, and nothing but the truth, so help you God?"

"I do."

Tess diAngeli approached the witness. "Ms. Bailey, would you tell us how you are employed?"

"I'm a sergeant with the New York City Police Department, assigned to the Twenty-second Precinct, in Manhattan."

"How long have you worked for the police department?"

"Four and a half years."

"Would you describe the events of the Sunday before Labor Day, two years ago, as they relate to this trial?"

"Around midday a woman by the name of Yolanda Lopez came into the precinct. She said she was worried about John and Amalia Briar, who lived at 777 Park Avenue."

"Did she say why she was worried?"

"Apparently they'd been sick for some time. They didn't answer the buzzer and the building staff was on strike. Ms. Lopez wanted an officer to break into the apartment. I telephoned the apartment. A man answered and I asked if John and Amalia Briar were having any kind of problem. He said they were fine."

"Did you break into the apartment at this time?"

"No. Since I'd been able to speak with someone on the premises, and they reported no emergency, that would be against departmental procedure. We classified Ms. Lopez as a false alarm."

"Ms. Bailey, would you describe the events of the Tuesday after Labor Day, as they relate to this trial?"

"Tuesday, a little after one P.M., Jack Briar came into the precinct. He said he had a lunch date with his father and stepmother. He was worried because they didn't answer their buzzer and their phone was off the hook. He said they'd been in failing health for some time. Since the building staff was on strike, he wanted an officer to break into the apartment."

"And how did you respond?"

"First I phoned the apartment. The phone was busy, and the operator confirmed that it was off the hook. Which suggested Mr. Briar was right, there might be some kind of mishap. So I went with him to 777 Park and broke into the apartment."

"How did you break in?"

"I used a police department crowbar and sledgehammer on the front door."

"Before you broke the door," diAngeli said, "did you notice signs of an earlier break-in?"

"At that door? No."

"When did you enter the apartment?"

"At one-thirty P.M., approximately."

"Would you describe what you found?"

"John Briar was lying on the floor of his bedroom, naked except for an adult diaper and a robe. No visible wounds, but there was no pulse; the body was cold."

"And did you find anyone else in the apartment?"

"Amalia Briar was lying in her bedroom—faceup—no visible wounds, but she was also dead."

"And did you find any person *alive* in the apartment?"

"There was a man in the kitchen—alive."

"Did he identify himself?"

"He didn't need to. I recognized him—it was Mickey Williams."

A stir passed through the courtroom.

"Do you mean Mickey Williams the ex–running back for the Houston Oilers?"

Sergeant Bailey nodded. "Yes."

"What was he doing in the kitchen?"

"He was sitting there. Eating spaghetti from a pot."

"Did he act surprised to see you?"

"He showed no reaction to anything. It was like he was in a trance."

Dotson Elihu jumped to his feet. "Objection. Conclusion."

"Sustained," Judge Bernheim said. "Jury will disregard witness's last remark."

Dotson Elihu was holding a sheaf of papers. "Sergeant Bailey—is this your report on the discovery of John and Amalia Briar's bodies?"

The officer examined the papers. "It is."

"You just testified that you found Amalia Briar faceup. But on page two of that report you say that you discovered her body facedown on the bed."

The officer leafed again through the pages. She looked back at Elihu, her expression wary.

"So which is the truth? Facedown or faceup?"

"Faceup."

"You're sure?"

"Absolutely."

"Then why do you say facedown in the report?"

"I made a mistake."

"You made a mistake? Why didn't you correct the mistake?"

"I did. But sometimes the computer loses information."

"Then your final, considered testimony, under oath, is that you discovered Amalia Briar lying how—facedown or faceup?"

"Faceup." Officer Bailey's voice had risen slightly.

"And did you examine the front door of the apartment for signs of a break-in before you broke in yourself?"

"Naturally." The witness's voice was inching into irritation now. "And I observed that there were no signs of a break-in."

"How long did you examine the door?"

Sergeant Bailey didn't hesitate. "Thirty seconds."

Elihu went to the defense table and reached into a battered briefcase. He crossed to the jury box, winding a white plastic kitchen timer. He set the timer on the rail. It had the lopsided tick of a juvenile's homemade bomb and it seemed to tick much longer than half a minute.

When the timer finally jangled, the witness gave a little start.

"That's thirty seconds. Is that how long you took?"

Thirty seconds was obviously an overestimate and Elihu had trapped her; but this lady did not retreat. "Approximately."

"Did you ask the crime scene photographer to photograph the door before you broke in?"

"There was no crime scene crew present. I didn't know for a fact that the apartment was a crime scene till I found the bodies."

"Are you saying there are *no* photographs of the door as it was before you destroyed it?"

"To my knowledge there are no such photographs."

"The People call Lieutenant Vincent Cardozo."

Cardozo took the stand, swore to tell the whole truth and nothing but.

Tess diAngeli rose from the prosecution table. She walked him through his record and career: eighteen years with the NYPD, twelve years a detective, eight years a lieutenant, seven years at the Twenty-second Precinct. Twice wounded in the line of duty. Two distinguished service citations.

"How soon after the discovery of the Briars' bodies did you arrive at their apartment?"

"Twelve minutes."

"Could you describe the state of the apartment as you found it?"

"Aside from the front door, which was broken in, most of the rooms were fairly neat. John Briar's bedroom was not neat. Mr. Briar was lying dead on the floor. He'd pulled the bedclothes down with him. A lamp was on the floor, broken. Articles were knocked off the tabletop."

"Based on your years of experience as a detective, would you say these were signs of a struggle?"

"Absolutely. No mistaking it."

"Do the police possess an inventory of the Briars' apartment?"

"We were given one by the estate's lawyer."

"Was anything of value missing from the apartment? Any jewelry, any artwork? Rare books? Anything of that sort?"

"Nothing was missing."

A movement at the defense table caught Cardozo's eye. The defendant and his lawyer, heads bent together, were reviewing some kind of checklist. Cardozo had never seen Corey Lyle in the flesh before, but he recognized him from photos: calm, centered, smiling a smile that suggested either complete innocence of the charges or complete indifference to them.

Cardozo had met Dotson Elihu a dozen times over the last decade, but he was intrigued to see him at the defense table today. Elihu had represented Lyle five years ago, when the government had failed to sustain an indictment on charges of conspiring to blow up the White Plains post office; he had represented Mickey Williams two years ago. Mickey was now the state's chief witness against Corey Lyle—and Elihu was again defending Lyle. Whatever happened to conflict of interest?

"How many people were in the apartment when you arrived?"

"Aside from the two victims, there was Sergeant Bailey. And a sergeant at the front door. And three sergeants inside. And a civilian in the kitchen."

"Who was the civilian?"

"Mickey Williams—the ex–running back."

"What was Mr. Williams doing in the kitchen?"

"Sitting. Eating spaghetti."

"Did he tell you at that time if he had witnessed the murders?"

"*Witnessed* was not the word he used. But based on his statements to me, he witnessed the murders. Decidedly."

Dotson Elihu crossed slowly to the witness box. "Lieutenant Cardozo—would you describe the state of Amalia Briar's room when you found her dead body?"

"Nothing upset, nothing obviously out of place. Except for the phone on the floor."

"Would you say the scene was like or unlike the scene in John Briar's bedroom?"

"Very unlike. At first glance, you'd think Amalia Briar died peacefully in her sleep."

DiAngeli leaped up. "Objection. Not responsive."

"Overruled."

Elihu smiled. "Lieutenant, did the police dust the premises for fingerprints?"

"Yes, we did."

"How many prints did the police find in the apartment?"

"Usable prints? Over a hundred."

"How many of these could the police identify?"

"Thirty-one."

"Which leaves sixty-nine unidentified?"

"That's right."

"So there could have been as many as sixty-nine as

yet unidentified people who left their prints in the apartment?"

"No, there were nine sets of duplicates."

"Then sixty as yet unidentified people could have left prints?"

"That would have been the maximum." Cardozo held up both hands, blunt fingers outstretched. "But a lot of people have ten prints."

Elihu tugged at his ear, playing it slow-witted, letting it show that he was playing. "Then an absolute minimum of six unidentified people left prints?"

"Theoretically, yes."

"When the police first searched the Briar residence, was there any evidence that an intruder had broken in and robbed the apartment?"

"No."

"Isn't it a fact that Amalia Briar for tax reasons did not insure her jewelry?" Elihu casually waved a sheet of official-looking paper. "Isn't it a fact that a missing diamond-and-emerald bracelet valued at eighty thousand dollars did not show up on the insurance inventory?"

Cardozo shook his head. "No record of any such bracelet has come to my attention."

Elihu strolled away from the stand. "You say two murder weapons were found? Could you describe them?"

"They were goose-down pillows."

"Were you able to recover prints from either of the pillows?"

"We recovered prints from both pillows."

"Whose prints?"

"Mickey Williams's."

"So did you arrest Mickey Williams?"

Cardozo glanced toward Tess. She gave a barely perceptible shake of the head. "No. I did not."

Elihu seemed puzzled. "In the light of Mickey Williams's presence at the scene and his prints on the murder weapons—why on earth didn't you arrest him? Wasn't he the first person you suspected of the murders?"

DiAngeli jumped up. "Objection."

"Overruled. Suspicion is part of this witness's job and he may testify as to his state of mind in this regard."

"I was under the impression," DiAngeli said, "that this was cross-examination."

Judge Bernheim shot the prosecutor a dead-eyed stare. "Your impression is correct and I've overruled you. Lieutenant Cardozo may respond."

"If you're asking, do I recall my state of mind? . . ." Cardozo pressed his fingers into a pyramid. "It crossed my mind that here were two dead bodies in a locked apartment, here was Mickey Williams sitting in the apartment, there was a good chance he knew what had happened."

"It didn't cross your mind there was an even better chance he had caused it to happen?"

"We didn't have the print results at that time, but yes—it crossed my mind."

"It crossed your mind, but you still did not arrest him?"

"I did not."

"Then what did you do? Allow him to walk away?"

"As it happened, Mr. Williams chose to come to the precinct with us."

"Mickey Williams went with you *voluntarily*?"

"Yes, sir."

"Are you telling this court that you found Mickey

Williams sitting at a murder scene, you invited him to a tête-à-tête at the precinct, and you never once considered the possibility of charging him, not even after his prints were identified on both murder weapons, not even on *suspicion*?"

"We charged and arraigned him. Charges were later dropped."

"Why?"

"There are two aspects to the crime." Cardozo held up two fingers. "Opportunity, which Mickey Williams clearly had. And motive, which it developed he did not."

"When did you determine that Mickey Williams had no motive?"

"Soon after our arrival at the precinct."

"But you questioned him over several days?"

"Yes." Cardozo glanced again at the prosecutor. "As a material witness."

ELEVEN

1:10 P.M.

In the jury room, a stocky, dark-haired man whistled for silence. "Ladies and gentlemen of the jury—and alternates—as your foreperson, I have a suggestion." A crooked front tooth made him look oddly innocent, almost likable. "Why don't we all take seats, and go around the table and officially introduce ourselves? My name's Ben Esposito. In real life I'm assistant director of the Department of Fraud for the U.S. Post Office."

"Don't tell me they commit fraud in the U.S. Post Office," a heavyset black man said. He was dressed like a partner in a law firm.

"Not with me on the job they don't." Ben smiled. "And what's your name, friend?"

"I'm P. C. Cabot. My real name's Paul, but people call me P.C. because those are my initials, and I'm an MTA motorman on the A line. PCC happens to be the initials of one of the best streetcars ever designed. Naturally, they stopped building them."

"Don't drink on the job, fella," Ben said. "I ride the A line to work."

The next juror moving clockwise was a small, dapper Chinese. "I'm Seymour Shen. I run a small chain of organic food stores."

And then Donna. "Hi, guys. My name is Donna Scomoda. I do voice-overs for TV commercials."

Next came a bald white juror. "Abe da Silva . . . I'm employed by the Center for Strategic and International Studies—which is better known by its acronym SIS—where I'm senior adviser."

"What the hell does SIS do?" asked a slender, aquiline-featured black woman four seats down.

"I often wonder myself," Abe said.

"Seriously. These million-dollar think tanks are sort of an unelected government."

"Introductions first," Ben said. "Coffee klatch later."

Next came the woman who had given Anne the betting sheet. "My name is Lara Duggan. I'm director of new faces for the Mystique Model Management Agency."

"Channel seven did an exposé on one of those agencies," Abe said.

"Yeah, that was us. Our fifteen minutes."

"My name's Shoshana Beaupre." A tall, serious-faced African-American juror smiled gravely. "I teach at a private school in Manhattan—St. Andrew's."

"What do you teach?" Abe said.

"Everything—with an emphasis on math."

Next came a willowy black juror with a profile off a Roman coin. "I'm Gloria Weston—I'm a full-time spokesperson and community activist for the East New York Coalition."

"What the hell do they do?" Ben asked.

"To put it in three little words, we right wrongs."

"Oh, yeah? And who pays?"

"A mix of private and city funds. Why, you want to see our balance sheet?"

"And be an accessory after the fact?" Ben grinned to show he was just joking. Gloria did not smile.

"My name is Ramon Culpeper." The young man was crisp as a male model in his madras jacket. "I run a franchise of mystic and spiritual shops. The Healing Crystal. We specialize in ayurvedic medicine and toiletries; crystals; books; meditation classes."

"Did you bring any samples?" Donna Scomoda said.

Ramon winked. "See me afterward."

"You're very big in minority neighborhoods," Gloria said.

"Hispanic neighborhoods," Ramon said.

Anne's turn. "I'm Kyra Talbot. I'm photography editor for *Savoir* magazine."

"My name is Paco Velez—I'm retired." A beat of silence passed. And another. He was a tall man with a widow's peak and dark glasses, and he obviously intended to say no more.

An overweight juror spoke up. "Hi, folks. I'm Thelma del Rio. Till last year I was a hospital dietitian; I now work for American Cyanimid, in new products. I just want to say that being here with all of you today is one of the proudest moments of my life—the realization of a ten-year dream, and a seven-year lawsuit. I'll bet I'm the only person in this room who had to sue to get onto this jury."

The jurors laughed.

Thelma explained: "New York State said I didn't have to serve on a jury because I'm two hundred fifty pounds overweight. As far as I'm concerned, that was the same as saying to hell with building access ramps for the disabled. So on the advice of my therapist I did what any red-blooded obsessive-compulsive American would do—I initiated class action."

"On the advice of your physical therapist?" Paco Velez asked.

"I'm not talking about my psychotherapist, honey. She's suing *me.*"

More laughter.

The bailiff rapped on the door and announced that the jurors would be having their lunches at Eugene's Patio, a restaurant two blocks from the courthouse specializing in burgers and Italian-American cuisine.

"The People call Harkness Lamont."

A man who must have been six-foot-four strode into the courtroom. Behind him, on a cleaning woman's squealing trolley, a guard pushed a three-foot TV.

The witness took the oath. Tess diAngeli asked him to describe his work.

"I'm an assistant D.A. with the Manhattan District Attorney's office." He spoke with a nasal Bostonian accent.

"Two years ago, on September twentieth, in connection with the murders of John and Amalia Briar, did you interrogate Mickey Williams?"

"I interrogated Mickey Williams on that date, in that connection, yes."

"Would you view the following videotape and tell the court if this is an accurate record of your interview with him?"

"Objection, Your Honor." Elihu pushed himself to his feet. "As my colleague well knows, the defense intends to call Mickey Williams as a witness. Ms. diAngeli never informed us that she intended to use this tape as part of her case."

For an instant diAngeli stood openmouthed. "The defense was given the entire tape three months ago."

"That is not the issue, Your Honor." Elihu shook his head angrily. "We object to the showing of this tape unless Mr. Williams is available for cross-examination. And he isn't."

Judge Bernheim seemed perplexed. "But, Mr. Elihu, didn't you just say you're going to call Mr. Williams as a defense witness?"

"We've subpoenaed him, Your Honor, but he hasn't answered the subpoena."

"Will counsel please approach the bench?"

Judge Bernheim and the lawyers had a whispered sidebar conference. In her seat next to Anne, Thelma del Rio craned forward in her chair and followed the dispute with absorbed attention.

Judge Bernheim's hands finally made an abrupt slicing motion. "I'll allow the tape to be shown."

The bailiff lowered the window shades. The prosecutor's assistant worked the controls on a VCR.

Dotson Elihu dropped into his seat, glowering. Corey Lyle touched the lawyer's hand and whispered something.

A picture came up on the TV screen: a man sat at a table in what could have been a motel room, staring at the camera. He had California-boy hair, glossy and bowl-cut. He needed a shave, and something in his manner suggested he had been sitting there for a week. He wrenched a cigarette loose from a crumpled pack of Marlboros, fumbled it to his lips, struck a kitchen match.

The assistant flicked a remote at the screen and the image froze at the instant when flame touched cigarette. Nicotine had left deep yellow patches on the man's fingers.

"Mr. Lamont," Tess diAngeli said, "can you identify the man on that TV screen?"

"That's Mickey Williams."

The man broke into movement, dropping the match into an ashtray piled high with butts. In his white buttoned-to-the-neck golf shirt, he looked like an athlete who had lost a little of his shape but none of his muscle.

"Were you acquainted with John and Amalia Briar?" an off-camera voice asked.

The figure on the screen froze again.

"Mr. Lamont," Tess diAngeli said, "is that your voice?"

The witness nodded. "That is my voice. Yes, ma'am."

"We were all members of Corey Lyle's group." On the TV, Mickey Williams spoke with a sweet, boyish lilt. "I used to pray with John Briar. When we weren't praying together, we were playing together."

"Did you know his wife, Amalia?" On the tape, Lamont's voice had a higher, more adenoidal quality than it did on the stand. It could almost have been a different man speaking.

"I met her two or three times."

"Do you recall the last time you saw them?"

"Yes." The eyes darted to the right. "I went to their apartment Friday before Labor Day."

"Were they alive at this time?"

"They were alive when I arrived."

"What did you do to John Briar?"

"I suffocated him with a pillow."

A rustle, like wind in a forest, swept the courtroom. Spectators craned to get better sight lines on the TV.

"When did you do this?" the voice asked.

"Early Saturday morning."

"And what did you do to Amalia Briar?"

"I suffocated her with a pillow."

"When did you suffocate Amalia Briar?"

"I suffocated her fifty-three hours after I suffocated John Briar."

"Did you perform these acts of your own free will?"

"I can't answer that. I have no idea what free will is. I can't say as I've experienced free will in the last thirty years."

"Were you ordered to perform these acts by some other person?"

Mickey Williams raised his eyes to the camera: cow-brown eyes, glowing but dead. "Corey Lyle ordered me to kill the Briars."

Dotson Elihu's fist hit the table. "Objection!"

"Stop the tape," Judge Bernheim said wearily.

On the TV screen, Mickey Williams froze in the act of lighting another Marlboro.

"Your Honor," Dotson Elihu shouted, "it's intolerable that such testimony should be sneaked in by the back door!" He wheeled, red-faced, and screamed at diAngeli. "Dr. Corey Lyle has the same right as any American—the right to confront his accusers! They shall not hide from cross-examination behind an electronic wall of tape!" And back to the judge. "Your Honor, I demand that you declare a mistrial!"

"Mr. Elihu, Mr. Elihu . . ." Judge Bernheim's hands made calming, easy-there, boy motions. She beckoned both attorneys to the bench.

On Madison Avenue, behind iron gates, students thronged the courtyard of the private school, shouting, pushing, leaping, squeezing every ounce of freedom they could out of afternoon recess.

Sergeant Britta Bailey watched and shuddered. Children were such animals. It chilled her to see how they formed cliques, how they ganged up on the weakest and ugliest. Their weapons were subtle: the jostle, the push, the turned back. Nothing that a teacher would notice. Instinctive little acts of disdain sure to embitter the victim.

Britta Bailey knew. She'd gone through it herself—almost fifteen years ago, but when she heard school kids shouting it seemed like the day before yesterday.

Her eyes kept coming back to one child in particular—an eleven-year-old boy with a deep summer tan that strikingly set off his blond hair and brown eyes. He was bouncing a ball off the wall, quick and sure of himself. There was something almost insolent about his grace and coordination, his indifference to his schoolmates.

Sergeant Bailey approached the boy. "Hi . . . what's your name?"

The boy caught the ball and turned. "Toby Talbot, ma'am."

"Toby, my name's Britta Bailey. I need a favor. There's a blue Pontiac parked on Madison Avenue. There's a man in the front seat. I'm going to walk away. I want you to turn around and just happen to look in that direction. See if you can get a good look at him without letting him know you're looking. I'll be waiting over there, inside that door, and you come tell me if you've ever seen him before, okay? You got the drill?"

"Yes, ma'am—I've got it."

Officer Bailey crossed the cobblestoned court and pushed through the glass-paned door. Her footsteps echoed up to nineteenth-century moldings. She watched through the window.

The boy was bouncing his rubber ball off the ivied wall again. But now that he knew he was being watched, his movements were tight and self-conscious. He fumbled a catch and the ball got away from him. He headed it off at the iron fence.

His gaze came up and he looked out through the spear-pointed pickets. On the avenue, traffic lumbered past—taxis and buses and upscale delivery trucks.

On the east side of Madison, a blue Pontiac had double-parked, motor idling. In the driver's seat, a man sat peering through the zoom viewfinder of a camera. He had the look of an overage skinhead. Hair shaved to the skull. Thick neck and shoulders. Noodle-veined temples.

The boy looked over at the man. The boy's expression was puzzled. But interested.

Sergeant Bailey wondered how much the kid needed spelled out for him—that the man was a pervert, that he was watching schoolkids, photographing them, that he was watching *Toby.*

The man lowered the camera. He let a beat pass, then waved. A very slow, very visible, very comic wave.

Britta Bailey's stomach turned over.

The boy glanced bashfully away. He hurried into the lobby.

"Recognize him?" Bailey asked.

"No, ma'am." The boy shook his head. "Ma'am, would you tell me something? Is he doing anything wrong?"

"We don't know, Toby. But I'm going to find out right now."

Wood tapped sharply on glass. The man turned.

A nightstick knocked on his passenger window. "Sir."

There was a way of saying *sir* that showed absolutely no respect, and this freckle-faced policewoman had mastered it. She motioned him to roll the window down.

"Yes, Officer?" He smiled up at her.

"You're double-parked." She had a cold, unwavering gaze and a voice just a little too high and tight, to match.

He kept the smile. "That's right."

"What are you doing here?"

"I'm a magazine photographer." He held up the camera, bristling with high-tech add-ons. "I'm doing a spread on education."

"You were here yesterday."

He nodded. "That's right."

"Let me see your registration and I.D."

He set down the camera and leaned across the seat and pushed the door open. The air-conditioning lowered the policewoman's guard, drew her closer. She placed a foot up on the car frame. It was a male gesture, and it needed more weight. It needed a boot, not that black lace-up go-to-funerals shoe she was wearing.

A bell sounded, and the schoolchildren began filing back into the building. He took out his wallet. He flipped through charge cards, dawdling until the yard was empty.

Her eyes were pale and watchful and nervous. "Would you hurry it up?"

"Sorry." He twisted in the seat, storing torque in his

right shoulder. He held out the wallet. "You know, I really didn't plan on this."

"Mm-hmm." She reached for the wallet. When she saw that he was wearing surgical gloves, her eyes jumped to his face. Big mistake.

He exploded into movement. His right hand clamped onto her left. Wristbone snapped. He yanked hard and fast, sliding backward on the seat. There was a split second's astonishment in her eyes, and she came flying full length into the car. His left hand grabbed her head and drove it into the open glove compartment. A tooth bounced off the accelerator pedal.

Holding her down with his right hand, he pulled the door shut. His eyes scanned the sidewalk for passersby. All clear for a half block in either direction.

She was whimpering like a little dog. Her neck strained against the pressure of his hand and arm.

"I'm sorry, but we're going to have to take a little drive." He gave her five inches, just enough leeway to slam her face into the leather seat. He pressed down with his full body weight, both hands around her neck.

When he released her, she rolled partway off the seat. He pushed her down into the space between the seat and the dashboard.

He twisted the key in the ignition. With a glance over his shoulder, he angled into the traffic.

TWELVE

3:20 P.M.

"On October third . . ." Tess diAngeli said, "did you interrogate the accused, Corey Lyle, with regard to the murders of John and Amalia Briar?"

"I did," Assistant District Attorney Lamont said.

"Would you view the following videotape," diAngeli said, "and tell the court if it's an accurate record of that interview?"

"Objection." Dotson Elihu rose to his feet, sighing. "The videotape contains statements made by Dr. Lyle in the absence of a lawyer. Since Dr. Lyle did not waive his right to counsel, the tape is inadmissible."

Judge Bernheim turned to the witness. "Did you advise the accused of his right to counsel?"

"I did, Your Honor."

"And did he request counsel?"

"He waived counsel," Lamont said. "It's on the tape."

"The tape may be shown from the point where the accused is advised of his right to counsel."

The prosecutor's assistant ran the videotape fast-forward. The image of Corey Lyle, staring out of the TV screen, hardly moved. But a curtain in the window behind him flapped as though amphetamined poltergeists were ripping it apart.

Checking the sound on earphones, the assistant located the frame he wanted and slowed the tape. The window curtain floated in a lazy breeze and the off-camera voice of Harkness Lamont said, "You're aware your statements could be used in a court of law."

"I'm hoping they will be," Corey Lyle's image said, "if they can help Mickey." Even on the TV the voice possessed astonishing resonance, as though it were speaking in an empty church.

"Do you wish to have counsel? You're entitled to it."

"Why would I wish that?"

"Several of your statements could be used against you."

Corey Lyle's image shaped a smile utterly without malice or irony. "I don't think that need worry us, do you?"

"It's my duty to advise you of your rights. If you want to continue this discussion, just the two of us, that's okay."

"At the moment my rights aren't an issue. It's Mickey that concerns me."

"Objection, Your Honor."

The prosecutor's assistant stopped the tape.

"That is clearly not a Miranda warning." Dotson Elihu heaved himself to his feet. "And my client clearly did not waive his right to counsel."

"I'm going to rule that it *is* a Miranda," Judge Bernheim said, "and your client waived. Overruled."

Elihu shot the jury an astonished look.

The assistant started the tape again and the off-screen voice asked, "Why's it your worry if Mickey's in a jam?"

"In any legal sense, Mickey is innocent of the murders. He misapprehended the doctrine of our group and acted on that misapprehension. I taught him the doctrine. I'd say that puts a certain responsibility on my shoulders, wouldn't you?"

"Two people are dead. Somebody's responsible."

"Then I'm responsible."

"You're going to have to explain that to me."

"Your Honor," Dotson Elihu cried, "I object to these out-of-context excerpts. They amount to compelling the defendant's testimony."

On the screen, all movement drained from the image.

"Must I remind you, Mr. Elihu," Judge Bernheim said, "the constitutional prohibition against self-incrimination does not apply to documents. A tape is a document. The People can give us these statements from the tape. If you feel your client's statements have been unfairly excerpted, you may later introduce the complete tape and set the record straight."

A juror muttered in front of Anne, "Oy!"

"The People may proceed," Judge Bernheim said.

The prosecutor's assistant again aimed the remote at the TV screen.

"Were there ever occasions when Mickey Williams acted without your advice or approval?"

"Mickey never did anything without seeking my advice. He's not a developed intellect. He prefers to obey an authority."

"And are you that authority?"

"At present, pretty much."

The image lurched, as though there had been some kind of electronic deletion.

"Did you speak to Mickey Williams on Friday of Labor Day weekend?"

The image nodded. "I asked him to go to the Briars' apartment and keep an eye on them."

"Okay, let me get this straight. You preceded Mickey to the apartment and let him in. You then left the apartment."

"That's correct."

"Did you speak to Mickey Williams again that weekend?"

"We spoke on the phone early Saturday morning."

"Who phoned who?"

"Mickey phoned me."

"Why?"

"To tell me that John Briar was dead."

"Did this news surprise you?"

"I'd been expecting it for some time."

"In other words, you had advance knowledge this event was going to occur?"

"That's correct, but not in the sense you think."

"You seem to be saying that you were involved."

"That's also correct, but in a way that would be hard for me to explain to you."

"Look, are you sure you don't want a lawyer?"

The prosecutor's assistant aimed the remote. The image froze, then vanished, leaving the TV screen with a hard, rubbery glare. The assistant removed the tape.

"Your Honor." Dotson Elihu stood. "I respectfully request that you declare a mistrial."

Judge Bernheim stared at him. "On what grounds, Mr. Elihu?"

"*That* was the Miranda warning. Right there where

the People turned off the tape. Everything preceding it is inadmissible."

"I disagree with you, Mr. Elihu. By my count that was the second Miranda."

After the day's testimony, four guards herded the jurors down through the basement and out to a bus that took them to their hotel. The World-Wide Inn was a glass-sheathed skyscraper at the edge of lower Manhattan's business district. Polished brass doors swung open onto a pink-and-gold lobby. The man at the desk had a list of room assignments, and Anne found she was sharing 1818 with Shoshana Beaupre, the schoolteacher.

As they stepped into the elevator, Shoshana asked, "Do you smoke?"

"I haven't for years."

"Do you mind if I smoke?"

"Doesn't bother me."

"Good." Shoshana had cheerful mink-brown eyes, and her lace blouse and calf-length floral skirt gave an impression of carefully understated neatness. "We're going to be friends."

Anne had no sensation of rising. The floor indicator stopped at 18. They followed the guard down a gray-carpeted hallway. He slid a card-key into the lock of 1818. The tiny room had two beds and a very low ceiling and a mirrored wall that made it seem six people had crowded in. Outside the window, skyscrapers reflected the cold pink beginnings of autumn sunset.

"Home," Shoshana said. "Do you believe it?"

"It's a little cramped," Anne said.

Shoshana made a quick check of the accommodations. "I think it's their way of telling us to reach a fast verdict."

"If I can help you in any way . . ." The guard set their luggage on the baggage rack and handed Anne the electronic card-key. "Just ask."

"I know you didn't expect to be taken up on that," Shoshana said, "but how about seeing if you can get that TV to work?"

The guard shook his head. "You're sequestered. No TV, no phone."

Shoshana frowned. "What if there's an emergency?"

"Then you get in touch with me." He winked.

Shoshana's silence let the suggestion glide to a crash landing. The guard tipped an imaginary hat and backed out of the door.

"I have a feeling he likes you," Anne said.

Shoshana clicked the bolt on the door. "And I have a feeling he's an orbiting spy satellite."

Anne began unpacking. "Do you want the right or left half of the closet?"

"If it's the same to you, I'll take the left." Shoshana shook a gym bag empty over one of the beds. Newspapers and magazines tumbled out. "Look what I sneaked past the gestapo." She held up a copy of the latest *Savoir.* "This is where you work, isn't it?"

"In the photography department."

Shoshana lit a mentholated cigarette and sat with her crossed leg swinging easily. "Does that mean you're a photographer?"

Anne tried to think how Kyra would answer that question. Evasively, of course. "I don't have an eye for taking pictures. I only have an eye for selecting them."

"Then you'll love this." Shoshana pulled a snapshot from her wallet. "These are my kids."

The photo showed a group of beaming eight-year-olds wearing Rollerblades and private-school blazers. No more than three out of the twenty or so faces were dark-skinned. The picture had been taken on an immaculate city street lined with trees and BMW's.

"What great-looking children," Anne said. "Are they your students?"

Shoshana nodded. "I took that picture up on East Ninety-second, right outside the school."

Anne turned. "They say the kids at Saint Andrew score the highest SAT's of any school in New York City."

"Except for the École Française. That's where your kid goes, right?"

Anne's hand, reaching to hang a sweater in the closet, stopped in midair. "How did you know that?"

"I'm psychic." Shoshana laughed. "And you mentioned it in voir dire."

"Of course. Toby's in sixth grade. I'm sorry I don't have any photos of him."

"He must be pretty damned bright. I hear the École is even tougher than St. Andrews."

"He *is* bright," Anne said. "And warm. And loving. He's a wonderful kid."

The guard unlocked the steel door and Dotson Elihu stepped into the windowless green-walled interview room.

Corey Lyle was seated at the far end of the table, eyes fixed on the darkened screen of the TV set. As the door clanged shut, his eyes floated up. He unfurled a smile and rose, pleasant and placid as a tabby cat stretching in the sun. "There you are, Dot. Thanks for coming by."

"diAngeli finally gave me the tape." Elihu took the videocassette from his briefcase and slipped it into the VCR. The TV screen lit up into a shimmering abstract painting. The colors abruptly resolved into a fuzzy but recognizable image: a dark-haired man fidgeting with a cup of coffee at a cigarette-scarred table in the Twenty-second Precinct.

"Rotten quality." Elihu frowned. "This must be a third-generation dupe. Apparently everyone's seen it but you and me."

A voice spoke from off-camera. "This is an interview of Jack Briar, conducted by Lieutenant Vincent Cardozo, four forty-five P.M., September eighth."

"The sound's pretty good," Corey observed.

Elihu raised a shushing hand and leaned forward in the metal chair, squinting.

"Mr. Briar, would you describe the events leading up to the discovery of your parents' bodies?"

Jack Briar's weary, bloodshot eyes flicked up. "I can't think of anything I haven't told you already."

"Let's go through it just once more for the record. Take your time."

In a shock-deadened voice, Jack Briar told his story.

Elihu opened Briar's deposition and checked off points as they occurred on the tape. The order was essentially the same, as was the information.

Yet—Elihu reflected—diAngeli had tried to withhold the tape. Why?

He had come to the next-to-last page of the deposition, when the screen turned into a black-and-white snowstorm and Briar's voice became a hissing white noise, like the sound of escaping steam.

Elihu stiffened. His eyes consulted his client's.

Corey's face was relaxed and at peace, eyes luminous. He seemed serenely unconnected to anything happening on the TV screen or in the space around him.

It came to Elihu with a jolt: Corey was meditating.

"I'm sorry to interrupt," Elihu said, "but do you see that?"

For just an instant, Corey seemed embarrassed. "Sorry . . . what did you say?"

"diAngeli erased part of the tape."

"Really? It seems all right now."

The image was back, and Briar's voice was clear. Elihu reversed the tape and played again through the erasure. A little over thirty seconds had been deleted.

"You know," Corey said, "there's a serious weak point in the prosecution's case. At the time the government building in White Plains was bombed, I—"

Elihu cut him off almost savagely. "You were never charged with that bombing, and I don't want to hear anything more about it. At least not from your lips."

Corey gazed at his attorney shrewdly. A breath lifted his tailored jacket. "As you wish. Perhaps you're right."

By the time Elihu stepped out of the state detention center, evening had sunk into night. He hurried north on Centre Street. Raindrops licked lightly at his face. He opened his umbrella. It wasn't till Canal Street that he managed to find a phone with its armored, vandal-proof cord still intact.

He didn't have exact change, so he dropped three dimes into the coin slot. It killed him to give Ma Bell the extra nickel. He tapped seven digits into the stainless-steel keypad.

A woman's voice answered on the fifth ring. "Hello?" The tone was distinctly unwelcoming.

"Alicia? Dotson. Emergency. Can I come over?"

"I wish you wouldn't. I have guests for dinner."

"And you didn't invite me?"

"You're a rotten conversationalist, Dotson. You pontificate."

"Alicia, be kind to an old bore. This will only take a moment."

Seven minutes later Dotson Elihu, badly winded, rapped on a Chinese-red door on the fourth story of a loft building on lower Broadway. A tall, frowning woman let him in. With her bobbed black hair and hipless shimmy dress and jangling loops of ceramic beads, Alicia Mordaunt could have stepped out of a snapshot album of Jazz Age flappers.

"Well?"

He handed her the videotape. "Part of it's been erased and I need to know what it was."

She led him down the corridor, past drunken laughter into a workroom paneled in perforated gray industrial soundproofing. State-of-the-art electronic gear, computers, and monitors were stacked from floor to ceiling.

She slipped the tape into a VCR. Watching on a monitor, she fast-forwarded to the patch of snow. "They recorded TV static over the original signals. It's either an accident or a very low-tech job. They obviously didn't have a magnetic eraser."

"Can you restore the signals they recorded over?"

"Let's see." She twisted dials and replayed. Ghost silhouettes flickered through the snow. Faint disembodied voices moaned beneath the white noise. "I may be able to pull up a degraded signal."

"How soon?"

The man with the shaved head slipped a plastic bag over his left boot. Then another over his right boot. He knotted both bags securely.

Throwing open the door of the darkened Pontiac, he pushed the U.S. government mail sack halfway out. The warm night air, choked with exhaust, swirled up to greet him.

He climbed over the sack. Grunting and tugging, he pulled it the rest of the way out.

Now he waited, eyes scanning, double-checking the darkness. Droplets of drizzle floated down, dewing his forearms and face.

Trees in leaf blocked the view from West End Avenue. Across the Hudson River, a co-op tower sequined with windows pillared the New Jersey sky.

Behind him, tires sang on the roadway of the West Side Highway.

He bent and hefted the mail sack up over his left shoulder. The ground beneath his boots made a faint squishing sound. It had the consistency of rotting newsprint laid over decomposing animals.

He carried the sack ten feet to the fence of the Sixtieth Street Terminal Conrail yard. He set it on the ground and undid the steel fasteners. He slid the canvas down. It made a silken sound slipping away from the Glad double-thick plastic mesh–reinforced thirty-gallon trash bags.

Using the blade of a box cutter, he slashed through the belt of mover's tape.

He peeled one black garbage bag up from her waist, over her torso, and off her head.

Sitting there still half-bagged on the damp ground, leaning against the fence, she had a wounded expression in her eyes. It could have been a plea for protection. It could have been an invitation to abuse.

He laid her down and yanked the other bag off her legs and feet. His surgical gloves squeaked. Gripping her around the waist, he turned her so she faced the chain link. He pushed her up. Her torso flopped forward into the barbed top rail.

A dog barked in the distance and another dog took up the refrain. The windows in the watchman's building stayed dark. He nudged her farther. Gave a thrust. Wire twanged as she went over.

THIRTEEN

Thursday, September 19
Second day of trial
7:25 A.M.

Lieutenant Vince Cardozo pulled his Honda to a stop outside the West 70th Street entrance to the Conrail yard. He propped his NYPD placard in the windshield.

Two plainclothesmen were canvassing parked cars, writing down license plate numbers.

Across the street a dozen squad cars and unmarked cars were jammed nose-to-nose like a twenty-car smashup. The rotating beacon on an ambulance was flashing.

The usual crowd of rubberneckers had gathered, standing about, waiting for someone to tell them what all the fuss was. TV news trucks had started arriving and reporters and cameramen were trying to talk their way past the police cordon.

Cardozo showed his shield. The young-looking sergeant entered his name, shield number, and time of arrival in the crime scene log.

"Where is she?"

"Right over there, Lieutenant." The sergeant pointed toward the steel-chain gate.

Crime scene tape and sawhorses cordoned off two hundred square yards inside and outside the rail yard. Detectives were poking hands and ballpoint pens and sticks and flashlights into every inch of the area, plastic-bagging anything that looked remotely like physical evidence. Forensic men crouched, scratching rocks with instruments that resembled dental probes. Photographers were snapping flash photos. Print technicians were pouring plaster of paris into footprints in the mud; others spray-gunned the chain-link fence with black powder and dusted with small brushes—not an easy job in the open air, with unpredictable breezes whipping off the Hudson River.

They had all done this job so many times before that there was nothing that needed saying or asking; they worked in grim silence, except for a detective with a tape measure, shouting out figures to another detective, who noted them on a sketch of the crime scene.

A stocky man with an almost bald head disengaged himself from the group and came forward. Cardozo recognized Lou Stein from Manhattan forensics.

"She's over here, Vince." Lou led him to the edge of the yard, where the crowd clustered thickest.

"What do we know?"

"Her badge says she's Britta Bailey. All we need is you to give us the final word."

Technicians and medical personnel made room for them. A body-bagged bundle the size of a huddled adult lay on a stretcher on the garbage-littered ground. Lou Stein's gloved hand raised the black plastic flap.

Cardozo stared down into the face of a uniformed female police officer. A spike of ice drove through his lower intestine. The dove-colored eyes of Britta Bailey stared back at him.

"It's Britta." He wanted to close his eyes. "How long do you figure she's been dead?"

"Rough estimate," Lou said, "nine, ten hours."

Dotson Elihu walked to the witness stand slowly, with a troubled expression. "Did you read Mickey Williams his Miranda rights?"

Tess diAngeli's chair screeched. "Objection!"

"Sustained," Judge Bernheim ruled. "Counselor, limit your questions to material raised in direct."

"Sorry, Your Honor." Elihu's eyes glided back to the witness. "Was Mickey Williams's lawyer present when that tape was made?"

"Objection."

"Overruled."

"When those segments were taped," Harkness Lamont said, "I don't recall a lawyer on hand to represent Mr. Williams."

"Mr. Lamont, can a prosecution be brought on the basis of a confession obtained in the absence of a lawyer representing the accused?"

The witness glanced toward Tess diAngeli. She made no move to object. "Only if the accused has waived his privilege."

"And did Mickey Williams waive his privilege?"

"Objection," diAngeli said. "Irrelevant."

"Your Honor . . ." Elihu turned toward the bench.

"It's hardly irrelevant to the jury's understanding of the government's legal strategy and the selective nature of this prosecution."

"Objection sustained," Judge Bernheim said. "There is a proper time and proper way for the defense to raise that point."

Elihu was silent for a moment. "If Mickey Williams did not waive his privilege, isn't it a fact that no prosecution can ever be brought against him—even though he confessed to the very crimes of which you now accuse Dr. Lyle?"

"Objection." diAngeli leaped up. "Argumentative, hypothetical, repetitive."

"Sustained, sustained, sustained."

Elihu stood still a moment. "Why did you wait three weeks after the Briars' deaths before you questioned Dr. Lyle?"

"Investigations sometimes move slowly."

Elihu stepped back. An artist taking a longer view of his subject. "Did you subpoena Dr. Lyle before questioning him?"

"Of course not." There was surprising venom in those three words. Something had broken through the assistant D.A.'s facade.

"Why do you say 'of course not' as though it should be obvious? It's not obvious to me. And I wouldn't be surprised if there aren't one or two members of the jury it's not so obvious to either."

"It should be obvious," the witness said evenly, "from the fact that there was no attorney present. If we had subpoenaed Corey Lyle, he would have had an attorney with him."

"And wasn't that the last thing you wanted?"

"I have no particular wants in that area."

"Was Dr. Lyle under arrest when you questioned him?"

"No."

"Then how did he happen to be in the police station? Did he just walk in?"

"So far as I know, yes. He said he wanted to talk with the attorney who had questioned Mr. Williams. Who happened to be me."

"But Dr. Lyle didn't say why he wanted this talk? He didn't say, 'I have come to confess to the crime that Mickey Williams committed'?"

"No, Corey Lyle did not say he had come to confess to any crime. Not at first. Not in so many words."

"The locale on that tape, what I could see of it, didn't look like a precinct. Was it a hotel?"

"The Gotham Squire Inn."

Elihu crossed to the defense table. He picked up a stack of what looked like room service orders. "And while you and Dr. Lyle were at this hotel, did you happen to order . . . drinks?"

The witness glanced at the papers in Elihu's hand and then at the prosecutor. "We did."

"How many drinks did you see the defendant consume?"

"I believe he had eighteen Scotch and sodas over a ten-hour period. Which surprised me because I'd heard he was religious and I'd have thought liquor was against his convictions."

"Is Benedictine against the pope's convictions, Mr. Lamont?"

"Objection."

"Sustained."

Elihu fanned through the stack of papers. "Did you succeed in getting a formal confession out of Dr. Lyle?"

"As the videotape shows, he gave us good grounds for charging him with murder."

"In other words, even after you'd been drinking all night with Dr. Lyle, you still couldn't get a confession out of him—not even a drunken one. *Then why in God's name charge him, when you already have a clear confession from Mickey Williams?*"

Lamont pulled back in the chair. "Because—in the first place—Corey Lyle admitted to being an accessory before the fact, which is legally the same as committing the crime himself. And in the second place, Mr. Williams's confession did not tell the whole story."

"Now let me get this straight. Was Mr. Williams holding back information?"

"Mr. Williams didn't have full knowledge of the circumstances or of his acts."

"Mickey Williams didn't have full knowledge of his *own acts*? On the snippets of tape that the prosecution has allowed us to see, he tells you he deliberately murdered two human beings. Are you saying Mickey Williams was *lying*?"

"No, I am not saying he was lying."

"Are you saying his testimony is a delusion?"

"No, I am not saying that."

"If Mickey Williams's testimony is not a lie, not a delusion . . ." Elihu's hands clamped back on to the brass railing. "Then why, sir, isn't *he* being prosecuted for his acts?"

"The reason we're not prosecuting Mickey Williams is that at the time of the murders, he was hypnotized."

A flurry passed through the courtroom.

From the expression on Elihu's face, it was obvious he had not expected the answer. "Your Honor, for the moment I have no further questions of this witness, but in view of the videotaped record of his astonishing professional misconduct—"

"Objection to that characterization!" diAngeli cried. "Mr. Lamont is not on trial!"

Elihu wheeled around. "After today he sure as hell ought to be!"

"Objection, prejudicial!"

"Look, let's keep on track," Judge Bernheim said. "Mr. Elihu, kindly moderate your tone. You said you have no further questions of this witness?"

"Not at this point, Your Honor." Elihu glowered at Harkness Lamont. "But the defense will be recalling him as a hostile witness."

Vince Cardozo leaned back in his swivel chair, one foot propped on an open desk drawer, and studied Sergeant Britta Bailey's two notebooks. She had been carrying both of them in her jacket at the time of her death.

When he opened the newer one, a small piece of yellowed newsprint, neatly scissored, fell out.

> *Virgo Aug. 23—Sep. 22:*
> *Look beyond immediate boundaries in love, creative endeavor, finance; present appearance of chaos masks future security.*

He wondered why the hell Britta would have kept an ancient magazine horoscope. He turned it over. The other side was a black-and-white photograph of Mickey Williams, grinning and healthy, looking very much the football bruiser in his business suit. Only a portion of the caption had survived Britta's scissors: MICKEY WILLIAMS, FORMER STAR HOUSTON OILERS RUNNING

Cardozo examined the notebook. Britta had made entries on the first four sheets only. The final entry was dated yesterday.

3 P.M. MADEMOISELLE.

He began putting it together in his mind. Britta had worked the eight-to-four shift yesterday. She'd logged in, but she never came back to the precinct to log out. Her civilian clothes were still in her locker.

At 3 P.M. she'd apparently gotten a call from the precinct to check on someone she referred to as Mademoiselle. Her last known contact with anyone.

Cardozo opened the door to the squad room.

Detective Greg Monteleone was pouring himself a cup of precinct coffee.

"Hey, Greg, you got a minute?" Cardozo showed him the notebook. "Who did Britta know called Mademoiselle?"

Greg shrugged. He was wearing a loose-fitting gray cotton shirt, open at the neck to show off his gold chain. Leave it to Greg to find a loud shade of gray. "Plenty of French restaurants in the neighborhood."

"Aren't New York French restaurants all Italian? I think we'd better have a look at yesterday's calls. See if anything came in around three P.M., a woman with a French accent or a French name. You might check 911 too—something could have got routed to the precinct."

Greg made a face as if Cardozo had just handed him a ptomaine burrito. "That could take all afternoon. I was hoping to get off early today."

Which explained that extra dollop of Old Spice he was wearing.

"Greg, she'll wait."

Cardozo returned to his desk and flipped through the older of Britta's notebooks. It smelled of rose sachet, as though she'd stored it in a drawer with sweaters. Though the pages were lined, her handwriting rarely stuck to the lines. The entries dated from August and September of two years ago. Britta had obviously resurrected the notebook for her testimony in the Corey Lyle trial.

One page had been altered. Britta had written: *J. Briar wearing robe dead on bedroom floor*

And then six words that looked like: *hers on lips in mo roat*

Cardozo squinted at the page. He could see erasures: one before *hers,* another before *roat.*

Why would Britta have gone to the trouble of erasing parts of words? If she'd made a mistake, why not cross it out, as she'd done on half the other pages in the notebook?

His mind played with the word fragments. *Roat,* on that page, in the context of *lips,* could be *throat.* Which made it a fair guess that *mo* had been *mouth.* So the partially erased line must originally have read: *hers on lips, in mouth and throat.*

He puzzled. What the hell was *hers*?

He scooted his chair across the cubicle to the filing cabinet. He opened the drawer where he kept his old notebooks. He found the notebook where Tess had pasted her masking tape.

He'd written: *J. Briar dead on floor struggle abrasions face forearms . . .*

Tess had covered the rest of the page. He tried tugging the tape, but it wanted to pull the paper with it.

He lifted the phone and dialed Ellie Siegel's extension in the squad room. He could see Ellie at her desk, dark-haired and serious, word processing a report. After ten rings she picked up. "What is it, Vince?"

"If you knew it was me, why didn't you answer?"

"I figure you can take ten steps through an open door."

"It's private."

"I can keep a secret."

"Have you got any nail polish remover?"

"On me? No. Why?"

"I want to lift masking tape from a notebook without pulling up the writing."

"Why do you need remover? Nail polish is a solvent."

"Okay, do you have any clear polish?"

"I wasn't suggesting Jungle Red."

A moment later, Ellie stepped into the cubicle smelling very faintly and very pleasantly of that new perfume she'd started wearing. She thunked a small designer bottle of transparent liquid down on the desktop.

"Please." He pushed the notebook toward her.

Ellie sat down, pulled the arm of the lamp closer, and unscrewed the bottle top. She lifted the brush out and drew the fine hairs along the upper edge of the tape and then the lower edge. She lifted as much of the tape as would lift, which was barely a half inch. She repeated the operation till she was able to lift the entire tape.

He saw what Tess had covered: *feathers in mouth*

"What the hell is so hush-hush about a man suffocated with a goosedown pillow? Why would a prosecutor care if it was mentioned in court?" He showed her Britta's notebook. "The same thing was covered in Britta's notes."

"Funny. Neither of you mentioned Amalia's mouth." Ellie's eyes pondered. "Dan Hippolito said Amalia died a natural death, right? But the state threw out his autopsy and went with Lalwani's. They're accusing Corey of conspiring to murder John *and* Amalia, right?"

"Right."

"Then the point isn't pillow feathers in John Briar's mouth. What you and Britta both noticed—and what Tess doesn't want coming out—is that there *weren't* any feathers in Amalia's mouth."

FOURTEEN

9:40 A.M.

"The People call Jack Briar."

In the jury box, Thelma del Rio shot Anne a quick, knowing glance—as if to say, *This is going to be good.*

The door flew open and a tall man—impeccably tailored in a three-piece bank-president charcoal gray—crossed to the stand. He had a lustrous brunette ponytail and the boyishly sprinting step of a TV emcee.

The bailiff held out the Bible. Jack Briar crossed himself. "So help me God."

Tess diAngeli asked him to tell the court about his work.

"I'm an author and journalist." Jack Briar settled back comfortably in the chair. He crossed his legs and described books and articles he'd published.

"What was your relationship with the deceased?"

"Johnny Briar was my dad and Amalia was my stepmother. But we weren't just family, we were dear, dear friends. There was very little about our lives we didn't confide to one another."

"How did they come to be acquainted with Corey Lyle?"

"I'm sorry to say, it was my fault. I introduced them." Jack Briar's gaze floated toward the ceiling. Portrait of a man lost in remembering. "I met Corey five and a half years ago. I was doing an article for *Gotham* magazine. Corey was the new guru in town. He had every appearance of being *the* lama for the lean decade."

Jack Briar described how the Corey Lyle cult reached across the social divides, involving not just rich whites but minorities too. How Corey maintained an active recruitment program in the inner city. How his people distributed food, clothing, medicine to the poor. How they sheltered the homeless.

diAngeli smiled, a sunny woman in a sunny room. "Why did you introduce your father and stepmother to Corey Lyle?"

"They couldn't seem to shed the weight they'd put on since Dad's retirement. They said to me, if they could have one wish in this world, it was to be thin and fit again. Well, I instantly thought of Corey. He'd had spectacular success slimming down fat socialites."

"You'd seen such cases?"

"Oh, yes. I saw many, many fatties transformed overnight into slenderellas."

"Mr. Briar, after you introduced your father and stepmother to Corey Lyle, did you personally observe any changes or transformations in them or in their lifestyle?"

"Yes, indeed. And I was astonished. The big change was, they scaled way down. They stopped giving big parties. They stopped drinking and they stopped all prescription drugs. They became very concerned with the hunger and misery in the world. They rerouted all their charitable gifts to Corey."

"And did you observe *physical* changes in your father and stepmother after they met Corey Lyle?"

"Indeed I did. In three months they went from monsters of flab to charmingly pudgy."

The prosecutor requested permission to show eight photographs on closed-circuit TV.

The first showed a man and woman so bloated that there was not a line or wrinkle in the face of either. Except for a desperate weariness in the eyes, they could have been roly-poly children playing at dress-up.

"This was taken at a fund-raiser for Senator Pat Moynihan," Jack Briar said. "It was the third day of Dad and Amalia's weight-loss treatment, so as you can see there really hadn't been any progress to speak of."

Over succeeding photographs, the Briars must have shed a good sixty pounds each. Opening night at the Metropolitan Opera they seemed nearer their true ages, seventy-one and seventy-nine, but strong and trim and smiling, eyes serenely cheerful.

"In the next three months, my father and stepmother went from pudgy to normal—then to fashionably slim—then to enviably slim."

At a gala for the Metropolitan Museum Costume Institute, the process had clearly gone too far—the Briars were skeletons in evening clothes.

"But it didn't stop."

In the final photo, a *Paris Review* revel on a yacht in the Hudson, the skeletons had the thickness of paper cutouts and their eyes shone with a fevered, visionary intensity.

"The last year of Amalia and Dad's lives, they never

ate anything but raw carrots. Never drank anything but carrot juice. Their complexions became yellow. And they . . . shriveled—there's no other word for it. I spoke with them about their weight loss. Shouldn't they be checked by a doctor? My stepmother answered that flesh was corrupt, a burden."

"Had you heard anyone else express such an idea before?"

"I'd heard Corey say the same thing in lectures."

"Did you discuss your father and stepmother's health with Corey Lyle?"

"I was forced to. The January before my father and stepmother were murdered, at a dinner for King Juan Carlos, I *begged* Corey, 'Look at my poor father and stepmother over there—eating carrots while the rest of us stuff ourselves on rack of lamb!' "

"How did Corey Lyle reply?"

"Corey said, 'They have chosen their road.' "

"How did you interpret this remark?"

"Naturally, I took it to mean that Corey had absolutely no intention of taking them off that awful diet, even if it wound up killing them."

"Objection. Witness is not a mind reader or a doctor."

"Overruled."

"Why did you feel it was up to Corey Lyle to take your father and stepmother off their diet?"

"There was no one else they'd listen to."

Tess diAngeli walked to the jury box. "Mr. Briar, did you ever witness Corey Lyle heal a sick person?"

"Only once. I saw Corey stop a child's nosebleed."

In word and hand movement, Jack Briar set the scene: a fund-raising party in Zuleika Carlyle's garden over on Sutton Place. Tulips in bloom. Sunshine to die for. Peter Duchin and a great backup trio. Champagne and beluga. Caterers rushing with silver trays. A tray colliding with a seven-year-old child.

"And you know how children's nosebleeds can be. Well, Corey just crouched down and told that child: 'You are relaxed and fully at ease. . . .' " The witness's voice seemed to belong to somebody else now: it was deeper, booming, yet oddly soft and just a bit seductive. " 'When I touch your hand it will rise.' Corey touched the child's hand."

Jack Briar's left hand lay on the railing of the witness box. His right hand touched it. "The child's hand rose." Jack Briar's left hand floated up into the air, pulling jurors' eyes.

"Corey said, 'When I count to three your nose will stop bleeding.' Then Corey counted: 'One . . . two . . . three . . .' " Jack Briar brought his hands to rest in his lap. "And the nosebleed stopped."

diAngeli smiled. "Mr. Briar, did you ever witness an act of Santería or animal sacrifice by a member of the Corey Lyle cult?"

At the mention of the word *Santería,* the juror in front of Anne nudged his neighbor.

"Not exactly," Jack Briar said. "Not with my own eyes."

"Did any member of the Corey Lyle cult tell you they had participated in such acts or knew of members who had?"

"Yes. Six months after I introduced Dad to Corey, he told me several members of Corey's circle asked him to join a select group that practiced animal sacrifice. This was the first inkling I had that something might be a little batty in the state of Denmark. But Dad's

Alzheimer's was kicking in and I couldn't be sure whether the bats were inside his head or outside."

"Did your father tell you the purpose of these sacrifices?"

"Yes, he did, and I must say he seemed a little baffled by the whole thing. Befuddlement and confused recall are early signs of Alzheimer's. But according to Dad, it had to do with getting sexual favors through the intervention of the gods."

"Objection!" Elihu was shaking his head in disbelief. "It's one thing for this witness to offer his expertise in diagnosing Alzheimer's, but to offer blatant hearsay is beyond the pale!"

Tess diAngeli appeared politely astonished. "Your Honor, statements by a dying person are exceptions to the hearsay rule."

"Ladies and gentlemen of the jury." Judge Bernheim's broad, unhappy mouth thinned into a flat line. "The reason we are reluctant to accept hearsay testimony is that in olden times, before we had the rule excluding it, a witness might say, Tinker told me that Evers killed Chance, and eyewitnesses to the alleged crime didn't have to be produced to hang Evers. So nowadays we limit witnesses to their own direct knowledge. But there is an exception—statements made by a dying person. The theory is you don't lie when you're about to confront your Maker. So the issue here is whether John Briar knew he was dying when the witness says he made these statements."

Judge Bernheim turned to the witness. "Mr. Briar, how long after these statements did your father die? Was it over a year and a day?"

Jack Briar had to think for a moment before he nodded. "I believe so, Your Honor."

"Then I'm going to rule that the statements are hearsay and inadmissible."

Tess diAngeli lost none of her self-possession. "Mr. Briar, when did you last see your father and stepmother alive?"

"Amalia invited me to the apartment two years ago last May."

"Was anyone else present?"

"Two other people: her part-time maid, who spoke no recognizable language I ever heard, and her lawyer, Felix Logan."

"And did you learn the purpose of this gathering?"

"Indeed I did. Amalia asked me and the maid to witness her signature on her will. I made a little joke: 'Well, I know two people who aren't inheriting—your maid and me.' I believe witnesses can't inherit, am I right?"

"Was this the first you knew that Amalia Briar's estate plans did not include you?"

"It was the first hint."

"Was your father present at any time at this meeting?"

"No, my father was sleeping in his bedroom. I looked in on him—but he didn't recognize me."

"Did you discuss his condition with your stepmother?"

"I tried to, but she said Dad had started a regime of Belgian carrots, and he was a little disoriented and it was perfectly normal and there was nothing to worry about."

"After witnessing your stepmother's will, did you ever speak to your father again?"

"Never."

"Did you speak to your stepmother again?"

"You'd better believe it. I made a point of phoning

three times a week at a minimum. I kept begging to see her: 'Amalia,' I pleaded, 'at least let me bring you a basket of fresh fruit. Corey isn't going to excommunicate you over a *tangerine*!' But she kept putting me off. Finally I pinned her down to lunch, Tuesday after Labor Day."

"Would you describe the events of that day?"

"I arrived at the appointed time. The building staff was on strike. No one answered the intercom. The phone was busy and the operator said it was off the hook. I finally went to the precinct and persuaded a lady cop to let me into the apartment. Poor gal had to break down the door with a *crowbar.*"

"Would you describe what you found?"

"Dad was lying on his bedroom floor, dead. Amalia was in her own bedroom. She seemed to be asleep. 'Amalia,' I said, 'something dreadful has happened to Dad!' I shook her. But she was dead too."

Tess diAngeli let a moment slide by. "And after that time, did you and Corey Lyle discuss your father's and stepmother's deaths?"

"Yes, we had a long talk."

"When and where was this?"

"It was at Saint Bartholomew's Church—at my father and stepmother's funeral. At that time there was a lot of speculation in the press about the role Mickey Williams had played in their deaths. Well, Corey came straight up to me after the service and said Mickey Williams was innocent."

"Do you recall Corey Lyle's exact words to you?"

Jack Briar glanced toward heaven. "Corey said, 'Mickey is no guiltier than a pistol. If anyone killed Amalia and Johnny, it was me—I loaded that pistol and pointed it and pulled the trigger.' "

As the jury filed out of court for the lunch break, Thelma del Rio turned to Anne. “If I didn’t hate carrots, I’d give that diet a try.”

“I wouldn’t try it for too long,” Anne said.

FIFTEEN

12:15 P.M.

Britta Bailey had been married to a cop, and they lived in a modest old wood-frame on a quiet street in Woodside. Obviously neither of them had been a groundskeeper. Cardozo stepped around flowerpots and dead ferns and pushed the buzzer.

Roger Bailey answered the door in his bathrobe. His face was unshaved and pale, made even paler by the boyish splash of freckles across the bridge of his nose.

"Sorry to wake you up," Cardozo said.

"Vince." Bailey looked at him with a puzzled frown. "I already heard about Britta."

Which made it a little easier for Cardozo. "I just dropped by to say how sorry I am."

"I know. Thanks." Bailey stepped away from the door. He had the slow movements of a man feeling his way through a fog. "Come on in."

Daylight slatted through the living room Levolors,

dappling the sofa. A coffee cup sat on the TV like a robin that had strayed in through the window.

Bailey took the cup into the kitchen. Cardozo followed and glanced around at copper pots too gleaming ever to have been used. Spices and cooking staples were racked in bright lettered jars that he had a feeling no one had ever opened. A stale smell of lemon-scented something floated in the air.

Bailey fixed two cups of coffee. His actions were dazed and mechanical. Crockery rattled. Coffee spilled. He brought an open package of Oreos from the counter and pushed it across the table. "Have some breakfast. Or lunch. Whatever."

"No, thanks." Cardozo patted his stomach. "Gotta watch the old waistline."

Bailey hung a cigarette inside his lower lip and struck a kitchen match. He was watching Cardozo, waiting for him to get to the point.

"Roger . . . at a time like this, I hate to bother you with questions, and if you'd rather postpone it—"

Bailey blew out a perfect smoke ring. "You have a job to do."

"Did Britta ever mention having a French friend or acquaintance? Someone she called Mademoiselle?"

"Mademoiselle? Not that I can recall."

"It was the last thing she wrote in her notebook. Maybe it was someone she met in the line of duty? Or a friend's nickname? Or someone who did her hair?"

"She went to the same haircutter I do. Unless Britta knew something I don't, he's a signore, not a mademoiselle."

"Writing *Mademoiselle* and no name suggests it was someone she'd met before."

"She never mentioned any mademoiselles to me." Bailey pulled at the cord of his bathrobe. "You know how it is when you're both cops, working different shifts. There's not much time to talk."

"She was carrying a newspaper photograph in her wallet." Cardozo took out the clipping. "Know anything about it?"

Bailey nodded. "I saw her clip this out."

"When?"

"Tuesday night. I came home after my shift, she had old magazines and articles spread out on the sofa. Said she was looking for a decent photograph of Mickey Williams. That was the last time I saw her alive."

Silence caved in.

"Any idea why she wanted a photo of Williams?"

"Said she might have to identify him." Bailey pushed a strand of dark hair back behind his ear. "You know Britta. She was like this kitchen. Always prepared."

"Identify him where? In a lineup? In court?"

"She didn't say. I didn't ask. Britta and me, we didn't talk a whole lot." Bailey stared down at the table. "Look—you're going to find out and I'd rather you found out from me. We hadn't been getting along for almost a year."

"I'm sorry to hear that." Cardozo's tone was low and sympathetic. "What was the trouble?"

"Nothing spectacular, no fights, no scenes—just in our own quiet way disagreeing more and more. Which is why there are two television sets. We weren't home together often, but when we were, she liked cop shows; I can't stand them. Sounds petty, but so's marriage."

Shock makes some people quiet. Others it makes chatty. Roger Bailey was one of the chatty ones. He seemed to have forgotten, or didn't care, that the spouse is always the first suspect in a homicide.

"Little things add up. In our case they were starting to add up to zero." He ground out a half-smoked cigarette in his saucer. "In fact, as soon as we could think of a way to break the news to her parents, we were planning to divorce."

"Whose idea was that?"

"She was the one who came out and said it."

"Did she give you a reason—besides cop shows?"

"Said she needed space to find herself. To tell the truth, I think she met somebody." He said it in the sort of voice a man uses to say it's seventy-two degrees outside.

"What makes you think that?"

"Some of her phone calls. Some of her excuses."

"Any idea who it might have been?"

"No idea. She'd developed a secretive side. And frankly it was a relief. Roommates don't argue as much as lovers."

"So you'd become roommates?"

Bailey nodded. "Long time. More coffee?"

"I'm fine, thanks. Roger, what shift were you working yesterday?"

"Four to midnight."

"And what did you do after your shift?"

"Showered, changed, and came straight home. Vince, I hate to make your work harder, but I'm telling you up front, I didn't kill her."

"I know you didn't. Any sign that she came home during the day?"

Bailey shook his head. "She didn't come back yesterday. I can tell because I left a note on the refrigerator. It's still there."

In the windowless green-walled interview room, Corey Lyle watched as Dotson Elihu played the restored section of the police videotape.

"My father had great sympathy for Mickey Williams." Jack Briar was a flickering green-edged shadow, his voice a tinny monotone. "Dad loaned Mickey his apartment during a cruise. When he returned unexpectedly, he discovered Mickey with an underage girl. He asked Mickey to return the key."

Corey Lyle drew his shoulders back. His eyes narrowed, grim and green and weary. "How does any of this help us?"

Dotson Elihu fixed his client with a lethally patient stare. "Mickey Williams is the Achilles' heel of the People's case. He's already got three convictions for child molestation. They've been erased from the national crime stats, but the paperwork is on file in Austin, Texas. He can't risk a fourth. With this tape, we create a reasonable suspicion that he was still molesting kids and John Briar saw him. Which gave Briar the power to put Mickey away for life. Which gave Mickey a motive to silence him. Which leaves you in the clear."

Something had altered in Corey's posture. He was sitting with his hands neatly clasped in his lap, chin down, eyelids lowered.

"Add to that Dan Hippolito's autopsy on Amalia, which suggests she died a natural death, and at the very least we'll get a hung jury—maybe even an acquittal."

"No." Corey shook his head. "We can't use that tape."

For an instant, shock took Elihu's power to speak. "And why the hell not?"

"Because Mickey told me about those children, in confidence."

"You *knew* about these kids and never mentioned it? Who are you trying to help, the prosecution?"

Corey's eyes refused all argument. "I will not betray a sacred confidence to save my own sinful skin."

"Core—this is me, Dot. You don't have to playact here. You know and I know that Mickey doesn't give a damn about you—he's throwing you to the dogs to save himself!"

"I'm not playacting. And it so happens Mickey cares deeply about me and the Fellowship. And in his own quiet way, he's helping me."

There was a tiny vibration, a movement of understanding inside Elihu's mind. "I shared my home with Mickey for two of the most horrible months of my life. I came to know his thinking and his proclivities. I don't like the sound of his helping you, and I don't want to hear any more about it."

In the side room at Eugene's Patio, Anne sat at the end of the jurors' table, waiting for the waitress to bring her order.

"Excuse me." Ben Esposito's hand rested on the empty chair beside her. He was wearing a wedding ring. "Is this seat taken?" He drew the chair out and sat and stared at a battered plastic menu. Above their heads a wooden ceiling fan revolved slowly. "What's good today?"

"I ordered health salad," Anne said.

"You shouldn't take nutritional crap from the food fascists. I'm going to have a cheeseburger. With bacon."

"The Coreyites are deep into kiddy porn." Thelma

del Rio was loading spaghetti and breaded chicken cutlet onto her fork. "The government has photos."

Anne looked up. "Where did you hear that?"

"During one of those sidebars."

"I didn't hear any of that. And I was sitting right next to you."

"You should get your hearing checked."

"Hey, Thelma, give it a break," Ben Esposito said. "We could have a mistrial if you repeat those things."

"Excuse me. I thought it was a free country."

Turning toward Anne, Ben lowered his voice. "There's one on every jury." He said it as though they were confidants. What he wanted, Anne sensed, was to show that a jury foreman could be like Type-O blood—and get along with anyone.

"Corey was giving the kids drugs." Now Thelma was talking to Shoshana. Poking at a plate of fruit salad, red Jell-O, and cottage cheese, Shoshana didn't look the least bit interested or bothered.

"Can you believe it?" Thelma said. "Drugs. To break down their inhibitions."

"Inhibitions?" Donna Scomoda said. "I've never met an inhibited kid in my life."

Half the jurors had ordered big meals. By the time they had all eaten and paid, the better part of an hour was used up.

"Thelma's inside poop gives me the jitters," Shoshana muttered. "I wish she'd keep it to herself."

Anne nodded. "Funny she's the only one that overhears it."

Two hours after lunch, Dotson Elihu was well into his cross-examination. "Is there any chance that we can look forward to your write-up of this trial in one of our national magazines?"

Jack Briar sat forward in the witness chair. His manner became confiding. "Yes, indeed. I'm writing this case up for *Savoir* magazine as a three-part series."

"Then you're being paid for your presence here?"

"By my publisher, naturally."

"Tell us, Mr. Briar . . ." Elihu strolled a short distance from the witness box. "Did your magazine fee go up when your father and stepmother were murdered?"

"Objection."

"Sustained."

"Did your magazine fee go up when your publisher learned you would testify at this trial?"

"Objection."

"Sustained."

"Mr. Briar," Elihu asked pleasantly, "you say your father told you he'd heard rumors of sexual activities involving cult members and children?"

"Objection." diAngeli sprang to her feet. "The witness made no such statement."

"But he did indeed," Elihu said. "On the police tape."

Corey Lyle's face whipped around to stare at his attorney. He shook his head two times, slowly.

"Your Honor, there is no such statement on any tape—nor has any such tape been introduced into evidence."

"Objection sustained." The judge glared at Elihu. "Mr. Elihu, this is cross-examination and you will question the witness accordingly. Now, I don't want to have to remind you again."

"Mr. Briar . . ." Dotson Elihu placed his hands on the railing of the witness box. "You testified that when you found your stepmother dead, you thought she was asleep. You say you shook her. How roughly did you shake her?"

"Why on earth would I shake an old woman roughly?"

"She'd cut you out of her will, hadn't she?"

"I wouldn't brutalize an elderly woman over a financial disagreement."

"Do you remember the body's original position before you shook it?"

Jack Briar was wary now. "Well, I—"

"Mr. Briar, will you please tell this court, under oath, exactly how Amalia Briar was positioned when you entered her bedroom?"

Jack Briar didn't answer.

"Could she have been lying on her side?" Elihu's tone was suddenly gentle, almost friendly. "With her face down?"

"I don't recall exactly. I don't think she was face-down."

"But you're not sure?"

"Not a hundred percent, no."

"Mr. Briar, is it not a fact that your father's will left his entire estate to your stepmother?"

"Objection—relevance."

Elihu wheeled. "Your Honor, I intend to show relevance."

"Overruled. Witness may answer."

"Yes, my father left his entire estate to his wife."

"And is it not a fact that one week after your father's death was discovered . . . you filed suit contesting his will?"

"That's true, I contested his will."

"On what grounds?"

"Objection." Tess diAngeli sprang to her feet. "This line of questioning has no bearing whatsoever on any material raised in direct."

"Overruled."

"Mr. Briar . . ." Elihu returned to the defense table and picked up a sheaf of court papers. "Did you not depose under oath that your father's marriage ceased being a marriage five years before his death, that Amalia Briar locked her bedroom door and refused him his conjugal rights?"

Tess diAngeli was on her feet again. "Your Honor, I—"

"Overruled."

Jack Briar drew himself up. "Shortly after I introduced my father and stepmother to Corey Lyle, my father told me Amalia had decided to take a vow of celibacy. She told me the same thing."

"Objection—hearsay!"

"Your honor." Elihu turned, sighing. "The People cannot impeach their own witness's sworn declaration to the New York probate court."

"Objection overruled."

Jack Briar continued. "The upshot was, my father and stepmother stopped having sexual relations. There was no secret about it. They told everyone."

"Did your father say he intended to be celibate as well?"

"He never mentioned the subject to me."

"Do you know if he was celibate after that point?"

"It was none of my business."

"Is that a *no*?"

"Yes." Jack Briar's face colored. "That's a *no.* I don't know."

"Then it's conceivable that your father met with another woman—or other women?"

"Anything's conceivable, I suppose, but he never mentioned such a relationship to me."

At the prosecutor's table, diAngeli scrawled on a sheet of scratch paper. Her assistant read the note and shook his head in the negative.

"To your knowledge, was your father in the habit of giving friends the key to his apartment?"

"Not to my knowledge. He certainly never gave one to me."

Elihu gave the point a moment to register: conceivably, one or more unnamed persons had had access to the apartment. "Mr. Briar, I didn't ask if your father gave *you* a key, I asked if he gave *friends* keys."

Jack Briar's face colored. "I don't know. I honestly can't conceive of it."

"Ellie," Cardozo said, "what are you working on?"

"Two homicides and a robbery." Ellie Siegel's fingers flew across the keyboard of her P.C. She didn't look up. "And twenty assorted lesser felonies. Why—what did you have in mind?"

"Would you have time to check out Roger Bailey's movements Wednesday evening?"

"He was working the four to midnight shift."

"I know that, but where? Who saw him?"

"I'll bet his partner saw him."

"Talk to his partner and make sure. Find out where he went after his shift. And another thing—Britta asked him for a divorce. He thinks she met somebody else but he doesn't know who. Look into that, okay?"

"Think he killed her?"
"He's hiding something."
"Most men are hiding something."
"Mmm. See if you can find out what."

SIXTEEN

Friday, September 20
Third day of trial
7:50 A.M.

In the deputy assistant medical examiner's office under First Avenue, Cardozo turned a page of the preliminary autopsy report on Britta Bailey. "Before the killer suffocated her, he hit her on the side of the face with a straight-edged object?"

Dan Hippolito nodded. "Which is how she lost her upper left incisor."

"What kind of straight-edged object?"

"Possibly the open door of an automobile glove compartment. Which would fit with the synthetic carpet fibers on her clothing and the synthetic leather fibers in her mouth and nostrils. Her face was pushed into the front seat of a car and held there till she stopped breathing."

Cardozo tried not to visualize it. Easier said than done.

"Pontiac uses that fiber," Dan said. "So do American-assembled Hondas. And NYPD cars don't."

Cardozo turned to the next page of the report. He scanned for a moment in silence. "Estimated time of death, somewhere between five and seven P.M. Wednesday?"

"That's going by the cottage cheese and the hydrochloric acid in her stomach."

Cardozo thought back. "The ground was wet under her body—but it didn't rain till two A.M. Thursday. So she was left in the rail yard after two. But if she was killed early Wednesday evening . . ."

"What bothers you about that?"

"The idea of driving around for seven hours with a corpse in the car."

"Who says he was driving around? He could have been parked. He could have been having dinner. Watching a movie."

"Then he's a sociopath."

"From what I've seen, it's a possibility."

Cardozo's mind kept trying out connections. "Funny. John Briar was suffocated by a sociopath and Britta was the first uniform on that scene. And two years later she turns up suffocated, possibly by a sociopath."

"Relax, Vince, you're reaching too hard." Dan pushed up from the desk and ambled to the counter where he kept his Juicematic machine. "There are a lot of sociopaths in this world, and statistically, strangulation is the third most common form of homicide in the United States."

"What do statistics say about killers changing their M.O.?"

"I'm making some fresh tangelo juice. Could I interest you in some?"

"No, thanks. Does an M.O. tend to stay constant over time, like handwriting?"

"Depends on the killer. Professionals tailor their M.O.'s to circumstances."

"And professionals are sociopaths."

"Have to be. But Britta and John Briar weren't the work of professionals. They were heat-of-passion jobs. The killers went in without a weapon and they improvised with the material at hand: a glove compartment door, a leather seat, a pillow."

That pillow nagged at Cardozo. "The prosecutor didn't want Britta or me testifying about goose down in John Briar's mouth and throat."

"That figures." Dan sliced citrus fruit and fed the slices one at a time into the screeching machine. "The presence of goose down implies that John Briar was murdered, but the *absence* of goose down implies that Amalia died a natural death."

"Which was your finding."

Dan nodded. "And since the charge is conspiracy to commit *two* murders, it's not a finding the state's going to let loose in court." He brought over two cups of juice and placed one on the table beside his guest. "I could see preferring to skip the whole issue of goose down."

Cardozo sipped. "This is good."

"You should get one of these machines."

"There's no room in my office."

"Throw out some files."

"I wish." Cardozo closed the report. "How did the D.A.'s office react to your findings on the Briars?"

"I never heard from the D.A.'s office."

"They didn't ask you to testify?"

Dan shook his head. "I never expected them to. Not

when Lalwani's findings suited them so much better than mine."

Cardozo recalled that just last week Hank Lalwani, the controversial medical examiner for Queens County, had been accused by a television network of slanting his findings to suit prosecutors. "And what were Lalwani's findings?"

"What you'd expect. He said they both were murdered."

"At present," the tall man with the high-cheekboned, closely shaved head said, "I'm in my eighth year as a crime scene technician with the NYPD."

Judge Bernheim interrupted: "Ladies and gentlemen of the jury, Mr. Kelly is certified as an expert. That means he's allowed to give us his opinion as a recognized professional in his field. It does not mean that his opinion necessarily has the weight of evidence. You yourselves are going to have to decide what weight you ultimately wish to attach to the opinion portion of his testimony."

"Mr. Kelly," Tess diAngeli said, "would you tell the jury a little about a crime scene technician's duties at the scene of a murder?"

Alvin Kelly described how minute particles and sometimes not-so-minute quantities of blood and skin, hair and saliva were invariably deposited at a scene of violent death. "Some belong to the victim, some to the killer or killers, and sometimes some belong to third parties." He told how he went about detecting the presence of such particles; how he collected them and preserved them.

"And would you explain to this jury exactly how you processed the scene of the Briar murders?"

As Alvin Kelly explained, diAngeli asked him to identify several dozen small plastic envelopes. Kelly considered each envelope in turn and stated that it contained a sample of tissue from John Briar or his wife, Amalia, that he had personally recovered this sample from the murder scene.

"Your Honor," diAngeli said, "I ask that the jury be allowed to examine this evidence."

For a moment the judge's gaze met the prosecutor's. A message passed. Annoyance. "Very well. If you insist."

The bailiff distributed the envelopes to the jury, like party favors. The immaculately packaged bits passed from juror to juror: white and brown dust, gray hairs, shreds of cloth—the last molecules left behind by John Briar and his wife, Amalia.

Cardozo figured Roger Bailey's captain would give him at least a week off; and eleven A.M. seemed a reasonable hour to phone a bereft husband who had nothing on his schedule but drink and sleep.

Bailey answered on the third ring. "Yeah?"

"Roger—Vince Cardozo. Did I wake you?"

"That's okay."

"How are you doing?"

"I don't know." He sounded ragged. "I went down yesterday to see her. They showed me a picture. To spare me the shock."

"Everyone gets a picture nowadays. No one sees the body but the examiner."

"She didn't look dead. The whole thing feels unreal.

The grief counselor says I should go through scrapbooks. Britta and I had a lot of memories. I'd forgot how many."

"Roger, I have one fast question. Did Britta have any heart or lung problems? Did a doctor ever prescribe anything?"

"Funny you should ask—I was just looking at pictures of Britta and me white-water rafting on our honeymoon. She was stronger than me. Had a heart like an ox. Never had any trouble. Not even a skipped beat. About her lungs—I never heard anything."

"Okay, Roger. I'll let you get back to your scrapbooks."

As Cardozo hung up the receiver he saw that Ellie Siegel had made herself at home in a chair. She arched an inquiring eyebrow. "How's he doing?"

Cardozo shook his head. "Grief therapist."

"Then they're monitoring him for suicide." The police chief had become alarmed about the suicide rate among cops: it was fourteen times the civilian rate and rising. "Widowers are in the second highest risk category. And Bailey's partner says he's been depressed for the last three months."

"And does his partner say where he was Wednesday night?"

"He spent the whole shift in the squad car."

"And afterward?"

"She drove him home."

"His partner's a she?"

"It happens, Vince. More and more. Her name's Edie Vasquez."

Cardozo tapped a pencil on the edge of the phone. "Any rumor of anything between them?"

Ellie sighed the sort of sigh that said all men, but

especially Vince Cardozo, had a one-track mind. Cardozo had a problem with Ellie's sighs.

"It happens, Ellie."

"I suppose you want me to check?"

"Tactfully."

Ellie stopped at the door and threw him a look. "By the way, if Britta had a love life, she wasn't telling anyone at the precinct."

"Keep digging."

SEVENTEEN

9:35 A.M.

"Dr. Lalwani . . ." Tess diAngeli had a welcoming smile for the witness. "Would you tell the jury a little about your work?"

"I'm assistant chief medical examiner for Queens County." Dr. Hank Lalwani appeared to have dressed for a state funeral. A tall, extremely thin, white-haired East Indian, he spoke in a melodious voice seasoned with a British accent. He detailed his curriculum vitae—degrees earned and honorary, previous employment, college lectureships, articles published in professional journals.

Judge Bernheim explained to the jury that the witness was an expert.

"Objection, Your Honor." Dotson Elihu shot to his feet. "The People gave the defense only Dr. Lalwani's written autopsy reports. The People did not turn over the tapes he recorded while performing the autopsies."

"Your Honor," diAngeli said, "the People turned over all medical records in their possession."

"The issue, Your Honor, is the medical records that were allowed to *escape* the People's possession."

"I can't see why this matter wasn't raised in pretrial." Judge Bernheim beckoned. "Counsel will approach the bench."

The attorneys conferred with the judge in low, buzzing voices.

"Mr. Lalwani . . ." Tess diAngeli returned to the witness. "Two years ago, on the twelfth of September, did you perform an autopsy on the body of John Briar?"

"I did."

"Could you outline your findings for us?"

"John Briar was a dark-complected Caucasian male of seventy-nine years of age. Examination of his body and organs revealed an extremely malnourished person—body weight was low, bones were deficient in calcium, intestines showed minor bloating and ulceration. . . ." He went on for several minutes.

"And what do such findings suggest to you?"

"They are symptoms of starvation and carotene excess. They indicate John Briar had been living on a diet of carrots for a year or so prior to death."

"Would such a diet be recommended by a doctor?"

"Objection."

"Ms. diAngeli," Judge Bernheim said, "you know better than that. In my court, you're going to have to lay a foundation for that question."

diAngeli turned to her witness. "Dr. Lalwani, are you board certified?"

"I am."

"And the nature of board certification is that you are

competent and licensed to practice general medicine on living patients, like any M.D.?"

"Yes, ma'am."

"As a licensed physician, do you feel qualified to answer the question: Would a diet of carrots be recommended by a doctor?"

"I do, and no responsible doctor would recommend it. Such a diet, pursued over a year to a year and a half, would be fatal."

"Was it malnutrition that caused John Briar's death?"

"No. Hemorrhaging at the back of the eyeballs showed that the cause of death was asphyxiation. Saturday before Labor Day, between midnight and two A.M., John Briar was smothered with his bed pillow."

"Your Honor, I request permission to show People's Exhibit Fifteen." A color photo of a malnourished seventy-nine-year-old male, lying naked beneath a disheveled bathrobe, came up on the TV screen. "Is this John Briar as he was found after his murder?"

"It is."

A stained, crumpled pillow lay next to his head.

"And is that the pillow the murderer used to suffocate his victim?"

"It is."

"Did you examine that pillow?"

"I did. I found saliva on the pillowcase. The DNA in the saliva matched John Briar's DNA."

"Permission to show People's Exhibit Sixteen." Another color photo came up. It showed a frighteningly thin old woman, naked on a stainless-steel autopsy table. "Is this a photograph of Amalia Briar?"

"It is," Lalwani said.

"Could you tell the jury your autopsy findings?"

"Amalia Briar was a fair-complected Caucasian female of approximately seventy-two years of age. Examination of her corpse revealed an extremely malnourished person, with bloating and ulceration of the lower intestine. She showed faint yellow pigmentation of the skin and nails, which is a common symptom of massive carotene excess. It suggested she'd been living on a diet of carrots for a year or so prior to death."

"Was it the diet of carrots and the resulting acute malnutrition that caused Mrs. Briar's death?"

"No."

diAngeli's dress flared into violet as she stepped through a shaft of sunlight. "Do you have any idea how asphyxiation occurred?"

"I have a very clear idea. I found carrot particles on the pillowcase. I also found carrot particles on Amalia Briar's upper molars and in her esophagus—her upper throat."

At the prosecutor's table, the assistant was peeling tape off the flaps of a cardboard carton.

"I conclude," Lalwani said, "that the murderer pressed the pillow into her face long enough to cut off her air supply. Due to her weakened state, she put up no struggle."

The assistant handed diAngeli two small pillows neatly bagged in plastic. Feathers had leaked into both bags. Even at this distance Anne could see stains.

diAngeli approached the witness stand, holding the bundle outstretched like holy relics soaked in the blood of a saint. "Is this the pillow that killed John Briar?"

Silence flowed through the court.

Lalwani considered the pillow, his lips tight and thin. "This is the pillow."

"And is this the pillow that killed Amalia Briar?"

"It is."

diAngeli turned. "Your Honor, the People ask that these pillows be marked People's Exhibit Number seventeen and eighteen."

The bailiff took the pillows to the court clerk's desk.

Judge Bernheim shifted papers, looking for something. "The pillows will be so marked."

diAngeli asked the witness if he had been able to determine the approximate time of Amalia Briar's death.

"Amalia Briar was asphyxiated sometime between five and six A.M. on Labor Day."

Cardozo had taken a moment to finish up some backlogged paperwork when the smell of Old Spice invaded the cubicle.

"Hey, Vince." Greg Monteleone's voice. Boyish and exultant. He was holding an enormous cheese Danish in one hand; an orange Post-it was sticking to the Danish. "A call came in Wednesday, three P.M. Woman with a French accent." He angled his thumb and stuck the Post-it to the desk lamp. "Britta Bailey caught the squeal."

"That took you twenty-four hours?"

"Couldn't get to it till this morning. Had a break in the Gonzales case. Sorry."

"What was the break?"

"False alarm."

Cardozo reminded himself to have a look at Greg's case reports. Something was going on besides work. Greg had started wearing that gold chain like a dog tag and he was basting himself in Old Spice.

Cardozo peeled the little orange square off the lamp. "What's this scribble?"

Greg tilted his head. "Mademoiselle Josette de Gramont. She phoned in the complaint. She works at that private school over on Madison—the École Française."

Dotson Elihu had a purposeful way of moving across empty space, which shaped the courtroom into an audience. There was a promise in that stride: *Keep your eyes open, folks, and you'll see something explode.*

"Dr. Lalwani . . . isn't it a fact that during your autopsy of John Briar, you tape-recorded your observations?"

A half-beat hesitation. "I did."

"Didn't you state on that tape that John Briar died of accidental self-suffocation?"

"I made no such statement."

Elihu was standing close now, hunched toward the witness. "Did you not also state on that tape that the torn bed pillow was pressed into John Briar's face *after* death?"

Lalwani shifted in his chair. "I made no such statement."

Elihu shook his head; a show of bemusement. "Your Honor, I request permission to play to the jury the relevant portion of this witness's autopsy tape."

"Your Honor," diAngeli said, "that tape cannot be played. Mr. Elihu is bluffing. As he is well aware—we do not possess it."

With an expression of astonishment, Elihu turned to the witness. "Dr. Lalwani, didn't you testify that you turned the tape of John Briar's autopsy over to the prosecution?"

"I normally turn such tapes over to the prosecution, but in this case I was unable to. We were short of tapes and I had to reuse the Briar tape to record an autopsy performed later the same day."

Elihu's incredulous gaze moved slowly across the jury, then back to Lalwani. "Then we have only your recollection as to what that tape contained?"

"No, I prepared a written report from the tape before it was recorded over."

Elihu strolled three steps, thinking, and stopped. "Did you tape-record your observations during the autopsy of Amalia Briar?"

"I did."

"And didn't you state on *that* tape that Amalia Briar died of accidental self-suffocation?"

"I did not."

"Then perhaps we could play the tape of Amalia Briar's autopsy and straighten this matter out. You *did* turn the tape of Amalia Briar's autopsy over to the prosecution?"

diAngeli leaped up. "Your Honor, I object. Counsel knows that both tapes were recorded over. This is repetitious and getting us nowhere."

"Mr. Elihu," the judge said, "do you have a point to make?"

"Yes, Your Honor. One tape might conceivably have been recorded over, as the witness claims. But for two autopsy tapes—both critical to the defense—to be recorded over goes way beyond probability."

"Objection—counsel is neither a witness nor an expert in probability."

"Your Honor, it hardly takes an expert in probability to smell wholesale suppression of evidence."

Judge Bernheim whacked her gavel on the bench. "The People are sustained, and the defense will please move forward."

"Your Honor, I request that the jury be shown People's Exhibit Seventeen."

"Objection." diAngeli shoved back her chair. "The witness was never questioned concerning that photograph."

Elihu tossed the prosecutor a courtly smile. "I'm not cross-examining on the photograph. I'm cross-examining on the dead woman. I request the photograph purely to refresh the witness's memory."

"Objection overruled," Judge Bernheim said. "The photograph is already in evidence. Show it."

A moment later the image of Amalia Briar, serenely dead on a raft of percale pillows, glowed on the TV screen.

"Dr. Lalwani—you claim that this is a photograph of a woman who was savagely murdered, a woman who died in abject terror?"

"She was near death and unable to defend herself. It took very little force to suffocate her. She may not even have been aware of what was happening."

"You say a pillow was used to suffocate John Briar, because the DNA of saliva on his pillow matched his own DNA."

"Correct."

"You mentioned no saliva on Amalia Briar's pillow, yet you claim *her* pillow was used to smother *her*. What evidence supports this conclusion?"

"Carrot particles on her pillow and in her mouth."

"I see. The carrot DNA on the pillow matched the carrot DNA in her mouth?"

"I didn't test the carrot DNA."

"You didn't test it." Elihu stroked his chin. "Now, Doctor, you say you found hemorrhaging at the back of

John Briar's eyeballs, and you say this proves he was suffocated."

"Correct."

"Did you find similar hemorrhaging at the back of Amalia Briar's eyeballs?"

"I did not. But in some cases—"

Elihu turned. "Doctor, are you familiar with sudden infant death syndrome?"

"Objection."

"I'm going to allow that question," Judge Bernheim said.

"Yes," Lalwani said in a guarded voice, "I'm familiar with the phenomenon."

"In SIDS, don't infants sometimes asphyxiate themselves?"

"They sometimes roll onto their stomach and position their mouth and nose in the pillow or bedclothes. If they lack the strength or coordination to roll to their side, they risk asphyxiation."

"What is the effect of long-term starvation upon an elderly person's strength and coordination?"

"Those abilities would be somewhat compromised."

"Could an elderly, starved, weakened, bedridden person such as Amalia Briar . . . suffocate herself?"

"Accidental suffocations among the elderly do occur. But Amalia Briar died faceup."

"But if she died facedown—hypothetically, now—would the evidence rule out accidental death?"

"Not necessarily, but she died faceup."

"Why bother to kill her if she was already so near death?"

"Are you asking me to read minds?"

"I'm asking you for an expert opinion. Why didn't the

murderer roll her onto her stomach if that would make death appear accidental?"

"In my opinion, the murderer did not care whether or not the death was detected as a murder."

EIGHTEEN

2:20 P.M.

Anne sat in the jury room, watching the sunlight walk across the floor. She could feel resentment filling the room like a cold, dark fluid.

Abe da Silva, the bald-headed juror, was tossing paper gliders at the wastebasket. Ramon Culpeper had laid out a game of cards on the conference table. Thelma del Rio peeked around his elbow. "Solitaire?"

"Not exactly."

"What kind of cards are they?"

"New Age."

P. C. Cabot scowled at his watch as though he suspected it of lying to him. "She tells us to be back at two sharp, and it's nearly two-thirty. What the hell do these judges *do*?"

"One of the Coreyites' victims almost died," Thelma was saying. "Surgeons had to work on her for *ten hours* to close her up."

"I didn't hear anything like that," Shoshana said.

"Thelma, please," Anne said. "I really wish we could talk about something else."

Thelma drew herself up to full sitting height, her features righteous. "I guess some people don't want to know what's happening to children nowadays."

"Some of us happen to love and care about kids," Anne said. "And we resent having their pain and suffering reduced to prurient gossip."

"Right on," Abe da Silva said.

"Well, I'm *sorry.*" Thelma mustered a look of dainty astonishment. "It's not as though I was trying to personally offend you, but I thought as jurors we ought to know the kind of evidence Judge Bernheim is suppressing."

"If the judge suppressed it," Seymour Shen said, "how did you happen to hear it?"

"I think Thelma's making it up," Donna Scomoda said.

"Hey. Didn't you hear me yesterday?" Ben Esposito said. "Don't discuss the case. Those are our orders."

Anne had a sudden screaming need to get away from this claustrophobic little room, to go out and breathe the exhaust-laden air of the street.

"Okay, everyone who bet on the games . . ." Lara Duggan rose from her seat. "Since we're sequestered, I may not be able to get the payoffs till after the verdict."

Groans from half the jurors.

"So anyone who wants to withdraw, can. On the other hand, depending on circumstances, I might be able to get the payoffs before the verdict."

"What do you mean," Abe da Silva said, " 'circumstances'?"

"That's all I'm going to say. If you want your money back, say so now."

There was a jangling of keys. The door opened and the bailiff's head popped in. "The judge is ready."

"You spoke with Sergeant Britta Bailey Wednesday," Cardozo said. It was a statement, but it was a question too.

"I did." Josette de Gramont, headmistress of the École Française on East 64th Street, sat with unbending spine behind an enormous carved wooden desk. She was a waif-thin woman with a giant gray coiffure. "That was the second time I spoke with her."

"What was the first time?"

The air in Mademoiselle's gray-curtained office smelled of potpourri. A shaft of refracted afternoon light fell on the fireplace.

"Last Tuesday I phoned the precinct to report a man in a car illegally double-parked on Madison Avenue. The children were playing in the schoolyard and I didn't like the way he was watching them." Mademoiselle de Gramont glanced down at her hands. Ancient, liver-spotted hands clasped together on the desktop. "Officer Bailey came to the school—but the man drove away before she could talk to him."

"What kind of car was he driving?"

"It looked new—it was blue—four doors."

"You don't recall the make?"

"American—but I'm not good at recognizing makes."

"Tell me about Wednesday."

"Wednesday he was back. This time he was photographing the children."

"From the car?"

She nodded. "He had a camera with a long lens."

"Telephoto."

"He seemed to have a particular interest in one of the boys—Toby Talbot."

Cardozo jotted the name in his notebook.

"Again I phoned Sergeant Bailey. She came and spoke to Toby. Then she went to speak to the man. I was called to the hallway and when I came back, he was gone."

"Did you see Sergeant Bailey after he left?"

"No."

"Did you see her speak to him?"

"I saw her approach the car and stand by the window, but I can't say I actually saw her speak with him."

"Did she by any chance show you a photograph and ask if it was the man in the car?"

"She didn't show me any photograph."

"Did you see her show Toby Talbot a photograph?"

"No, I didn't. But that doesn't prove anything."

"Could I speak with Toby Talbot?"

"I'll have to get his mother's permission." Mademoiselle de Gramont found the number in her Rolodex. She lifted the telephone receiver and dialed.

In the corridor on the other side of the half-opened door, children passed, dressed in navy blue school uniforms. They didn't run; they walked. They weren't shouting; they were conversing. In French. It struck Cardozo as eerie.

Mademoiselle hung up the phone. "I could only get a recorded message. Mrs. Talbot is on jury duty. Without her permission, I can't allow you to speak to the boy."

"Perhaps I could speak with Toby Talbot's father?"

"Toby's parents are divorced. I believe his father lives in Seattle."

"Then who's taking care of Toby?"

"Mrs. Talbot has a Dutch au pair who looks after the boy."

"I'd like to speak with her. Could you give me Mrs. Talbot's home phone?"

Bare feet twitching beneath her on the living room sofa, Kyra Talbot stubbed out the eighth cigarette she'd chain-smoked in the last half hour. She hated herself for giving in to the craving, but her nerves were screaming.

As she ate, she glanced through the noon mail. Bills, bills, junk, and a letter from the co-op. But no airline tickets.

"Juliana," she shouted, "the travel agency was supposed to leave an envelope with the doorman."

Juliana stepped in from the kitchen. "He didn't mention it to me."

"I hope to God they haven't screwed up. Would you go downstairs and double-check?"

Juliana grimaced. "Cigarettes and junk food and checking with the doorman every half hour—are you getting a little compulsive?"

"I'm getting a little crazy, and your attitude isn't helping."

"Me? Attitude?" Juliana strode to the front door and slammed it behind her.

Kyra unwrapped the sandwich Juliana had brought her from the deli—low-fat cream cheese on date-nut bread. The first bite tasted like burnt leaves on cardboard. She opened the letter from the co-op. It was a bank notice informing the treasurer that her last check for the monthly maintenance had bounced.

Frowning, she got out her checkbook and her last statement. She did a quick computation with her calculator. Deduct the outstanding checks for Con Ed and Nynex and MasterCard, for Toby's tuition at the École, for the mortgage. Add the three-thousand-dollar overdraft line. Deduct the check for the maintenance, and she should show a net balance of . . .

Minus three dollars and two cents.

She realized what had happened: Some computer had bounced her check because of a piddling three dollars. She had to smile. So what if all her checks bounced? So what if the co-op evicted her or the school expelled Toby? For all it mattered, let Con Ed turn off her lights. Neither she nor Toby was going to be around long enough to be bothered.

And then a thought darkened her mind. What if the Voyageur check had bounced too?

But there was no check. I used my company travel card.

She paced to the window and stared down at traffic flowing along Barrow Street. No sign of the minivan from Voyageur Travel.

What if someone in the accounting department caught the unauthorized charge? What if I wind up stuck here in New York?

The front door flew open and Juliana bounced in. "Voyageur, finally."

She stood aside, and Sally, the travel agent from Voyageur, came briskly across the room, an envelope clutched in one hand. "Sorry to bust in, but I need your signature."

Damn, Kyra thought, *I'm supposed to be on jury duty—no one can know I'm here.*

"What a disaster!" Sally said brightly. "They canceled your Concorde."

Kyra's heart gave a painful thump. "Canceled?"

"Not to worry, I got you onto Air France, first class. If

you'll just sign . . ." Sally handed over the Air France tickets for Kyra and Toby and an American Express charge form with the card number already written in. "I've never seen your apartment before." She turned to study a painting on the wall. "That's a Hockney, isn't it?"

"My mother bought it years ago, before he was expensive." Kyra scratched her signature at the bottom of the charge form. "Concorde will refund, won't they?"

"Or you could credit it against your return flight."

"I'm not sure of my return plans."

"Really? And usually you're so sure of everything." Sally took the charge form and studied it before slipping it into her briefcase. "Anything else you need?"

"Not a thing."

"Then I'd better run."

Kyra saw the travel agent to the front door. When she returned to the living room, Juliana had flicked on the TV and was channel-surfing with the remote.

"Are you an idiot, or what?" Kyra said.

"Beg your pardon?"

"You know I'm supposed to be on jury duty. How could you come waltzing in here with that woman?"

Juliana shrugged. "She said she couldn't leave the tickets without your signature."

"You always have an excuse for screwing up."

"What the hell was I supposed to do? You've been wailing all day about those tickets."

That word *wailing* did it. "I've just about had it with you."

"Likewise."

"Fine. Turn off that TV and pack your bags and get out of my home."

The color drained from Juliana's cheeks. "You mean—"

"I mean you're fired."

Juliana flung the remote down onto the sofa. "It'll be a pleasure. And this time, when you change your mind, I'm not coming back."

"Don't worry." Kyra went into the kitchen and buzzed the doorman on the intercom. "Hello, Joey? What time do you go off duty today?"

"Four P.M., ma'am, same as every Friday."

"An emergency's come up." She was taking a chance, but there was no choice. "I wonder if you'd be able to come up to the apartment for a moment?"

Three minutes later, the doorman stood in Kyra's hallway. He arched an eyebrow at the sound of drawers slamming in Juliana's bedroom.

"I had to fire Juliana," Kyra explained.

"I'm sorry to hear that."

"Would you be able to go to Toby's school at five and bring him home? Just give the headmistress this note." She handed him a sheet of stationery, neatly folded over. "Naturally, I'll pay you for your trouble. Would a hundred dollars be sufficient?"

The doorman smiled broadly. "Very sufficient, ma'am."

Kyra waited for the sound of the front door closing. She used the phone in the kitchen and dialed the École Française and asked to speak with the headmistress. She disguised her voice. "Mademoiselle, this is Kyra Talbot's secretary."

"How may I help you?"

"Juliana van Dieren is no longer authorized to pick up Toby from school. Mrs. Talbot has had to fire her.

Joseph la Plata will pick Toby up this afternoon. He'll show you a note from Mrs. Talbot."

Dotson Elihu's face imitated perplexity. "Isn't this unusual behavior for a murderer?"

In the witness box, Dr. Lalwani leaned back in his chair. "You can't generalize. Nothing is unusual behavior for a borderline."

"Borderline what, Doctor?"

At counsel's table, diAngeli drove a palm against her forehead. She jotted something on a pad and passed it to her assistant.

"Borderline personality. It's a psychiatric term."

"You've examined the accused?"

"I have not."

"Dr. Lalwani, are you licensed in psychiatry?"

"I am not, but I've read extensively in the field."

"Perhaps you can offer some psychiatric explanation for John Briar's being so violently suffocated that he was thrown to the floor, while his wife was so gently suffocated that she appears to have died calmly in her sleep?"

"I can't speak for the killer's thought process."

"But you just did. You said he was borderline."

"I was speaking hypothetically."

"*Dr.* Lalwani—speaking nonhypothetically, have you ever been censured by any medical or legal board of ethics?"

"I have been censured by the state board of education of Alabama," Lalwani said quietly. "The board claimed that—"

"Are you aware," Elihu interrupted, "that Dr. Daniel Hippolito of New York County performed autopsies on the bodies of John and Amalia Briar four days before yours?"

"Objection!" diAngeli cried. "Irrelevant!"

"Your Honor, I'll show relevance."

"Overruled. Witness will answer."

Lalwani folded his arms across his chest. "An exploratory autopsy was performed before mine, but I did not discuss it with Dr. Hippolito."

"Didn't you and Dr. Hippolito discuss his conclusion that Amalia Briar predeceased her husband by four hours?"

"We did not. I know of no such conclusion drawn by any competent authority."

"You did not discuss with Dr. Hippolito his conclusion that Amalia Briar died of natural causes?"

"I had no such discussion."

Elihu wheeled around. "Your Honor, the defense will call Dr. Daniel Hippolito. He will testify as to gaping flaws in Dr. Lalwani's methodology. He will further testify that Amalia Briar died Friday night, four hours before her husband, not Monday morning."

"Your Honor," diAngeli cried, "I object to unsupported claims of nonexistent evidence being made in a transparent attempt to gull the jury!"

"The objection is sustained. But Ms. diAngeli, please don't characterize your colleague's statements. And Mr. Elihu, I don't want to have to warn you a second time that you are not to employ the preview tactic in my court."

"My apologies. No further questions."

Tess diAngeli rose from her chair and strolled easily to the witness box. "Dr. Lalwani, why were you censured by the state board of education of Alabama?"

"For referring in my testimony to the evolutionary

theory of the famed Communist agnostic, Charles Darwin."

There was laughter in the court. Judge Bernheim hammered her gavel. "If any of you feel you must applaud or laugh, take it outside those doors."

"We found Britta Bailey's body yesterday morning." Cardozo was sitting at his desk with the phone propped to his ear and a mug of precinct coffee growing lukewarm at his elbow. "In the West Side Conrail yard."

"Oh, no." Even over the phone, Tess diAngeli's shock was palpable.

"She was carrying your phone number."

"I gave her my number. She was nervous about testifying."

"Did she phone you yesterday?"

"Britta and I haven't spoken since she testified."

"Maybe she left a message with someone?"

"I'll check."

"Britta was also carrying Mickey Williams's photograph."

Silence. And then: "What's that supposed to mean?"

"I thought you might tell me."

"Vince, I was not an intimate of this woman."

"Relax, I'm not accusing you of anything."

"I'm not accusing you of accusing me."

"Did you suggest Britta might have to identify Mickey in court?"

"I did not."

"Tuesday and Wednesday a man was hanging around the schoolyard at the École Française over on Madison. He had a camera. He seemed to be especially interested in an eleven-year-old by the name of Toby Talbot. The school called Britta, and Britta confronted the man. He may have been the last person to see her alive. Sixteen hours later she was found dead."

"Christ. Is the boy safe?"

"The boy's in school, but I can't question him without his mother's permission."

"You say that as though it had something to do with me."

"It does. The mother's name is Kyra Talbot and she's serving on a jury. Any chance you can locate her?"

"Kyra Talbot is serving on my jury and they're sequestered. If you want to talk to her, you'll have to ask Judge Bernheim, and I can tell you right now she'll turn you down flat."

"Maybe not. I think Britta was carrying Mickey Williams's photo to see if any of the kids recognized him."

"And did they?"

"I won't know till I speak to Toby Talbot."

"Vince, you're giving me mirrors and smoke."

"You say that a lot lately."

"Because you've been doing it a lot lately."

"Come on. We both saw Mickey's record before the feds shredded it. His M.O. is hanging around schoolyards. And Britta saw the record too. She was also the first uniform on the scene of the Briar killings—so she had a fair idea of your star witness's capabilities."

"There's no way Mickey could have done *anything.* He's been in the federal witness relocation program for almost two years."

"Unfortunately, federal protection isn't the same thing as federal restraint. Look at the situation. It's crazy. Two years ago, Mickey was a suspect in two murders and the court released him in Dotson Elihu's recognizance. Now charges against Mickey have been dropped, Corey Lyle's accused, and Elihu's representing Corey. And his *old* client is chief witness against his *new* client. Doesn't that strike you as a little too cozy?"

"Elihu has always represented the Coreyites. While Mickey Williams was friendly to them, he represented Mickey. When Mickey became hostile, Elihu dropped him. There's no irregularity."

"Then if it isn't giving away a government secret, can you tell me if Mickey was in New York City this past week?"

"What if he was? You want to yank one of my jurors out of sequestration and possibly screw up a sixty-million-dollar trial, but you don't know who this man in the schoolyard is. You're just pulling Mickey's name out of a hat. From what you're telling me, you don't even have a witness who got a good look at him."

"Not yet. But I might if the judge excused Talbot from the jury and used an alternate instead."

"Why would she do that? You haven't established compelling need. Judge Bernheim's aiming at a Supreme Court nomination. She's got to keep this trial on track. She's not going to waste an alternate that she may need down the road to avoid a mistrial. Look how many alternates the O.J. trial used up. She'd have to be crazy. Or in love with you."

"You yourself once said, Mickey's dangerous."

"Dangerous, maybe, but not an idiot. He wouldn't cruise for chicken while he's testifying for the federal government."

"Wouldn't he? His record didn't suggest he had a handle on his compulsions."

"Vince, I've got a hell of a lot to do tonight. Could we save the rest of this talk till you have something a little more solid?"

"That's a date."

She had already hung up.

Cardozo lowered the receiver into the cradle. He leaned back in his swivel chair, thinking: *She's scared. Why?*

Tess diAngeli searched her desktop. She found the number of Mickey Williams's guard, lifted the telephone, and punched it in. She sat tapping nervous fingers.

A man answered. "Security."

"Rick? It's Tess diAngeli." Though the door was shut, she lowered her voice. "I need some information. Do you happen to recall where Mickey was this past Tuesday and Wednesday afternoon?"

"He was with his girlfriend."

"You're absolutely sure?"

"If you mean, was I in the bedroom with them, no, I wasn't. I dropped him off at her place around two P.M., picked him up around five."

"What did you do in between? Observe the premises?"

"Hell, no. I went to a movie. It's not as though anyone's gunning for the guy. Or are they?"

Then Mickey had a window of opportunity, Tess realized. *Damn. If he's starting to stalk kids again, this could be a disaster.* "Rick—don't ever leave Mickey unobserved. And I want you to start keeping a log on his movements."

NINETEEN

Saturday, September 21
Fourth day of trial
8:55 A.M.

"There's not a chance," Ellie Siegel said, "that anything was going on between Roger Bailey and his partner."

"How can you be so sure?" Cardozo slathered cream cheese on a pumpernickel bagel. They were having breakfast in a rear booth in the Lexington Coffee Shop.

"Vince, that gunk is going to kill your arteries."

He gave her a look and dolloped marmalade on top of the cream cheese. "I asked you a question."

"How can I be sure? Edie's gay. She's out and she heads the gay officers' alliance at her precinct." Ellie pulled the bag of chamomile tea out of her cup, wrung it dry, and deposited it neatly in the saucer. "I agree with you, Vince—generally speaking, where there's smoke, something's burning. But if I could venture an opinion, there isn't even smoke here. Furthermore, Britta and Edie were good friends."

"How good is good?"

"Britta sounded Edie out, how did she think Roger would react to the idea of a divorce. Edie said go for it."

"Doesn't that seem peculiar to you, the wife bending the ear of the husband's partner?"

"Not when they're all cops."

"Any chance anything was going on between Edie and Britta?"

Beneath waved dark hair, Ellie's brown eyes were impatient. "Give me a break."

"Do me a favor. Check Edie's movements Wednesday night after her shift."

Judge Bernheim had decided, in the interest of moving the trial along as quickly as possible, to hear testimony Saturday. At nine thirty-five Tess diAngeli called her eighth witness, the doorman at the Park Avenue building where the Briars had lived.

"After Corey Lyle began visiting the apartment of John and Amalia Briar," diAngeli asked, "what security measures were in effect to protect former Secretary Briar and his wife?"

"The same as for the other tenants. If a visitor or a delivery arrived, I rang on the intercom. Visitors went up the front elevators, deliveries went up the rear."

"In the two years before his death, did you ever see John Briar bring strange women into his apartment?"

"The only woman I ever saw him with was his wife."

"Around this time, did unescorted women begin visiting the Briar apartment?"

"Unescorted? No."

"Did you ever see any woman besides Mrs. Briar or

the maid let herself into the apartment with her own key?"

"No."

"And what security measures were in effect the night the former secretary and his wife were murdered?"

"Besides the lock on the front door, there was no security, because there was no doorman on duty, not on Labor Day weekend. The staff went on strike midnight Friday."

"Who was on duty Friday evening before midnight?"

"I was."

"Would you describe the traffic to and from the Briars' apartment before midnight?"

The witness took a moment to consider. "The Briars' servant left around eight. Corey Lyle went up around ten. Around eleven Mickey Williams arrived. The Briars hadn't said anything about expecting him. I called up on the intercom. A man said to send Mr. Williams up."

"Was it John Briar who answered the intercom?"

"If it was Mr. Briar, his voice sounded a whole lot healthier than it had lately."

"Objection. Conclusion."

"Sustained."

"Were you familiar enough with Corey Lyle's voice to recognize it over an intercom?"

"Objection—leading the witness."

"Sustained."

"If it wasn't former Treasury Secretary Briar who answered the intercom, who else—from your knowledge of the comings and goings in that apartment—could it have been?"

"Him." The witness nodded toward the defense table. "Corey Lyle."

"Mr. LaMontagna," diAngeli said, "before you went

on strike at midnight, did you see Corey Lyle leave the apartment?"

"No, ma'am, I didn't."

"Did you see Mickey Williams leave the apartment?"

"No, ma'am."

Cardozo shaded his eyes and peered into the window of the shop that called itself Antiquity Americana. Between shimmering reflections of Madison Avenue traffic he could make out a jumble of furniture and duck decoys and quilts, and a blond hairdo that appeared to be chatting with a red hairdo.

He pressed the button beside the door. There was a buzz and the door swung open.

Both hairdos turned, but it was the blonde that spoke. "Could I help you, sir?" An affable smile flashed beneath cold gray eyes.

He inhaled an almost intoxicating mix of varnish and potpourri. "I'd like to speak to someone who was in this shop last Wednesday afternoon."

The smile died. "This is with reference to . . . ?"

He opened his wallet to the gold shield. "Something that happened in the street around four o'clock." This was the twelfth shop on the block where he'd asked, and so far he'd had no luck.

The redhead spoke. "Carla might be able to help. Walk on through to the back room."

Cardozo stepped through a steel doorway. A young woman was crouched on the floor blow-torching the finish from an enormous tiger maple armchair.

"Excuse me," he said.

The air was suffocating and heavy, the blowtorch as loud as a jet plane.

He moved closer. He saw that the chair had an over-size circular back that flipped down and rested on the arms so that it became a table. "Excuse me," he shouted.

The head turned, eyes visored behind a dark plastic shield.

Cardozo held out his I.D.

The young woman turned off the flame and set the blowtorch down on the floor.

"Nice chair," he said.

"Early twentieth-century. Mormon."

He looked into peanut-shaped eyes and smiled his broadest smile, inviting hers. "If you're Carla, they said you might be able to help me."

"I'm Carla and I'll be glad to try."

"You were in the shop last Wednesday afternoon around four?"

She nodded.

He held out an envelope. "Could you look at these pictures and tell me if you happened to see this woman? She was in the street and you might have noticed her through the window."

She snapped off her gloves and sprang to her feet. She went to a tiny sink in the corner and lathered her hands with a bar of industrial-looking red soap. She rinsed and dried and tossed the paper towel into an empty carton.

"Let's have a look." She took the envelope and drew the glossies out and looked at them one by one: Britta in lacy white at her wedding, beaming. Britta in cutoff jeans at the precinct barbecue last June, grinning, gesturing with a chicken leg. Britta at her Police Academy graduation five years ago, in full uniform, a good ten pounds lighter, trying her damnedest to look serious.

"She's a cop?"

"She was."

She caught the past tense and turned her gaze and looked at him. "I saw her. She was in uniform. She came out from the schoolyard and started talking to a guy in a blue 'ninety-four Pontiac—double-parked. Jersey license. Weird-looking guy."

Cardozo opened his wallet and took out Britta's magazine photo of Mickey Williams. He'd covered the caption with masking tape. "Was this the man?"

She frowned. "I wouldn't want to say for sure. It could have been, but he'd shaved his head. And when he leaned into the sun, something gold glinted in his left ear. Looked to me like it could have been an earring."

Cardozo jotted a note. "Did you happen to hear any conversation between Sergeant Bailey and this man?"

"No, the shop door was closed, but I had the impression she was questioning him and he was showing her his wallet."

"Did he seem to be angry or hostile?"

"I couldn't see it all, I was waiting on a customer. But one minute she was on the street looking like she was about to write him a ticket. And the next moment she kind of—this sounds weird, but she kind of fell into the car with him."

Cardozo frowned. "*Fell* into the car?"

"It looked that way. And then I couldn't see her at all, and he was at the wheel, and the car drove away."

The way Cardozo reconstructed events, the man pulled Britta into the car; to Carla, watching from the antique shop, it looked as though Britta fell in. Now, if Mademoiselle de Gramont had seen the same man as Carla—

and Cardozo was assuming she had—there was a possibility that she too might have caught a glint of gold earring in the left ear.

Cardozo lifted his receiver and tapped in the number of the École Française. A machine with a French accent told him the École would not be open until Monday. If he wished to speak with Josette de Gramont, he could reach her at home.

He dialed the home number. Another machine with the same accent told him he could reach Mademoiselle at the École.

He dropped the receiver into the cradle, exasperated. The voices of two detectives floated into his cubicle from the squad room. They were arguing about the Los Angeles Rams.

He glanced at his watch. Five after eleven. Two hours since he'd last tried Kyra Talbot. He wanted to talk to her au pair. He tried again. A busy signal came back at him, bell-like and tireless. He dialed zero and asked to verify the number.

There were three ear-popping clicks and a furiously amplified busy signal. "I'm sorry, sir. That line is out of order."

"What's the problem?"

"It could be a malfunction with the customer's equipment. Or a work crew could have cut a cable. It should be taken care of within twelve hours."

"Cash or charge?" the man at the counter asked.

"Cash." Kyra Talbot set her parcels down and opened her purse and handed him a ten.

Something brushed her forearm. She turned. Across

the aisle a man with a shaved head, his back toward her, was studying a rack of joke greeting cards.

"Five ninety-eight and two is six, and four makes ten. Would you like a bag for those other parcels?"

"Thanks—you're an angel." She tucked the Advil into her purse and consulted her notebook. Most of the items on the list headed MUST DO BEFORE 7 P.M. SATURDAY had been checked off: *Toby's passport / my passport / foreign currency / trav checks / toilet paper / vitamins / echinacea.* But there was no check beside *electric current adapter.*

Damn, she thought. She'd been running around town for two days and she was dead-tired. *They must sell adapters over there. I'm going to take a chance.*

The counterman handed her an *I Love NY* plastic bag stuffed with her last-minute purchases. She swung the door of the drugstore open and stepped out onto the sidewalk. She stood a moment, troubled, wondering why putting the parcels in one bag made them feel lighter than they had separately.

She was about to recount when the traffic light changed and a pedestrian surge carried her across Lexington Avenue. She turned downtown and turned again on East 81st. Halfway down the deserted block, something made her stop. A kind of dim echo. She couldn't tell if she'd heard it or if she was just remembering it. She'd been aware of it several times this morning.

She glanced behind her. There was nothing moving on the block, not a pedestrian, not a wisp of traffic.

She walked toward her sister Anne's building, just a little faster now.

It came again—the sound of her own steps, but not quite. There was a split-second delay. As if someone were trying to walk in her footprints.

I'm imagining this, she told herself. *It's been a frantic two days and my mind's overloaded.*

"G'morning, Mrs. Bingham. Beautiful day."

She smiled at the doorman and hurried into the lobby.

The man with the shaved head stopped at the entrance to 118 East 81st Street.

"Help you?" the doorman challenged.

"I'm from the druggist's. Mrs. Bingham forgot one of her packages."

"I'll see she gets it."

"She has to sign for it."

The doorman nodded toward the elevators. "Eleven-E. She just went up."

TWENTY

12:40 P.M.

The intercom buzzed like a fly caught in an electric zapper. Kyra pressed the button.

"Mrs. Bingham, a man from the drugstore is bringing up a package you forgot."

The doorbell dingdonged. She flipped the dead bolt.A shadowy male figure stood in the doorway, silhouetted against the flickering hall fluorescents. She squinted to make out his face.

He held out a small brown paper–wrapped package.

"Thank you." She reached for it, but he pulled it away. Almost teasingly.

"You have to sign for it. But I lost my pen." His voice had a mischievous resonance.

"I'm sure I can find a pen. Just a minute." She went and foraged through papers on the worktable.

"And I'm out of receipts," he said. "You'll have to write one."

Sighing, she found a pen and a sheet of Anne's stationery. "What do you want me to write?"

She turned. He was no longer at the door, but standing two feet from her. Light fell slantwise across the shaved skull, the brown eyes glowing with peek-a-boo, I-see-you malevolence.

She took a shocked, lurching step backward. "Get out of here, or I'll scream. I'm not kidding."

He unfurled a slow, lopsided grin.

She slashed out with the pen, broad swipes across his chest.

He slapped it from her fingers. A rat-trap of a hand caught her left wrist. "Pick that pen up."

He twisted her wrist behind her, hard.

She picked up the pen.

"Write exactly what I tell you: 'Dear Mademoiselle: This is to inform you that Toby's father, Catch Talbot—' "

"No!" She tried to jerk loose. Couldn't.

"Write! 'Catch Talbot has my authorization to pick up Toby after today's school excursion and bring him home. With many thanks, Kyra Talbot.' "

He shoved an envelope at her. "Address it. 'Mademoiselle.' "

She obeyed, then handed him the letter and envelope.

He stood there, reading what she had written. She drove the pen at his left eye.

A work-booted foot kicked her leg out from under her. She slammed down against the floor. She cried out.

"Stop screaming." He picked up a green velvet throw pillow from the sofa. "I'm only going to tell you once."

She tried to push the pillow away, but it crushed her hands, crushed her face, blotted out light and sound and air. Suffocation pressed down and the pen clattered from her hand.

"And after Dr. Lyle became a regular visitor . . ." Dotson Elihu faced the witness box, hands in his pockets. "Did you notice any change in the sorts of people the Briars entertained?"

"The people changed." The doorman's face was grave. "Till three years ago, the Briars invited decent people. Well-dressed. Said thank-you when you held the door. Tipped you if you called a cab in the rain."

"And after three years ago?"

"The Briars began getting nonsocialites."

"What do you mean when you say 'nonsocialites'?"

"Minority people. Blacks—Hispanics—Orientals. Some dressed practically like street people."

Elihu stepped back, putting space between himself and the witness. "Are you saying the Briars admitted street people to their home?"

"Objection." diAngeli stood. "Calls for conclusion."

"Sustained."

The witness turned to the judge. "Some tenants wouldn't even ride in the elevator with those people."

"Mr. LaMontagna." The judge's voice was stern. "Don't talk to me." The gavel pointed to Elihu. "Talk to him."

"Mr. LaMontagna." Elihu flashed a smile that seemed to say, *It's us guys against her, buddy.* "On that Friday evening before Labor Day, when you announced Mr. Williams, can you say with absolute certainty whose voice answered the intercom? After all, it's not a high-tech digital intercom, is it?"

The witness gave a laugh. "It sure isn't."

"So even though the voice didn't sound exactly like John Briar's, it still could have been him and the intercom could have distorted his voice?"

"Objection. Hypothetical."

"Overruled."

"Yes, sir, that's very possible."

Elihu allowed a moment's silence for the point to sink in. "Did anyone go up to the apartment with Mr. Williams?"

"No."

"Did anyone besides Dr. Lyle arrive before or after Mr. Williams and go up to the apartment?"

"I never saw them."

"Could anyone have gone up to the Briars' apartment after midnight?"

"Objection. Hypothetical."

Judge Bernheim sighed. "Mr. Elihu, the information you want could be put on the record with a different question."

Elihu nodded. "Mr. LaMontagna—based on your seven years' experience as a door person at 777 Park Avenue—could a visitor have gone up to the Briars' apartment after midnight?"

"Not unless they had a key to the front door."

In a gray and pale-green drawing room on the twelfth floor of the Vista Hotel, Tess diAngeli paced with the telephone. "You were supposed to have him here at one-fifteen sharp. It's one-twenty."

"He's watching a movie."

"What are you two, film critics? I told you to keep a log and not let Mickey out of your sight."

"For Chrissake, what am I supposed to do, change his diapers? I'm in the theater with him, isn't that enough?"

"What theater?"

"Adult Playtime. Forty-fourth and Eighth."

"Can you see him?"

"He's watching the film. I'm in the lobby with the *Wall Street Journal.*"

Tess gritted in rage. "How long has he been in there?"

"Two hours and seven minutes."

"If he's given you the slip, it'll mean your job."

"Relax. He's there."

"Then get him out right now and get him down here."

Twenty minutes later, Tess was rehearsing Mickey Williams's testimony. "And were you sentenced to serve time?"

Seated on the sofa six feet from her, Mickey nodded. "They put me in a trade school in Texarkana." Tension pushed his voice high into his adenoids. Coming out of the body of a former running back dressed in too-tight polo shirt and corduroys, the effect was cartoonish.

We'll have to dress him better for court, Tess realized. *Will off-the-rack fit?*

"It was really a kind of reformatory," Mickey said. "I learned welding."

On the other side of the room, Tess diAngeli's assistant rapped a wooden ruler on the edge of the table.

Mickey blinked guiltily. "Did I do it wrong?"

"You said you learned welding before Tess asked."

Compared to Williams, Brad Chambers was built like a pretzel, but he spoke from the chest, sonorously. Tess wished Mickey and her assistant could trade voices for the duration of the trial.

"You're speaking just a little too fast, Mickey." As a courtroom lawyer, she knew that speed of speech was voluntary; pitch of voice, much less so. Yet the two were physiologically linked, and if she could get Mickey to speak slowly, the pitch of his voice would come down. If the voice came down, the jury would be far more apt to believe him. "And whatever you do, don't *ever* answer a question before I've asked it. Because if you get away from the script, you may volunteer something that we haven't had a chance to discuss. It may seem unimportant, but it could be just the opening the defense needs."

"In other words, I goofed again." Mickey's head drooped. "I'm sorry."

Tess couldn't shake the suspicion that this dopiness was deliberate on Mickey's part. *Why's he trying to convince me he's an idiot?* "You didn't goof. You're doing fine."

Mickey beamed.

"Now, I'm going to ask you once again: Were you sentenced to serve time?"

"They put me in a trade school in Texarkana." Much better. The words were slow, the voice mid-range. "It was a kind of reformatory."

"What did you learn in Texarkana?"

"I learned welding."

Tess glanced at her legal pad. There were still three pages of points to cover, and barely ten minutes left of her lunch hour. "How long were you in this institution?"

"Three years—till a minister and his wife adopted me."

Brad Chambers's ruler rapped again on the table.

"You answered before I asked," Tess said.

"Shit." Mickey blushed. "Sorry. It's just that there's so much to remember. . . ."

"Mickey, would you excuse us a moment?" Bertram Bogdan, Justice Department trial consultant, rose from the easy chair, brushing the wrinkles out of his dark suit. "Have yourself a glass of soda."

Tess and Brad followed Bogdan into the bedroom. He shut the door. "Mickey's voice is going to be a real turn-off for the jurors. It rises under tension, so let's keep him from tensing up."

"I'm afraid I haven't got that kind of control over him."

"It's not him we have to control, Tess." Bogdan's dark eyes nailed her. "It's you."

That interested Tess, because it struck her as 180 degrees bass-ackwards. Yet the government was paying Bogdan $1,250 for one hour of consulting: as much as they paid Tess for a week's backbreaking trial work. He must be doing something right.

"When you're making eye contact," Bogdan said, "Mickey's okay. When you break eye contact he feels he's annoyed you and that's when the whining, begging tone starts. Are you aware how much you're avoiding eye contact? Do you know the reason?"

Now that she thought of it, she realized he was right. "This is an awful thing to say about my own witness. He embarrasses me."

"Why?"

"I don't know. It's something physical. He's so big and messy—and that shaved head looks like a rat's ass."

"Then you're just going to have to repeat to yourself, *I am proud of this witness.*"

"I am proud of this witness," Tess muttered. She'd been working fifteen minutes a day with Bogdan's affirmation cards, and they struck her as government-subsidized voodoo. *"He is a credit to the case."*

"If you believe it," Bogdan said, "the witness believes it. And if the witness believes it, the jurors believe it."

When they returned to the drawing room, Mickey was hunched over the coffee table, glum-faced.

"What's the matter?" Tess said.

"Corey's a good person." A deep sigh came out of Mickey. The right vocal quality, at last. "And I'm saying *shitty* things about him."

"He's not a good person." Tess's eyes locked onto Mickey's. *I'm dealing with a child,* she reminded herself. *And I am proud of this child.* "He's not good in any morally or legally meaningful sense of the term."

"He was good to me and I'm being rotten to him." Mickey's voice was climbing again. "He saved my life and I'm—"

"No, Mickey," Tess said. "Five days from now you'll be saving your own life."

At 2:30 P.M., the blue government '94 Pontiac pulled up at the curb in front of 60 Centre Street. Tess diAngeli stuffed papers into her briefcase and stepped out of the car. "Thanks for the lift."

"Always a pleasure, ma'am." Mickey closed the passenger door and watched Tess race up the courthouse steps.

"Nice legs," his guard commented.

"They're all right." Mickey burped quietly into his fist. "Let's get out of here."

The guard eased back into traffic, peeled left, and

headed uptown on Lafayette. Two blocks north of Canal, Mickey told him to pull over.

"Go see a movie." Mickey handed the guard forty dollars. "And leave the keys in the car."

TWENTY-ONE

2:30 P.M.

"The People call Felix Logan."

A well-tailored, overweight man in his thirties stepped up to the witness stand and took the oath. Tess diAngeli asked him to describe his work.

"I was John and Amalia Briar's lawyer. At present I represent their estate."

Tess diAngeli handed the witness a document and asked if he had ever seen it before.

"This is Amalia Briar's last will and testament. I drew it up for her."

"Whom did Amalia Briar name as her beneficiary?"

"John and Amalia Briar each wrote wills leaving their estates to the other."

"Was there any stipulation in John Briar's will as to the length of time his wife had to survive him in order to inherit?"

"Forty-eight hours or more. It's a standard provision,

in case both spouses die in the same plane crash, for instance, and exact times of death can't be fixed."

"Since John Briar did in fact predecease his wife by a little more than forty-eight hours, his estate became hers?"

"That's correct."

"Whom did Amalia Briar name as her heirs?"

"In the event John predeceased Amalia by forty-eight hours or more, her will named Corey Lyle sole beneficiary."

"Was Corey Lyle aware of this fact?"

"Oh, yes. Yes, indeed." Felix Logan's eyes rested, silently accusatory, on the defendant. "Amalia Briar asked me to show Corey Lyle her will."

"Did she tell you why?"

"So Corey Lyle could establish a tax-exempt foundation and avoid inheritance taxes."

Corey Lyle gazed at the witness with serene detachment. A sad smile touched the line of his mouth. It was as though his face was saying, *I know your pain, brother. I share it.*

"Was Corey Lyle aware of the forty-eight-hour provision in John Briar's will?"

Felix Logan nodded. "He asked about the forty-eight-hour provision in Amalia's will, and I explained that both wills contained it."

At 3:30 P.M., on Madison and 64th, a dozen women waited outside the iron gate of the ivy-covered nineteenth-century mansion that housed the École Française.

Sitting in a double-parked blue Pontiac across the avenue, motor idling, a man watched them.

A small blue van drew up to the entrance. A short woman in black stepped briskly down from the driver's seat and unlocked the gates. Waif-thin, with a giant gray coiffure, she had the posture of a lamppost.

She climbed back into the van and drove into the small cobblestoned courtyard. The doors of the van flew open and a dozen children hit the cobblestones running, screaming, pushing, jumping.

The women surged through the gate, plucked their charges from the swarm, hurried them homeward. In sixty seconds only two people remained: the little gray-haired lady, frowning at her watch, and an eleven-year-old boy.

The boy pulled a rubber ball from his back pocket. He spat on the ball, kneaded it in his palms, and hurled it at the limestone wall.

The man watched: his mind registered the pattern of the boy's leaps into the air. There was something irresistible about a boy who knew his own strengths.

In the street, a truck backfired. The boy turned. He gazed out through the iron pickets. His eyes looked directly at the man in the Pontiac.

The man gave a just-between-us wave.

The boy covered his uncertainty with a smile and looked away.

The man's adrenaline was break-dancing in his veins. *Now,* he decided.

The light was against him, but there was a break in traffic. He stepped out of the Pontiac. In ten quick strides he crossed the avenue and entered the courtyard. "Mademoiselle."

The old woman looked over at him.

He flashed a daddy smile. "I've come to pick up Toby."

Suspicion rippled out from the old woman's eyes. "I have no authorization," she snapped with a hint of a French accent.

"His mother gave me a note." The man reached into the pocket of his raincoat and handed her the note.

The old woman studied it. Studied the man with the shaved head and the brown eyes and the small gold ring in his left ear. "Toby, you are to go with your father."

"Since John Briar allegedly predeceased his wife by forty-eight hours"—Dotson Elihu's tone was almost mocking in its skepticism—"his estate went in its entirety to her?"

Felix Logan nodded. "That's correct."

"But if Amalia Briar had *predeceased* her husband, her estate would have gone in its entirety to him?"

"Again, provided he survived her by at least forty-eight hours."

Elihu stepped closer to the witness box. "But in the event John Briar *survived* his wife—to whom did he then bequeath his estate?"

"To his son."

Elihu nodded slowly. "Then Corey Lyle's alleged motive depends on John Briar dying forty-eight hours before his wife. Otherwise the combined estates pass to Jack Briar. Leaving Dr. Lyle with no motive and the state with no case."

"Objection. Argumentative."

"Sustained."

Elihu walked four careful steps away from the witness box. He turned. "We know a murderer cannot legally profit by his crime. So if Corey Lyle is found guilty—who inherits the combined estates?"

"Jack Briar inherits."

Elihu's tone became accusatorial. "In other words, *Jack Briar's sole hope of getting the inheritance is for the state to win this case?*"

The witness looked toward the prosecutor. She made no move to object. "That's correct."

"Have you ever been in the employ of Jack Briar?"

"Five years ago Jack—Mr. Briar—asked me to handle the closing on his co-op."

"Have you ever been in the employ of the defendant?"

"Of course not."

"Have you ever drawn up any legal document for the defendant?"

The witness placed a hand on the railing. A jeweled cuff link winked. "No."

"Have you ever drawn up any legal document for the defendant's signature?"

"At the request of Amalia Briar, I—"

"Just answer the question. Yes or no?"

"Yes, but—"

"What was the document?"

"Incorporation papers for a tax-exempt foundation."

"And was this foundation the entity that Amalia Briar named sole heir?"

"Yes."

"So, technically, she didn't leave her fortune to the defendant—but to a legal entity devised by you."

"Technically, yes. But the defendant would still—"

"But in drawing up those papers you also represented the defendant, so by testifying against him today aren't you breaching legal ethics?"

"The law's clear on that point—"

"Yes or no, please."

"No. He's not my client."

"Your Honor." Elihu's voice curled with disgust. "I have no further questions of this witness."

Judge Bernheim asked if the People wished to redirect.

Tess diAngeli strode to the stand. "Who controls the foundation to which Amalia Briar left her fortune and her husband's?"

"The defendant controls it."

"Did the defendant ever engage your services or pay you any salary or fee for any service?"

"Never."

"So there's no way in which he could be legally considered a client?"

"No way at all."

"Are there any instances in which client-attorney privilege does not apply?"

"It doesn't apply when the attorney knows his client intends to commit a crime."

"No further questions."

Dotson Elihu rose. "Mr. Logan, have you ever been charged with a felony?"

The witness's lips drew tight. "Like many lawyers, I've been frivolously charged."

"With what?"

"Malfeasance."

"Malfeasance—that means a crime against a client, such as conflict of interest or deception or theft?"

"It can cover those acts, but it also covers far less serious acts. It's a very common charge brought by disgruntled clients."

"And doubtless you have many of those?"

"Objection."

"Sustained."

Elihu seemed pleased as he ambled back to the defense table. "No further questions."

Cardozo lifted the receiver and once again tapped in the number of the École Française. This time a woman's voice answered. " 'Allo?"

"Ms. de Gramont? It's Vince Cardozo again from the Twenty-second Precinct. I have a question about the man who was watching Toby Talbot from that blue car. Could you see his left ear? Did you happen to notice if he was wearing an earring?"

"No, but I saw his left ear this afternoon when he picked up Toby, and he was wearing one."

Cardozo jerked forward in his swivel chair. "He picked Toby up this afternoon?"

"Right after the school excursion. It turns out he's Catch Talbot—Toby's father."

"Did he show you any kind of identification?"

"He gave me a note from Mrs. Talbot authorizing him to take Toby."

"Ms. de Gramont, this is very important. Do you still have that note?"

Mademoiselle Josette de Gramont opened the drawer of her mahogany desk. She took out a sheet of stationery the color of crème brûlée and handed it across the desktop.

Cardozo held it by the corner. The note was dated today, September 21. The handwriting was a mix of loops and detached vertical strokes.

Dear Mademoiselle: This is to inform you that Toby's father, Catch Talbot, has my authorization to pick up Toby after today's school excursion and bring him home. With many thanks, Kyra Talbot.

"Is this Mrs. Talbot's handwriting?"

"As nearly as I could tell. If you'd like to judge for yourself . . ." Mademoiselle de Gramont went to a file cabinet and pulled out Kyra Talbot's application to enroll her son in the École.

Cardozo studied the loops and strokes. He was no expert, but they seemed to match the note. "Why was this note necessary? Isn't Toby a little old to have to be picked up from school?"

"Yes, but his mother was strict on the point. Either she or the au pair dropped him off and picked him up. I don't know why, but those were her instructions."

"Who picked Toby up this last week?"

"The au pair. Except for Friday. Friday a man by the name of La Plata picked Toby up. He said he was the doorman."

"And did he have a note from Mrs. Talbot?"

Mademoiselle de Gramont handed Cardozo a second sheet of stationery. The paper and the handwriting matched the first.

September 20. Dear Mademoiselle: Mr. Joseph La Plata, our doorman, has my authorization to pick up Toby after school today and bring him home. With many thanks, Kyra Talbot.

Cardozo frowned. "Was there an envelope with either of these notes?"

"There was with Mr. Talbot's." She handed him an

envelope addressed with the single word *Mademoiselle.* "He was a gentleman."

"Had you ever met him before today?"

She reflected. "I met him once before—six years ago, when Toby enrolled."

"How is it you didn't recognize him last Wednesday?"

"He was too far away."

Cardozo studied the envelope. The return address was engraved across the flap: APT 11-E, 118 EAST 81ST STREET, NEW YORK N.Y. 10028. There was no sender's name. The trademark TIFFANY & CO. MAKERS NEW YORK was embossed under the flap.

"I'd like to keep these notes and the envelope," he said.

"I'll have to make copies."

She switched on the Xerox machine and made copies and gave him back the originals.

"By any chance," Cardozo said, "did you happen to notice the color of Catch Talbot's eyes?"

"I couldn't help but notice. They were deep brown."

Cardozo stepped through the door of 118 East 81st Street. The small lobby was lined with smoked mirrors and corn plants potted in copper tubs.

A doorman moved forward to intercept him. "Help you?"

Cardozo flipped his wallet open to the gold shield. "I'd like to have a word with Kyra Talbot."

"Kyra Talbot? Never heard of her."

"She lives in Eleven-E."

"No, she doesn't, not in this building. Sure you want 118? Because Eleven-E is Anne Bingham." He pointed to the tenant directory on the wall. *Anne Bingham 11-E.*

Cardozo took the envelope from his pocket and checked the address. He frowned. "Could you buzz Ms. Bingham for me?"

The doorman pushed an intercom button. No one answered.

"Could you give me her phone number?" Cardozo said.

Cardozo went to the pay phone on the corner of Lexington and dialed Anne Bingham's number. After two rings an answering machine unleashed a stream of synthesizer baroque. "Hi. You've reached the office of Ding-a-ling Music, Anne Bingham, CEO." The voice was young and perky, with an appealing musical lilt. "If you'd care to leave a message at the beep, I'll get back to you as soon as possible. That's a promise. Thanks."

Beep.

"Lieutenant Vince Cardozo, Twenty-second Precinct. I'd appreciate hearing from you as soon as you get this message." He left his number and broke the connection. Fishing another quarter out of his pocket, he dialed the École Française.

" 'Allo?"

"Ms. de Gramont, Vince Cardozo again. There seems to be a mix-up. The address on that note isn't Kyra Talbot's. It's the home of Anne Bingham. You wouldn't happen to know that name?"

"Bingham? No, I'm sorry. We have no Bingham at the École."

"Do you have Kyra Talbot's home address?"

"Just a moment." There was a silence. And then: "Six Barrow Street. Do you want her phone number?"

Cardozo swung the glass door open and stepped into a marble lobby hung with monster orchid paintings. Muzak sprayed down from ceiling speakers like a fine mist of pesticide.

A tall doorman with a veneered smile stepped from behind a desk. The name *Louis* was stitched in purple script on a uniform that could have been designed by a Costa Rican dictator's mistress. "Sir?"

Cardozo showed his shield. "Did Catch Talbot bring Toby home about an hour ago?"

"Catch Talbot?"

"His father."

"I don't know any father."

"A big man with a shaved head. Could be wearing an earring in his left ear."

"Never seen anyone like that around here. Anyway, Toby left last night."

"Left? Where did he go?"

"He didn't say." Louis shrugged. "He took a load of packages and suitcases in a taxi."

"Do me a favor. Would you buzz Toby's apartment?"

"Glad to, but no one's home." Louis went to the switchboard and buzzed 9-H. No answer. "Haven't seen Mrs. Talbot or Juliana for two or three days." He buzzed again. "Sorry."

Feet propped on the open desk drawer, Cardozo flipped open his notebook and reviewed his information on the man who may have been the last person to see Britta Bailey alive.

Tall. Heavy. Shaved head. Photographing children from illegally parked American-make blue car. Brown eyes.

Ring in left ear. Corduroy trousers, raincoat. Well-spoken. Uses name Catch Talbot. May be Toby T.'s father.

It wasn't much and it wasn't nearly enough. The only remotely corroborated details seemed to be the hairstyle and the brown eyes. As for the name, there was no such person listed with any phone company in a fifty-mile radius. There was a Catch Talbot listed in Seattle, but it was a business phone and a recorded voice said to call back Monday between nine and five.

Cardozo pushed up from his chair and stepped into the squad room. Twelve of the sixteen desks were deserted. The mayor's austerity budget had decreed Saturdays, Sundays, and holidays low-crime days. Detective Greg Monteleone sat staring at a triplicate form in the carriage of his typewriter.

"Greg, you got a minute?"

"Obviously not now, I don't."

"Would you run a check on charge-card activities over the past week, anyone you can find by the name of Catch Talbot? We're especially interested in any charges in the New York City area."

"Does Mickey Williams ever wear a ring in his left ear?"

Cardozo was sitting with Tess diAngeli in her office, a partitioned space on the eighth story of the state court building. A weekend nocturnal quiet flowed through the floor.

"I've never seen him wearing one," she said.

"But the man who picked up Toby had a shaved head. You said Mickey does too."

"Unfortunately, quite a few men shave their heads nowadays."

"What color are Mickey's eyes?"

"Brown."

"The man in the car had brown eyes."

Tess shrugged. "Did any of your witnesses recognize him?"

"One said there's a good resemblance to Britta's photo of Mickey Williams."

A shadow glided across the frosted glass door. Tess waited for a pair of lonely feet to scurry past in the corridor. "You're yanking my chain, Vince. You don't have a single witness who can say the man in that car was Mickey."

Cardozo nodded. "That's right. In fact, Mademoiselle de Gramont says he was Toby's father."

Tess diAngeli's head snapped around. "Then what the hell are you bothering me for?"

"Doesn't it seem peculiar—a father sits in a car taking photos of his kid? And drives away when a cop challenges him?"

"So? There are peculiar fathers. Vince, why are you dumping all this on me?"

"Because that man is the last person who saw Britta alive. I need to find him, and Kyra Talbot can help me."

"Forget it, Vince. The government has invested over four years and forty-nine *million* dollars in this case. They're going to keep her sequestered."

"If Kyra Talbot's sequestered, how did she manage to write these?" He handed Tess the notes, cased in protective Mylar.

She skimmed them, then flung them down. "Give me a break. Obviously she wrote them ahead of time and post-dated them."

TWENTY-TWO

8:20 P.M.

In the hotel coffee shop, Anne watched Shoshana transfer keys, coins, and cosmetics from her purse to the Formica tabletop.

"It hides from me; I swear it hides." Shoshana finally found a little brown bottle, opened it, and tapped it against the palm of her hand. A solitary pill rolled out. She closed one eye and peered down the bottle. "Do you believe it? This is my last."

"What is it?"

"Prozac, what else? From here on, I'm flying without a parachute." Shoshana tossed the pill into her mouth and belted it back with a slug of iced tea.

Anne tried to smile, but the smile felt forced and false. "I think I'll skip dessert. I have a headache. Would you excuse me?" She pushed up from the table.

"See ya." Shoshana waved and began shoveling debris back into her purse.

Anne told the uniformed jury guard by the door that she was going up to her room.

Anne fitted the card-key into the lock of room 1818. The door swung open onto darkness. She flicked the light on, went into the bathroom, and took an Advil with tap water. She began running a bath.

There was a shrill warbling sound in the other room. Her heart gave a jump. She stopped the water. The sound came again.

The telephone, she realized. But weren't outside calls supposed to be blocked?

Maybe it was an electric surge on the line. Or maybe calls from inside the hotel weren't blocked.

She crossed the bedroom and lifted the receiver. "Hello?"

There was a clicking sound like a bicycle chain ripping loose. And then a man's voice: "Kyra Talbot?"

It was a voice like none she had ever heard before—it seemed alien, fraudulent, as though he—or she—was pushing it down to alter the sound.

"Yes, this is she."

"Don't repeat what I'm about to say to anyone. If you ever want to see your son alive again, vote Corey Lyle not guilty."

The threat caught her like a rock to the skull. There was a click followed by a dentist's drill of a dial tone. It took her a stunned moment to remember that she still had two hands. She broke the connection and punched zero.

After three maddeningly leisurely rings, a woman answered. "World Wide Inn."

"This is Kyra Talbot—one of the sequestered jurors. I've got to speak to Judge Bernheim right away."

"Hang up the phone and you'll be contacted."

"You don't understand. It's an emergency. *It can't wait.*"

"I understand, ma'am. You'll be contacted."

It was three minutes of racing thoughts and ice in the pit of her stomach before the phone finally rang. She snatched it up. "Hello?"

"Ms. Talbot?" A man. Young sounding. "This is Josh Hormel, Judge Bernheim's assistant."

"I've got to speak to the judge immediately."

"Could you give me some idea what the problem is?"

The warning echoed in her head. *Don't repeat this to anyone.* "I can't. It's . . . personal."

"I'm afraid the judge won't be available till Monday. I'll tell her you wish to speak to her."

Anne grabbed her purse and made sure the door was locked behind her. She jabbed the elevator button and almost collided with Shoshana stepping off.

"Hey." Shoshana arched an inquisitive eyebrow. "Thought you had a headache. Where are you running?"

"I'll be right back." Anne jabbed the button for the ground floor and held her finger on *emergency call* all the way down. *Please, God,* she prayed, *let it be a mistake. Let it be a horrible, sick prank. Let Toby be safe.*

With its gold-leaf walls, the lobby had the costume-jeweled iridescence of an overlit nightclub. She dashed through milling patrons to the front desk. "Excuse me."

The sandy-haired, very young desk clerk gave her a startled look. "Yes, ma'am?"

"Someone just phoned my room. I need to know who he was and how the call got put through."

"I'm afraid I can't help you. Calls to the rooms are put through automatically."

"But I'm a juror—I'm sequestered. My phone's supposed to be cut off."

He shook his head. "I don't know anything about sequesterment."

"Who does?"

The clerk placed a short, low-voiced phone call. Thirty seconds later a tall man in a business suit came striding across the lobby and introduced himself as the manager.

Anne explained that she was sequestered and she wanted to check on a call that had come to room 1818.

The manager's eyes were dubious. "Chris, let me have that outside line." He tapped in a seven-digit number and held the receiver so Anne could hear.

"I'm sorry," a recorded female voice was saying. "The number you have dialed cannot be accessed at this time."

"Anyone who calls your room," the manager said, "gets that message. Your number's blocked."

"*Somebody* called, and they weren't blocked." She turned on her heel and raced through startled patrons toward the street door.

"Ma'am!" the manager shouted behind her. "Madam!"

Anne pushed through revolving glass doors. The September night caught her like a warm washrag slapped in her face. A taxi braked in a bath of sparks and a man stepped out. She grabbed the cab door from him and slid into the backseat.

"Could you take me to Six Barrow Street? That's just off Fourth Street, west of Sixth Avenue."

The cab eased into a traffic jam. Through the open

window horns blared and brakes squealed. A police siren yodeled and a blue-and-white cruiser pulled into the street ahead of them, lights flashing. The cab swerved and braked.

The driver, a slender black man in a *Terminator* T-shirt, turned his head. "Hey, lady . . ." He had a Jamaican accent. "What did you do? Rob a bank?"

Two officers were running toward the cab, revolvers drawn. "Kyra Talbot?"

"Mrs. Talbot . . ." Judge Bernheim was wearing diamond earrings and a black evening dress. The air in her chambers was dry and cold, like flowing particles of iced silicon, and she hadn't taken off her brocade bolero. "Would you care to explain why you told the guard you were going to your room and then left the hotel?"

Anne had to push words through disaster scenarios exploding in her head. "That wasn't the way it happened."

"Then how *did* it happen?" The judge's tone was withering.

"After dinner I went up to my room. I was running a bath. I received a threatening phone call. A man or woman—I couldn't tell—said if I ever wanted to see my son alive again, I had to vote Corey Lyle not guilty."

The judge stared in drop-jawed shock. "Stop right there. How did you get a telephone into your room?"

"I didn't. The call came on the hotel phone."

"That phone is blocked—there's no way a call could have gotten through."

"Your Honor, there is a way, and a little boy could be in danger."

Gina Bernheim shot her a long, evaluating glance. "What time did this call come?"

"A little after eight-thirty."

"Why didn't you contact me immediately?"

"I tried to."

The judge sighed. "Was anyone else in the room with you?"

"I was alone."

Judge Bernheim lifted the telephone receiver and pushed two buttons. "Harvey, run a check on any incoming phone calls to Mrs. Talbot's room this evening." She replaced the receiver and consulted the scrawl on a yellow legal pad. "You left the hotel at twelve minutes after nine and got into a taxi. You asked the driver to take you to Six Barrow Street. Why?"

"That's my home. I wanted to make sure my son was safe."

"Are you totally ignorant of the law, or do you just think it doesn't apply to you?"

"I'm not completely ignorant. My father's a lawyer. You may know him. Leon Brandsetter?"

Judge Bernheim stiffened. "You're his *daughter*?"

"One of them."

"You were asked in voir dire if there were any lawyers in your family. Why in God's name didn't you say *yes*? You'd have been excused and we wouldn't be going through all this."

Don't tell me—Kyra missed a chance to get off the jury? "I'm sorry. I guess I wasn't thinking."

"Evidently. What's your phone number?"

"My phone—?" For one whirlpooling moment Anne couldn't remember Kyra's number. And then it popped into her memory.

The judge dialed and grimaced. "Busy." She dialed

zero, identified herself, and asked the operator to interrupt.

"I see." She lowered the receiver and glanced up. "That line's out of order."

Anne's mind ricocheted between terrifying possibilities. "I left Toby with my sister. They could be at her place." She managed to remember her own number.

The judge dialed. Anne sat forward on the chair, straining to overhear.

After a moment the judge cleared her throat. "Yes. This is Judge Gina Bernheim." She had the voice of someone who loathed speaking to answering machines. "I'm calling for . . ." She covered the receiver. "What's your sister's name?"

"Kyra—" Anne bit her tongue.

"Your *sister,* Mrs. Talbot."

"Anne Bingham."

"I'm calling for Anne Bingham. This is an emergency. Would you please get in touch with me as soon as possible?" The judge left her number.

There was a knock on the door. A young man in blue jeans and a Brooks Brothers shirt handed the judge a printout. She scanned rapidly. Her gaze swung around to Anne. "According to the record, there've been no calls to your room since you were sequestered."

"The record is mistaken, Your Honor."

Judge Bernheim glanced at her assistant.

"There's a call block on sequestered jurors' rooms," he explained. "Caller I.D. automatically registers any incoming attempts. If anyone had placed a call to your room, it wouldn't have gotten through, but there'd be a record of their number and the time they tried."

Anne gritted her teeth. "I understand how the system's supposed to work—but it didn't work tonight."

The judge's eyes iced over. "When you monkey with justice, Mrs. Talbot, you're monkeying with the DNA of civilization. You're also monkeying with me. I have one word of free legal advice: *don't.* We'd better have a talk with that lawyer of yours. What's his number?"

Twenty minutes later, Mark Wells burst into the room wearing squash shorts and a windbreaker. "I apologize for my clothes, Your Honor." He was out of breath; sweat had plastered locks of brown hair to his forehead.

"Sorry to interrupt your game," Judge Bernheim said. "Have a seat, Mr. Wells."

Mark sat in the chair beside Anne and flashed her a smile.

In a rapid monotone, Judge Bernheim summarized the situation. She handed Mark the telephone printout. "As you can see, there's no record of any phone call."

"Yes, I see." He darted Anne a pained look.

"Once a jury is impaneled," Judge Bernheim said, "any attempt to get off fraudulently is a felony."

"Your Honor, I doubt my client was fully aware of the legal implications of her action."

"*My* action?" Anne cried. "Their recording system goofed! There *was* a phone call!"

"Kyra . . . please." Mark's hands made placating gestures. "Let me handle this?"

"Why don't you take Mrs. Talbot into the next room," Judge Bernheim suggested. "Talk with her."

The door closed, and they were alone in the walnut-paneled anteroom. Anne handed Mark a dollar.

"What's this?"

"Your retainer. We're covered now by client-attorney privilege, right?"

"We are." Mark tucked the dollar into his billfold. "So you might as well tell me the truth. Is this another attempt to get off the jury, or did you really get a threatening call?"

"I'm not lying. I didn't recognize the voice. It could have been a man or a woman. It sounded . . . disguised. They said if I didn't vote to acquit—I'd never see Toby alive again. Mark, *help* me."

"I'll do everything I can."

"Get me off this jury. I've got to warn Kyra."

His brow furrowed. "Warn *Kyra*?"

"And if it's too late for that, I've got to find Toby."

"Wait a minute. You said 'warn Kyra.' "

She nodded. "Because I'm not Kyra. I'm Anne."

His eyes skittered disbelievingly across her face.

"Last Tuesday I took my sister's place on the jury."

His face turned ashen. "That's crazy. That's irresponsible. Not to mention illegal."

"She had an overloaded schedule and we thought you'd get her off—me off."

"My God—don't you realize what you two have done? Not only have you caused a mistrial—you've probably aborted Gina Bernheim's bid for a seat on the Supreme Court. There's only one way you can get off this jury now. You have to tell her everything."

She stood by the window, staring down at the streetlights in Foley Square. "And if I tell her everything—what happens?"

"There'll be a mistrial. You'll be guilty of felony and conspiracy to commit felony."

"Conspiring with Kyra?"

"Naturally."

"Which makes her a felon too?"

"Of course."

"And who gets custody of Toby if Kyra's a felon?"

"She'll lose him. Catch will get custody."

Anne felt a tightening in her chest. "That would kill her." She turned. "I can't do it to her."

"You mean you're *not* going to tell the judge?"

She shook her head. "I'll keep quiet and stay on the jury. You'll have to warn Kyra."

"As your lawyer, Anne, it's my duty to advise you that—"

"As my lawyer, you can't repeat anything I've told you." She took his hand. "Come on."

Judge Bernheim's eyes were expectant as Anne and Mark stepped through the door.

"Your Honor," Anne said, "I have to make an admission. There was no threatening phone call."

Gina Bernheim bristled with the indignation of a queen on her throne. "You're admitting you lied?"

"My client deeply regrets her action," Mark said.

The judge tapped a ballpoint pen on the edge of her desk. "Your client is in grave trouble, Mr. Wells."

"My client appeals to the understanding and compassion of the court."

The judge studied Anne skeptically. "Mrs. Talbot, it's within my discretion to overlook your actions. But if I do so, I must have your assurance and your attorney's that you'll discuss tonight's events with *no one.*"

TWENTY-THREE

Sunday, September 22
7:10 A.M.

Footsteps. Something fell to the floor with a clatter. Panic slid over Anne like a new layer of skin. She sneaked one eye open.

Morning light slatted the walls of room 1818. Shoshana rose up from between the beds, slipping a cassette into a Walkman. The earphones had yellow Mickey Mouse ears. The yellow matched her sweatshirt top. It didn't match her spinach-green spandex bottoms.

"Halloween?" Anne mumbled. "Already?"

"Lara and Abe and I and one of the guards are going for a jog. Why don't you come? It'll fine-tune your system."

There was something too bright and unpitying about Shoshana's energy—it reminded Anne of the blades of a thresher, mowing down all laggards and late risers.

"I'll take a rain check." She pulled the pillow over her head.

"Kyra Talbot's line is out of order." Tommy Thomas showed the super his work order. "We have to get into the apartment."

The super mused over the computer-generated order. "Who reported this? Because there hasn't been anyone in that apartment for two days."

"Our computer reported it."

The super's swarthy face wrinkled and his eyes went to Cardozo. "And who are you?"

Cardozo handed over the fake Nynex I.D. that Tommy had provided him.

Tommy Thomas was Cardozo's telephone connection. The phone company, unlike the police, didn't need a court order to get into a private residence; all it needed was the wrong kind of busy signal. Cardozo had done Tommy a few favors over the years; Tommy owed him a few. This was one of them.

The super pulled his fingers through his frizzy brown hair. "No one else in the building has complained."

"It's not affecting other phones in the building." Tommy Thomas's sandy-brown hair was salon-cut and he wore a lightweight dark gray suit and carried a small leather tool case. He was an extremely trustworthy-looking guy. "It's affecting phones in the neighborhood."

"I don't know . . ."

"Mr. Marcowitz," Tommy said, "this is an emergency."

The super reached up to the wall of his office, where tenants' duplicate keys hung. "Come with me."

When no one answered the buzzer, the super unlocked the door. "Mrs. Talbot?" he shouted.

No answer.

"Let me know when you're through," he said.

Cardozo stepped into the apartment. Despite the disorder, he had to marvel at the sheer abundance of the lifestyle: deep chairs and sofas; oriental rugs; tabletops loaded with silver and crystal; a forty-inch TV and state-of-the-art home electronics; shelves crammed with books and CDs.

"No matter how you slice it," Tommy Thomas said, "more *is* more."

Cardozo nodded.

The kitchen was a warehouse of cooking and cutting and grinding and juicing appliances. The bedrooms had personal computers. The shelves in the master bathroom looked like a Madison Avenue cosmetics-and-bath shop.

Cardozo examined a photo cube on the mirrored vanity. All the snapshots showed the same freckle-faced towheaded boy, running, jumping, throwing a Frisbee. He took a shot of the boy reading a comic book and slid it carefully into the credit-card pocket of his wallet.

"Eureka." Tommy Thomas had found a receiver underneath the canopied bed. The phone lay on the floor two feet away. "This got knocked off the table."

A marmalade cat scurried across the rug into the hallway.

"And I think the perpetrator just got away."

At nine-fifteen, Mark Wells folded the Week in Review section of the *New York Times,* came in from the terrace to his living room, and once again dialed Kyra's phone number. This time her machine picked up, chirpy and indomitable. "Hi. This is Kyra. There's no one home. If you want to speak to me, or Toby, or Juliana, please leave a message at the beep and one of us will get back to you."

Mark frowned. It didn't make sense to him. The line had been busy last night, and busy again at seven this morning—so someone must have been home and gone out again.

Or was Kyra screening her calls, hiding behind her answering machine?

"If anyone's there, pick up. It's Mark. Emergency."

No pickup.

"Look, I've spoken with Anne. I know everything and naturally I'm concerned. What's going on? Where are you? Phone me. Leave a message. Please."

"They're letting us see a movie this afternoon," Anne told Shoshana. "Are you coming?"

"I wasn't planning to. It sounds like one of those shoot-'em-ups."

"Please come. I have to do something—and I need help."

On the giant screen, a white stretch limo rammed into a hearse. Brakes squealed. Machine guns rattled. A three-hundred-pound male comedian, dressed as a nun, crawled out from under a pushcart of stuffed O.J. dolls.

Four rows from the rear of the darkened theater, Anne nudged Shoshana and whispered, "Let's go."

Anne squeezed past the knees of other jurors. "Excuse me." She waited a moment in the aisle.

Shoshana caught up and they climbed the incline

toward the red EXIT sign. A female jury guard stepped into their path.

"We're going to the ladies' room," Anne said.

The guard nodded. "Downstairs to your left."

A red velvet corridor brought them to a small, deserted art deco lounge. A circus strong-man logo decorated one door; a lissome pinup girl the other. Anne pushed the pinup girl.

The small black-and-white tiled washroom had two sinks and two stalls, both open. The air carried an eye-bashing sting of camphor.

"Close one of the stall doors and wait by the sink," Anne said. "If anyone tries to go into that stall, tell them I'm using it and you're waiting for me."

Shoshana's face was dubious. "And where are you going to be?"

"You don't want to know."

In keeping with the nostalgia motif of the theater's decor, the phone booth was an old-fashioned World War II design with a little fan that went on when Anne closed the folding door. She dropped a quarter into the slot and pushed the buttons for Kyra's number.

The line was busy.

She hung up, waited forty-five seconds, and tried again.

Still busy.

See, she told herself, *everything's okay—Kyra wouldn't be chatting on the phone if there was any kind of trouble.*

She waited thirty seconds and tried Kyra's number again.

Still busy. She pushed zero. "Operator—could you verify a number for me?" She gave Kyra's number.

"That line is busy," the operator said.

"There's conversation on the line?"

"Yes, ma'am."

Anne consulted her watch. There was still eighty minutes till the movie broke.

She decided to chance it.

Spurred by the promise of a ten-dollar tip, the taxi driver avoided traffic jams and street fairs and slam-braked to a stop beside a little flower-bordered park in Greenwich Village. "Close enough?"

Anne shoved fifteen dollars into the change gate. "Fine." The light was against her, but there was a break in traffic. She ran.

Outside the red-brick high-rise, the doorman leaned against a pillar, smoking a cigarette. The name *Joey* was lettered in gold script on his uniform lapel. "In a serious rush today, Kyra?"

"You know it." Anne opened her purse and made a show of searching through it. "Damn. I left my key in the apartment. Is Toby up there?"

"Haven't seen the Tobester since Friday night."

"Could you let me in?"

"No problema." Joey flicked his cigarette into the gutter. "You go on up and I'll get the passkey."

Anne crossed the lobby.

"Mrs. Talbot," a gray-haired but young-faced woman called from the white leather sofa. "We haven't been formally introduced, but I know your son, Toby? I'm Sadie Hooper, your neighbor in Nine-J?"

"Yes, Mrs. Hooper?"

"I noticed you had a stack of games piled in the corridor Friday night? If you're throwing out any toys or games, we could use them at the community center."

"I'll remember that, Mrs. Hooper."

"Sadie. Please."

Anne stepped into the elevator and pressed nine.

Jumbled sections of Saturday's and Sunday's *New York Times* lay piled on Kyra's doormat. Anne pressed the buzzer.

No answer. Joey arrived with the key and opened the door.

"Thanks, Joey." She picked up all the pieces of the *Times* and laid them on the hall table.

"Looks like you could use a cleanup crew in here."

Was that a hint for moonlighting cash? "I'll let you know, Joey. Thanks." Smile nailed to her face, she closed the door behind him, firmly.

She stood in the hallway. "Hello? Anyone home?"

Whoever had been on the phone must have gone out again.

She walked quickly to Toby's room. The toys and games were gone. The closet was open. There were no clothes on the hangers, and the shelves were bare.

She threw open the closet door in Juliana's room. There was not a shoe, not a dress, not a single article of clothing.

She went to Kyra's room. The closets and drawers were full, but Kyra kept them overstuffed and it was hard to tell if any clothes were missing. The bathroom shelves and the top of the dressing table seemed as expensively cluttered as ever.

She heard a scurrying sound beneath the bed. She knelt down and reached into the dark space. Something furry pounced on her hand. She drew her arm back. Toby's kitten was hanging on to her wrist. She cradled him and petted him.

"Hey, Max, where'd everyone go?"

Her eye fell on the answering machine. She saw that two messages had come in. She pressed *replay.*

"If anyone's there, pick up. It's Mark. . . ."

She fast-forwarded to the second message. "Would you like an all-expenses paid vacation in sunny Saint Kitts? Of course you would." She understood why the line had been busy. The sales pitch went on four minutes. She gritted her teeth and pressed *reset.*

The cat, leaping and dashing across the bedspread, had discovered something wedged between the pillows and the quilted headboard.

"What have you found, Max?" She lifted a pillow, and there was Kyra's cellular phone.

TWENTY-FOUR

6:40 P.M.

"Could I ask you a favor? Would you double-bag those?"

The long line behind him snaked halfway down the baked goods and canned fruits aisle. Only two other checkouts were open, and they were equally crowded.

The checkout girl gave him a sullenly minimal glance and began bagging the groceries into double plastic bags.

"We forgot potato chips," Toby said.

"Just as well. Potato chips are loaded with additives and chemicals. I'll tell you what *is* good for you, though." He pointed to a display rack. "All-natural carrot chips." He handed the boy a crisp twenty-dollar bill. "Why don't you go get some?"

They carried their bags across the parking lot. He unlocked the car.

Captive heat spiraled out, carrying a stale smell of baked upholstery. He placed his grocery bags in the backseat. Soy milk. Organic eggs. Oatmeal. Green beans. Free-range chicken. Good stuff. All fresh, nothing frozen.

He lifted the bags from Toby's arms. This was the fun stuff. Fresh fruit. Yogurt. Organic rice crackers. Healthful snacky things.

Toby just stood there.

"Come on, kiddo. Hop in."

The kid's eyes were tired. "Mom's going to be worried about me."

"Mom knows you're getting good wholesome food. Wait till you taste my barbecued chicken."

"How does Mom know what you're feeding me? I'll bet she doesn't even know where I am."

He crouched, eye-to-eye, man-to-man. "Forget your mom—you're with me."

The kid's fists slammed into him. The unexpected force threw him back against the car. His butt slammed down against asphalt.

Two cars down, he heard a woman's laugh. Something contracted along his spine.

Never, you tell yourself. *I'd never hit a child. Never in a million years.* And then you hear a woman laugh at you and every promise you ever made to yourself or to your shrink is dissolved.

He pushed up and swung. Fist connected with skull and Toby, white face of shock, dappled red, was spinning away from him.

"Toby—get your goddamned ass back here!" He chased the kid, but his left hip felt as though he was running with a thirty-pound hacksaw in his cartilage. Horns blared. Brakes screamed. Wheels skidded.

He lunged and caught the kid in a bone-crushing hug and pulled him up onto the sidewalk. Shouting and kicking and punching, the kid struggled to pull loose.

A group of shoppers from Leroy's Discount Pharmacy stopped to watch, safely out of range of fists and feet.

He threw them an annoyed grimace. "Slight family disagreement, that's all. Please go away."

"Doesn't look so slight to me," a big woman in pink overalls said. "What's that in his hair?" She stepped forward.

The man shouldered her away. "Everything's under control."

The woman touched a fingertip to the side of the kid's head. She stared at her fingertip. Her features scrunched into a knot. "That's blood!"

"What's going on?" someone shouted.

"This kid's bleeding!"

"I've had a small disagreement with my son. It's resolved. Now I'll thank all you good citizens to kindly butt the hell out."

The kid reached out and caught the woman's arm. "He's not my father."

"What?" She searched the young face for some sign that this was a tall tale. She saw nothing but pain and a desperate, wide-eyed honesty.

"Call a cop!" she screamed to the gathering crowd. "This man's a kidnapper!"

Lieutenant Bill Benton gave the kid time, let him tell his story in his own way.

Every now and then Benton typed an observation into

the computer. The computer shared desk space with framed photos of his wife and four-year-old daughter.

"Tell me something, Toby. If he wasn't your father, why did you go with him?"

The boy gazed at him, blond hair tousled, face swollen and bruised and betraying absolutely nothing.

The tape recorder clicked to a stop. Benton snapped the cassette out. He lifted papers, searching for a ballpoint pen to mark the label. The desktop was strewn with photographs and still-unread sections of last Friday's Scotsville *Journal.*

"Did he threaten you?" Benton asked.

The boy gave an abrupt shake of the head. "No."

"Offer you money?"

"No, sir."

"What was it, then?"

The boy seemed embarrassed. "He said he'd take me hiking."

Benton grinned. "I guess you don't get too much hiking in New York City."

"No, sir." No grin.

"That's why you came to Scotsville."

"Yes, sir."

"Let's see if your mom's home yet." Benton lifted the phone receiver and once again tapped in the Manhattan number. The machine answered. He waited for the beep. "It's Lieutenant Bill Benton again. We've got Toby. Give a ring." He left his number again, and pushed up from his chair.

The boy rose at the same time. Benton realized he was in the presence of manners.

"You like magazines, Toby? We have a roomful." Benton pulled open the frosted glass door. He spoke to the sergeant at the desk outside. "Herb, would you take care of Toby here? See he gets some magazines and a Coke or whatever he needs. And send Talbot in."

A moment later the man who claimed to be the boy's father stepped into Benton's office. He moved with a kind of defiant jock swagger and dropped into one of the Rutgers University–decal chairs. He shot Benton an openly sizing-up glance that was almost contemptuous.

"Could I trouble you for some I.D.?" Benton said.

The man reached into his jacket and pulled out a wallet as thick as his fist. He handed it across the desk. The wallet had a noticeable new leather smell. A ladder of credit cards swung free.

Benton flipped through plastic windows, studying the faces that stared out at him. He angled the Gurney and Gurney company pass to the desk lamp. The photo glared with the same overfocused, angry brown eyes as the man sitting in his alma mater chair. Same tight lips. Hair shaved in the same skinhead cut. Benton wondered why the hell a businessman would want to look like a punk. "How long have you worked for Gurney and Gurney?"

"Eighteen years."

"According to the date, your company I.D. was issued fifteen days ago."

"New I.D.s are issued annually in September."

"What brings you to New Jersey, Mr. Talbot?"

"Annual vacation."

"Been to Atlantic City?"

"Not yet."

If he was lying, if he was a freak preying on eleven-year-old kids, he showed extraordinarily careful planning to have a wallet full of fake I.D.s made up in the victim's last name. "This driver's license isn't a month old."

"My driver's license has a habit of expiring every four years, August twenty-seventh."

Benton ignored the sarcasm. It would be easy to lose the thread of civility; easy and a mistake. The man did not radiate trustability, but he could still be telling the truth. "I'm going to have to call your company."

"You're not going to get an answer on Sunday."

"We'll see." Benton lifted the phone and tapped 9 for a line and 1 for long distance. He tapped in the Seattle area code and the cutesy company number ending in 1234.

A machine answered, female. "You have reached the Seattle offices of Gurney and Gurney, attorneys-at-law. Office hours are Monday through Friday—"

Benton pressed *disconnect.* "Is there anyone who can vouch for you? Someone at home maybe?"

"I live alone."

Bill Benton swiveled in his chair. Outside the office window, the last sun of a perfect fall day reflected off the warehouse across the vacant lot. "Well, Mr. Talbot, looks like we have us a problem."

Cardozo typed the last words on the last of the blue triplicates: *No further progress to report on this investigation at this time.*

It was an update on a tourist who'd been murdered outside an East 73rd Street singles bar in 1978. Cardozo pulled the report out of the carriage, signed it, added it to the inch-high stack.

The phone rang. He lifted the receiver and propped it between his shoulder and ear. "Cardozo."

"Vince, it's Tess." She sounded antsy. "I thought you were going to phone me."

"Was I? What about?"

"That guy at the kids' school—what have you found out? Was it Toby Talbot's father?"

"No further progress to report on Catch Talbot."

"I'm worried, Vince. I asked Mickey's guard about Tuesday and Wednesday. Turns out Mickey had a window of opportunity both afternoons—two to five. And yesterday. Eleven-oh-five to one-fifteen."

Silence begat silence.

"Something else bothers me," Tess said. "He says Mickey has a pierced left ear."

"Does he look like the father?" Lieutenant Lars Fiumefreddo of the Scotsville police force was a big, practical man who smiled more and more as the months between him and retirement dwindled down. "Does he sound like the father?"

"He and the kid have the same way of speaking." Lieutenant Bill Benton glanced at the ventilation grille in the dropped ceiling, aware that it could carry voices out just as easily as it piped stale air in. "That's about all. It's a tone."

Lars Fiumefreddo's eyes turned skeptical behind their thin, clean glasses. "You checked missing kids in Manhattan?"

"I checked. Nothing. The kid's eleven. Legally, that's a person, not a kid, and they don't list him till he's been gone forty-eight hours."

Lars Fiumefreddo stared a moment at his coffee. "Worst-case scenario. You give the kid back to Talbot, and Talbot turns out not to be Talbot, and an abuser to boot. Or a kidnapper. Your worst case is unacceptable." He laid the plastic spoon across an ashtray. "So you keep the kid in protective custody overnight. Tomorrow someone in Manhattan or Seattle will answer the phone and one way or the other you'll have verification."

"And if Talbot *is* the father, he sues." Bill Benton didn't want it to be his wrong judgment call that spilled more red ink on the county books.

"You've got reasonable doubt. The man was seen beating the kid. The kid says it's not his father. I.D.s can be faked. You're looking out for the kid's welfare. Any judge or jury in the state would give you a medal."

It was dark in Bill Benton's office. The big man who might or might not be Catch Talbot was sitting in shadow, so still that he hardly seemed to be there at all.

Bill Benton flicked on the overhead light. He crossed to the desk. "You can go, Mr. Talbot."

The thin wood arms of the Rutgers chair creaked, taking all of the man's weight as he pushed up. "Where's Toby?"

"Toby's going to stay with us for the night."

The face darkened. "What the hell are you trying to pull?"

"When we can't make telephone confirmation, in a case like this, we prefer to play it safe. As a father I think you can understand."

The man stood regarding Bill Benton with no expression whatsoever, then turned and socked the door open and vanished.

A sign in the Sixth Precinct on West 10th Street stated: ALL VISITORS MUST STOP AT DESK. There was no choice: the desk blocked the corridor. On the other side of the barricade, a half dozen uniformed cops drifted in and out of cubicles.

"Excuse me," Mark called.

Experienced eyes deftly avoided his.

Behind him, a bicycle fell over with a clatter. One of the cops, startled, looked around. Eye contact. "Help you?" The offer was grudging.

"Yes, thank you. I'd like to report a—"

"Excuse me." A gray-haired woman rose from a chair. "I've been waiting twenty minutes."

"What's the problem?" the cop asked.

"I was walking down Charles Street, and this"—she held up a two-foot square of inch-thick plywood—"this falls out of the top story of 162 and almost kills me."

The cop shook his head. "You want Department of Buildings and Maintenance."

The woman was indignant. "It's not a question of maintenance. Some idiot's throwing crap out the window—they could hit a cop, for Chrissake."

"Ninety-five Jay Street, lady." The cop scrawled the address on the back of a Chinese restaurant flyer and shoved it across the desktop. His eyes came around to Mark. "What's your problem?"

"I'd like to report a missing child."

"Child's name, residence, age, and how long missing?"

"Toby Talbot, Six Barrow Street, eleven years old, two days."

The cop turned. "Hey, Lou, we got a missing kid."

A redheaded woman in blue jeans stuck her head out of a cubicle. She held a bagel in one hand, coffee in the other. She glanced at Mark, squeezed around the desk, and gestured with the bagel. "Upstairs."

Mark followed her up into an office with three metal

desks. She sat down, searched a drawer for a grimy-looking triplicate form. She wound it into a model-T electric typewriter. "Who's missing?"

He repeated Toby's name, age, and address.

She typed with two fingers. "Sit down."

He sat.

She nodded toward the half-chewed bagel. "Have some bagel."

"No, thanks."

"What's your relationship to Toby?"

He flashed that if he wasn't a relative she'd throw the case to the Department of Parks. "Uncle."

"When was Toby born?"

"Twelve years ago, this Wednesday. And I have a photo." He laid the snapshot on the desktop. It showed Kyra, himself, and Toby at Coney Island. "That was taken a little over a year ago."

"We'll get to the photo in a minute. When did you last see Toby—day, place, and hour—and what was he wearing?"

Anne didn't have to invent a headache; she had one. Her brain was running in overdrive, disaster scenarios tumbling over one another. She pushed her pecan pie away, untouched. "I'm going up to the room."

"You're not having your pie?" Shoshana looked shocked. "It's good."

"You have mine." Anne left the coffee shop. "I'm going upstairs," she told the guard. "Really." She took the elevator up to her room. She dredged Kyra's cellular phone from its hiding place in the closet and took it into the bathroom. Tapping in Kyra's number, she locked the door and turned on the bath water.

"Please leave a message at the beep," Kyra's recorded voice was saying, *"and one of us will get back to you."*

"Hi. It's me. Look, I'm worried. Are you okay? Is Toby okay? We need to talk, but you'd better not phone me. I'll call tomorrow morning around seven, okay?"

She phoned her own apartment and left the same message. Then she phoned Mark and got his machine.

"Hi. It's Anne, Sunday evening. Would you check with the École Française tomorrow and see if Toby showed up for school? I'll phone you tomorrow at eight P.M. sharp."

TWENTY-FIVE

Monday, September 23
Fifth day of trial
9:40 A.M.

Lieutenant Bill Benton lifted the receiver and dialed Kyra Talbot's number in Manhattan. He got the machine again. At the beep, he gave his name and phone number and asked Mrs. Talbot to phone as soon as possible.

He looked at his watch. Nine-forty. Over two hours till anyone would be answering a business phone in Seattle.

He went down the corridor to Lars Fiumefreddo's office. Lars was off for the day and the shrink had commandeered his space. She'd pushed two chairs together to form a makeshift bed and Toby Talbot, looking blissfully distant from earthly woes, was curled on his side clutching an inflatable pillow.

"He's asleep," Sondra van Orden said. Sondra was

the county equivalent of a traveling priest: she served four police jurisdictions as psychiatric evaluator, youth counselor, and—if a cop needed it—short-term therapist. "I gave him a mild over-the-counter sedative. Can we talk outside?"

They went to the water cooler. She downed half a cup of Bear Springs's finest.

"I ran a polygraph," she said.

"And?"

"Toby's lying about everything except his name and his age. The needle jumped off the chart."

"Is that surprising? You said he's upset."

"True; he has conflicts with his dad to resolve. But there's a measurable difference between upset and lying. This is lying." She dropped her paper cup into the trash. "I also ran a polygraph on Catch Talbot."

Benton was startled. "When?"

"I finished twenty minutes ago."

"Why?"

"He said you'd ordered it."

"I didn't."

She shrugged. "Talbot may have lied about that, but he's telling the truth about his name, his residence, and his relationship to Toby. The polygraph says he's Toby's father."

"What if he knows how to beat the polygraph?"

"Bill, you've done your job. The polygraph results are on record. Let the kid go and thrash it out with his dad."

"It's the thrashing that worries me."

An explosion of voices echoed down the corridor. "Hey, Lieutenant! There's a man in a hurry to see you!"

The man in a hurry was the man who had just convinced a polygraph he was Catch Talbot. Now he was trying to push past the sergeant into Bill Benton's office.

"You won't find me in there," Benton said.

He wheeled around, red-faced and panting like an attack dog. "I passed that lie detector and I want Toby."

"I understand, and you'll get your son." Bill Benton was wondering how the hell he was going to stall Talbot till someone answered the phone in Seattle. "But I'm going to have to ask you to wait just a little longer."

"I've been waiting since eight o'clock last night."

"Your son can't be moved right now."

"Why not?"

Benton waited for Sondra van Orden to speak up. She didn't.

"Toby's asleep," Benton said.

"Asleep at a quarter to ten in the morning?" Disdain rippled. "What the hell did you people do, drug him?"

Benton shot Sondra a beseeching glance: *Help me out of this.*

She was no help at all. "Bill, we have no legal right to hold the boy."

Shrinks, Bill Benton reflected, *should not be allowed to get night school law degrees.*

"If you'll come this way, Mr. Talbot." She led Talbot around the bend in the corridor. Benton followed.

The frosted glass door of Lars Fiumefreddo's office was shut. Sondra rapped. "Toby?" She opened the door.

The two chairs were still pushed together. The inflatable pillow still lay on one of them.

The boy was gone.

The sound of the organ was like a patient breathing on a respirator—it seemed to accentuate the hush around it. The church was full, a blue sea of uniforms. Faces were grim.

Churches are always full for cops' funerals, Cardozo thought. *Faces are always grim.*

Candles glowed upon flowers and wreaths banked either side of the marble altar. Cardozo's gaze drifted up to the crucifix. It was a large dark mahogany cross with the crucified Savior carved in ivory. The crown of thorns was an intricately chiseled band of mahogany.

He tried to empty his heart of rage and focus instead on eternity and God's merciful justice. Rage kept blanking out eternity.

Detective Ellie Siegel, somber in navy blue, slid into the pew beside him. "Edie Vasquez is clean," she whispered. "The morning of Thursday the nineteenth, after her shift, she went down to Pandora's Box. The bartender vouches for her."

"What's Pandora's Box?"

"An after-hours gay girls' club in Chelsea." Ellie looked down at the printed memorial program: *Church of St. Mary, Martyr: Sanford Avenue, Flushing; requiem mass for Britta Maureen Bailey.* "The bartender also happens to be Edie's lover, and she says there's no way Edie would be seeing another woman."

The mayor made a late, noisy entrance with a flying wedge of Armani-suited gofers and media reps and bodyguards. There was a sound of oak doors slamming. The congregation rose to their feet. Six pallbearers, cops from the Twenty-second Precinct in full-dress uniform, slowly wheeled Britta's coffin up the aisle. It was draped in lilies and a New York City flag.

"What makes the bartender so sure of Edie?"

"They're together every moment Edie's not on the job. And have been since they met three months ago."

"Honeymoon. It won't last."

"Cynic."

Three priests vested in white came out from behind the altar. Cardozo opened the hymnal to look for the first hymn.

"What about the bus to *New York*?" the man groaned.

"There's none direct." Lieutenant Bill Benton studied the bus schedules. It gave him a headache to focus on the small print in the vibrating, dancing wash of fluorescent light. "Toby could just about have made the bus to Elizabeth. If he missed that, there's the bus to Kearney. At Kearney he could make a connection to New York."

"The Kearney bus goes on to Union City," Sondra van Orden said. "He could take the PATH train."

"Let me see those schedules." The man grabbed them from Benton's hand. Bus stops. Train stops. Arrival times. Departure times. Angry eyes narrowed into brown slits. "Toby will arrive at the Port Authority terminal in New York at one-oh-seven. We have to head him off."

"We're only a twelve-man force. At the moment we only have a four-man capability."

"You Nazis owe me this! I'll sue!" A fist slammed down on the desk. There was a scream of wood splitting. A blizzard of glass shards gusted over the floor.

Benton held out a paper napkin. "Your hand."

The photograph of Bill Benton's wife and daughter lay on the linoleum, blood dripping down on it from the heel of Talbot's ripped palm. Benton knelt and picked the photograph up and gently wiped it off.

Lucy-Anne Westervelt fixed her eyes carefully on the lines of *Healing Words,* a doctor's research into the medical effects of prayer. The book kept bucking in her hand as the bus rumbled its way across the New Jersey marshland toward Manhattan. She turned the page and glanced at the boy in the seat beside her.

His head was tipped back against the leatherette. His eyes were shut and, judging by the rise and fall of his shirt, he was asleep. It seemed odd to Lucy-Anne: a boy traveling alone into the city, wearing only a striped green Ralph Lauren polo shirt on a day when temperatures were in the low fifties and the weather bureau was predicting rain.

A shadow brushed her thoughts. Today wasn't a holiday. Why wasn't the boy in school?

She studied the sleeping form. He didn't look like a runaway—on the other hand, it was obvious no mother had been near him in the last twelve hours: his face needed washing, and his hair could use a combing, and his shirt was badly rumpled, causing Lucy-Anne to suspect he'd slept in it.

He stretched his arms and opened his eyes. He turned to look out the window at an empty brown meadow.

"Did you have yourself a good sleep, young man?" As a former third-grade teacher, Lucy-Anne knew you can't teach children respect without showing it, and that was why she called him *young man.* "You were dead to the world."

The boy forced a brief little effort of a smile.

Lucy-Anne closed *Healing Words.* "Do you live in Kearney?"

"No, ma'am." His voice had a numb, quiet quality.

"Then you must live in New York?"

"Yes, ma'am."

"Whereabouts?" *I'm six times your age,* she thought, *but it's not so long since I played hooky and fibbed to my elders, too.*

"Downtown."

"Whereabouts downtown?"

"The Village."

"That's a lovely part of town."

Breasting a chattering tide of young students, Mark Wells climbed the curving flight of marble stairs and searched for room 103.

The door was ajar; a bespectacled woman with steeply piled gray hair sat at a carved desk, marking the pages of blue examination booklets.

He knocked. "Mademoiselle de Gramont? One of the teachers suggested I speak with you."

She rose, motioning him into the room. A curious sweet scent hovered in the air. "How may I help you?"

"I'm looking for Toby Talbot. I'm his uncle—Mark Wells." The lie came quite naturally now.

She quickly shut the door. "Toby did not come to school today. I phoned his home and nobody answered."

"When did you last see him?"

"I haven't seen Toby since his father picked him up last—"

"His *father*?"

"Last Saturday. He gave me a note from Toby's mother."

No way, Mark thought. "Could I trouble you to show me that note?"

Annoyance flared across her face. She took a sheet of paper from her desk, laid it over the window of a Xerox machine, and pushed a button. Greenish light flashed. She handed him the copy.

> Dear Mademoiselle: This is to inform you that Toby's father, Catch Talbot, has my authorization to pick up Toby after today's school excursion and bring him home. With many thanks, Kyra Talbot.

The handwriting was undeniably Kyra's—large and extroverted, with extravagantly looped *b*'s and *h*'s and *k*'s. But when she handed him a copy of the envelope, he saw that the printed address—118 East 81st—was Anne Bingham's.

"And you haven't seen the boy since?"

She shook her head. "There's been no call, no explanation."

Mark ran the information through his mind, trying to make some sense of it. "Mademoiselle, could you describe the man who gave you this note?"

"The people call Jeptha Randolf."

With six enormous strides, a lanky, suntanned man in his early sixties crossed to the stand and took the oath.

Tess diAngeli asked the witness to describe his work.

"For the last thirty-seven years I've been with the BATF—the Bureau of Alcohol, Tobacco, and Firearms." His dark suit and striped tie were Wall Street, but his accent was Alabama. "At present I'm assistant deputy director of security operations for the eastern United States."

"Have you been monitoring the activities of Corey Lyle and his cult?"

"Yes, I have, for eight and a half years."

"Why is the BATF concerned with their activities?"

"We'd heard reports of mail fraud, charge card fraud, income tax fraud, drug and gun dealing, child abuse, and involvement in domestic bombings."

"Objection." Dotson Elihu pushed himself to standing. "Those allegations are irrelevant and are raised solely to prejudice these proceedings."

"Your Honor," diAngeli said, "the People intend to demonstrate relevance."

"I'll give you a little leeway here," Judge Bernheim said. "We'll allow the witness to testify to crimes mentioned in his agents' reports."

"Mr. Randolf," diAngeli asked, "were your agents able to document legal irregularities in the cult's activities?"

"Yes, indeed. Enough gray-zone activity to warrant sending in an undercover agent."

"And did you send in an agent?"

"Not exactly. We recruited a cult member. Her name's Yolanda Lopez. Her nine-year-old daughter, Lisa, was also a member. Mrs. Lopez came to us with a complaint that Corey Lyle had used her little girl as a human bomb in an attempt to blow up—"

Elihu sprang up. "Objection!"

"Overruled."

Randolf continued. "To blow up the IRS building in Manhattan. The bomb malfunctioned and the explosive leaked. The little girl was badly injured and required eighteen separate skin grafts. We arranged for the operations and sent Mrs. Lopez back in to surveil the cult."

"And did Mrs. Lopez uncover proof of illegal activity?"

"In less than a month, she was sending back reports of tax fraud, crooked fund-raising, illegal import of Czech plastic explosives—"

"Objection." Dotson Elihu rose. "How is alleged felony by parties unnamed relevant to the charge against Dr. Lyle?"

"Overruled."

DiAngeli smiled. "Did Mrs. Lopez send back reports mentioning John and Amalia Briar?"

"Five months after she went back in, she told me Corey had something real dirty cooking with John and Amalia Briar."

"Objection!" Elihu leaped up. "Hearsay!"

"Mr. Randolf," the judge said, "are you referring to a written report by Agent Lopez?"

"No, ma'am, this instance was a phone talk."

"Was this phone talk recorded?"

"No, ma'am."

"I'm going to have to sustain the objection."

DiAngeli stood, frowning. "Mr. Randolf—five months after you sent Mrs. Lopez back into the cult, did you instruct her to tape her discussions with Corey Lyle?"

"Yes, ma'am, I did. Soon as the Briar murder plot came up."

"Objection." Elihu was on his feet again. "We're smack back to hearsay."

"If it please Your Honor," diAngeli said, "it's a simple matter to clear this up. I ask permission to play the court one of Yolanda Lopez's tapes—which we are prepared to offer in evidence as People's Exhibit fifty-two."

"Young man," Lucy-Anne Westervelt asked as the bus nosed to a stop on the upper-level ramp of the Port Authority, "would you help me with my bag?"

"Sure." The boy pulled her suitcase from the overhead rack. They joined the passengers filing out.

"I suppose you're heading down to the Village?"

"Eventually." The boy seemed to be scanning the crowd, searching for someone.

"Can I give you a lift in a cab?" Lucy-Anne suggested. She stepped onto the down escalator.

The boy followed. Lucy-Anne knew he didn't want to come with her; but he was holding her bag, and he was well brought-up.

"Which way are you headed?" he said.

"Downtown," Lucy-Anne lied.

Down on the first level the scene was bad: kids with opportunistic, purse-snatching gazes, loitering in running shoes. Beggars stationed at newsstands and candy and soda machines, rattling cups. Homeless men curled up in corners on nests of Big Mac wrappings and thrown-away newspaper. Crazies screaming conversations with themselves. Lucy-Anne smelled crack deals and concealed firearms and children lured into prostitution.

"I'm not going downtown right away." The boy stopped. He set Lucy-Anne's suitcase down. It became a rock of stillness in a sea of hurrying feet. "It was nice meeting you."

Lucy-Anne was aware of another population in the bus terminal—cops circulating everywhere, male and female, officers barely twenty years old, with holster-heavy hips and the cynical eyes of octogenarians.

"I have to go uptown first." She picked up her suitcase. "I can drop you off anywhere you're going."

"Thanks, but I'd better not." The boy's eyes had stopped searching. He was staring at something.

Lucy-Anne turned, following the direction of his gaze.

A man with a shaved head was standing thirty feet away in front of a Dunkin' Donuts window, staring back at the boy.

Lucy-Anne didn't like it; she didn't like it one bit. She reached out her free hand and caught the elbow of the nearest cop. "Officer!"

The cop whirled, one hand on his holster.

"This little boy—"

The officer's face tightened. A red, rough-textured face. "Is the kid bothering you, lady?"

"This little boy is a truant—he should be in school."

Something slammed into Lucy-Anne's suitcase, knocking it from her surprised hand. The boy dove into the crowd.

"Young man!" she called.

The suitcase spun across the floor. She ran and caught it, but when she turned around, the little boy was gone. Her eye went to Dunkin' Donuts.

The man with the shaved head had vanished too.

TWENTY-SIX

12:07 P.M.

Lieutenant Bill Benton angled his wrist. The hands of his watch pointed to 12:07—9:07 in Seattle. Somebody ought to be answering that company phone in Seattle by now.

He found the envelope he'd written the number on. The call clicked through and a woman with an upbeat voice and a bad head cold answered. "Gurney and Gurney, attorneys-at-law. May I help you?"

"Could I speak with Catch Talbot, please?"

"May I ask who's calling?"

"Lieutenant William Benton, Scotsville Police, New Jersey."

"Just a moment, I'll put you through."

Bill Benton's fingertips danced on the edge of his desk.

"Yes, Lieutenant." The male voice was bemused. "This is Catch Talbot. How can I help you?"

The minute he heard that voice, Bill Benton had a

sinking feeling how this talk was going to go. "Mr. Talbot, were you by any chance in Scotsville, New Jersey, last night?" He didn't bother asking *or two hours ago*? That would have sounded too crazy.

"Last night? Are you kidding?"

"No, sir, I'm not kidding."

"I've never been in Scotsville in my life."

"Have you lost a wallet recently or any I.D.s—charge cards, driver's license?"

"Not that I know of."

"Do you have an eleven-year-old son by the name of Toby?"

"Yes, I do." The voice tightened. "Is something the matter? Is Toby in some kind of trouble?"

"No, sir. Someone tried to use your I.D. and we're just checking."

"I don't understand. What does Toby have to do with this?"

"You've cleared the matter up, Mr. Talbot. Thank you." Bill Benton snapped a finger down on the disconnect bar.

Sondra van Orden sat with her legs crossed, foot arcing slowly back and forth. She was staring at the toe of her shoe, avoiding Benton's eyes.

"Sondra, honey . . ." He pushed to standing. "You and me and that polygraph are in deep doodoo."

"*How long can they hang on?*" the high-voiced male said.

"Only God knows that," the woman said.

The voices came from the pocket-size tape recorder that Tess diAngeli held in her hand. She walked slowly along the jury box, moving as if she were carved of flowing water.

"If they're not dead by September fifteenth," the deep-voiced male said, *"we'll be in a bad financial way."*

DiAngeli stopped the tape. A shudder of silence passed. "Do you recognize this tape?"

"I do," Jeptha Randolf said. "That tape was recorded by Yolanda Lopez two years ago, August fourth."

"Objection!" Dotson Elihu rose angrily. "The People have introduced no evidence that Ms. Lopez recorded that tape."

"Sustained. Counselor, lay a foundation."

DiAngeli snapped the cassette out of the recorder. "Do you have reason to believe this tape was recorded by your agent Yolanda Lopez?"

"I do." Jeptha Randolf nodded. "Yolanda Lopez gave me that tape in compliance with my request for tapes of her conversations with Corey Lyle."

"Can you identify the voices on the tape?"

"The woman's voice is Yolie's—Yolanda's. The deeper male voice is Corey's. The other is—"

"Your Honor, I object." Dotson Elihu was working very hard at appearing shocked. "The People have submitted absolutely no proof as to the identity of any of the voices on that tape."

"Surely a government expert can be trusted," di-Angeli said, "to identify the voice of his own operative on a tape of his own operation?"

"Your Honor," Elihu cried, "a witness who admits hiring amateur sleuths could just as easily hire amateur actors."

Judge Bernheim's eyes shot staples into Elihu. "Overruled. The witness is competent to identify the voice of his own agent."

DiAngeli removed the tape from the recorder and inserted a second. "Mr. Randolf, would you listen to this tape and tell me if you recognize it?"

"They're near," the deep male voice said. *"Very near."*

"Thank the merciful Lord," the woman's voice said.

"We have to keep a vigil over them," the man said. *"We want his wife to live forty-eight hours longer than him."*

DiAngeli stopped the tape. "Do you recognize this conversation?"

"I do. That tape was given to me by Yolanda Lopez on August twelfth, two years ago, in compliance with my request for records of her conversations with Corey Lyle."

"Had you heard any of these voices before?"

"Yes, I'd heard them on Ms. Lopez's previous tape."

DiAngeli turned to the bench. "The People request permission to introduce these tapes as People's Exhibits fifty-two and fifty-three."

"Let them be so marked," Judge Bernheim said.

DiAngeli turned toward her witness. "Did Yolanda Lopez attempt to contact you Labor Day weekend?"

"Yes. At six A.M. Saturday, she phoned headquarters and left a message on the answering machine."

"With the court's permission," DiAngeli said, "I would like the witness to tell the jury if this is a recording of that message."

"This is Yolanda." The woman's voice was screaming. *"I'm in the Briars' apartment—Saturday morning. Send somebody up—it's an emergency—Corey's hypnotized Mickey—Mickey's gone crazy—he's killed John and he says he's going to kill Amalia. I've locked her bedroom and I'm in here with her—but that door won't keep him out. Send help! Please! Oh, God!"*

There was a click and silence.

"That's the message," Randolf said.

Tess diAngeli asked that the tape be introduced into evidence. She again faced her witness. "Did Ms. Lopez attempt to contact you a second time that Labor Day weekend?"

"She phoned again eleven A.M. Sunday and left a message."

The voice had reached hysteria. *"This is Yolanda—Sunday morning—Mickey's locked me out of the apartment—he's murdered John and he's in there murdering Amalia—you've got to send help!"*

"Did Ms. Lopez attempt to contact you again that weekend?"

"She phoned at eleven A.M. Monday and left a third message."

The voice was drained. *"This is Yolanda—I'm at the Briars'—John and Amalia have died."*

"Hi. You've reached the office of Ding-a-ling Music, Anne Bingham, CEO. If you'd care to leave a message at the beep, I'll get back to you as soon as possible. That's a promise. Thanks."

"Hi. This is Lieutenant Vince Cardozo at the Twenty-second Precinct again. Calling Monday afternoon."

Something rapped sharply on the open cubicle door. Cardozo turned and saw Greg Monteleone. He signaled Greg to hold on just a second.

"I'd appreciate it if you'd phone me at your earliest convenience." He left his number. "Thank you." He looked up. "What have you got, Greg?"

Greg stepped into the cubicle and the air swooned with Old Spice aftershave. Today he was wearing a bright turquoise shirt with cowboy-style mother-of-pearl buttons. "There seems to be just one Catch Talbot in the U.S.A. Hope it's the right one." He laid a fax on the desk. "Lives in Seattle and has a Visa card."

Cardozo's eye zigzagged in a quick sampling scan over the column of computerized laser print. Right away something puzzled him. "You double-checked this, Greg? Because according to these dates, Catch Talbot was charging dessert in Seattle and dinner in New York City on the same day."

Greg nodded. "Thursday last week. I noticed that too."

Cardozo lifted the top sheet. A second sheet listed Catch Talbot's home address, his business address, his home and work phones. "Even if there was a Concorde flying between Seattle and New York, that would still take some very fast jetting." He tapped the work number into the phone. A secretary in Seattle with a bad head cold put him through to Talbot.

"Catch Talbot." A honey-edged baritone. The voice of a man pitching blue-chip annuities.

"Mr. Talbot, this is Lieutenant Vince Cardozo of the Twenty-second Precinct in New York City."

"How can I help you, Lieutenant?"

"Were you by any chance in New York this past week?"

"I've been right here in Seattle for the last three months. You're the second call I've had from East Coast police—a New Jersey lieutenant wanted to know if I'd been in Jersey last night."

Cardozo grabbed a pen. "Do you recall the lieutenant's name or the town he was calling from?"

"Bill Benton, Scotsville. Would you care to tell me what's going on?"

"Are you the holder of Visa card 444-467-894?"

"Let me check. . . . Yes, I am. Is there a problem?"

"Are you aware that someone in New York has been using your card?"

"I'll stop that card immediately. Thank you. You New York police are certainly alert."

"Just one other question, Mr. Talbot. Do you have a son studying at the École Française in New York City?"

A beat of silence. "Yes, I do, and the officer from New Jersey asked about Toby too."

"When did you last see your son?"

"Around this time last year."

"When were you last in touch with your ex-wife?"

"She phoned Friday the thirteenth and said a custody hearing had to be canceled. Four days later her lawyer phoned and said the same thing." An edge of alarm was creeping into his voice. "Look, I'd like to know why you're so interested in my son and my ex-wife."

"A policewoman is dead. Your son spoke to her the afternoon she died and we need to question him. To do that we need your ex-wife's permission, but she's on jury duty and I haven't been able to reach her."

A beat of silence. "Lieutenant, what's going on? Should I fly East?"

"At this point I don't see that it would serve much purpose."

"You'll tell me if there's anything I should know?"

"You can count on it. Thanks for your help, Mr. Talbot."

Cardozo dialed Mademoiselle de Gramont at the École Française. "Has Toby Talbot come to school today?"

"He has not." She sounded personally offended. "We've had no word about him and no one's answering his home phone."

Just to double-check, Cardozo dialed Kyra Talbot's apartment. A machine picked up.

"Hi. This is Kyra. There's no one home." The recorded female voice oozed cultivation and competence. "If you want to speak to me, or Toby, or Juliana, please leave a message at the beep and one of us will get back to you."

He left his name and number, broke the connection, and dialed the precinct in Scotsville, New Jersey. "Lieutenant Bill Benton, please."

"How much of the taxpayers' money"—Dotson Elihu strode to the witness box—"has the Bureau of Alcohol, Tobacco, and Firearms squandered in its pursuit of Dr. Lyle?"

"Objection," Tess diAngeli cried. "Counsel knows that federal law prohibits such disclosure."

"Sustained," Judge Bernheim said.

Elihu turned. "Mr. Randolf . . . strictly speaking, is child pornography part of BATF's mandate?"

Jeptha Randolf nodded regretfully. "Whenever it's accompanied by alcohol and firearm abuse."

"Well and good, but where in the BATF charter does it say that child abuse is the province of your department rather than of the Justice Department?"

"Objection."

"Sustained."

Elihu paused and turned, stepping back in the direction of the press benches. In his mind, he seemed to be exploring some new possibility, some shifted direction of attack. "Was any evidence of actual child abuse ever collected by your agency—any eyewitness accounts or photos matching children known to be linked to the Corey Lyle Fellowship?"

"Yes, indeed. Sworn depositions. DNA evidence."

Elihu pounced. "You found Dr. Lyle's DNA on the persons of these children?"

"Objection!" Tess diAngeli jumped to her feet. "The witness cannot reveal data in ongoing investigations!"

"This court," Elihu said, orating now, "is not bound by secret memoranda of agreement between renegade federal agencies and their hired accomplices!"

"Mr. Elihu." Judge Bernheim shot him a toxic glance. "You seem determined to push this case into the Supreme Court."

"If that's what it takes to get a straight answer out of Mr. Randolf, you bet I am."

"The Supreme Court has enough trouble. Objection sustained."

Elihu faced the witness. "Mr. Randolf, could you tell this court the name of one single child abused by anyone connected to Dr. Lyle?"

"Mr. Elihu," Judge Bernheim demanded, "how is this line of questioning germane?"

Elihu faced the bench. "Child abuse is the red flag the government is waving in this jury's face—and I agree with Your Honor: it is *not* germane to the charge."

"Objection," DiAngeli cried. "Mr. Elihu is sneak-previewing his summation."

Elihu spun. "Objection to that characterization."

"Fellas . . ." Judge Bernheim placed both hands on the bench. "Stop it—the two of you. I'm going to sustain the objection to naming the children."

"Your Honor," Elihu said, "you are buying into the People's argument. You are assuming that there are actual children who can actually be named. My point is—"

"The bench, Mr. Elihu, buys into nothing. I have seen many instances of young people drowning in emotional, moral, and physical abuse. I am not prepared to heap the acid of publicity upon the scars of their degradation."

"Your Honor, on the basis of that remark, I move—"

"Denied."

Elihu arranged his face into a courteous mask and turned back to the witness. "Could you tell us the name of one single eyewitness to the alleged abuse of children by anyone connected to Dr. Lyle?"

"Mr. Elihu," Judge Bernheim said, "hold it right there. You are very close to contempt."

"Your Honor, either this is a trial under the Constitution or it's a star-chamber proceeding."

"Mr. Elihu, you are cross-examining, not lecturing a freshman civics class."

Elihu turned. "Mr. Randolf, you said that Dr. Lyle's organization was suspected of child abuse. Then why did you allow the nine-year-old child of Yolanda Lopez to be taken into the cult?"

"Yolanda Lopez took her own daughter into the cult. We had nothing to do with it. It happened before we established contact."

"This woman took her own child into a cult that you were allegedly investigating for child abuse, and you regarded her as a trustworthy agent?"

"Are you asking me a question?"

"I sure as hell am."

"Mrs. Lopez was the best option available to us. And she proved to be a damned fine agent."

"Isn't it a fact that Yolanda Lopez habitually prostituted her daughter Lisa to wealthy and influential pedophiles? Didn't she have two such charges against her when she first approached you?"

"That is false."

"And didn't she offer her services in exchange for the complete expunging of her record?"

"That is a contemptible lie."

"Yolanda Lopez told you John and Amalia Briar had died natural deaths." There was fire in Elihu's eyes. "Isn't that a fact?"

"That is false."

"Isn't it a fact that you fabricated evidence so as to implicate Corey Lyle in two murders that never happened?"

"That is false."

"Didn't you script Yolanda's phone calls after the Briars' deaths and alter the phone records so it appeared that John Briar died forty-eight hours before Amalia? And didn't you thus create a motive for Corey Lyle's supposedly ordering the Briars to be murdered?"

"That is false. The BATF answering machine is secure. The records can't be tampered with."

Seated at a table for four in Eugene's Patio, Anne searched the menu for something that didn't have mayo and wasn't fried.

"You know who I wouldn't mind sending to death row?" Thelma del Rio buttered a bread stick. "Dotson Elihu."

Ramon Culpeper nodded in agreement. "I'm sick of him saying 'Is it not a fact that . . .' And then he tosses out some B.S."

Ben Esposito pulled reading glasses from his checked

blue shirt. *"Isn't it a fact that your child is an extraterrestrial hooker?"* he suggested.

"Isn't it a fact Martians killed John and Amalia?" Thelma said.

"Isn't it a fact we shouldn't be discussing the trial?" Anne said.

"We're not. We're talking about that nitwit." Thelma turned a page of the menu. "Has anyone tried the breaded fish sticks?"

TWENTY-SEVEN

2:50 P.M.

"Was this the boy?" Cardozo handed Lieutenant Bill Benton the photo.

Benton crossed to the window. New Jersey sun fell in slatted shafts across his thin, intelligent features. He studied the picture of Toby Talbot sprawled on a lawn reading a Batman comic. "That's him, all right."

"And was this the man?" Cardozo handed Benton the newspaper photo of Mickey Williams with masking tape over the caption.

A scowl stole across Benton's face. "Hair was completely different. This guy looks familiar, but . . . maybe the jaw was a little heavier. Could have been he just needed a shave."

"And the boy said the man *wasn't* his father?"

Benton nodded. "But the guy had a wallet full of Catch Talbot I.D.s. So we had no grounds for holding him."

"The boy wasn't hurt?"

"Not bad enough to charge assault. Fathers are allowed to spank their sons in New Jersey. Within reason. Of course, when we finally reached Seattle, and the *real* Catch Talbot was there, that was a different story. But by then it was too late."

There was a knock at the door and a bearded face popped into the office. "I'm looking for Lieutenant Benton."

"Richie. You got my message." Cardozo jumped up and pumped Richie Gallagher's hand. "Lieutenant, meet Richard Gallagher, one of our best sketch artists. And he makes out-of-state house calls. Richie, Lieutenant Bill Benton."

"Good to meet you." Richie sat, opened his artist's carrying case, and extracted a folio-size drawing tablet and a set of charcoals. He skidded his chair around so Benton could see the sketch take shape. "How would you describe the head? Long and egg shaped? Round and ball shaped? Block shaped?"

"Long-headed," Benton said.

With three strokes of charcoal, an egg shape materialized. With four more strokes it grew two rudimentary eyes; with another stroke, a mouth.

"Hairstyle?"

"Skinhead."

"How would you describe the eyes?"

"Brown. Narrow. Cold."

Leroy's Discount Pharmacy smelled of bath soap, and the gray-haired clerk behind the counter had a smile that smelled of licorice. "Yes, sir, how can I help you?"

Cardozo laid his shield on the counter. "There was a

fight in front of your store yesterday evening—a man and a young boy?"

"Sure was."

"Did the man look like either of these fellows?" Cardozo laid the newspaper photo of Mickey Williams next to a photocopy of Richie's sketch.

The clerk nodded. "Yeah, he did, kinda."

"Which one?"

"Kinda like both."

"Any possibility the man could have been inside the store before the fight?"

"Could've been. I don't recall. Sunday's our busiest day."

"Maybe he bought something?"

"It's possible, sure."

"Would you mind checking your charge receipts? The name I'm looking for is Catch Talbot. As in *catch* a baseball."

The clerk pressed the change button on the cash register and began searching through a bundle of charge carbons. "Mean bastard," he muttered.

"You found him?"

"Sorry." The clerk slipped a red elastic band back around the bundle. "If he bought anything, he must've paid cash."

Cardozo ran the chronology through his mind: the man who'd called himself Catch Talbot picked the kid up from school Saturday, fought with him Sunday, lost him Monday, and disappeared. "Could I use your phone?"

"Help yourself."

The clerk slid a telephone across the countertop and Cardozo dialed Greg Monteleone's extension at the precinct.

"Monteleone."

"Greg, Vince. Would you check whether any missing persons report has been filed on Toby Talbot?"

The deep male voice once again filled the courtroom. *"We want his wife to live forty-eight hours longer than him. . . ."*

Elihu stopped the tape machine. "Mr. Randolf, how do you interpret the remark you just heard?"

"Corey Lyle states that—"

Elihu slammed a fist onto the witness box. "Come on, Mr. Randolf, you're not going to sneak that one past. The People have not demonstrated *who* the hell's voice is on that tape."

"The voice states that Amalia Briar must be killed no sooner than forty-eight hours after her husband."

"Then the jury and I must have missed something. Does the man at any time use the word *killed*? Doesn't he say Amalia Briar must *live*? In fact, couldn't this tape, far from showing any kind of conspiracy to murder . . . show intention to *prolong* life for forty-eight hours?"

In the jury box, next to Anne, Thelma del Rio shifted irritably. "Gimme a break," she muttered.

"In my opinion, in the context of this investigation, that is not what the tape says."

Elihu's eyes were a cool swell of amazement. "Mr. Randolf, if it isn't going to give away any professional or personal secrets, just where the hell were you on Labor Day weekend when your agent was allegedly leaving all those desperate messages on your machine?"

"I was on holiday."

"Where?"

"Objection."

"Sustained."

"Let's see if I have this right. You and your bureau are winding up a multimillion-dollar eight-and-a-half-year investigation. You skip town on vacation, leaving an untrained agent in place without so much as a phone number where she can reach you. Now, even for a tenured employee of a big-spending government agency, isn't that pretty casual behavior?"

"We didn't expect the case to break till after Labor Day."

"You had the timing worked out ahead of time?"

"Objection."

"Sustained."

"Mr. Randolf, isn't the Treasury Department's security budget under attack? Wouldn't a guilty verdict in today's case save the bureau from draconian personnel and budget cuts?"

"Objection!"

"Sustained."

"Mr. Randolf, during all your investigation of Corey Lyle, how many criminal accusations against him did you turn up?"

"I'd say somewhere in the neighborhood of thirty-five."

"And did any result in criminal charges?"

"We preferred not to charge Corey Lyle till we had a rock-solid case."

"In other words, until the deaths of John and Amalia Briar, you had no case against him?"

"We had a case. We wanted to be sure of it."

"Precisely my point. No further questions."

Mark Wells's secretary was dressed in form-fitting, hey-look-at-me colors that left no curve unhugged. "May I help you?"

"Vince Cardozo, New York City police." He flipped open his shield case. "I'd like a word with Mr. Wells. Concerning the missing person report he filed."

A startle reflex showed in her green-shadowed eyes. "I'll see if Mr. Wells is free." She lifted the phone and spoke in a scarcely audible murmur. The fingers of her right hand were tipped in fresh red nail polish that matched the glossy red on her lips. She hadn't yet painted the nails of the left. Or maybe, Cardozo speculated, unsymmetrical was the look in Wall Street law firms.

"You can go right in, sir."

Mark Wells met him at the door—a tall man dressed like a magazine ad. His worried eyes didn't go with the jaunty millionaire look. "You've found Toby?" He closed the door and motioned toward the leather chairs. "Please."

Cardozo sat. His eyes roamed book-lined walls. A Harvard Law diploma hung above a trophy for the Racquet and Tennis Club squash semifinals. "Sorry. I'm looking for him too. A cop was murdered, and Toby Talbot was one of the last people to speak with her. He also seems to be acquainted with one of the suspects. They were seen in New Jersey this morning."

Mark Wells shot him a panicked look. "A suspected *murderer* has him?"

"The man is using the name Catch Talbot. But the real Catch Talbot is in Seattle. The impostor picked your nephew up from school last Saturday. He had a note from your sister."

Wells's fingers jittered on the desktop. "Look. Kyra's not my sister—she's my client. Saying I was Toby's uncle was the only way I could get those precinct people to listen to me."

"If you're not family, how did you know Toby was missing?"

"Kyra told me."

"Kyra Talbot's serving on a sequestered jury. How did she know?"

Wells lifted the phone. "No calls, Miss Emerson." He covered his eyes a moment, as if fending off a migraine. "I'd rather you didn't repeat this. Saturday night Kyra received a threatening phone call. She was told to acquit Corey Lyle or she'd never see Toby alive again."

"Did she recognize the voice?" Cardozo said.

"No. She couldn't even tell if it was a man's or a woman's."

"And how did you find all this out?"

"Judge Bernheim phoned me. There was no record of the call and she felt Kyra was lying—trying to get off the jury. So Kyra and I had a discussion. I explained that the government would go very hard on her if she caused a mistrial in a forty-million-dollar prosecution. And as a felon, she'd lose custody of her son. The upshot was, she decided to withdraw her story and stay on the jury."

"But did she retract her story to you?"

"No."

"And you believe her story?"

"I believe her. There just isn't the proof to back her up."

If Kyra Talbot was telling the truth, Cardozo could finally see a scenario that knit the pieces together. One of Corey Lyle's skinheads had grabbed Toby Talbot in order to pressure the jury. Britta Bailey had gotten in the way of his preparations and he'd killed her.

There was only one problem with that scenario: in all probability the skinhead was the state's star witness *against* Corey Lyle.

Cardozo laid the photocopied sketch on the desktop. "This man claims to be Toby Talbot's father. Do you know him?"

Wells examined the sketch. He shook his head. "It's not Catch. He wouldn't be caught dead in a haircut like this. Makes him look like a recruiter for the Michigan Militia."

Cardozo brought out the news photo. "And this?"

Mark Wells studied it. "Certainly is an old picture. There's a generic resemblance, I suppose. Catch always was a jock. Football and boxing. But I don't think this is him."

Cardozo frowned. "I promised I'd call Talbot. Can I use your phone?"

"Absolutely." Wells lifted the receiver. "Miss Emerson, could you get hold of Catch Talbot in Seattle?"

A moment later the phone buzzed, and a secretary in Seattle with a bad cold told Cardozo that Catch Talbot had been called away from the office on an emergency.

As soon as Cardozo left the office, Mark asked his secretary to get hold of the investigator who did jobs for the firm.

An hour later, Mark sat at a booth in a deserted coffee shop. An overweight, acne'd man by the name of Peter Connolly watched his shaking hand spill coffee into a saucer.

"This has to be absolutely confidential," Mark said.

"It always is, Mr. Wells."

"One of our clients has vanished," Mark explained.

Connolly's face remained stony and unsurprised even when Mark described the jury switch and the kidnapping. Connolly took notes and asked one question about the terms of Toby's trust.

"I'll get back to you," he said.

"How can I help you, Lieutenant?" the manager said.

"A Visa charge card was forged," Cardozo said, "and several unauthorized charges were made on it. One of them was made here in the Oak Room, Thursday the nineteenth." He handed the manager the fax of Catch Talbot's Visa transactions, with the sale date, the post date, and the Visa card reference number neatly highlighted. "I need a description of the man who used the card."

The manager's jaw set itself forward. "We're not liable. Once the computer gives us that authorization number, the charge is cleared."

"No one's blaming the Oak Room."

"I can show you the original dinner check."

"That would be a help."

The manager opened a wooden drawer in a wall of filing cabinets. Thousands of restaurant checks with stapled charge card flimsies had been filed by date. He searched for almost three minutes before handing Cardozo a check for four beverage, two bottles wine, two soup, two salad, two prime rib, two coffee, four cognac, and tax. Total, $167.80. It looked like a merry time had been had.

Two carbon flimsies were attached. One was Visa, signed *Catch Talbot.* The other was American Express, signed *Gordon Gibbs.* Talbot and Gibbs had split the bill and tipped a generous twenty percent.

"Could I get a copy of the Talbot signature?"

"No problem. But as for describing the gentleman . . ." The manager shook his head.

"What about the waiter who served them? Server seven? He might remember two guys sitting at table twelve, killing off two bottles of wine and four cognacs and splitting the bill—and leaving a good tip."

"Don't get your hopes up."

Cardozo followed the manager across the hallway. In the paneled bar, lights softly glowed on polished brass and crystal and oak. Evening was already dark in the windows. Even though all the chairs at the bar and most of the tables were taken, the sound of voices was subdued.

"You got a minute, Jimmy?"

A tall, black-haired waiter glanced up from the cash register.

"Lieutenant Cardozo here has some questions about this charge." The manager handed the waiter the check. "Do you happen to remember the customers?"

"It's Talbot I'm interested in," Cardozo said.

The waiter's eyes flicked from Cardozo to the check. "This was almost two weeks ago. Sorry. But you know who might be able to help you? Dr. Gibbs is sitting over at his regular table—by the corner window."

"Dr. Gibbs?"

The heavyset, cheerful-looking man with the trimmed white beard and half-glasses glanced up from the editorial page of the *New York Times.* "Yes?"

"Vince Cardozo. New York police." He flipped open

his shield case. "Sorry to bother you. I need some information on Catch Talbot."

"Well, well, so that old rascal Catch has got himself in Dutch with the fuzz." Gibbs smiled. "Have a seat."

"You two had dinner here on Thursday the nineteenth?"

"Yes, we did."

"When did you first meet him?"

"That evening. He phoned in the afternoon and introduced himself and asked to see me."

"Why did he phone you?"

Gibbs took a swallow of his martini and gave Cardozo a long, evaluating glance. "Catch was new in town—and having difficulties. So, naturally, as a fellow member of P-Wok, he contacted me. I'm director of the New York chapter."

"I'm sorry—I don't know what P-Wok is."

"Pops Without Kids. We're a self-help group of fathers who feel we've been shafted by the favoritism divorce courts show women. We have chapters in eleven major American cities."

"What sort of difficulties did Catch Talbot say he was having?"

"Family problems—he was fighting his ex-wife for custody of his son."

"Could you describe him?"

"He had hair shaved to the skull . . . brown eyes. He was heavily built . . . well-dressed."

"Was he either of these men?"

Gibbs studied the photo and the sketch. "Rotten likenesses. He looked more like the photograph, but his hair was more like the drawing."

"Did he give you a New York address?"

"No."

"Have you seen him since that dinner?"

"We were ships in the night." Gibbs shook his head. "Now tell me, Lieutenant, why does this man interest you so much?"

"Catch Talbot was in Seattle the evening of September nineteenth. A thief was using his charge card."

Gibbs seemed unsurprised. "Well, well—looks as though I was taken in. Lucky I didn't write him that prescription."

"What prescription?"

"He asked if I could get him some anabolic steroids."

"Steroids?" Cardozo's eyebrows went up. "The synthetic testosterone that bodybuilders use?"

Gibbs nodded. "Apparently some fellow at a gym in Seattle convinced him it was an easy way of building lean body mass."

Gibbs was gazing not at Cardozo's eyes but a little to the side, at his left ear. Cardozo flashed that he was holding back: maybe not exactly lying, but not telling the whole story either.

"How long has he been using steroids?"

"He told me he'd been working out with them for nine months or so, taking out his aggression on barbells."

"What kind of aggression?"

"I gathered he'd had some financial setbacks."

"But you didn't give him the steroids?"

"How could I, Lieutenant? They're a government-regulated substance. I said he'd have to come in for an examination first. He never took me up on it." Gibbs glanced at his watch. "Good Lord—you're going to have to excuse me, but I'm about to be late for a dinner engagement." He laid a twenty-dollar bill under his glass. "It's been a pleasure meeting you, Lieutenant."

TWENTY-EIGHT

6:15 P.M.

After two hours of hide-and-seek on the West Side subway and six hours in two kick-boxer double-features, Toby let himself into the apartment. "Mom?"

Silence answered.

He stood a moment in the dark, sifting sounds. A water pipe whispered in the wall. Voices murmured indistinctly from a neighbor's TV. A smell of Kitty Litter hovered.

He snapped on the light. "Mom?"

A pattering noise came from the kitchen.

He slid his keys between his fingers, brass knuckles in case he had to defend himself. He tiptoed through the dining room, drew a deep breath, and pushed the kitchen door open.

Glass crashed to the floor and shattered. Something leaped through the shadows.

He snapped on the light. A smashed jar of mustard lay oozing on the floor and Max the cat, all marmalade bristles and arched spine, crouched hissing in the corner.

"It's okay, fella, it's only me."

Toby bent down. His lips touched the cat's nose. The cat purred subaudibly.

Toby crossed to the refrigerator and searched for a can of Friskie Treats. Max began dashing in circles.

Except for Joey the doorman, the lobby of Six Barrow Street was deserted. Joey glanced toward the elevators; both were resting on the ground floor. He glanced toward the entrance. The coast was clear.

He pulled a piece of paper out of his uniform pocket. A hundred-dollar bill, folded in the paper, fluttered to the polished granite floor. He stooped and picked it up. Easiest hundred he'd ever made.

He lifted the telephone receiver and dialed the number written on the paper. He spoke softly. "Mr. Talbot? This is Joey the doorman at Six Barrow?"

"Any news for me, Joey?"

"Your son just came in. He's up in the apartment now."

"Alone?"

"Alone."

Anne locked the bathroom door, opened the bath faucets, and tapped Mark's number into the cell phone.

He answered before she even heard a ring. "Yes?"

"It's me."

"Where the hell are you?"

"I'm in the hotel."

"Then what are you doing phoning?"

"I smuggled Kyra's cellular phone in."

"Christ, you're really going for the maximum sentence."

"Mark, I didn't *plan* this."

"It might be better if one of you had."

"Did you check Toby's school?"

"He didn't show up today. But he went on the school excursion Saturday. A man calling himself Catch Talbot picked him up. He gave Mademoiselle a note signed by Kyra."

"His *father* has him?"

"Not necessarily. Mademoiselle's description doesn't fit. He would have had to shave his head and change the color of his eyes. Anyway, Catch is in Seattle."

"Then who took Toby?"

"The cop who came to see me today thinks it was a Coreyite. He says Toby and the man were seen in New Jersey this morning."

"Oh, Lord. And where's Kyra during all of this?"

"Her office says she's on jury duty; no one answers the phone at home."

"How could she just *disappear*?"

"I don't know. But I feel a hell of a lot better now that the police are involved."

Cardozo sipped at his tea, watching Tess over the cup. She'd changed from court clothes into slacks and an old cardigan.

"Why didn't you tell me Kyra Talbot got a threatening call?" he said.

"Because she was lying. And she admitted it."

They were sitting at a booth in a dimly lit all-night eatery on Canal and Centre. The place had a vaguely

Chinese atmosphere—a mural of the Great Wall, paper dragons dangling from ceiling fans, undocumented waiters. The menus were written in English and Chinese and Spanish.

"Why would she lie?"

"To get off the jury."

"I wonder. If Kyra's *not* lying and there *was* a threat, it would start to make sense. A Coreyite skinhead stalks a juror's kid; Britta Bailey sees him—maybe she even recognizes him—so he has to kill her. He snatches the kid and phones Kyra Talbot. He tells her she has to hang the jury or he'll hurt Toby."

Tess shook her head. "The lines are blocked; there's no way anyone could have phoned her hotel room. Besides, there'd be a record of any call even attempted to a juror's room—and there isn't."

"The drugstore owner in Scotsville saw the skinhead." Cardozo showed her the sketch and the photo. "And he says he looked like both these pictures."

She shrugged. "It's not proof. And if that's supposed to be Mickey, it's a lousy picture."

Cardozo glanced to make sure the next booth was empty. "How much do you remember about Kyra Talbot's voir dire? Did she mention her son's name, his school, her ex-husband's name, his residence, his job?"

"Probably."

"Is there any way that voir dire could have gotten out to any of the Coreyites?"

She reflected a moment. "One very easy way. Elihu could have passed it on."

"That would put Elihu over the line."

"He's been over the line for a decade now."

Cardozo leaned forward. "Tess—I have to talk to Mickey Williams. Give me his address."

Tess's cool, direct gaze was still direct, but it was no longer cool. "Vince, I'm handling this."

"You're not handling it well."

"If I gave you that information, I'd be flushing my career down the toilet."

"I'm not going to rat on you."

"Says who?"

"Come on, Tess. Mickey's using you. He's sitting on both sides of the fence. Saving his ass by testifying, saving Corey by kidnapping the kid."

"I don't believe it. Mickey's not dumb enough to think it up and he's not smart enough to pull it off."

"Oh, no? You yourself said there were windows of opportunity."

"Opportunity isn't proof."

"Okay, then tell me this: Where was Mickey last Sunday from six to eleven P.M.? Where was he Monday morning from nine to noon?"

Tess made a face and tapped a number into her cell phone. "Rick? Tess. I need some information. Where was Mickey last Sunday evening, six to eleven? . . . And what about Monday, nine to noon? . . . Thanks." She slipped the phone back into her purse and gazed levelly at Cardozo. "The guard says Mickey was at his girlfriend's from five P.M. Sunday till one P.M. Monday. She lives on the Upper West Side. The guard was in a car watching the building. There are two entrances and he could see them both."

"That's a twenty-hour shift. You really believe this guard never dozed off or stepped out to take a piss? You're covering too many asses, Tess—Mickey's and yours and that guard's. What happens if Mickey harms the kid? Because you know he's going to. It'll be on your conscience. And your résumé. This could be your chance to save a human life."

"Sorry, Vince." She slapped ten dollars on the table and snapped her purse shut. "Nice try, but no sale."

Toby took the cat carrier down from the closet and set it on the hallway floor. Max was sniffing around, wondering what was up. Carrier meant vet, and he'd never made a nighttime trip to the vet before.

A car honked in the street, and then two cars and then a dozen, rising in short-tempered chorus.

Max scampered into the living room, vaulted across a chair, and hopped up onto the window ledge. The window was open six inches. Toby dove after the cat, captured it, and slammed the window shut. Double-glazed silence descended.

Down in the street, a taxi was trying to get through the maze of street peddlers and jaywalking tourists. A man in a white wool watch cap leaped out of the cab and thrust money into the driver's window. The cap slipped to the side and Toby caught a glimpse of a completely shaved head. His heart dropped.

The man barreled down the sidewalk and disappeared under the awning of Six Barrow Street. Two minutes later, the apartment doorbell rang.

Max dashed to the front door.

Toby switched off the living room light. He crept into the front hallway and placed his ear to the door.

A scratching key searched for the lock. Found it with a click. Turned.

The door flew open. A figure stood silhouetted. "Hey, Tobester! What are you doing in the dark?"

He recognized the voice of Joey the doorman. "What do you want, Joey?"

"Got a message for you."

The silhouette stepped into the apartment.

"Who from?"

"From your dad."

Toby tried to see around the silhouette, to see if there was a second silhouette skulking. "Listen to me, Joey. He's not my father."

"Come on, Tobester." Two footsteps forward. "Of course your father's your father. He says pack your bag because you're going back to the country. I envy you, pal."

In the space behind Joey something moved, blacking out the corridor light.

Toby wheeled around and dashed down the hallway into the kitchen. Momentum sent him skidding across the linoleum and *thunk* into the back door.

He undid the chain and twisted the lock. The bolt snapped back. He yanked the door open.

The man with the shaved head stood on the landing, grinning. "Hey, Toby, all set?" He tossed a white wool watch cap up into the air and caught it. *Get me, I'm a circus clown.*

Toby wheeled, skidded around the kitchen table, back into the hallway. Smack into Joey the doorman.

"C'mon, Tobester, what's the big rush?" Joey clamped a hand around Toby's arm, lifting him partway off his feet, pushing him back toward the kitchen.

"Excuse me," a voice called out behind them. "I said, *excuse me*! Do you realize your front door is open?" It was Mr. Hooper from next door, gray-haired and just a little bit concerned. "Your cat just got into the hall."

Toby slipped out of Joey's grip. "Wow, thanks, Mr. Hooper!"

He scooped up the cat carrier and bolted into the corridor. Max was pawing at the elevator door. He grabbed the cat just as the elevator opened.

Mrs. Hooper, tall and sweet-smelling, had one high-heeled foot off the elevator when Toby bumped into her. "Why, Toby! What in the—?"

"Push *lobby*!"

Her face was an uncomprehending blank. He shoved a hand past her and pushed the *lobby* button.

"Excuse *me,* young man!"

The door started to close. Just as Mrs. Hooper reached to stop it, the head with the white wool cap popped up on the other side of the crack.

Toby seized Mrs. Hooper's arm and yanked her back. An enormous hand was grabbing through the door. The door tried to close on it and then snapped back.

Toby leaned against the *door close* button.

The hand and forearm snaked around the batting door. Fingers strained to reach the control panel.

Toby picked up the cat carrier and drove it into the arm.

The arm flung the cat carrier away. The carrier lid sprang open and a bristling ball of Max, claws extended, arced yowling into the air and sank its teeth into the hand.

Mrs. Hooper screamed.

Max hit the floor at the same time as the spatter of blood. The hand vanished and a voice cried, *"Goddamn you!"* The door slammed shut and the elevator began its descent.

"Mrs. Hooper, I'm really sorry and I'll explain later."

Toby pushed Max into the carrier and snapped the lid shut.

The door opened and he dashed across the lobby.

In her office, Tess lifted the phone and tapped in the number of Mickey's guard.

"Yeah?"

"Rick—Tess. How's Mickey?"

"Mickey's being a good boy."

"Are you keeping the log?"

"Sure am."

"Good. Anything I should know about?"

"Not yet."

"Phone me if anything develops."

"You bet."

TWENTY-NINE

Tuesday, September 24
Sixth day of trial
8:50 A.M.

Cardozo liked to think he had eyes wide open to the varieties of chiseling in the world. But looking over Greg Monteleone's expense vouchers, he felt like a virologist who had isolated a killer strain of expense-account padding.

Flowers to cheer up hospitalized informant; Park Avenue doctor to prescribe tranquilizers for nervous witness A; restaurant meals for nervous witnesses B and C; taxis to take nervous witness D to and from the emergency room.

Cardozo pushed his chair away from the desk, as though distance could help him see the context. As though context was a light you could shine on things that would change black to white.

He acknowledged the power of money and the paradox that people would do sleazy things to get twenty bucks that they wouldn't dream of doing for two thousand. It wasn't as though Greg was the first to steal from the police budget. Contractors did it; mayors did it; commissioners did it; and did it a hundred times worse.

But cops shouldn't do it.

There was a knock at the open door. "Got hold of Catch Talbot's MasterCard charges." Today Greg was wearing an open-necked pink orchid Hawaiian shirt. Two gold chains winked in the cleavage as he laid the fax on the desk.

Cardozo scanned September posting dates and an unbroken column of Seattle, Washington. "Say, Greg, I was looking at some of your expenses on the Gonzales case. I take it some of those witnesses are attractive young females?"

"Reasonably." Greg shrugged. "Why?"

Cardozo's eye hit a charge at Spook Boutique in New York City on September sixteenth. And another at Philmar's Car Rental in Newark the same day. And a third at the Tru-Val Supermarket in Scotsville, New Jersey, on the twenty-second. He grabbed the Manhattan phone directory and found the listing for Spook Boutique: 526 Little West Twelfth Street. "Didn't you use to work vice over on Little West Twelfth? Ever hear of an outfit called Spook Boutique?"

"Must be a new one." Greg was thoughtful. "Sounds kinda necro."

The phone gave a peremptory buzz.

"Cardozo."

"Vince." Ellie Siegel's voice managed to telescope competence and calm and good humor into a single syllable. "You have a visitor."

Cardozo leaned around in his swivel chair and peered into the squad room. A man in a summer-weight business suit stood fidgeting beside Ellie's desk. From the back, his most salient features were broad, heavy shoulders and thick brown hair.

"I don't recognize the back. What's his name?"

"Catch Talbot. From Seattle."

"Christ. Send him in."

Talbot turned, and Cardozo saw haunted blue eyes in a face shadowed by sleeplessness.

"Mr. Talbot? Vince Cardozo." He stood, mustering politeness, and met his visitor at the door. "Good to meet you."

Talbot fumbled his hand around Cardozo's and gave him a beseeching look. "I'm here to help."

"I've completed my review of the taped material." Judge Bernheim gazed out over packed benches. "I'll allow the People to offer all taped exhibits except the tape of September third."

"Your Honor." Tess diAngeli rose. "The People respectfully object to the exclusion. In *Gorley* v. *McClintock,* the seventh district court of appeals ruled that—"

"Ms. diAngeli, I've gone just about as far as I'm inclined to in accommodating the People. Please call your witness."

"Yes, Your Honor." Tess diAngeli turned. "The People call Yolanda Lopez."

The door opened, and a delicate-boned, dark-complected woman in a high-necked white lace dress crossed uncertainly to the stand.

"Mrs. Lopez . . ." Tess diAngeli fixed the witness with a sympathetic gaze. "What is your occupation?"

"At present I'm on leave of absence from the Bureau

of Alcohol, Tobacco, and Firearms. I guess right now my profession is single mother."

"Would you describe your work for the BATF?"

"Two years and three months ago, they asked me to act as their undercover agent in the Corey Lyle cult. They wanted me to look for evidence of drug use and drug dealing. Tax fraud. Mail fraud and charge card fraud." Yolanda Lopez hesitated. "And bombings."

"Your Honor, I object." Dotson Elihu pushed to his feet. "The defendant is not accused of tax fraud or bombings. Nor has evidence of any such activities been produced."

"The witness is not accusing the defendant," diAngeli said. "She's describing the activities she was asked to monitor."

"Objection overruled."

"Mrs. Lopez," Tess diAngeli said, "prior to your employment by the BATF, did Corey Lyle give you any specific duties in the cult?"

"Bookkeeper."

"Had you had any training in bookkeeping or accounting?"

"I studied accounting at St. John's Junior College night school—in Galveston. Eight credits."

"And when you worked on Corey's books, were you able to come to any conclusion as to the state of his finances?"

"He was broke. He had five thousand in two CD's—that was his assets. On the debit side, he'd drawn down the full quarter million on his credit line. Citibank was trying to get judgments to repossess his cars. For over two years he hadn't made payments on a one-point-one-million-dollar loan from Chemical. He was behind on his mortgage on two town houses; the bank was due to take possession September fifteenth."

"The fifteenth of September?"

"Yes, ma'am."

DiAngeli turned toward the jurors. "The jury will please note that date." And back to her witness. "Did Corey Lyle have any other outstanding debts?"

"He had a federal tax lien for nine hundred thousand dollars."

"Did he ever discuss with you how he intended to clear up his IRS difficulties?"

"He said he was going to blow up their computers."

Elihu jumped to his feet. "Objection!"

Cardozo laid the fax of Talbot's MasterCard charges on the desk.

As Talbot studied the list, his eyebrows shelved out over weary eyes. "I didn't make these charges in New York and New Jersey. I wasn't even here."

"Any idea who could have done it?"

"Aren't there rings of thieves who specialize in charge cards?"

"There are—but I'll tell you why I don't think they're involved. Last Thursday, a man with a shaved head and brown eyes—a man claiming to be you—had dinner at the Plaza with a doctor by the name of Gordon Gibbs. Gibbs is director of the local chapter of Pops Without Kids . . . P-Wok. Do you know anything about them?"

"I've been a member since my divorce."

"Then the man using your charge cards knows a few things about you."

"But apparently not what I look like."

Cardozo nodded. "Last week a man with the same

appearance was seen in a parked car outside the École Française. He was watching your son, Toby. One of our officers challenged him. She vanished and was murdered the same night. Last Saturday, the same man—still claiming to be you—showed up again at the École. He had a note purportedly from your ex-wife, authorizing him to take Toby." Cardozo handed Talbot the note. "Is this Mrs. Talbot's handwriting?"

"Oh, God." Talbot sat with his head in his hands. "If it's not, it's a damned good imitation."

"Last Sunday in Scotsville, New Jersey, the same man had a public fight with Toby. The local police detained him. He had a wallet full of your I.D.s."

Talbot gripped the arms of the chair. "Was Toby hurt?"

"A few scratches. Nothing serious."

"Where is he now?"

"Toby and the man both disappeared Monday morning. So far as we know, they disappeared separately. We haven't been able to trace either one of them."

Catch Talbot let out a long sigh of exasperation.

"The phone threat," Cardozo said, "suggests that Corey Lyle's supporters or cult members are involved."

"Christ, no. Most of those people are nuts."

Something in the inflection caught Cardozo's ear. "You've had dealings with them?"

"Indirectly."

"Tell me about it."

"It doesn't have any bearing."

"I'd still like to hear."

"A little over two years ago the Seattle Welfare Board sued one of Corey Lyle's culties. I defended him pro bono. Seattle Welfare were bastards, and the Coreyites were loons, but he was a good man." Talbot smiled ruefully. "And we won."

"What was his name?"

"Mickey Williams."

Cardozo sat forward. "The ex-football player?"

"You know him?"

"Mr. Talbot, think back carefully. Did you ever tell Mickey Williams your son's name, or school, or your ex-wife's name?"

"Some of those things may have come up in conversation."

"Did he ever see your charge card?"

"Possibly. We ate at a vegetarian place—I don't recall if they took charge cards."

"Who's a vegetarian—you or Mickey?"

"He is. And for two and a half years now, I've been trying to get the toxins out of my life and diet." Catch Talbot stopped. "Now, wait a minute, you don't think Mickey could . . ."

"What would you say Mickey's attitude was toward Corey Lyle?"

"Unmitigated adoration."

"Which puts him in a tough situation now, since he's testifying against Lyle."

"*Against* him? That's not possible. There's no way on earth Mickey would ever—"

"The government may have made him an offer he couldn't resist. Or they may have pressured him into it. Either way, he still would want Lyle to get off. Which gives him a motive to make that call to Mrs. Talbot. And to kidnap your son."

"No way." Catch Talbot shook his head. "Mickey Williams and I are *friends.*"

Cardozo observed Talbot. He saw a man who was exhausted and frightened, a man whose defenses were coming apart and whose emotions were beginning to sluice through the cracks. A man who—like a million others in times of stress—clung to the familiar: old habits, old convictions, old friends.

"Would you happen to know where your old pal Mickey is living at the moment?"

"At the moment?" Talbot considered. "I don't recall." He glanced at his watch. "But I could ask my secretary."

Cardozo pushed the phone across the desk. "Dial nine."

Talbot phoned Seattle. "Peggy? It's me. What's the most recent address we have for Mickey Williams?" After a moment he reached for a ballpoint and pad. "You're sure? Thanks. Talk to you later." He hung up the phone and jotted. "Scandinavian Seamen's Residence, Fifteen White Street."

"White Street, New York?"

"Seattle. He lived there during the suit. Then he came to New York."

"Where in New York?"

"I don't know."

"Why did he come here?"

"Because a dying friend was asking for him."

"I don't suppose that dying friend was John Briar?"

"It was, and I've seen the news reports. But the Mickey I knew was a decent guy and a man of honor. He'd never harm another human being—let alone a dying old man or a defenseless child."

After reading Mickey Williams's criminal record, Cardozo found Talbot's faith hard to swallow. But he didn't mention the record. It was better to hold out some hope. "Have you thought of checking whether the precincts and hospitals have any record of Toby?"

Talbot made another notation on the scratch pad, pocketed the sheet of paper, and pushed quickly to his feet. "Incidentally, I haven't been able to get hold of Kyra's sister—Anne Bingham. Have you?"

Cardozo glanced up. "Anne Bingham is Kyra Talbot's sister?"

"Her twin sister."

"Miss or Mrs.?"

"Mrs."

"Would you excuse me just a second? I'll get those hospitals for you."

Cardozo stopped by Greg Monteleone's desk in the squad room. "Check out any charge cards belonging to a Mrs. Anne Bingham, 118 East Eighty-first Street. And while you're at it, check out Kyra Talbot's."

Greg scowled. "How do you spell *Kyra*?"

Cardozo spelled it. "And do me a favor. I'm sending Catch Talbot to check out hospitals. Keep an eye on him. Discreetly. He's in worse shape than he realizes."

THIRTY

12:40 P.M.

"Mrs. Lopez," Tess diAngeli asked, "two years before you became an agent for the government, did you bring your seven-year-old daughter into the Corey Lyle cult?"

Yolanda Lopez sat with her head angled down. "I did."

"Why?"

"Lisa had emotional problems. She needed a father. I felt Corey could help."

"Would it be fair to say that at the time Lisa joined the cult, you trusted Corey Lyle?"

Yolanda Lopez nodded. "With my life."

"And after your daughter joined, did your trust continue?"

"I began to have doubts when he separated Lisa and me. He said Lisa needed the open air—so he moved her to John Briar's estate in Connecticut. I stayed in New York in cult headquarters."

"When did you next see your daughter?"

"A year later."

"Where was this?"

"In the burn center at St. Vincent's Hospital in Manhattan."

"Objection." Dotson Elihu shoved wearily to his feet. "Irrelevant."

"Your Honor, the People will demonstrate relevance."

"Overruled."

DiAngeli turned to the witness. "Why was your daughter in the burn center?"

"Because she wore a belt of explosives into the IRS building. The explosive leaked and she got third-degree burns over a quarter of her body."

"Who instructed her to wear the belt?"

"Objection. Relevance."

DiAngeli whirled. "Your Honor, this goes straight to the character of the accused."

"Overruled. Witness may answer the question."

Yolanda Lopez's gaze pinned the defendant. "Corey Lyle told Lisa to wear the belt or she wouldn't get to heaven."

"Objection. Hearsay."

"Ms. DiAngeli," the judge said, "lay a foundation or I'll have to sustain."

"*They're near death.*" The voice resonating from the tiny tape recorder filled the courtroom like a genie from a bottle. *"We have to keep a vigil over them. We want his wife to live forty-eight hours longer than him."*

Tess diAngeli stopped the machine. "Mrs. Lopez, do you recognize the tape?"

"Yes. I recorded it August tenth."

"Do you recognize the woman's voice on that tape?"

"It's my voice."

"Who were you speaking with when you recorded that tape?"

"With Corey and Mickey Williams."

"And whose was the last voice we heard?"

"That was Corey."

"Did Corey Lyle tell you the names of the elderly couple who were near death?"

"John and Amalia Briar."

"Objection!" Dotson Elihu leaped to his feet. "Those names are nowhere mentioned on that tape!"

"Overruled. The witness may testify from her memory."

Tess diAngeli approached the witness box. Her voice became compassionate and caring. "Mrs. Lopez, could you tell the court what happened on Labor Day weekend following this conversation?"

"Corey told me and Mickey to come to the Briars' apartment midnight Friday. He said the Briars' maid had to go to Pakistan for a family funeral, and he didn't want them to be alone."

"Did you know at that time if there was any plan on the part of Corey Lyle and Mickey Williams to kill John and Amalia Briar?"

"At that time I knew there was a plan that the Briars had to die before September fifteenth."

"Objection." Dotson Elihu stood. "No such plan has been established."

"Your Honor." Tess diAngeli appealed to the bench. "People's exhibit demonstrates—"

"A hope," Elihu cut in, "is not a plan."

"Objection overruled." Judge Bernheim glowered. "Mr. Elihu, you'll get your chance in cross."

DiAngeli faced her witness. "Mrs. Lopez, how did you get into the apartment?"

"Corey let us in."

"Were John and Amalia Briar alive when you arrived?"

"Yes."

"Did Corey Lyle give you specific instructions at that time?"

"He told Mickey to sit with John, and he told me to sit with Amalia. He told us to feed them carrot puree and carrot juice."

"Did you hear Corey Lyle give Mickey Williams any other instructions?"

"No. Corey took Mickey into John's bedroom. I didn't go with them."

"Did he leave you and Mickey Williams in the apartment?"

"Yes. He left us at two A.M."

"Were the Briars alive when he left?"

"Amalia was. I don't know about John."

"When did you next see John Briar?"

"Around seven A.M. I heard Mickey chanting in the living room. He sounded crazy, so I—"

"Objection." Elihu jumped up. "Conclusion. This witness is not an expert. Not remotely."

"Sustained, but Mr. Elihu, spare us your footnotes."

"When did you next see John Briar?" diAngeli repeated.

"Around seven A.M. I went to John's bedroom to make sure he was all right, and . . ." She faltered.

"And what condition was John Briar in when you found him?"

"He was lying on the floor." Yolanda Lopez drew in a

long breath. "Dead. I could see there'd been a fight, and I knew Corey had somehow flipped Mickey out."

"Objection!" Dotson Elihu rose shouting. "This kind of tabloid conjecture by a paid government *informer* has no more place in a court of law than outright perjury!"

Yolanda Lopez crumpled against the partition of the witness box. A stir passed through the spectators' benches.

"Your Honor," diAngeli cried, "would the bench instruct my colleague to temper his attacks on this witness? She's been through a horrible ordeal."

Judge Bernheim whispered to the bailiff. He helped Yolanda Lopez to her feet and guided her out of the court.

"Ladies and gentlemen of the jury," Judge Bernheim said, "it sometimes happens that witnesses do become overexcited or collapse during direct or cross-examination. This is not to affect your standards of judgment in evaluating their testimony."

Little West Twelfth Street looked like a bomb-testing site. Most of the storefronts were boarded up. Skeletonized car wrecks lined the curbs.

Cardozo found number 526, a four-story brick tenement with peeling blue paint. A timber buttress running from the cobbled gutter braced an ominous second-story hernia. A hand-lettered card spelling SPOOK BOUTIQUE had been shoved partway into one of the buzzer slots. He pressed the button.

The steel door opened with a ratchety buzz. A moldy smell floated in the air. He took the dark, narrow staircase two flights up till he saw light.

A tinkling bead curtain swayed at the end of the landing. He stepped through and looked around him. A poster solicited funds for the Corey Lyle Defense Fund: FOR THE LOVE OF LIBERTY, CONTRIBUTE! Electronic gear was arranged in glass cabinets. Bookshelves lined two walls. He took down a book: *Spooking Big Sam—How to Find Out if He's Spooking You and What to Do About It.*

The door behind him closed. He wheeled around.

A short, heavyset woman with close-cropped, iron-gray hair stood smack in his path. She must have been hiding behind the door. "Help you?"

He replaced the book on the shelf. "Who's Big Sam?"

"The hybrid progeny of Uncle Sam and Big Brother." Her tone was mild, matter-of-fact. Her T-shirt said: LET GO AND LET GOD.

Cardozo took his time making a selection. He could feel the clerk watching him and he didn't want it to look random. He bypassed books on crystals and past-life therapy and chose *Freak the Fiend: Establish and Document Your Alternate Identity and Drive Big Sam Bonkers.*

The clerk rang the book up on the computerized cash register. "With a ten percent discount for hardcover, that comes to twenty-four seventy-five."

Cardozo realized his NYPD shield would get him nowhere in this environment. He took out his Visa card. "And I'd like to make a contribution to the Corey Lyle Defense Fund. Twenty dollars. Can you put it on the card?"

"Can do."

"I'll make that forty dollars," Cardozo said, "if you can give me some information."

Suspicious eyes fixed on him. "What kind of information?"

"A man by the name of Catch Talbot made a twenty-four-hundred-dollar purchase from you last Wednesday. Would you by any chance recall the gentleman?"

"Sorry. Wednesday's my day off."

"Could you tell me what he bought?" Cardozo gave her the order number.

The clerk went to the bead curtain and glanced into the hallway. She sat at the computer. She punched up a file and searched the data. "Mitchelson Medusa-type microminiaturized solid state block-defeater with redirecting capability. Bell and Howard signal inverter."

"What's a signal inverter?"

"Disguises the voice."

"And a block-defeater?"

Her eyes flicked up. "It bypasses blocked telephone lines and redirects caller I.D. to a false number or no number at all."

Which, Cardozo reflected, might explain how Kyra Talbot got her threatening phone call and why there was no record of it. "Could I see Mr. Talbot's order?"

The clerk pressed a key on the computer and a small dot-matrix printer spat out a length of two-inch-wide tape.

Cardozo studied the print. It was almost too faint to make out. "Does this say *head cleaner*?"

"Triple-X VCR head cleaner." She tapped the display case where several pale blue canisters had been piled in a pyramid.

He crouched to read the label. *A deep inhalation is required to clean the head. Saturdate cloth and apply to nose and mouth. Do not use paper towel.*

"Saturdate?" he said.

"They're from Mexico." She winked. "The government doesn't allow us to sell chloroform."

"After you found John Briar dead," Tess diAngeli said, "what were your actions?"

Yolanda Lopez, back in the witness box after a half-hour absence, looked drained and exhausted. "I locked myself into Amalia's room. I phoned the BATF. A machine answered. I left a message. But it was a holiday weekend—so I phoned 911. They said an ambulance would be over in twenty minutes. I waited an hour and phoned again. They said the ambulance had come and no one was at the address. So I went to the police. I told them John Briar was dead and Amalia was in danger."

"Did the police help you?"

Yolanda Lopez shook her head. "Sergeant Bailey phoned the apartment. She spoke with a man who said he was John Briar. He said he was fine. She spoke with Amalia, and Amalia was fine too. So there was nothing the police could do."

There was a flurry of movement at the defense table. "Your Honor!" Elihu sprang to his feet. "I demand that you declare an immediate mistrial! John Briar was alive and spoke to the police a good twelve hours *after* the time the People's coroner has alleged he died. The People have been in possession of this evidence and they have knowingly withheld it."

Judge Bernheim turned to the prosecutor. "Ms. diAngeli?"

"Your Honor, I never heard the witness mention this information before this moment."

"Your Honor, is this a court of law or a vaudeville theater?"

"That's up to you, Mr. Elihu."

"Haven't we had enough of the People's mind reading and the People's hearsay and the People's cover-up?

I *demand* that Sergeant Britta Bailey be recalled to the stand to be properly examined on this crucial point."

"That's not possible," Tess diAngeli said.

Elihu whirled. "I'd like to know what law forbids it."

"Your Honor," diAngeli said, "may I approach?"

Judge Bernheim asked both attorneys to approach the bench. After five minutes of whispering, Judge Bernheim informed the court that Officer Britta Bailey would not be recalled to the stand. "I shall review this witness's previous depositions and grand jury testimony. Pending the outcome of that review, direct examination may continue."

Tess diAngeli smiled encouragingly at the witness, as if to say, *We're almost home.* "Mrs. Lopez, after the police refused to investigate, what did you then do?"

"I spent the day running from hospital to hospital—trying to persuade a doctor, a nurse, somebody to come back to the apartment and help. No one would come." Yolanda Lopez looked down guiltily at her hands. As though they had somehow failed.

"When you were unable to get medical help, what did you then do?"

"I kept phoning BATF, but I always got the answering machine. So I spent Saturday night in the entrance hall outside the apartment—ringing the bell and pounding on the door."

"And did you see Mickey Williams again?"

"Labor Day morning, he finally opened the door. He said, 'It's done. They're gone.' "

In the jury room, afternoon light streamed through the window.

"I'm starved," Thelma del Rio said. "There should be a law: morning sessions end at one sharp."

"If John was dead," Lara Duggan said, "how could he have answered the phone?"

"I'm not going to think about it," Anne said, "till we have all the evidence."

"It *wasn't* John who answered," Seymour Shen said. "It was Mickey."

Lara made a confused face. "I didn't hear anyone prove that."

"Sometimes," Thelma del Rio said, "you have to use your head just a little."

"Hey," Ben Esposito said. "No discussion."

THIRTY-ONE

3:40 P.M.

Catch Talbot pushed through the revolving door into the lobby of St. Andrea Polyclinic. He joined the line at the information desk. A blue-haired matron was fielding inquiries.

He cleared his throat. "Excuse me."

She gave him a look that said, *Go ahead, take another piece of my sanity.*

"I'm looking for an eleven-year-old by the name of Toby Talbot?"

She typed the name into her computer. He could see the cursor on the monitor, blinking in a column of T's that went from *Tabachnik* straight to *Taylor*. No *Talbot.*

"Sorry, we have no patient by that name."

"Could he have been released?"

"He was never admitted to pediatric."

"What about the adult wards? Maybe there was a mix-up in the records."

Fingers danced over the computer keyboard. She shook her head. "Sorry."

"Have you admitted any unidentified eleven-year-old boys since Monday morning?"

She entered more data. "We had a young burn victim, male, yesterday."

Catch had to think very hard about getting his next breath. "May I see him?"

"He was transferred the same day to the burn center at St. Vincent's, Manhattan."

"Thank you." As Catch turned, he saw a heavyset man in line behind him, wearing a jacket over a Hawaiian shirt. The man quickly looked away.

"Help you, sir?" The smiling clerk with the name tag *Mitzi* had to shout.

Cardozo showed his I.D. Mitzi lost the smile.

Philmar's Car Rental agency was crowded and bad-tempered, echoing like a fast-food joint. Jet planes passing overhead added to the din.

"A man by the name of Catch Talbot rented a car from you last Wednesday. I'd like to see that contract." Cardozo gave her the transaction number.

Mitzi consulted with coworkers, searched drawers, and finally produced a pink sheet with unreadably small print and a barely legible carbon scrawl filling in the blanks.

Cardozo noted that the blue '94 Pontiac was not due to be returned for ten days. He copied the license number, 12F73, and Catch Talbot's New Jersey address, the Holiday Inn in Kearney. "Thanks, Mitzi. I appreciate it."

"Isn't it a fact"—Dotson Elihu's tone was let's-work-this-out-together helpful—"that John and Amalia Briar were both dead when you left the apartment, and both voices that Officer Bailey heard on the phone were Mickey Williams?"

"No." Yolanda Lopez's eyes were burning moistly. "Amalia was alive—there was still a chance. Why would I phone BATF if she was dead?"

"I'm glad you asked that question. I don't quite understand . . . if you were seeking help so desperately, why did you repeatedly phone an answering machine that you knew no one was answering?"

"I phoned because those were my instructions and I hoped someone would get my message in time."

"But after phoning and never once getting through—why didn't you return to Amalia Briar's bedside and protect her yourself?"

"I tried to—but I couldn't get into the apartment. Mickey wouldn't open the door."

"So you sat vigil outside the apartment for over twenty-four hours—pounding on the door?"

"Yes!"

Dotson Elihu looked politely astonished. "Did anyone *hear* or *see* you during this time?"

"I don't know."

"Did you sleep in the hallway?"

"I can't remember."

"Did you *urinate* or *defecate* in the hallway during these twenty-four hours?"

"Objection!" Tess diAngeli cried. "Hectoring the witness!"

"Counselor," Judge Bernheim warned, "save your scatological humor for your poker club."

Elihu inclined his head just sufficiently to suggest respect. "My apologies, Your Honor, if I've offended the court's sensibilities. However, as a sage once remarked, biology is destiny, and I'm sure the jury is as curious as I to know how Ms. Lopez managed to evade it for so long a stretch of time."

Cardozo laid his shield unobtrusively on the countertop. The desk clerk of the Kearney Holiday Inn flinched.

"Did you have a Catch Talbot registered here September eighteenth?"

The clerk entered the name into her computer. A river of print flowed up the monitor screen. "We show no one by that name registered then or now."

"Could I speak with house security?"

She tapped a number into the phone. "Mr. Higgins—a police officer to speak with you."

"He calls himself Catch Talbot. He could be using other names as well."

Higgins examined the sketch and then the photograph. A scowl creased his sallow, jowly face.

"Over the weekend he might have had an eleven-year-old boy with him." Cardozo handed Higgins the snapshot of Toby Talbot.

Higgins squinted a long, considering moment. "Haven't seen the boy."

"What about the man?"

Higgins shook his head. "If a skinhead registered here, believe me, I'd have made it a point to notice. Sorry."

Dotson Elihu turned slowly toward the witness, holding an official-looking document at arm's length. His face was grave. "Ms. Lopez—out of all this alleged conspiracy to murder John and Amalia Briar, how is it you managed to record only three minutes of innocuous conversation that bear even remotely on this case? How is it you couldn't record a single instance where Dr. Lyle even once mentioned the Briars by name?"

"Corey mentioned their names all the time! He was always talking about getting them to die!"

"And why didn't you tape those conversations?"

"I did. But that tape was—" She caught herself.

Elihu's eyes came around. "That tape was what, Ms. Lopez?"

"It was lost."

"How was it lost?" Dotson Elihu's tone was soft; almost compassionate.

But Yolanda Lopez sank away from his concern into the corner of her chair. "I was carrying the tape in my purse and it was stolen."

Dotson Elihu's gaze bored into the witness. "Ms. Lopez, isn't it a fact that you made only one call to the BATF on Labor Day weekend, and that was on Sunday—and this is the call?"

He pressed a button on the audiocassette player. A sound of labored, jerky breathing pulsed from the plastic box and then a woman's voice. *"This is Yolanda—I'm at the Briars'; Johnny and Amalia have died."*

Elihu stopped the tape.

"I made that call Monday," she said, "not Sunday."

Elihu stared at her skeptically, craftily. "Now I'm going to play another call you made to your favorite answering machine. You may care to revise your recollection as to the day and time you made it."

Dotson Elihu pushed a button. Hysteria exploded. *"This is Yolanda. I'm in the Briars' apartment—Saturday morning. Send somebody up—it's an emergency. Corey's hypnotized Mickey. Mickey's gone crazy—he's killed John and he says he's going to kill Amalia. I've locked her bedroom door and I'm in here with her—but that door won't keep him out. Send help! Please! Oh, God!"*

With two loud clicks, Elihu stopped the tape.

"I made that call Saturday morning," Yolanda Lopez said. "That's the first call I made."

"And this call?" Elihu snapped another tape into the player.

"This is Yolanda—Sunday morning—Mickey's locked me out of the apartment—he's murdered John and he's in there murdering Amalia—you've got to send help!"

"That's the second call I made. That was Sunday."

"Then you couldn't have made that call from the Briars'. So where did you call from?"

"A pay phone in the street."

"So in your first call on Saturday you shriek that John has been murdered. Then a day later you call and shriek that Mickey's murdering Amalia too. And a day later you call and calmly announce that John and Amalia have died. Now, when people are murdered, the normal description is *they were murdered,* not *they've died.* What happened? Did two murders suddenly turn to natural deaths?"

"Murdered people die too!" the witness screamed. "I'm sorry if you don't like the way I speak English!"

"On the contrary, Ms. Lopez. Your English is charming." Elihu stared at the witness with saddened, this-kills-me-more-than-it-kills-you eyes. "Tell me, Ms. Lopez, when were you finally able to reach your employer on the phone?"

"Monday night."

"And on Monday night didn't he tell you to make two more phone calls to the answering machine? Didn't he tell you to phone and give false days and times?"

"That's not true."

"Didn't he tell you to be sure this time to mention murder and madness and Mickey Williams?"

"That's not true."

"And weren't those Monday night calls the two you claim you made Saturday and Sunday? And weren't they scripted for you by the BATF?"

"That's not true."

"Ms. Lopez, didn't the BATF script the testimony that you've given here today?"

"That's not true."

"Isn't it a fact that there was no conspiracy before the Briars died? Isn't your whole story about a hypnotic conspiracy between Dr. Lyle and Mickey Williams a fabrication? Didn't you and Mickey Williams and the BATF work out this entire preposterous farrago *after* the Briars died?"

"That's not true."

"Ms. Lopez—you claim you found John Briar murdered the Saturday before Labor Day. You claim you reported his death to Sergeant Britta Bailey of the Twenty-second Precinct on Saturday. You then make the incredible claim that Sergeant Bailey refused to help."

"She did refuse."

"But according to Sergeant Bailey's testimony, it was Sunday when you reported John and Amalia Briar sick and in trouble—but you made no mention of John

Briar's murder. How do you explain the contradiction between Sergeant Bailey's testimony and yours?"

"She made a mistake."

"I submit that *you* made the mistake—in fact, you're lying: John Briar was not dead when you went to the precinct."

"Everything I said is the truth! I swear to God!"

Elihu turned toward the jury. "A pity we can't recall Sergeant Bailey to the stand. It would be interesting to establish once and for all which of the prosecutor's witnesses is lying."

"Objection."

"Sustained."

The manager of the Scotsville Tru-Val Supermarket referred to the piece of scratch paper where Cardozo had jotted the MasterCard transaction number. She tapped the data into the keyboard.

Something electronic yelped.

"Sorry about that." She cleared and reentered. The computer went to work, conjuring memories. The screen flashed a question. She tapped another key. A screen full of data flashed. "Do you want a copy of the itemized receipt?"

"Please."

She pressed a key. A printer clattered. She ripped off a ribbon of curling paper.

Cardozo examined the purple markings. *Pro* was obviously produce, and *dry* dairy. His eye went to the final figure: *cash returned $0.00.* Just above, *cash tendered $0.00.* Above that, *67.19.* "How many bags would this order fill?" he asked.

"We'd bag it in four or five."

"That's a lot to carry. Was this a delivery?"

"We don't deliver after four on Sundays. This was rung up at five forty-two. The customer took the groceries herself."

"Himself." Cardozo showed her the drawing and the photo. "His name's Catch Talbot. Ever seen him?"

"Not that I recall."

"He might have had a kid with him." Cardozo showed her the snapshot.

She shook her head.

"Would you do me a favor?" Cardozo handed her a photocopy of the drawing with the caption HAVE YOU SEEN THIS MAN? and his precinct phone. "Could you put this up on your bulletin board?"

Cardozo stood in the supermarket parking lot, gazing out at the low suburban sprawl and the belt of green woods beyond. An airplane swept past overhead, jets drilling the sky.

Cars cruised, looking for spaces near the supermarket.

A second parking lot, just beyond the hedge, was empty except for two cars. A woman in short shorts was loading packages into a red Datsun. The other car, a blue '94 Pontiac, was parked at the far end of the lot. Late afternoon sun reflected from the rolled-up windows, making it seem as if someone were tossing lit matches in the backseat.

Cardozo crossed the empty lot. Sun-softened tarmac sucked at his shoes.

The Pontiac had a Jersey license, 12F73, and there was a little *Philmar's Car Rental* plate in the corner. Cardozo bent down at the driver's window.

He could see that there was only half a steering wheel. At first he thought it might be an innovative design touch, but then he saw the jagged splinters of plastic where the wheel had been shattered.

Four bulging brown paper bags had been placed on the backseat. A yellow fluid oozed from one of them.

He took a thin plastic glove from his pocket and tried the door handle. The door was unlocked. A hot stench of rancid meat and spoiled milk exploded into the air. There was something else in the sickening mix, a faint metallic note.

He climbed into the backseat and poked through the paper bags, face angled away from the fumes. The groceries—what survived of them—matched Catch Talbot's itemized receipt.

THIRTY-TWO

5:10 P.M.

Dotson Elihu turned and took three slow, full-weighted steps toward the witness box. "Ms. Lopez, would you call yourself a good mother? A natural mother?"

"I hope so."

"After what you claim Dr. Lyle did to your little girl . . . it would be natural for you to hate him. What are your feelings toward him?"

"I hate him."

"And do you want to see Dr. Lyle in prison?"

"If he did that to a child of yours, wouldn't you want him in prison too?"

"Isn't it a fact that you want to put Dr. Lyle in jail so badly, that you'd give the testimony you have today, regardless of truth or falsity?"

"My testimony is the truth."

"That's not what I'm asking. *Isn't it a fact that you have a motive to lie to this court?*"

"I'm not lying."

"That's not the question. Listen closely. *Escuchame bien.* Do you not, as the mother of Lisa Lopez, have a motive to lie to *this court*? *No tiene usted motivo para—*"

"I speak English and I have no reason to lie to this court."

"Really?" Dotson Elihu smiled. "No further questions."

Tess diAngeli beamed a smile of reassurance. "Ms. Lopez, have you lied today on the witness stand?"

"No."

Peter Connolly nodded grimly as Mark Wells slid into the booth at the back of the coffee shop. "You may have run into a guy by the name of Joey la Plata?"

"Not that I can recall," Mark said.

"The doorman in Kyra Talbot's building? He says Kyra was spooked all last week. From Tuesday on she shut herself in the apartment. Friday she went a little loopy—Joey's words—and fired her au pair girl. She paid Joey to pick up Toby and bring him back from school. She kept asking if anyone followed them."

"*Followed* them?"

Connolly nodded. "Joey said no, but Kyra was worried. So he helped get the bags into a taxi, and Kyra and the kid took off."

"Where'd they go?"

"According to the taxi sheets, they went to 118 East 81st."

Mark frowned. "Her sister's apartment."

"No one answers the intercom. The answering machine picks up but it doesn't take messages. The trail's dead."

Mark started at the word. "Dead?"

"Last Friday Kyra bought two one-way tickets for the Saturday night flight to Paris. But she never used them."

Mark stared. "My God."

"At this point, Mr. Wells, I think you need the police, not me."

In the jury room, Donna Scomoda seized Anne's arm. "Can you believe Elihu? Is he a Nazi or is he a Nazi?"

"The way he treated that poor Lopez woman!" Thelma del Rio said.

"He was certainly rude to her," Anne said. "But a trial isn't a tea party. And he made some points."

"Points?" Gloria Weston groaned. "Give me a break."

Mark Wells strode into his Central Park West lobby, high-fived the Puerto Rican doorman, and collected his mail. Riding up to his tenth-floor apartment, he reviewed the day's assortment of bills, junk mail, and magazines he'd never subscribed to.

There was only one letter in the lot. The stationery was heavy, dove-gray. The envelope had been addressed by hand; large, looping handwriting. Female. Confident. Kyra's.

He turned the envelope over and studied the flap. A return address was simply, elegantly engraved: *Apt. 11-E, 118 East 81st Street, New York, NY 10021.* He recognized Anne Bingham's address.

He let himself into the apartment, tossed the junk mail onto the hall table, and ripped the gray envelope open.

Friday. My dearest Mark, by the time you read this you will have been worrying where on earth I am.

The phone rang at eight on the dot. He was waiting. "Hello?"

"Mark, it's Anne." She spoke softly. Water was running in the background. "Have you heard anything about Toby or Kyra?"

"He didn't show up at school. But I've had a note from Kyra. Let me read it to you: *'My dearest Mark, By the time you read this, you will have been worrying where on earth I am. Toby and I will be in Paris, at the Hotel France et Choiseul till we can find an apartment—' "*

"Paris? Why on earth would she—"

"I've been concerned how much Toby misses his father. It's natural in a boy his age. But he idealizes Catch, and has no idea of the kind of man his father really is. I've shielded him from that.

" 'Toby and I have been having problems, and I honestly believe in his present state he would choose to live with his father. And Catch would turn him against me. I couldn't bear to lose Toby.

" 'Forgive me for not confiding in you sooner, but I knew what you would say. I've decided I've no alternative but to take matters into my own hands. I hope one day you'll understand and forgive—your loving Kyra.' "

A silence passed.

"I can't believe it," Anne said. "When's the note dated?"

"Friday. Postmarked Saturday A.M. It could have been mailed Friday and picked up Saturday. It's written on stationery with your address."

"That's the Tiffany stationery she gave me last Christmas. It matches hers."

"How did she get hold of yours?"

"I gave her the key to my apartment so she could water the plants. But if she's in Paris . . ."

"She's not. She didn't use her plane tickets. I phoned the France and Choiseul to double-check. She and Toby were due Sunday morning, but they haven't showed up. Anne—I'm worried."

"Do you suppose she could still be at my place?"

"I just phoned, but the answering machine is on the blink."

Anne covered the mouthpiece and called something, then whispered: "Gotta go. My roommate wants the bathroom. Talk to you tomorrow, same time."

Mark poured himself a Chivas on the rocks and phoned Lieutenant Cardozo's number.

"Cardozo."

"It's Mark Wells. We have to talk."

Cardozo laid the note down on Mark Wells's coffee table. "You're sure this is Kyra Talbot's handwriting?"

"It sure would fool me." Mark Wells leaned forward and added a generous splash of Scotch to his drink. He offered to pour a shot into Cardozo's diet Pepsi.

Cardozo shook his head. He took Kyra Talbot's other notes from his pocket. He smoothed out the Mylar and compared. The verticals in the Mademoiselle notes were more slashing, as though they had been written under pressure. The loops in the Mark Wells note were loopier, lazy little works of art. The stationery was the same in all three notes.

"Why would she use her sister's stationery? Where would she get it?"

"She has a key to her sister's apartment."

Cardozo reflected. "You wouldn't happen to have any samples of Anne Bingham's handwriting, would you?"

Wells hesitated. "It's sort of personal. . . ." He pushed himself out of the chair and wobbled to the bookcase. He returned with an *Oxford Book of English Verse.* "The flyleaf."

Cardozo opened the book.

Mark—
Love, a twilight of the heart, eludes a little time's deceit
—Anne

The most obvious difference between the writing in the notes and in the book was that Anne Bingham was left-handed.

"What's the quote from?"

"I don't know." Wells shook his head. "I searched, but it's not in the book."

Catch Talbot pushed wearily through the West 13th Street entrance of St. Vincent's Hospital. Merciless fluorescent light gave red plastic benches and Formica counters the look of a fast-food joint.

As he approached the reception desk, a gray-haired woman scowled over the counter at him.

"I'm looking for an eleven-year-old male burn victim. He was transferred yesterday from St. Andrea in Newark."

"Name?"

"Toby Talbot."

She studied the computer monitor and shook her head. "I show no Toby Talbot."

"Then he may be listed as unidentified."

"Are you sure Kyra Talbot is still sequestered?" Cardozo was standing at a pay phone on Amsterdam Avenue, a finger to one ear to block the siren of a fire truck. "Because she wrote a note to her lawyer, dated Friday, saying she was leaving for Paris Saturday. The postmark was New York 10021, Saturday A.M."

"That doesn't mean anything." Tess diAngeli sounded dead tired. "She could have had someone else mail it for her."

"Funny kind of note to write her lawyer if she didn't intend to go through with it."

"She obviously has a flair for fiction."

"Maybe a little less of a flair than you think. Have you ever heard of a phone-block defeater with I.D.-redirection capacity?"

"No."

"It bypasses call-blocking and it can defeat caller I.D. Last week a man using Catch Talbot's stolen charge card bought one from an espionage shop called the Spook Boutique."

"What does that prove?"

"Proves Kyra Talbot could have gotten a phone threat."

"Vince, she admits she invented that call."

"Her lawyer says she was telling the truth when she reported the call. He says she changed her story because she's afraid of losing her son."

"Then her lawyer's full of bull-bleep."

"The man using Talbot's charge cards bears an uncanny resemblance to the man who took Toby Talbot from the École Française. And *that* man bears an uncanny resemblance to your star witness."

"Vince, you're giving me the same old smoke and mirrors."

"It's a little more solid than that. The *real* Catch Talbot defended Mickey Williams in a Seattle lawsuit. They're friends."

A beat of silence. And then, defensive: "So?"

"So Mickey has seen Talbot's charge cards. And he knows who Talbot's ex-wife is and who his son is and where Toby goes to school."

"I haven't got time or energy for this. Good night."

There was a click and a dial tone. *Running scared,* Cardozo thought. He dropped another quarter into the slot and dialed Anne Bingham's number. Her answering machine picked up.

"Hi. You've reached the office of Ding-a-ling Music, Anne Bingham, CEO. If you'd care to leave a message at the beep, I'll get back to you as soon as possible. That's a promise. Thanks."

But instead of a single beep, there were a dozen or so.

"Miss Bingham," he began.

A click interrupted him, followed by a dial tone.

"Damn!" He realized what must have happened: Anne Bingham hadn't picked up her messages, with the result that sometime since he'd last phoned, her message tape had filled up and the machine automatically disconnected any further callers.

The doorman was leaning against the brick wall of 118 East 81st, smoking the tail end of a cigarette.

Cardozo flipped open his shield case. "I'm trying to get hold of Anne Bingham."

"Haven't seen her since last Saturday."

"Do me a favor." Cardozo took a business card and a fresh twenty from his wallet and tucked them into the doorman's breast pocket. "Contact me the minute she shows up."

Clutching his visitor's pass, Catch Talbot stepped off the elevator and looked for the nurses' station. He smelled burnt coffee and ethyl alcohol. A candy-striper shot out of the service door. Her cart broadsided him. Fruit and candies and canned juice and gifts spilled to the floor.

"Sorry." He crouched and helped her rearrange her pyramid.

"My fault." She smiled. "Paperback books on the bottom, dolls on top."

He handed her a stuffed baby dinosaur. "I'm looking for the nurses' station."

She pointed. "Right down there."

He stepped around a Latino family holding a clutch of silver balloons. A young nurse shaking down thermometers glanced over at him. Her eyes breathed a careful fog of apathy.

"Hi." He forced a smile. "I'm looking for an unidentified burn victim? Eleven-year-old boy?"

"A kid was transferred from Newark yesterday. Caucasian."

"That's the one. Could I see him? He may be my son."

The way the nurse was looking at him, he felt like wax under a blowtorch.

"They shouldn't have sent you up here," she said. "He died this morning. Never regained consciousness."

"My God. Is there any way I could—see the body?"

At that moment the elevator opened, and Catch saw the man in the Hawaiian shirt step off.

Tess diAngeli lifted the phone and tapped in the number of Mickey's guard.

"I'm sorry," a recorded voice told her. "The mobile phone number you have dialed is currently outside of the service area. Please try your call again later."

She broke the connection and dialed the number of her contact at the Justice Department.

A patrician voice growled, "Yes?"

"Foster—it's Tess."

A silence bubbled across the line.

"Tess diAngeli."

"Well, hello. How are you, my dear?"

"I'm having trouble getting hold of Rick Burnett—Mickey's guard. His mobile phone says he's outside the service area."

"That's not surprising. Mickey's under surveillance, not arrest."

"Rick's starting to worry me. He's been giving Mickey windows of opportunity."

"Tess, you're not part of the federal chain of command. I don't want you interfering."

"Mickey is my witness. The case depends on him. If he's running around unsupervised, he could compromise the whole prosecution."

"I'm quite cognizant of that possibility. And I'm on top of it, believe me. Mickey won't get into any trouble. You have my word."

THIRTY-THREE

Wednesday, September 25
Seventh day of trial
10:20 A.M.

"Do you know of any cases," Tess diAngeli asked, "where one person has exercised posthypnotic control over another for days or even weeks?"

The witness—a dark-haired man of forty-five or so—gave a sad-faced nod. "The psychiatric literature of the last quarter century is full of such instances—the Manson cult, the Koresh cult, the Jones cult, the Islamic fundamentalist terrorists operational in Europe and the United States."

"Have you yourself ever dealt with any such instances?"

"Your Honor," Dotson Elihu interrupted, pushing to his feet. "I object to the presence of Ms. Yolanda Lopez in this courtroom." He gestured toward the rows of spectators. Yolanda Lopez, unobtrusive in a high-neck pale blue dress, was sitting quietly on the aisle in the third row. "Her very visible presence is a clear attempt to influence the jury."

"Mrs. Lopez has completed her testimony," Judge Bernheim said. "Unless you intend to call her as a witness, there's no reason she can't view these proceedings."

Tess diAngeli, frozen in mid-gesture like a stop-frame TV image, broke into smiling, flowing movement. "Dr. Martins, would a person given a posthypnotic suggestion recall executing that suggestion?"

"The subject would be aware of his or her acts—and would recall them—but it would be as if he or she were watching someone else perform them. He or she would wonder: Why am I doing this? Why can't I make myself stop?"

"Did you ever have occasion to examine a young girl by the name of Lisa Lopez?"

"Yes, I did."

"And did Lisa Lopez exhibit signs of posthypnotic suggestion?"

"Yes, indeed. She'd been hypnotized by Corey Lyle. I was able to pull up the hypnotic commands."

"And what were these commands?"

"Commands to perform terrorist acts."

"Objection!" Dotson Elihu leaped up. "The charge is conspiracy to murder, not terrorism!"

"Overruled."

Tess diAngeli circled back to the witness box. "Dr. Martins, did you ever have occasion to examine Mickey Williams?"

"Yes, I did."

"Would you tell the court your findings?"

"As a child, Mickey Williams was repeatedly abused by his father. Almost three decades later, Mickey still bears the physical trauma of Williams senior's sadistic mistreatment."

"Objection." Dotson Elihu shoved himself wearily to his feet. "Since Mickey Williams is apparently beyond prosecution for the murders he admits committing, how on earth does his deprived childhood relate to the case before us?"

"Your Honor." Tess diAngeli's voice glowed with indignation. "It is precisely *because* of his childhood conditioning—a conditioning well understood by Corey Lyle—that Mr. Williams was so easily manipulated by the defendant."

"Overruled."

DiAngeli turned again to her witness. "Does Mickey Williams still feel anger over his abuse by his father?"

The doctor nodded somberly. "Mickey has enormous rage locked within himself."

"Does this rage ever break through into his awareness?"

"Not into his awareness per se, but into his actions—and like water breaking a dam, it is uncontrollable: it seeks to obliterate the object."

"Can Mickey and his rage be manipulated by others?"

"Very easily. Mickey is highly vulnerable to suggestion, to manipulation, and certainly to hypnosis."

"Could he carry out posthypnotic suggestions that were morally repugnant to him? Such as a suggestion to murder an elderly couple?"

"Objection! Hypothetical!"

"An expert may answer a hypothetical question. Overruled."

"He would have no difficulty," the witness said, "carrying out such a suggestion."

DiAngeli moved toward the witness box. "When you examined Mickey Williams, did he exhibit signs of post-hypnotic suggestion?"

"Yes, indeed. He'd been hypnotized by Corey Lyle. I was able to pull up the hypnotic commands."

"And what were these commands?"

"The commands were to murder John Briar and his wife Amalia."

"Objection!" Dotson Elihu shouted. "There is no evidence for such an irresponsible assertion other than the uncorroborated conjecture of this witness!"

"Overruled."

Greg Monteleone stepped into the cubicle. "Got that information you wanted. The Bingham and Talbot charge cards." Today he was wearing fire-engine red suspenders that clashed with his heliotrope shirt. He laid four faxes on Cardozo's desk.

"Thanks." Cardozo glanced up. "How's it coming with Catch Talbot?"

"He's keeping busy—checking out hospitals. Hitting a few bars."

Cardozo held up a two-inch stack of blue telephone message chits. "And calling here every minute."

"You should phone him, Vince—give him an update."

"There is no update."

"He'd still like to hear from you . . . he's edgy, depressed. And he may be getting a little paranoid, wondering why I'm on his tail."

"He saw you?"

"I was getting off an elevator in Saint Vincent's burn unit—he was getting on." Greg shrugged. "Bad luck and freak timing."

"Can't be helped now." Cardozo studied the charge reports. Anne Bingham's showed no activity since Monday, September 16. But Kyra Talbot's showed that she spent eighty-five dollars last Saturday at an establishment called Flip Your Wig.

No expenditures since.

"What do you know about this place Flip Your Wig?"

"Sounds like a New Age shrink or a hairdresser."

"Or possibly a wig shop in the hotel where she's sequestered." Cardozo reached for the phone directory.

Dotson Elihu crossed to the witness box with a sort of dawdling, senior-citizen swagger. He smiled at the witness. "Dr. Martins—you've had professional training in the field of hypnosis, have you not?"

"Yes, I've trained extensively."

"Extensively." Elihu seemed to measure the weight of the word. "You claim that Corey Lyle performed *prodigies* of hypnotic suggestion—twisted human wills like rubber bands—yet isn't it a fact that he was never professionally trained in hypnosis?"

"Manson wasn't trained, Koresh wasn't, Jones wasn't, the ayatollahs aren't—their hypnotic gift is a combination of intuitive skill and on-the-job training."

Dotson Elihu leaned into the witness box, zestfully belligerent now. *"Isn't it a fact that Corey Lyle was never trained as a hypnotist?"*

Dr. Martins's face flushed. "I don't know."

Dotson Elihu drew back, satisfied. He took a three-step stroll. "Dr. Martins—you say you've had personal experiences inducing posthypnotic suggestion—have you published these experiences in any professional journal, such as the *New England Journal of Hypnotherapy*?"

"I have not. There are considerations of confidentiality, security of ongoing operations."

"Yet you're not afraid of compromising security by testifying here—or is today's testimony an instance of an ongoing operation?"

"Objection!"

"Sustained."

"Dr. Martins . . . would you describe to the court how you recovered Corey Lyle's alleged hypnotic commands to Mickey Williams and Lisa Lopez?"

"By hypnotizing them."

"You had Mickey Williams and Lisa Lopez under hypnosis, and you told them to recall commands implanted by another person, and they did so?"

"Yes, indeed. Precisely."

Elihu drew in a deep breath. "While you had Mickey Williams hypnotized . . . if you told him his recollection would be that he murdered John and Amalia Briar under instructions from Dr. Lyle—would this be his recollection?"

"Objection," Tess diAngeli cried. "Hypothetical!"

"The witness is an expert!" Elihu shouted. "Experts may answer hypotheticals!"

"Mr. Elihu," Judge Bernheim said, "are you shouting at your learned colleague or at me?"

"I would never shout at Your Honor."

"You're out of order if you shout at anyone."

"I apologize, Your Honor."

"Overruled. Witness may answer."

Out in Foley Square, a police siren screamed past, dappling the stillness.

"My answer to that question," Martins said, "is that

it's within the parameters of conceivability—but barely."

A bell tinkled as Cardozo stepped through the doorway of Flip Your Wig, a small hairdressing salon on West 4th Street. A sweet, nutty smell of heated shampoo floated in the air. Scraps of conversation mixed with the sound of a Barbra Streisand record and the humming of hair dryers. Four white-smocked women sat in barber chairs, gazing into the mirror, while men in blue jeans fussed with their hair.

"Help you, sir?" A white-haired, slightly disheveled polar bear of a man approached. Brown solution was dripping off the fingers of his surgical gloves.

Cardozo showed his shield and introduced himself. "I need a little information on one of your customers. Kyra Talbot."

"Well, well, well. I'm Woody. Kyra's stylist." He snapped the gloves off, balled them, and lobbed them into a wastebasket. "I can always make a moment for the NYPD."

"Mrs. Talbot's records show she made a charge here Saturday."

"Oh yes, indeed."

"You did her hair?"

"Me and a few helping hands. It was an emergency."

"What kind of emergency?"

"The worst. She ran in without an appointment. Wanted a trim, rinse, and set. Said she had to look sensational. She wasn't spelling anything out, but she asked for the name of a hairstylist in Paris. And she wasn't talking about Paris, Texas."

THIRTY-FOUR

1:40 P.M.

"Before Britta and I testified," Cardozo said, "you covered up some lines in her notebook and mine." He laid the two notebooks down on the desk. "I'd be curious to know why."

They were sitting in room 509, Tess's broom-closet-size workspace, lunching on delicatessen takeout. She moved a file, making room, and opened the notebooks. She looked at the page where Britta had pulled up the tape and half the writing. She looked at the page where Cardozo had dissolved the tape and the ballpoint was still legible.

"Come on, Vince. We're living in the real world. No prosecutor's going to shine a spotlight on evidence that doesn't help her case. And there happens to be honest disagreement as to exactly how Amalia Briar died."

"Who disagreed?"

"There were two autopsies. We went with the autopsy we liked. It was a judgment call."

He gave her a long, appraising look. "If you knew the evidence was cooked, why didn't you just turn the case down?"

She slapped the notebooks shut. "Listen, my friend—this is not a decade for idealism. Since my building went co-op, my salary barely covers living costs. I still owe on a ten-year-old student loan and they just hiked the interest. Turning down assignments is a sure way of not getting a promotion, and if I don't get promoted this year I'll be looking for a new job."

"Okay, I get the picture."

"No, you don't. I put in five years' indentured servitude prosecuting cases for United States Tax Court—not knowing how I was going to meet the mortgage or the deductible on my health insurance. At long last I've got a chance to cop a little economic peace of mind—and I'm not throwing it away."

"Okay, okay. Sorry I asked."

She sat motionless and silent, gazing down at her fingernails. "I didn't mean to shout." She swiveled a full circle in her chair. When she came around again she was smiling. *See? I can be a Barbie doll.* "Vince, I told you we were making a deal with a demon so we could catch the devil. I was level with you from the get-go. What the hell more do you want from me?"

"I want that demon's address."

She slammed down a plastic cup beside her half-finished pastrami on rye. Diet Sprite splashed a stack of depositions. "We've been through this before. No way."

"I'm ready to barter."

"You haven't got a thing I want. And I've got to get back to court."

"How about the name of a witness who saw Kyra Talbot break sequestration last Saturday?"

Her eyes came up slowly. "I hope to God you're kidding."

He shook his head. "Woody Chandler. He does hair at Flip Your Wig at Charles and West Fourth. He'll be there till eight P.M. tonight."

She scrawled on a legal pad. "Are you going to tell anyone else?"

"Not if we have a deal."

She pushed out a sigh. "Mickey's using the name Matthew Warner. The government's rented him a garden apartment at 72 West Twelfth Street."

"Mr. Langdell," Tess diAngeli said, "would you tell the court your profession?"

"I am a polygraphologist." The witness was a tall man with red hair and a torso like a door. "I give polygraph tests."

"Your Honor." Dotson Elihu was up on his feet. "I object to the certifying of this witness as an expert. The scientific value and reliability of the polygraph has yet to be established."

Judge Bernheim gave him a hard, impatient look. "The court is satisfied that this witness is an expert. People will proceed."

Tess diAngeli asked the witness to summarize his qualifications. Langdell stated that his services were much used by NYPD detectives and New York County prosecutors. He had formerly served as a New York state trooper and a United States marine.

"On January seventh of last year," Tess diAngeli asked, "did you administer a polygraph test to Mickey Williams?"

"Objection." Elihu sprang to his feet. "Polygraph results are not admissible in this court."

"Polygraph results aren't admissible as evidence of a *defendant's* innocence or guilt," diAngeli shot back, "but need I remind my colleague that Mr. Williams is not the defendant?"

"And need I remind my colleague that he sure as hell ought to be!"

"Mr. Elihu, you are one millimeter away from contempt." Judge Bernheim's eyelids quivered at half-mast. "One more remark like that and you'll spend the night in the Cellblock Inn. Your objection is overruled. Jury will disregard Mr. Elihu's outburst."

Tess diAngeli shot the witness a glance of hardship borne together. "Mr. Langdell, on January seventh of last year, did you administer a polygraph test to Mickey Williams?"

"I did."

"Did you ask Mr. Williams if Corey Lyle had hypnotized him to kill John and Amalia Briar?"

"I did."

"How did Mr. Williams answer?"

"He answered affirmatively."

"How did the polygraph evaluate his reply?"

"The polygraph registered that Mr. Williams was telling the truth."

"Mr. Langdell"—Dotson Elihu strode forward with his head lowered like a bull's—"when a lawyer gathers polygraph evidence for courtroom purposes, isn't it the usual practice to go to a variety of polygraph experts, and keep the results that favor your client, and bribe the other experts to shut up?"

"Objection."

"Your Honor." Elihu wheeled to face the bench. "The witness is a qualified expert and the defense is allowed to cross-examine on the usual practices of his profession."

Judge Bernheim nodded curtly. "I'll have to overrule."

"To my knowledge," the witness said quietly, pleasantly, "that is not the usual procedure."

"Were you the first polygraph expert Mickey consulted?"

"I have no idea."

"Was Mickey Williams accompanied by a lawyer from the BATF when he consulted you?"

"Objection."

"Sustained."

"Isn't it true that you can defeat a polygraph by pressing your toes tightly together and puckering up your anal sphincter?"

"No." For the first time, the witness's voice betrayed something like impatience. "That's a frequently heard old wives' tale—and it's absolutely false."

"Did you run a polygraph test on the defendant?"

"Objection!"

"Sustained."

Dotson Elihu faced the prosecutor, smiling. "No further questions."

"Your Honor," Tess diAngeli said, "since the People's next witness will be a nine-year-old child, we ask that the courtroom be cleared of spectators and media."

"Objection!" Dotson Elihu roared. "The defendant is entitled to a public trial."

Judge Bernheim overruled. "The courtroom will be cleared." It took almost five minutes for the guards to empty the courtroom of spectators and press. Only one figure was permitted to remain in the spectator benches: Yolanda Lopez, solitary and vigilant in the third row.

"The People call Lisa Lopez."

Elihu leapt up. "Your Honor, I've reviewed this witness's statements, and they have nothing whatever to do with conspiracy to murder John and Amalia Briar. Her testimony can only be irrelevant and prejudicial. I object to her taking the stand."

Tess diAngeli faced the bench. "Your Honor, the People will demonstrate relevance. The witness's testimony goes directly to the character and behavior of the accused."

"The witness may testify," Judge Bernheim said. "Call Lisa Lopez."

A door opened and a uniformed matron walked a little girl across the court to the witness stand. The girl wore a spotless white frock that seemed to shimmer against the deep tan of her skin. She appeared younger than nine. She had long dark hair gathered in braids, and large, melancholy brown eyes. She climbed up into the stand and took the oath.

Tess diAngeli gazed at the child with the smile that is every child's dream: the smile of the loving mother, of the fond older sister, of the teacher encouraging a favorite pupil. "How are you today, Lisa?"

"Okay, thank you." The little girl sat there soft but tense, like spun glass, trying to look confident.

"Lisa, would you tell us when you first met Corey Lyle?"

"I met Uncle Corey three years ago."

"Was that when your mother brought you into Uncle Corey's group?"

The girl nodded.

"Lisa, you have to answer 'yes' or 'no.' "

"Yes."

"Lisa, did Uncle Corey separate you from your mother?"

"Yes." She nodded. "He made me live in the country."

"Were you ever alone with Uncle Corey?"

"Lots of times."

"What did Uncle Corey do when he was alone with you?"

"He told me stories."

"Stories about what?"

"Heaven. And hell."

"What did he tell you about hell?"

"It's an awful place. They burn children."

"What did he say about heaven?"

"There's ice cream. And angels. And no one gets burned."

"Did Uncle Corey say you were going to heaven or hell?"

"He said I'd go to hell unless I helped him."

"What did he want you to do for him?"

"He said I had to go to the Internal—" The girl broke off and bit her lip.

"Take your time, Lisa. You had to go where?"

"The Internal Revenue Office. He said I had to tell them a story."

"What kind of a story?"

"It wasn't a true story."

"And did you go to Internal Revenue and tell the story?"

"No."

"Did Uncle Corey punish you for not obeying him?"

"He locked my doll in the basement."

"Did he do anything else?"

"He showed me a cat. . . ." The child cast her eyes down. "He said . . . if I didn't do what he wanted . . . he was going to kill the cat."

"And did you do what he wanted?"

"No."

"And did he kill the cat?"

The child gazed steadily at the floor.

"Did you see Uncle Corey kill the cat?"

The child's eyes lifted. All expression had bled from them. "Yes."

The prosecutor gave the child a moment. "And after Uncle Corey killed the cat, did you do what he wanted?"

"He said if I didn't he'd kill my mommy."

"And after he threatened to kill your mother, did you go to the Internal Revenue Office?"

"Yes."

"Did Uncle Corey make you wear special clothes?"

"He made me wear a belt under my blouse."

"What kind of belt?"

"It was a heavy white belt. He said Internal Revenue was evil and the belt would protect me."

"What happened when you went to Internal Revenue?"

The child stared at Tess diAngeli with a drowning gaze.

"Take your time, Lisa."

"The belt leaked, and it burned me."

"And did you require eighteen skin grafts as a result?"

"Your Honor . . ." Dotson Elihu pushed to his feet. "Out of deference to the witness's obvious confusion and vulnerability, I've made no objections so far."

Judge Bernheim's expression made it plain that the court was in no mood for Dotson Elihu's charity. "Mr. Elihu, if you have an objection, state it."

"So far this witness's testimony has been hearsay and responses to shamelessly leading questions. I ask that it be stricken from the record."

"Request denied."

"Your Honor, if it were not a child in the witness box, none of this testimony would be allowed."

"But it *is* a child in the witness box, Mr. Elihu. Sit."

West 12th was a quiet, tree-lined street of old brownstones, and 72 was a pink stucco building that looked as though it had originally been a two-family town house. Now it was converted into flats. Luxury flats, according to a broker's sign at the entrance. The fountain in the courtyard had trickling water and a prancing Pan—and the mailboxes showed a Liebling/Warner in apartment 1B.

Cardozo pushed the buzzer and got no answer.

"No one's in that apartment." A lanky young man steered a wheeled cello case into the courtyard. "Gwen's subletting it."

Cardozo took out his shield. "I need to talk to her tenant."

"I've only seen him around here once." The young man opened the mailbox for 2B and pulled out a handful of bills.

Cardozo showed the sketch. "Was this the man?"

"Looks kinda like him." The young man shrugged. "Big guy, right?"

"Is there a super who might have a key?"

"I have a key. For emergency." The young man ripped up an unopened envelope and dropped it into a wastebasket. "What did he do?"

"He may have information in an ongoing investigation. Could you let me into the apartment?"

"There's no one there."

"So what difference could it make?"

The cellist hesitated. "I'm having a problem with the police. Parking ticket. Think you could help me?"

"Sure."

The cellist led Cardozo down a corridor and unlocked the door. A faint musty smell flowed out. The blinds of the French windows had been angled against the garden sun. The small living room had been furnished in painted wicker furniture and framed botany prints. An answering machine sat on the telephone table, and Cardozo could see there had been no messages.

"Why don't you go get the ticket?" Cardozo suggested.

"I'll be right back." There was a sound of a cello thunking up the stairs and then the thumping of feet overhead.

Cardozo examined an efficiency kitchen tucked into an alcove. The refrigerator and dishwasher were empty. He opened the bedroom closet. Empty. The chest of drawers. Empty. He lifted a corner of the bedspread. No sheets.

The telephone gave half a ring, cut short by the click of the answering machine. He stepped into the living room and boosted the volume on the machine.

Instead of an outgoing message, he heard the clicks

and beeps of automatic call-forwarding. There were three rings on another line and then another machine picked up. "Hi there," a woman's voice said. "I welcome your call. No one is home at present—please leave your name, your number, the date and time of your call, and I will get back to you as soon as possible."

There was a beep, a click, a dial tone, and a disconnect.

Tommy Thomas could help, Cardozo realized. *Just by listening to those beeps, Tommy could tell where Mickey's forwarding his calls.*

He lifted the receiver and tapped in Tommy's work number. A strange voice answered. "Tom Thomas's line."

"Could I speak with Mr. Thomas, please?"

"I'm sorry, but Mr. Thomas is on a scuba-diving vacation this week in Saint Kitt's."

THIRTY-FIVE

4:35 P.M.

Elihu approached the witness box. He had the earnest-lawyer-who's-also-a-concerned-father look down pat. He waited till Lisa Lopez's dark eyes peeped up at him. "What a pretty dress, Lisa."

"Thank you."

"I want you to try to remember something, Lisa." His voice was kind; a Goldilocks-and-the-Three-Bears voice for reading a child to sleep. "Did you ever see Uncle Corey kill any animals besides the cat?"

"Horses," she answered.

"Objection!" DiAngeli cried. "Confusing the witness!"

"The witness doesn't seem confused to me," Elihu said. "She volunteered the word *horses* quite clearly."

Bernheim pondered. "I'm going to overrule that objection."

"Now, tell me, Lisa. Did Uncle Corey ever call spirits?"

"Objection!"

"Your Honor." Elihu pivoted toward the bench. "I have a right to a little leeway in order to show the jury just how far this wee lass's imagination can take her."

"The objection is sustained," Judge Bernheim said. "Lisa, I want you to ignore that question. And Counselor, can't we just *once* show a little consideration? We're dealing with a child who has barely survived a terrifying ordeal."

Elihu crouched down by the witness box. "Now, Lisa, I want you to close your eyes and think back very hard. Did Uncle Corey ever fly or grow horns?"

"Objection."

"Sustained. Lisa, I don't want you to answer that question."

"But Your Honor," Lisa said, "Uncle Corey *did* fly."

"Lisa." Judge Bernheim's face was stern. "Don't answer the question after I've told you not to. Jury will disregard the witness's answer and it will be stricken."

Dotson Elihu smiled. "Thank you, Lisa. No further questions."

Tess diAngeli moved forward swiftly. "Lisa—you're sure you saw Uncle Corey fly?" Her manner had the threatening suggestion of a fourth-grade teacher. "You saw him fly with your own eyes?"

Lisa bit her lower lip. "He told me he could fly."

"But did you *see* him fly?"

Lisa Lopez shifted uncomfortably in the chair. Her eyes flicked downward. "Well . . . not exactly."

"And did you really see Uncle Corey kill a horse? With your own eyes?"

Lisa shook her head. "No. But I know he did because he made me drink a pot of horse's blood."

"And what did the blood taste like?"

"I pretended it tasted yucky." Lisa grinned. "But it tasted like V-8 juice."

"Thank you, Lisa. No further questions."

As Tess pushed through the door of Flip Your Wig, an eager young woman sprang up from her chair. "May I help you, ma'am?"

Tess scowled at the minuscule scrawl on the scrap of yellow paper. "I'd like to speak with Moody, please?"

"You mean Woody." A tic of annoyance twitched at the girl's mouth. "Woody!"

A large man with platinum-white hair looked up from a brunette head slathered in solution and paper curlers. "Sorry. Can't take any more."

Tess put on her best captivate-the-jury smile and threaded her way through barber chairs and heat lamps and dryers. "It's not about my hair."

Woody shot her head a look. "Really."

"My name's Tess diAngeli. I'm with the Justice Department." She sensed ears turning their way, voices under hair dryers suddenly falling silent. "Could I just have a word with you?"

Woody stepped to the sink and rinsed his gloves.

Tess waited for him to towel his forearms dry. "It's about one of your clients." She lowered her voice. "Kyra Talbot."

He looked puzzled and a little alarmed. "You're the second inquiry. What kind of trouble is she in?"

"Possibly no trouble at all. But did you do her hair last Saturday?"

"I want to know when Kyra Talbot is in her room and when she's not." Tess diAngeli's voice, explanatory and commonsensical, spread out like a soft light under the dropped ceiling of room 1819. "When she is, I want to know if she's alone or with her roommate. If someone else is with her, I want to know who that person is. We have no video on 1818, but this afternoon we installed mikes in the bedroom and bathroom, so you're going to have to listen for her door. When you hear someone coming out, open the door to the corridor a crack—repeat, a crack—and look. She doesn't pass this room to get to the elevator, so chances are she won't be looking in this direction. But play it safe; don't be obvious."

In one of the armchairs Brad Chambers sat, face fixed in an attentive frown. In the other chair, a young woman with eyeglasses and brown hair was taking notes.

"When she's not in her room, I want to know where she goes and who she meets. Even if it's just downstairs to get a pack of cigarettes. It had better not be anywhere else, but she's slipped through security before and it could happen again. It's not your job to prevent her slipping away, it's your job to know where she goes."

Brad Chambers nodded.

"Kyra Talbot is going to be less attentive to a woman following her," Tess said, "so Angie . . ."

The young woman looked up.

"You do the following. If you believe she's noticed you or is getting suspicious, then Brad will take over. But, Brad, if you're following, wear your contacts. She's seen your glasses in court."

Anne moved aside a bedroom curtain and squinted out into the darkness. Night had swallowed up the details of the skyline, but the silhouette was still there, etched in light reflected from low clouds.

She took the cellular phone into the bathroom, opened the faucets, and dialed Mark. "Hi—it's me. Any news?"

"Nothing yet."

"Oh, Christ."

"Don't worry . . . we're going to find them—alive and safe."

His tone of voice was such an obvious lie that she wanted to hurl the phone against the wall.

"Mark, do me a favor. *Don't* cheer me up. It reminds me of my father."

"Well," he said. "How's the trial?"

"Today a little girl testified. She said Corey forced her to wear a belt loaded with plastic explosives. And made her go to Internal Revenue to blow the office up."

"It was on the news," Mark said. "The belt malfunctioned and she wound up with burns over a quarter of her body."

His matter-of-factness brought home to Anne how quickly real-life horror lost its sting. The media turned it into a TV movie. All that was missing was the table for your stockinged feet and the box of munchies from the local deli.

"I'm surprised that testimony was allowed. Corey isn't charged with causing the child's injuries. What's more, a grand jury heard Lisa Lopez's evidence and refused to indict him."

"Are you arguing *for* him?" Anne said.

"Just playing devil's advocate."

"This isn't play, Mark. Toby's missing and Corey has harmed children."

"Possibly."

"And a psychiatrist said Corey hypnotized Mickey Williams to commit the murders."

"And do you believe that?"

"I don't know. But the government's making a good case that Corey Lyle's a monster. And if we don't find Toby, I'm going to have to argue for Lyle's release."

"*We're going to find Toby.* So stop worrying."

The cellular phone, balanced on the edge of the sink, gave a soft ring. Catch Talbot climbed out of the tub, wrapped himself in a towel, and lifted the receiver. "Hello?"

"Catch?" He recognized the voice of Peggy Cedilla, his secretary at Gurney and Gurney in Seattle. She still had that head cold and she sounded agitated.

"Peggy—what's the matter?"

"You had a call from your broker. The Canadian mine shares you bought on margin—they're still going down. He had to sell."

Catch had a sense that just when the bottom of his life had dropped out, just when he'd hit rock bottom, rock bottom was dropping out too. "So much for hot insider tips on gold stocks. Where does that leave me?"

"A quarter million in the hole. Or a half, if you count Jake de Clairville. He's been phoning. He says he never authorized you to put any part of the estate into mine shares."

"Never authorized? That's nuts. Only five weeks ago we had a long phone talk about it. He was crazy about the idea."

"I can't find any paper on it. Jake wants you to make good the loss. Or he's going to sue."

A kind of slow astonishment pulled at Catch. Pacing with the phone from strange bathroom to strange bedroom, still drowsy from his half-hour soak, he felt he'd floated into a nightmare. "If I had any sense, I'd probably put a bullet through my brain."

"You're not serious."

"No. I don't have a gun." He sat on the edge of the strange bed. Beyond gray-curtained windows, skyscrapers glowed against the night. "Did I remember to stop my MasterCard?"

"I stopped it Monday, remember?"

"I'm losing my short-term memory."

"You're under a lot of stress."

"I wonder if I'm going crazy."

"You're the sanest man I know. Tell me what's happening in New York."

"The police suggested I check hospitals to see if Toby turned up. So I've been checking."

"And?"

"I think the police followed me."

"What makes you think that?"

"I kept seeing the same man. I think he was in the precinct."

"You could be imagining. You're under a lot of stress."

"Possibly." He always said *possibly* when he didn't feel up to a discussion with Peggy.

"What did you find in the hospitals?"

"Nothing."

"Catch, far be it from me to speak out of turn, but . . ."

"But what?"

"Maybe I shouldn't say this."

"Say it."

"Have you considered the possibility that maybe your ex is behind this?"

"Kyra's been on a sequestered jury since last Wednesday. Toby vanished Saturday. And it was a man who picked him up."

"Then she's got a male accomplice. I don't trust that woman. Just speaking to her on the phone, she's devious."

"I don't know," Catch sighed. "I'll give it some thought."

"I wish I were there right now to rub your back."

"Mmm. Me too."

"Get some sleep. Things will look better tomorrow. I love you."

"Me too. G'night."

Cardozo set his coffee down on the desk and tapped Tess diAngeli's number into the phone.

"DiAngeli." She sounded rushed and irritable.

"Tess—Vince. I stopped by Mickey's apartment on West Twelfth. Thought you'd be interested—he hasn't lived there for over a month. He's rigged up an answering machine that forwards his calls somewhere else."

He could hear shock in her silence.

And then, in her most unflappable courtroom voice, "Dumb of him to play games with the feds. But I can't think of any New York law he'd be breaking."

"I can think of a few possibilities. Like kidnapping and murder. By the way, when does he testify?"

There was an instant's hesitation. "What are you planning to do?"

"Relax. I just want to catch his act."

"He testifies tomorrow morning. But, Vince—don't try anything tricky."

"Tricky?"

"Like arresting him. Because you'll be going up

against the federal government. You'll lose your job, your pension, and maybe a few other things too."

Today Mickey's guard answered. "Security."

"Rick? It's Tess. You were out of the mobile-phone service area yesterday."

"Mickey went to Jersey. Withersoever Mickey goeth—"

"I want to see the surveillance log."

"Sorry."

"What do you mean, 'sorry'?"

"The contents are federal property. The feds say I can't even discuss them with you."

"For God's sake." She broke the connection and tapped in another number. "Foster—it's Tess."

"Yes, my dear?"

"Since when am I not allowed to see the surveillance log on my own witness?"

"It's inconvenient, I know, but that's the way we do things at Justice. Stop worrying. I gave you my word of honor."

She sensed something badly askew. "Words of honor are no use to me. Not even yours. Unless you're willing to take the stand."

His voice was suddenly as flat as a knife blade. "What do you need?"

"I need to know what's in that log."

"You'll have it tomorrow."

THIRTY-SIX

Thursday, September 26
Eighth day of trial
First day of deliberation
9:35 A.M.

Cardozo flashed his shield and the armed guard waved him through the metal detector into the courtroom. Most of the benches were already crammed with chattering spectators. He saw an empty place and made a beeline to grab it.

Just as he sat, there was a flurry of movement at the front of the court. The jury filed into the jury box.

Cardozo knew Kyra Talbot was number 10 and he knew number 10 would be sitting in the second row toward the right. Still, when his eye found her, he felt a jolt.

I know her.

He remembered a conversation in the elevator and a woman who had been friendly and funny and a little bit crazy. And who got attacked by a Coreyite picketer the next day. And who didn't remember him when he came to her aid.

Today, with her eyes cast downward, there was nothing friendly or funny about her. Fidgeting and biting her lips, she seemed antsy and preoccupied.

The bailiff strode forward. "All rise. The Supreme Court of the Southern District of New York, Judge Gina Bernheim presiding, is in session."

"I've completed my review of Yolanda Lopez's interviews by the police and by the assistant district attorney." Judge Bernheim's granite-solemn gaze swept the courtroom. "I've also reviewed Ms. diAngeli's notes and audiotapes. I find no mention in any of that material that a man identifying himself as John Briar answered the phone when Sergeant Bailey called the apartment."

At the defense table, Dotson Elihu seized a pen and made a stabbing notation on a legal pad.

"I'm satisfied that the first time Ms. Lopez communicated this information to the prosecution was last Tuesday, in this court. I'm therefore ruling that the prosecutor complied fully with the law. The People may call their next witness."

"The People," Tess diAngeli said, "call Mickey Williams."

Dotson Elihu shot to his feet. "Your Honor, we notified the People of our intention to call this witness. But Mickey Williams is in the federal witness relocation program, and he has been unavailable to us."

Judge Bernheim's eyes flicked to Tess diAngeli.

"Your Honor, that's false. We offered to let Mr. Elihu deal with Mickey Williams on exactly the same basis as the People dealt with him—by secure fax forwarding through an automatic shunt."

"Your Honor," Elihu protested, "we attempted to do just that, and all we could get was an officious bureaucrat who claimed Mr. Williams is residing in some kind of nerve clinic and is in much too precarious a condition to be disturbed."

"Objection to the prejudicial nature of that remark!" diAngeli shouted.

"At no time," Elihu shouted, "did the People indicate their intention of preemptively calling this witness. If Mickey Williams is allowed to take the stand this morning, I will move that Your Honor declare an immediate mistrial!"

"And your motion will be denied. The People are entitled to present their case. People's witness may testify."

The door flew open. Something large and male stood there in shadow. A heavyset man came hesitantly into the courtroom. With his hair shaved to the scalp, his loose seersucker trousers and rumpled black jacket, he bore little resemblance to the gridiron star that Cardozo remembered. The Mickey Williams of the all-American and Pro Bowl days had been honed and lithe, every ounce of him geared to speed. This man looked as though he exercised by opening beer cans.

A wave of murmuring shock washed through the courtroom. The man next to Cardozo whispered, "What *happened*?" and Cardozo whispered, "Hot fudge sundaes and booze."

The painful thing was, Mickey seemed to know he

was an object of shock: Cardozo could see it in his blinking brown eyes.

Mickey took the oath and sat in the witness chair. Tess diAngeli led him gently through the preliminary questions. She had the manner of a deeply concerned social worker guiding a frightened child. "Have you ever been convicted of or charged with a felony?"

"Lord, what felony haven't I been convicted of! Well, the very first one was assault with a deadly weapon. Bread knife."

DiAngeli's lips thinned. Cardozo could see that something about the witness's answer bothered her. "Who did you assault?"

"My father." Mickey's voice broke like a teenager's. Embarrassment pulsed red in his face.

"Would you tell the ladies and gentlemen of the jury why you assaulted your father?"

"He shot my mother pretty bad, and he was about to do the same for me and Rilda-Mae—my little sister."

As Mickey sat back and turned his head, something glistened in his left ear. Cardozo leaned forward in his seat and squinted. Mickey was wearing a small gold earring.

"How old were you at the time?"

"Ten."

A clammy certainty slithered through Cardozo's mind. *It's him.*

"Were you sentenced to serve time?"

"They put me in a trade school in Texarkana. It was really a kind of reformatory. I learned welding."

The hair, the eyes, the earring. They fit Mademoiselle's description of the man who took Toby.

"How long were you in this institution?"

"Three years—till a minister and his wife adopted

me. They were Pentacostalists. We didn't see eye-to-eye. I ran away—joined a rodeo. I was always big for my age."

Cardozo's eye went to the jury box. Kyra Talbot was staring at the witness with an expression of shock.

Does she know him? he wondered. *Why's she looking at him like that?*

"And did your troubles with the law continue?"

Mickey grinned uneasily. "Regular as clockwork. I was drunk from the time I turned thirteen till I was fifteen. Sobered up in prison. Got released. Stayed drunk till I was seventeen. Sobered up in prison again."

Dotson Elihu rose from the defense table. "Your Honor, I object to the presence of Ms. Lisa Lopez in this room." He nodded toward the third row in the spectator section, where the little Hispanic girl, starched and immaculate in a fresh white dress, sat in the aisle seat beside her mother.

"Do you intend to call Lisa Lopez as a witness?" the judge asked.

"I do not, Your Honor. But her presence is clearly part of an orchestrated attempt by the People to—"

"Overruled."

Tess diAngeli gazed at her witness for a long, evaluating moment. "And after your second stay in state prison?"

Mickey pulled at his earring. "I got out and assaulted a security guard at a Wendy's restaurant. They caught that one on the security video; it made national TV."

DiAngeli stood with her arms folded. Annoyance flicked across her face. She hammered the witness with a tight-jawed stare. As if she were trying to signal him.

"A recruiter for Texas A and M saw me and paid my bail, got me off, offered me a football scholarship.

Should have been the happy ending, but I was too deep into drinking and drugging and self-will run riot."

Cardozo flashed what the trouble was: the testimony was not following diAngeli's script. She had lost control of her witness. Stage fright had got him, and he was babbling.

"After I graduated, I married a lovely young woman. Hope to hell we won't have to drag her into any of this. Screwed up my marriage."

"He married that movie actress," the man next to Cardozo whispered. "She ditched him."

DiAngeli uncrossed her arms. "How did you happen to meet Corey Lyle?"

"That's quite a story." Mickey gazed at the defendant with eyes that seemed to say, *My whole life I dreamed of loving someone and then of all people on God's earth I picked you.* "I was up for the third time on a charge of exposing myself at a playground. It could have meant prison. But the judge offered me a deal: prison or join the Corey Lyle cult. I didn't want to do hard time, so Corey seemed the way to go."

"And how did you and Corey Lyle get along?"

"Corey treated me like no one else ever had in my life. He was gentle with me. He was wonderful with me." Mickey smiled a smile of uncomplicated love, like a child's. "He lifted my headaches. He lifted my sleeping trouble. He lifted my compulsion to drink. He lifted my compulsion to exhibit myself."

"How did he do all this?"

"Just sitting with me—talking."

"Do you recall anything specific Corey Lyle said in these talks that helped you?"

Mickey stared at the defendant. "He told me to relax. Sometimes he lit a candle and told me to look at the flame. He told me when he touched my arm it would rise. And he'd touch my arm and it would rise." Mickey's beefy arm floated up from the rail of the witness box, demonstrating. "He'd tell me to close my eyes—and after that it's kind of blurry."

"Would you say Corey Lyle hypnotized you?"

"Objection."

"Sustained."

DiAngeli walked back to her table and consulted a piece of paper. "Mr. Williams, did you ever hear Corey Lyle use the phrase 'share the miracle'?"

"All the time."

"Would you explain what you understood Corey Lyle to mean?"

"Part of the Fellowship tradition was prayer shares. Members were paired off so they could help one another with prayer and meditation."

"Who were you paired off with?"

"I was paired off with Johnny Briar."

"Would you describe your impressions of John Briar?"

"Johnny went to extremes. I'd see him fast, then I'd see him binge on desserts. I'd see him go celibate for months. His wife was celibate and he thought he ought to try. But then he'd fall off the wagon and we'd go whoring together."

"Whoring? But wasn't this against cult regulations?"

"There weren't regulations—there were guidelines. And Corey was pretty gentle about enforcing them."

"Do you mean Corey Lyle was lax on sin?"

"Lax? He was gentle, not lax. But he said sins had to be atoned for. There was no getting around God's law."

"Did you and Corey Lyle ever discuss how you might atone for your sins?"

"He said if I performed an act of purification, my offenses against young girls would be forgiven and I could cut down my time in purgatory."

"Did he suggest any particular act of purification?"

"Yes, he did. He told me to go to the Briars' apartment Friday evening, Labor Day weekend—and kill them."

"And did you?"

Mickey's eyes dropped. At that instant he projected frailty, vulnerability—and fear. "I always did what Corey said."

"Who let you into the apartment?"

"Corey let me in."

"Did you and Corey Lyle have a conversation at that time?"

"Yes. He took me into Johnny's room and lit a candle and told me to look at the flame. I don't remember our whole talk, but he told me that at one A.M. I had to suffocate Johnny with a pillow."

Cardozo glanced at Corey Lyle, sitting relaxed and serious, but not at all solemn or worried, at his lawyer's side.

"Did Corey Lyle give you any further instructions?"

"He said to make sure Amalia stayed alive till six A.M. Monday."

"And what was to happen at six A.M. Monday?"

"He wanted me to suffocate her too."

DiAngeli allowed the words a moment to echo and die. "Can you recall killing John and Amalia Briar?"

"Yes, I recall doing it—but it was like I was watching someone else. I knew I was doing it but it didn't seem real. I didn't understand—Why am I doing this? Why can't I make myself stop? Johnny was somebody that I loved—and I wouldn't have hurt a little old lady like

Amalia for all the world—and yet I had no choice except to do what I did. It was like . . ." Mickey put both hands over his face. "It was like Corey was inside me, making me kill."

There was a knock and a rattle of keys. The steel door swung open and Dotson Elihu stood stoop-shouldered in the doorway, clutching to his gut a tattered, overstuffed briefcase.

Corey Lyle looked up. He laid down his plastic fork and wiped tuna salad from his mouth. "Hi there, Dot. How are we doing?"

Elihu waited till the door clicked shut behind him. "Not so good." He pulled Jack Briar's police tape from his briefcase. "This videocassette is our last hope. This afternoon in cross, I want to destroy Mickey with it. I want to jump right in to his record of child molestation and Jack Briar's statements to the police."

Corey gazed at his lawyer a long, refusing moment. "I won't allow it. I will not betray a disciple."

"Ex-disciple."

"Mickey's strayed, but he's not lost."

"What the hell do you think he's doing to you? He's a killer, and in case you haven't noticed, it's you he's killing. *You owe him nothing!* Only one of you can get out of this—you, or Mickey. My job is to make sure it's you."

Corey quietly folded his hands on the table. "Did Jesus cast Judas out?"

"Core—we're talking about you, not Jesus. There's a difference, or hadn't you noticed?"

Corey's expression was suddenly ferocious. "If you use anything on that tape to attack Mickey, I'll fire you on the spot and take over my own defense."

"Then you're going to spend the rest of your life behind bars."

Corey smiled. He wasn't giving it much, but it was still a recognizable smile. "Not necessarily."

"Bull! Look at those jurors. They hate your guts. They hate your fancy clothes and your salon-cut hair and they hate your cockamamy serenity."

"All we need is one juror holding out for acquittal."

"No juror is going to be idiot enough to do that."

"Don't be so sure. God moves in mysterious ways."

"Leave the Almighty out of this—He's not taking the stand."

"And neither is this tape." Corey seized the cassette and smashed it open against the edge of the table. Like a child destroying a doll, he ripped out handfuls of magnetic tape.

Elihu watched in disbelief. "Core, I've always known you were a lot of things. . . . But till this moment I never thought you were an idiot. You just committed suicide."

THIRTY-SEVEN

2:30 P.M.

Cardozo watched Dotson Elihu draw in a deep breath, bracing himself for an escalation of hostilities.

"Mr. Williams—why did you wait fifty-three hours between killing John Briar and killing his wife?"

"Because Corey said 'Kill Johnny at one A.M. Saturday morning and kill Amalia six A.M. Monday.' "

The times struck Cardozo as oddly precise and oddly pointless. Why fifty-three hours when all the will required was forty-eight? Had Mickey and Corey synchronized watches Friday evening at the sound of a starter's pistol?

"But isn't it a fact that Dr. Lyle did *not* order you to kill Amalia Briar? Isn't it a fact that Dr. Lyle did *not* order you to kill John Briar?"

Mickey's brow wrinkled. "No, sir. Corey told me to kill them."

"Isn't it a fact that John and Amalia Briar were both

alive Sunday morning? Didn't they die natural deaths Sunday evening?"

Mickey shook his head. "No."

It was an obvious strategy, Cardozo reflected; undermine the state's case by blasting the witness with alternate scenarios, and hope one or two jurors find them credible. He checked the jury box to see if any of the jurors were buying it. Several were frowning, and Kyra Talbot was shaking her head.

"Isn't it a fact that Monday night, before the police questioned you about the murders, you and other persons"—Elihu stared a moment at the prosecutor—"worked out the whole story of Dr. Lyle hypnotizing you?"

"Objection." Tess diAngeli sighed. "Mr. Williams was never arrested for these murders."

"An astonishing oversight!" Elihu spat.

"Objection sustained." Judge Bernheim gazed down at the defense attorney. "Tonight, Mr. Elihu, you are a guest of the federal prison system. Proceed."

"I appreciate the hospitality, Your Honor." A sly half-smile twinkled. "Mr. Williams, did you not make a phone call from the Briars' apartment to the BATF at seven forty-one Monday evening? And did you not talk to your government handlers until eight fifty-nine P.M.?"

"That's not true."

Cardozo watched Elihu's face go through the motions of perplexity. He strode to the defense table and snatched up a document that looked, from twenty feet away, very much like a Nynex phone bill. "Mr. Williams—Yolanda Lopez has testified that she made only one phone call from the Briars' apartment—a call to the BATF Saturday morning. Yet the Briars' Nynex record for Monday, September seventh, shows a call made that evening to the BATF, lasting well over an hour. If *you* didn't make the call and your friend Yolanda López didn't, then who did? The corpse of John Briar?"

Canny old bastard, Cardozo thought.

Mickey sat as though he had been struck, rigid and red-faced, brown eyes bulging with pinprick pupils. "I don't . . . I didn't see . . . I mean, I . . ."

Cardozo saw that this was exactly the reaction Elihu had been probing for: panic and confusion. Mickey's eyes flicked an appeal toward the prosecutor.

"Objection." Tess diAngeli sprang to her feet. "That alleged phone record was not raised in direct and it's never been offered in evidence."

"Sustained."

Elihu threw a glance toward the jury: *See what I have to put up with for the sake of justice?* "Mr. Williams, isn't it a fact that BATF instructed you to suffocate John and Amalia Briar's *dead* bodies with a pillow?"

Mickey blinked. The shift of subject seemed to have thrown him. "No, sir."

Elihu thumped a hand on the witness box. Cardozo could feel him closing in now. He had bracketed his quarry and he was centered on it and the next question would shake it from the bush.

"In exchange for the testimony you give in this trial, hasn't the BATF promised you immunity from charges arising from your admissions?"

"Objection!"

"Sustained."

"No, sir," Mickey Williams said, "the BATF hasn't promised me immunity from anything."

Judge Bernheim glanced toward the witness. "Mr. Williams, please do not answer a question when I have sustained an objection. The answer will be struck and the jurors will disregard it."

"Mr. Williams," Elihu said, "has any agency of the federal government offered judicial lenience in exchange for your delivering their scripted testimony in this trial?"

"Objection!"

"Sustained."

"Your Honor," Elihu shouted, "this jury is being kept in the dark as to the true nature of the government's witnesses in this trial! There is not a word in their case that has not been suborned, scripted, and paid for!"

"Counselor—you are one millimeter away from being the government's guest for a week! That will be enough!"

Dotson Elihu moved away from the witness stand and slowly turned. "Mr. Williams . . . you said you were given a choice of joining Corey Lyle's group or going to prison for a crime you'd committed three times. Could you tell us what that crime was?"

DiAngeli leapt up. "Objection!"

"Sustained. Mr. Elihu, you're on cross. Stick to material raised in direct."

"But, Your Honor, the witness himself brought up—"

"Objection sustained."

Elihu sighed and faced the witness. "Mr. Williams, did you once take part in an experimental parole program in the state of Texas?"

Mickey Williams nodded. "I was paroled, yes."

"And did you not break parole by moving to the state of Washington and later to New York?"

"Objection. Irrelevant."

Elihu wheeled around. "Your Honor, this goes directly to the witness's credibility."

"I'm reminding you for the last time, Counselor—you're on cross. Kindly stick to issues raised in direct."

Elihu pondered a long moment before putting his next question. "Mr. Williams, didn't the state of Texas seek to extradite you from New York?"

"Yes, but federal court decided—"

"Objection!"

"Sustained. Mr. Elihu, I don't want to have to warn you again."

Elihu flicked a bow of his head toward the bench. He beamed a *trust me* smile to the witness. "Mr. Williams, as a condition of your Texas parole, were you not required to undergo shock treatment?"

DiAngeli jumped up so fast that her chair fell crashing over. "Objection!"

Elihu shouted over her. "In fact, Mr. Williams, haven't your brain cells been subjected to over sixty electronic scramblings?"

"Objection sustained!" Even Judge Bernheim was shouting now. The fury on her face would have flattened a billboard. *"Mr. Elihu, you are a disgrace to your profession!"*

"And isn't it a disgrace," Elihu snapped back, "when government agents trowel-feed testimony into the brain of a mental incompetent and showcase him as their star witness? How far has justice in America fallen?"

"Not so far as you're hoping, Mr. Elihu, because you just got yourself a three-week reservation in the hoosegow. Now, either cross-examine the witness or excuse him. But you will not continue this sadistic grandstanding in my court."

"Your Honor, on the basis of that remark, I respectfully request that you declare a mistrial."

"Denied."

Elihu nodded. He seemed satisfied—more than satisfied. "In that case . . . I have no further questions to put to this witness."

Judge Bernheim turned now to the prosecutor. "Ms. diAngeli?"

The man next to Cardozo whispered, "DiAngeli's gotta rebut those shock treatments."

Tess diAngeli rose slowly to her feet. "Your Honor, the People rest their case."

A ripple of murmurs and whispers fanned out through the court.

"Your Honor," Dotson Elihu cried, "I move for acquittal."

"What grounds?"

"The People have now rested. By law the court is entitled to enter a verdict of acquittal if the People have failed to prove any element of the crime."

"Counselor, the court has heard evidence of a quantity and nature clearly sufficient to sustain a verdict of guilty."

"Your Honor, that's a prejudicial remark. I move for—"

"Mr. Elihu, this court has just about had it with your nugatory niggling. Motion denied."

"It's clear my client can expect no justice in this court. The defense has no recourse but to rest its case."

"I beg your pardon?"

"The defense rests."

A tidal wave of buzzing and chattering broke through the courtroom. Judge Bernheim, wild as a dog digging for a lost bone, could not find her gavel. "Order!" she screamed. "Order in this court this minute!"

Cardozo had parked his battered green Honda in a Centre Street bus stop; he'd propped his NYPD placard in the windshield to defend against those meter maids who were out to balance the city budget on parking fines. He slid into the driver's seat, switched on the ignition, and waited.

A crowd surged down the steps of the federal courthouse. Mickey Williams, a shaved head higher than anyone else, moved deliberately through the throng. At the foot of the steps he headed north with an easy, strolling gait. A mike-wielding sob sister from one of the afternoon news shows ran alongside, and they appeared to be having an earnest chat.

Mickey's head bobbed east on Bayard, and Cardozo leaned on his horn and cut across three lanes of law-abiding vehicles.

Right away the neighborhood changed. The telephones had signs in Chinese and the cash machine at the corner bank had a pagoda roof.

Mickey strolled across Baxter to a little park where five children were screaming Cantonese and playing a game with a Hula Hoop and a red Frisbee. He watched them. He seemed especially interested in the little girl whose polka-dot skirt kept flying up every time she tried to hoop the flying Frisbee. Cardozo was surprised some Chinese parent didn't send for the local Tongs.

A dark blue Pontiac with a federal license plate nosed to the curb and beeped its horn. A door opened. The driver—a burley man in shirt-sleeves—stepped out. He shouted something. The words didn't carry, but the angry tone did.

Mickey crossed to the car. The driver handed him a

set of keys. They shook hands. Mickey got into the front seat. The door swung shut.

The driver stood on the sidewalk, watching as the Pontiac eased north on Mott. Cardozo eased along three cars behind it.

"In conclusion, ladies and gentlemen of the jury—" Tess diAngeli's eyes swept slowly across the jurors. "I ask you to imagine those last forty-eight hours of Amalia Briar's life—that poor, sick, suffering, terrified old lady—as she came face-to-face with terror and death in her own undefended bedroom. Ask yourselves: Would I wish to go through this horror myself? Would I wish this on my mother? Would I wish this on any human being? And unless you can answer *yes*—you owe it to yourselves and to every person and principle you hold sacred—to return a verdict of guilty as charged."

Traffic congealed to a crawl along the peddler-packed stretch of upper Broadway. Cardozo could see a shifting sliver of the government Pontiac five cars ahead.

At West 106th Street, now christened Duke Ellington Boulevard, the Pontiac swung left, and when Cardozo finally reached the intersection he saw it crawling south on West End. He hooked a sharp left and followed.

There was an eardrum-puncturing blip of siren and a voice on a bullhorn barked, "You in the green Honda—pull over."

Cardozo glanced over his shoulder. There was no other green Honda in sight, and a blue-and-white police cruiser was spinning its lights at him. He pulled to the curb.

An overweight, mean-looking boy stepped out of the cruiser and ambled to Cardozo's window. "The sign back there says no left turn eight A.M. to eight P.M."

"I'm sorry, Officer, I didn't see it."

"Please cut your motor."

Cardozo didn't cut his motor. He pulled out his shield case and flipped it open.

The copped blinked. "Sorry, Lieutenant." He touched the brim of his cap and stepped away.

Cardozo pulled back into traffic. He'd lost sixty seconds, and the light at 104th Street was green, and there was no sign of the blue government Pontiac.

"What kind of case requires grants of immunity to the true murderers and conspirators?" Dotson Elihu crossed his arms and glared at the prosecutor. "What kind of a case requires wholesale suppression of genuine evidence and the procurement of false testimony? I'll tell you. *A frame-up.*"

He turned and placed his hands on the railing of the jury box. His eyes rested darkly on each juror in turn. "Ladies and gentlemen, if this is still a court of law and not an altar of sacrifice to political expedience—then you have no choice in the face of such arrogant, brazen trampling of our constitution but to bring back a verdict of not guilty."

THIRTY-EIGHT

1:10 P.M.

"I can't *believe* what Elihu did to Mickey Williams." At a corner table in Eugene's Patio, Shoshana sliced angrily into a turkey enchilada. "I've never seen anything so cruel."

Anne pushed her fork at her fruit salad. "But he has a point. How reliable can Mickey's testimony be if he's had his brain fried?"

Shoshana's eyes blazed. The skin beneath them looked puffy and tender. "We obviously have different ways of thinking."

"That's why there are twelve of us," Anne said. "Maybe we should talk about something else."

"The charge against the defendant is conspiracy to commit murder. The charge is *not* murder." Judge Bernheim had been speaking for almost an hour now, her voice slow and explanatory as a teacher's. "Bear this distinction in mind. To be guilty of conspiring to murder, there is no need for the murder to actually occur. What is required is that the accused plans to commit murder with at least one coconspirator, and that one of them—not necessarily the accused—takes at least one step toward the realization of that conspiracy. The step can be something as small as a phone call—or the purchase of some item needed in execution of the plan . . . a screwdriver . . . a map . . . or a gun.

"Beware of easy solutions to complex questions. A just verdict cannot be settled by slogans. It demands concentrated attention, much mental work, and above all, patience. God bless you and good luck to you all."

The jurors took their seats around the table. Each place had a legal pad and ballpoint pen.

"Ladies and gentlemen of the jury . . ." Ben Esposito raised his hands, calling for silence. "Before we begin discussing the evidence—it might save time to take a vote and see how close we are to agreement."

"Secret ballot," Thelma del Rio said.

Ben's eyes came up slowly, TV sitcom double-take slow-burn style. "You mean little scraps of paper?"

She nodded. "Little scraps of paper folded over."

"What's the point?" said P. C. Cabot, the well-dressed subway motorman.

Thelma's eyes were tight with determination. "The point is so we can reach a verdict without fear of coercion."

"Who's coercing?" Lara Duggan said.

"As a member of a multiple minority," Thelma said, "I can tell you, the majority always coerces."

"Right on," Gloria Weston said.

"This is stupid." P. C. Cabot's fingers were drumming on the table. "The minute anyone opens their mouth we're going to know how they're voting."

"Maybe. Maybe not." Sitting absolutely erect, Thelma seemed hard and sure of herself, a crusader on the attack. "I want a closed ballot and I have a right to it."

"You don't have a right to impose it on everyone else."

"Excuse me," Ben said, "but anyone who wants a closed ballot has a right."

"Oh, yeah?" P. C. Cabot said. "Anyone opposed?"

Seven hands went up.

Anne's stayed down. She noticed that Shoshana's stayed down too. Abe da Silva, the bald juror, kept his hand down. So did Donna. And Lara Duggan.

"Doesn't matter who's opposed," Ben said. "Thelma wants it, Thelma's got a right." He ripped a sheet of blank paper into twelve strips and passed them counter-clockwise. "Keep one and pass the others on. Write your verdict and fold the paper and pass it back."

Cupping the little ribbon of paper behind her left hand, Anne wrote the words *not guilty,* folded the paper, and passed it to Paco Velez.

Ben dropped the ballots into a brown paper bag, shook it, and emptied them in a little mound on the tabletop. His face was grim as he counted them. "Okay, guys, here's how we stand. Not guilty—four."

Anne's heart jumped. *I've got three allies!* Her eyes scanned the table. *Who?*

"Guilty—eight. Far as I'm concerned, we're heading in the right direction. But four of us need a little convincing. Discussion is open."

"There's a lot of tape we never got," Anne said. "Phone tapes, conversation tapes, autopsy tapes."

"No one mentioned lost *phone* tapes," P.C. said.

"I thought someone did. Could we look into that?"

Ben grunted. "Anyone else want to look into it?"

"I'd like to look into it," Anne said, "no matter who else does or doesn't."

"That's your right." Ben made a note on his pad.

"And what about the phone bill Elihu had?" Abe da Silva said. "The call someone made Labor Day from the Briars' apartment to the BATF?"

Is Abe an ally? Anne wondered.

"The alleged phone call," Ben said. "It was never in evidence."

"Why not?"

"Because the People have a right to choose how they'll present their case."

"What happened to the lady cop?" Lara Duggan said. "How come they wouldn't let her be recalled?"

And could Lara be one?

"Because she was killed," Thelma del Rio said.

Abe da Silva scowled. "I didn't hear anything about a lady cop getting killed."

"They discussed it in sidebar," Thelma said. "We aren't suppose to know."

"Damn it," Ben said. "If we're not supposed to know, don't tell us."

"I'd like to see Mickey Williams's record," Paco Velez said. "I want to see the kind of person we're being asked to believe."

That's a pro-Corey comment if I ever heard one, Anne thought. *Paco's definitely on my side.*

"We're not allowed to know his record," Abe da Silva said. "That's prejudicial."

"He's a witness," Anne said, "not a defendant. Besides, the record came up in testimony. I'd like to see it too."

"All right." Ben sighed. "We can try to get Mickey's record." He went to the door and jiggled the handle. "Hey, bailiff!"

It was five-thirty when Catch Talbot stepped into Cardozo's office at the precinct. "I've spent the last forty-eight hours in precincts and hospitals." There was something uncertain in his walk, a sort of blinking, I'm-lost-please-help-me confusion. "No one's seen Toby."

"Have a seat," Cardozo said.

"I think I know what happened." Hunched on the spare chair, Talbot stared straight into Cardozo's eyes. "Kyra's responsible."

"Kyra?" Cardozo didn't like Talbot's facial expression, his tone of voice. Because there was no expression, no inflection. It was as though grief or worry or two days of fruitless searching had stupefied the guy and left nothing in his head but the wriggling worms of obsession. Obsessives, Cardozo had found, were impossible to reason with.

Nevertheless, he made the attempt. "What about the man impersonating you who had dinner with Dr. Gibbs?"

"He's Kyra's accomplice."

"How would he or your ex-wife know your charge card number?"

"I've had the same card since Kyra and I were married."

"What's her motive?"

"To establish that I was here when Toby disappeared. To implicate me and clear herself."

In his work, Cardozo had dealt with many a divorced, angry cop; he recognized the paranoia that breaking up often engendered. He was careful to take a nonchallenging, nonconfrontational tone. "Clear herself of what?"

"Abducting Toby."

Uh-oh, Cardozo thought.

"This week a hearing was scheduled to decide whether Kyra or I get Toby. She canceled the hearing. She's using jury duty as a smoke screen, because she's terrified she won't get custody. Once she's off the jury, she'll take Toby outside the court's jurisdiction. Then she'll have the income from his trust to herself."

Cardozo reflected on that word *trust* and the unexpected light it cast on the puzzle. "What trust?"

"Toby's grandmother on his mother's side was a very wealthy woman. She left him the bulk of her estate in trust."

"How much?"

"Depending on the stock market, twelve to fifteen million. To a woman of Kyra's spending habits the guardian's fees could be a lifesaver."

Cardozo ran the theory through his mind. It jibed with the note Kyra had sent her lawyer; it jibed with her disappearing. But . . . "How could she hope to access the trust if she's kidnapped her own son and taken him out of the state?"

"It wouldn't count as kidnapping. At twelve, Toby's free to choose which parent he wants to live with; and he tends to choose whichever parent he's with at the moment."

"But how could she get the money out of the state? Wouldn't the trust be frozen?"

"Not since New York liberalized its laws. A parent with custody can take the children anywhere, even if the ex-spouse has visitation rights."

Cardozo reflected. The theory made a crazy kind of sense. "But how do you explain the threatening phone call?"

"Frankly, I don't think there *was* a call. I think Kyra invented it to cover her tracks."

"Look, Catch, I understand divorce has left you with resentments toward your ex-wife. But let's be realistic. She's on jury duty. Sequestered. She obviously hasn't got Toby with her. So where's she hiding him?"

Talbot pondered. "She could have sent him somewhere with that au pair girl. Or her sister could be helping."

"Her sister hasn't been seen since Saturday."

"The day Toby disappeared." Talbot's eyes flicked up. "Then *Anne* took Toby."

Cardozo felt he was trying to nail Jell-O to a wall. "A *man* took Toby."

"Then he's Kyra's accomplice. They're all in on it together."

Cardozo didn't like the turn the conversation was taking: the wife was a criminal mastermind; everyone was involved in Toby's kidnapping. Next, Talbot would claim that the government was tapping his phone.

Talbot scribbled a number on a scratch pad. "Anytime you need to reach me—this is my cellular phone. Call me direct. Hotel switchboards have a habit of listening in."

Cardozo tucked the slip of paper into his wallet. "Would you excuse me just a moment?"

He went into the squad room and spoke softly to Greg Monteleone. "Get Catch Talbot out of here. The poor guy's flipped."

"Where do you want me to take him?"

"Take him to a movie. Take him to a bar. Just keep him occupied and out of trouble. And out of my hair."

Cardozo closed the door of his cubicle and tried the number again.

Tess answered on the third ring. "DiAngeli." She was obviously in a piss-poor mood.

"Tess—Vince. I've been trying to reach you for hours."

"Some of us rest after we deliver summations."

"It's over already?"

"Everything but the verdict. What's on your mind?"

"I was in court this morning. Mickey's got quite a presentation. That shaved head and that earring."

"I could have murdered him when he showed up with that earring."

"Remember the man who took Toby Talbot from school? The man who drove off with Britta Bailey?"

"What about him?"

"Mickey fits the description."

"So do dozens of men."

"I followed him from the courthouse. He spent ten minutes ogling little girls in Chinatown."

"So?"

"That may not bother you, but it sure spooked his friend in the blue Pontiac with the government license plates. He gave Mickey a tongue-lashing."

"This is pointless, Vince."

"If we could ever find this guy, we've got enough to bring him in for questioning. It would be a start."

"My hands are tied."

Cardozo felt his nerves rising on an arc of impatience. "Murdering Britta and kidnapping Toby are *new* crimes. They were committed after you made that lousy deal."

"Get it through your head, will you?" She was shouting. "The federal government doesn't give a damn what Mickey's done. Who he's molested, who he's murdered. They want this case. Period." She was silent for a moment. And then, in a calmer, more conciliatory voice, "Maybe after the verdict is in I could get a bench warrant."

"We've got to bring him in today. This afternoon. Before he harms the Talbot kid. Assuming he hasn't already."

"The guard hasn't reported seeing him with a child."

"His guard is goofing off. You said yourself, he's leaving windows of opportunity left and right."

"That's been changed. The guard's keeping a surveillance log. Mickey's every move is written down."

"Have you seen this log?"

"Not yet—but I expect to in the next hour."

"I get it. The log is in the mail. For your information, Mickey's guard gave him the keys to the Pontiac and Mickey drove off alone. Unescorted. Unsupervised. I tailed him to the Upper West Side, but I lost him. Tess, the feds are pulling your chain."

She didn't answer.

"Come on—when Mickey's not on that stand, where the hell is he? What's he doing? Does his guard know? Do you? Does anyone?"

"I've got another call. I'll talk to you later."

Tess searched her desktop. Even though her contact at Justice had promised her the surveillance log, nothing had come in. She lifted the phone and punched in his number.

"I'm sorry," a recorded voice told her. "The mobile phone number you have dialed is currently outside of the service area. Please try your call again later."

"The hell with you, Foster." She broke the connection and phoned Mickey's guard.

A male voice said, "Yeah?"

"Rick?"

"This is Stan."

"This is Tess diAngeli at the Manhattan D.A.'s office."

"Hi, Tess, what's up?"

"What's happened to Rick?"

"Rick's been reassigned."

"Why?"

"Who knows."

"Who's watching Mickey?"

"Me."

"Where is he now?"

"I'll know in a few minutes. It's almost time for him to call."

"For him to call? But aren't you surveilling him?"

"Passive surveillance."

"What does that mean?"

"He phones three times a day and checks in."

"Then where are you?"

"Headquarters. World Trade Center."

For one jaw-dropped instant Tess was speechless. And then understanding hit like a wrecking ball. Justice had double-crossed her, and they had been doing it all along.

"Thanks, Stan."

She hung up the phone and spun a slow circle in her chair.

THIRTY-NINE

10:55 P.M.

Ben counted the results of the latest vote. "Not guilty—two. Guilty—ten."

Anne felt a whisper of panic in her blood. In eight hours, four not-guilty votes had whittled themselves down to two. In her mind, she heard the voice on the phone: *If you ever want to see your son alive again* . . .

Covering a yawn with his hand, Ben pushed the ballots into a paper bag. "It's taking all night, but we're getting there."

"What about the other autopsy?" Anne said. "It said Amalia died first. And if she died before her husband, Corey Lyle doesn't inherit and there's no reason for him to want them dead."

Ben Esposito's lips thinned with annoyance. "There was no second autopsy introduced into evidence."

"But you heard Dotson Elihu."

"That's not evidence," P.C. said. "That's fabrication."

"I disagree," Anne said. "And Elihu raised another point: what if the Briars both died *natural* deaths?"

"Who cares how they died?" Gloria said. "Johnny and Amalia are not the point. They were politically retro society trash. No one's weeping for them. But Corey could have killed *innocent kids*—your kids, my kids. And if we let him go, that's exactly what he's going to do."

"The charge isn't what Corey Lyle might do," Anne said. "It's what he *did* do."

"Bullshit!" Gloria shouted. "Get real for once in your la-di-da life! Our verdict has to send a message that enough is enough!"

"Sending messages isn't our job."

"In other words, if you're rich as Rockefeller and connected as Kissinger, you can blow up all the buildings and kill all the people you want? Send that message from your magazine, Ms. Talbot. But don't try to send it from this jury room."

"We're sworn to try Corey Lyle on the charge," Anne said quietly, "not on accusations he hasn't had a chance to answer."

"Ms. Talbot's view is almost funny," Seymour Shen said, "when you consider that Corey didn't bother to answer *any* charge."

"For God's sake," Anne cried, "that's his right. Are we back in the old witch-hunting days?"

"There's nothing wrong with a witch-hunt," Thelma said, "if the witch happens to be a murderer. And for your information, Corey *confessed.*"

"You mean that videotape where Corey told the D.A. he was morally responsible?" Anne slapped the table. "That was no confession. That was a collection of carefully edited sound bites."

"We weren't allowed to see the rest of it." Thelma's eyes were sly. "Elihu kept it out. But believe me—there was enough on that tape to convict."

"Why should we take your word for that?"

"Because I saw two lawyers and a judge arguing over it and I'm a damned good lip-reader."

"How do you happen to read lips?"

"My parents were deaf-mutes, so I picked it up."

"I'm sorry," Anne said, "I'm kind of slow—how did you pick up lip-reading if your parents were deaf-mutes? You weren't reading *their* lips."

"They watched television with the sound turned off. I had to lip-read to get the jokes on *All in the Family.*"

"Why did they turn the sound off if they were deaf? What difference did it make?"

"Hey, hey," Ben said. "Thelma's not on trial here."

"She's giving unsworn testimony," Anne said. "She claims she was lip-reading the sidebar conferences, but even if she was, we're not supposed to know what goes on in those discussions. And I for one think she's been embroidering."

Thelma pushed up on her arms, rising halfway out of her chair. "I resent that!"

"Hey, come on." Ben thumped the table. "The issue is not Thelma's lip-reading, the issue is two people have died horrible deaths, and are we going to let the killer get away with it or not? Ten jurors say hell no . . . and two of us"—his eyes lingered accusingly on Anne—"say let him go on a technicality . . . any technicality."

"It's not a technicality!" she cried. "The whole case against him is full of holes."

Donna yawned. "Haven't we been through this before?"

"Twenty times so far," P. C. Cabot said.

On the other side of the door, something jingled like Santa's sleigh bells. A key turned and the bailiff thrust a smiling face into the jury room. "Judge Bernheim says you've suffered enough. You can go back to the hotel."

Anne opened the bath taps all the way. Water pounded into the tub and steam began clouding the air. She tapped Mark's number into the cellular phone.

On the fifth ring there was a click. "Hello?" Mark's voice, with a baroque concerto buzzing manically in the background.

"Mark—it's me. Sorry to be so late. We started deliberating today."

"How come so soon?"

"The defense didn't present a case."

Mark whistled.

"Mark, do you remember how Mademoiselle described that man who picked Toby up from the École, the man who claimed to be Catch?"

"She said he was heavyset and had a shaved head."

"And crackle-glass brown eyes that look druggy and hyped, like laser discs spinning off-track?"

"She didn't describe them quite that vividly. I believe the exact word she used was *brown.*"

"I've seen him."

"Where?"

"On the stand in court today. He's the government's star witness—Mickey Williams."

"Now, wait a minute. Toby wouldn't just walk out of school with a complete stranger pretending to be his father."

"Toby's a needy, impressionable boy who misses his dad. Mickey Williams is a football hero. Half the eleven-year-old boys in America would leap at the chance to spend an afternoon with him."

"Give me a break. Mickey Williams is not taking time off from testimony to kidnap an eleven-year-old boy. He'd have to have a very skewed reality principle."

"That's the point. He got early parole in Texas by submitting to a course of sixty shock treatments. It came out in testimony."

"Come on, Anne. If it *is* the same guy, what's he trying to accomplish? He's state's witness *against* Corey Lyle—why the hell would he want to hang the jury?"

"Because he worships Lyle—you should have seen the way he looked at him today in court."

"Then why's he testifying for the *prosecution*?"

"Because that's the deal."

"What deal?"

"Okay—here's what I *think* happened. My father argued a federal extradition case—*Mathis* v. *Doe.* Have you ever heard of it?"

"Sure I have."

"Leon defended a Texas parolee who broke parole by leaving Texas. Which is exactly what Mickey Williams did. Mark, this is going to sound crazy—but *what if Mickey Williams is Doe*? The chronology fits. When Mickey murdered the Briars, Texas would have learned his whereabouts and sued for his extradition."

"What took Texas so long?"

"Maybe Texas couldn't trace him. Maybe Mickey laid low. Maybe the murders were his first felony since breaking parole. Now can you tell me who the judge was in Mathis v. Doe?"

"Robert MacLeod."

"That fits. Leon's old law partner. And wouldn't

Judge Bernheim have had to okay the immunity deal with Mickey?"

"Absolutely."

"Which is why she almost had a fit when I said I was Leon's daughter."

"Come on, that doesn't even make sense. If Bernheim didn't want Leon's daughter on the jury, why didn't she just excuse Kyra?"

"Because Kyra *didn't say* who her father was. When I came down to stand in for her, she was already empaneled. She *wanted* to get on the jury and she wanted *me* to take her place."

"That's crazy."

"I don't know why Kyra did it—but I'm pretty sure what Leon did. He orchestrated a deal: in exchange for testifying against Corey Lyle, Mickey got freedom in *Mathis* v. *Doe* and immunity in the Briar murders."

"You think Leon and MacLeod and Bernheim *conspired*?"

"Mark, they were making *conference* calls."

"Now, just hold it a minute. You're getting sequesterment fever. Even if there *was* a deal, and even if MacLeod and Bernheim were mixed up in it, Leon's client wouldn't be snatching Leon's grandson."

"Wrong. He's got two good reasons. He wants to hang the jury and he's pressuring Leon to keep quiet."

"Quiet about what?"

She explained about Leon's alleged phone calls. "Mickey admitted in testimony that he's a compulsive exhibitionist. He was sitting in Leon's cabin staring at the photographs of those lawyers' daughters. The photos are autographed. The names are in the Rolodex. He had the motive, he had the opportunity. *He made those calls.*"

"Monkey see, monkey phone? Isn't that a little simplistic?"

"Why else would Leon be taking the blame?"

"Didn't it ever occur to you that Leon could be telling the truth? He could be an old goat who gets his jollies phoning little girls."

"No way on earth. Leon's a monster, but not *that* kind."

"Or he could be an old-fashioned idealist who refuses to rat on *any* client."

"Come on, Mark. Mickey can't afford to be convicted of another sex offense—so he's pressuring Leon to take the blame."

"Mmm—well, you're right about another offense. The penalty for repeaters in New York is life. And New York might send him back to Texas. The penalty there can be castration."

"That's it. That's Mickey's motive."

"Okay, you've got the motive, but where's the weapon? What's Mickey's hold on Leon?"

"He can go public about the deal."

"He'd be committing suicide."

"People with electro-scrambled brains may not *care.*"

"Look. There's one big problem with your theory, and there's no explaining it away. Mickey Williams can't possibly be Doe."

"Why not?"

"He'd have to have had a lot more done to him than sixty shock treatments. I happen to have read a little about *Mathis* v. *Doe.* The judicial abstract refers to Doe as *she.*"

"She?" Anne suddenly remembered Leon's phone victim in Chicago—Candace Loffler—and her certainty

that the obscene caller had been a woman *trying* to sound like a man. "You're sure?"

"I saw it in cold type with my own eyes. Doe is a woman."

FORTY

Friday, September 27
Second day of deliberation
9:30 A.M.

The door closed. The bailiff's key clicked in the lock and the twelve jurors were alone in the jury room. Morning sun poured through the window, blindingly bright. P. C. Cabot walked over to angle the blinds.

"Before we get to the business of the day," Ben Esposito said, "let's take a vote and see if the Holy Spirit has moved any of us to new wisdom during the night."

The sound of ripping paper was like sand running down a drainpipe. Twelve ballots made their way around the table.

Anne wrote two words—*not guilty.*

The jurors passed their ballots back. Ben scooped them into his brown paper bag, shook them, poured them out onto the table, and counted the votes.

Anne glanced at Paco, at Abe, and Lara. *Is one of you still my ally?*

"We've made progress," Ben said. "Eleven guilty, one not guilty."

Anne had a sensation like a pane of glass snapping in her breast. *I'm alone.*

"We've spent half a day explaining our position." Ben's eyes nailed her. "Maybe, just out of courtesy, the holdout could explain his or her position to us."

"I asked to see Mickey Williams's criminal record," she said.

Ben shook his head. "It wasn't in evidence."

"The man's an admitted monster. How can we possibly believe him?"

"Aren't you forgetting something?" Donna Scomoda said. "The lie detector says he was telling the truth. So does the psychiatrist."

"Are we supposed to park our brains in Foley Square just because the court says the lie detector man and the psychiatrist are experts?"

"The psychiatrist hypnotized him. It's a medical fact that you don't lie under hypnosis."

"I didn't hear anyone say that in court."

"You didn't hear anyone in court say the earth is round," Ramon Culpeper said, "but it is."

"Look," Donna said. "I'm a nurse. I know from hypnosis."

"You're not a sworn witness. You're only a juror, like the rest of us."

"Like *some* of the rest of us."

"What's that supposed to mean?"

"It means, are you just plain mule-headed or are you Corey Lyle's paid agent?"

"I resent that."

"And maybe some of us resent you nitpicking the witnesses apart. Seems nothing's good enough proof for you. What the hell do you need?"

"Facts."

"We've had plenty of facts," Seymour Shen said.

"Name me one fact in this entire case that hasn't been contradicted."

"That little Lopez girl," Ben said. "No one contradicted her."

"Okay—she told a good sob story and no one had the guts to challenge her. But we're supposed to *believe* her?"

Gloria Weston thunked both elbows on the table. "And what's so hard about believing Lisa Lopez?"

"Come on," Anne said. "There wasn't a single piece of evidence supporting that child's testimony." *How would Kyra handle this? Ridicule.* "Flying sorcerers? Horse-blood cocktails? Give me a break. It was pure movie-of-the-week: everything but the bloodhounds nipping at her heels."

"Maybe to you it's twaddle," Gloria screamed, "but to a lot of minority kids it's their daily life."

I'm getting sucked into arguments. Losing sight of my purpose. The aim is to keep Toby alive. Period. Anne tamped down her adrenaline. Tried to. "Please don't shout at me."

"Why the hell not?" Gloria glared with a hatefulness that caught Anne like a chop in the throat. "You've been shouting elitist crap at us since we began deliberating."

"Amen," P. C. Cabot muttered.

Eleven faces stared, spewing silent rage.

How long can I hold out against this? Anne realized she was praying for a miracle; and she realized she wasn't going to get one. Not from these people.

There's no point taking another vote. The next vote will be the same as the last.

Which left her only one option.

She turned toward the foreman. "May I speak to the bailiff, please?"

"Now, cool down a minute, everyone." Ben's hands made urgent, placating gestures. "We're all under a strain. Nerves get frayed. Tempers are short. But Gloria didn't mean anything, did you, Gloria?"

"Like hell I didn't."

"Come on, girls, can't we settle this between ourselves?"

"I want to see the bailiff," Anne said. "Now."

As Cardozo dialed Anne Bingham's number, laughter from the squad room vibrated against the wall of his cubicle. Bingham's machine gave him a string of beeps and disconnected. Just as he laid the receiver back in the cradle, the phone rang. "Cardozo."

Silence. Breathing. "Lieutenant Vincent Cardozo?" A man's voice.

"That's right."

"This is Jerry McCauley." He said it as though the name ought to mean something. "Remember? Jerry, the doorman at 118 East Eighty-first? You asked me to contact you if Anne Bingham showed up?"

"Right."

"The reason I'm phoning, a neighbor reported a gas leak in Bingham's apartment. I was just up there, and it doesn't smell like gas. Smells like someone's died. A man from Con Ed's breaking in right now. Thought you'd want to know."

The bailiff rapped sharply on the oak-paneled door. A voice called, "Come in!"

He swung the door open. "Your Honor, one of the jurors would like a word with you."

Anne steeled herself and stepped into the judge's chambers.

"Yes, Mrs. Talbot?" Judge Bernheim folded her *New York Times*, but she did not rise from her desk.

"Thank you for seeing me."

"The jury can't deliberate while you're gone, so sit down and get to the point."

Anne sat in the leather armchair. "I have a confession to make. If you'll look in the bottom drawer of my closet, you'll find a cellular phone that I smuggled into the hotel."

Expression drained from the judge's face. "Tell me this is another one of your jokes."

"It's not."

The judge folded her arms. "Then you and I and the State of New York have a problem. Have you used this phone since you've been sequestered?"

Anne nodded. "Five or six times."

Judge Bernheim rose to her feet, ferocious. "What right entitles you to violate your oath as a juror?"

"I didn't have a choice. It was an emergency."

"*What* was an emergency?"

"The phone call threatening Toby."

"Saturday you said there was no such phone call. And now you say there *was*?"

"I lied. There was a phone call and I was terrified for Toby and my sister. I still am. I went to her apartment to warn them, but—"

"You went to her apartment?"

"Yes, Your Honor."

"When did you do this?"

"Sunday, but—"

"You went to your sister's apartment *last Sunday*?"

"But they weren't there, so I brought her cellular phone back with me. To stay in touch."

"To stay in touch?" Judge Bernheim's eyes bulged from her head. "Do you realize what you've done? You've aborted this trial and cost the government fifty million dollars!"

"I take full responsibility, Your Honor. And I want to make one thing absolutely clear: my roommate isn't involved. She knows nothing about this."

"We'll have to see about that, won't we? In the meantime, I'm charging you with jury tampering. I'm setting bail that will get you into the *Guinness Book of World Records.* You won't see sunlight for twenty years." Judge Bernheim seized a pencil from the desk and snapped it in two. "Furthermore: there's no way a New York court is going to judge you a fit mother. I will personally see to it that your ex-husband is granted full custody of your child."

"Your Honor," Anne said quietly, "that's not going to make any difference."

"Says you."

"It's not going to make any difference, because I'm not Kyra Talbot."

Judge Bernheim's face was suddenly a blank, giving nothing.

"I'm Kyra Talbot's twin. My name is Anne Bingham."

"In view of circumstances just revealed to me in chambers, I have no choice but to declare these proceedings a mistrial."

Judge Bernheim gazed grimly toward the jury box.

"Ladies and gentlemen of the jury—thank you for the time and effort you've put into performing your duty. I'm sorry that your service has been nullified by the irresponsible behavior of one person. All jurors except juror ten are excused. Please see the bailiff and he will give you your certificates. Be sure the court has your Social Security numbers, otherwise your checks cannot be mailed to you."

Judge Bernheim's eyes swung toward the prosecutor. "Ms. diAngeli. The People have eighty days in which to reinstate charges against Corey Lyle or to drop them."

Tess diAngeli broke off a whispered conference with her assistant. "Your Honor, the People cannot make that decision today."

"In that case, I have no choice but to release Corey Lyle on continued bail." The judge stared down at the defense table. "Mr. Lyle, you shall not leave this jurisdiction. You may be recalled within eighty days to face these charges, should they be reinstated. But in the meantime you are free to go."

Corey Lyle had a startled look. He bent toward his lawyer.

"Juror Ten," Judge Bernheim commanded, "approach the bench."

Anne rose from her seat. The bailiff held the gate. She stepped down to floor level and crossed to the bench.

Judge Bernheim had the look of a tired lioness.

"Congratulations, Kyra Talbot or Anne Bingham or whatever you decide to call yourself. You will soon have achieved your heart's desire—permanent exemption from jury duty. As well as from ever voting again."

She drew back in her chair. She spoke rapidly now, with clipped contempt.

"You have cost the government close to fifty million dollars. You have made a mockery of the efforts of hundreds of dedicated men and women working almost a decade. And you will bear the full retributive weight of the law for your actions. You are remanded to custody and this court is adjourned."

Judge Bernheim's gavel slammed down onto the shuddering bench. An armed guard stepped forward.

"All rise," the bailiff commanded.

The spectators rose. Judge Bernheim stood, drawing her robe around her. An absolute stillness suffused the courtroom as she glided granite-faced to the door.

A slam shattered the silence. The benches broke into movement.

Corey Lyle—crisp in his navy blazer and red striped tie—rose from his chair. He pulled a pair of dark glasses from his pocket and fitted them over his eyes. Masked now, he smiled a triumphant smile.

At the rear of the courtroom, a guard's voice howled, "Hey! She's got my gun!"

A hundred-voiced scream ignited and spiked upward. Leaping and spilling across benches, spectators shouldered and jammed in a stampede to clear the aisle.

Yolanda Lopez, eyes blazing, pushed forward through the whirlpooling panic. Gripping a police service revolver in her right hand, she stopped six feet from Corey Lyle and pointed the gun barrel at his chest.

"Yolanda—don't!" Corey Lyle's voice was pushed high and shrill. "Don't! In the name of God—"

The first shot cracked out. Corey Lyle stumbled three steps backward.

A second shot.

The defense table broke his sideways fall. He slid slowly to the linoleum and lay there, eyes staring upward at the ceiling.

Papers fluttered down.

Yolanda stepped up to the body and fired three shots straight into his face.

Anne's guard sprang from the cover of the prosecutor's table. He dove in a running crouch and grabbed Yolanda Lopez.

FORTY-ONE

11:40 A.M.

"Madhouse around here today." The guard led Anne through pale cigarette-stained corridors. "We haven't had a courtroom shooting in months."

"Where did she get the gun?"

"Grabbed it from a guard. What a guard's doing, leaving his holster unbuckled, don't ask me."

He opened the door of a small office crammed with metal filing cabinets. The walls were painted puce and the air-conditioning hit like a slap in the face with an iced catfish.

"That one works." He pointed to the phone on the desk. "You better call a lawyer."

The guard left and a key clicked in the lock. She lifted the receiver and tapped in Mark's direct line at work.

"Mark Wells."

"The secret word is *mistrial.*"

"Anne? Hung jury already?"

"Jury tampering. I told Judge Bernheim I'm Anne."

A beat of silence.

"That would do it," Mark said.

"That's not all. When Bernheim declared a mistrial, Yolanda Lopez grabbed a guard's revolver and shot Corey Lyle dead."

"Jesus."

"Mark, can you get me out of here?"

"What's your bail?"

"Two point five million."

Mark whistled. "I'll try."

The elevator stopped on eleven. A gassy smell floated in the air, faint and familiar. Cardozo followed his nose down the long gray-carpeted corridor to the door of 11-E. The smell grew thicker, with the stomach-turning sweetness of rotted pastries.

He pushed the doorbell. A moment later the door opened and a foul odor gushed out. The doorman stood there, a wet paper towel pressed over his nose and mouth.

"Okay, Jerry, what have we got?"

Jerry shrugged a shoulder. "The Con Ed man's in there looking. He says it's not a gas leak."

Cardozo stepped into the apartment. The air felt hypersaturated, like a rain forest. He saw at a glance that Anne Bingham's living room was a workplace. It had been given a light airbrushing of decor—two Chinese vases on a bookshelf, jungle-bird pattern curtains that matched the coverings on the chair and the convertible sofa. But over half the space was taken up by a worktable piled with computer and electronic gear, angled for easy access to the keyboards of a bank of synthesizers.

There was a monotonous humming sound. The windows were open, and the air conditioner was running on high fan. Cardozo frowned.

A crystal vase of dead cut flowers had been knocked over on the coffee table. A lamp lay at the edge of the threadbare Oriental rug, its shade crushed. A potted corn plant, upended in the corner, trailed a comet-tail of soil. A goldfish lay dead on the rug amid the shards of its shattered bowl.

Cardozo hurried down the hallway to the bathroom. The door was ajar and the stink was overpowering. For a moment he had to brace himself against the door frame, fighting back a gag reflex.

He snapped on the light.

The bathroom was tiled in pink ceramic. A bath mat in matching pink had been crumpled against the toilet stand, and a pink towel lay across the sink.

Cardozo's eye flicked across a narrow dribble of caked rust running from the sink to the tub. There was a swaying movement at the edge of the shower curtain where water pattered softly on plastic.

He pushed back the curtain.

The showerhead had been left dribbling. The opening in the overflow plate siphoned off the excess. The bathwater had reached the color and consistency of gazpacho.

A fully clothed woman lay in the tub on her side, an island of gray in the fetid dark slime. With gaping mouth and staring green eyes, the face had a look of abject terror.

Cardozo felt a disorienting stab of recognition. The woman was Kyra Talbot.

Cardozo's stomach turned over. "Hey, Jerry!"

Jerry's head poked into the bathroom. His eyes recoiled.

"Do you recognize her?"

Jerry nodded. "She's the owner of this apartment. Anne Bingham."

Anne turned at the sound of a key clicking in the lock. The door of the dusty little room flew open, and Mark Wells—hair flying and necktie over his shoulder—burst in. He wasn't alone.

"Anne, do you know Kyra's boss, Nort Stanley?"

She shook the hand of a bald man with Coke-bottle eyeglasses.

"God," he said, "you're a dead ringer for Kyra."

"Here's the deal." Mark's voice was a breathless rasp, as if he'd been running and negotiating at the same time. "Nort's posting your bail, plus you get a fifty-thousand-dollar advance against two hundred fifty thousand."

"What am I getting an advance for?"

There was a beat of hesitation, as if Mark was mystified that she should be mystified. "You'll write a three-part series on the trial. For the *Manhattanite.*"

"I'm not a writer."

"You are now."

"We want you, Annie." Behind the wire-rimmed glasses, Nort Stanley's eyes had a hungry, focused glow. "We want you bad."

Mark opened his briefcase and shoved papers at her. "Initial the bottom of each page and sign the last."

The corridor echoed with the pandemonium of a street carnival.

"The next few minutes are going to be tough. So hang tight." Mark sliced a path through the mob.

Outside the courthouse, bodies crushed and voices hollered and minicams of five networks jostled. Anne and Mark broke loose from the crowd and ran.

The sun was shining, the sky was a benevolent blue. The afternoon air was choked with exhaust, but to Anne it had the clean smell of freedom.

Mark's green Mercedes was double-parked in a no-parking stretch of Centre Street. He gunned the motor and the car was already in motion as she dropped into the seat. Soft beige leather cushioned her fall.

Mark angled up Centre and turned right on Canal, smack into the middle of a honking traffic jam. Pedestrians and pushcarts clogged the sidewalks.

Anne felt energy rippling out from the brawling, sprawling world of Chinese superettes and electronic hot shops and vendors and discount stores. It was fall. The season when the city geared up. New York was loud and bright and brash again.

"Have you heard anything from Kyra or Toby?"

Mark shook his head. "Not a thing."

"What if the Coreyites have them both?"

"Now that Corey's dead, there's no reason to harm them. The Coreyites aren't about to complicate their legal problems with another pair of murders."

"I wish I had your optimism."

"Not optimism—cynicism." Mark patted her knee. It was an oddly unthinking movement, as though they had been touching one another for years. "Now, where can I give you a lift to?"

"I'd love a nice long stop at my bathtub."

He swung a sharp left onto Bowery. "Coming up."

As they turned onto Anne's block they could see two blue-and-white squad cars and an NYPD Emergency Service van nose-to-nose in front of her building.

Mark braked.

A group of uniformed officers had taken over the lobby. Anxious clusters of tenants milled. A redheaded sergeant told Anne and Mark he was sorry, but for the moment there was no traffic in or out of the building.

Anne felt the pressure of Mark's finger on her elbow. A signal. *Let me handle this.*

"Mrs. Bingham lives in eleven-E, and I'm her lawyer. My client needs to get into her apartment."

For an instant of charged silence the sergeant stared at Anne. "Mrs. Anne Bingham?" As though there was something in that name that made her a celebrity; or a freak. "You can go right up, ma'am."

The sergeant cleared their way to the elevator. Anne could feel tenants' eyes on her, resentful, wondering how she rated privileged treatment. They rode up in silence. Mark's eyes were calm and she tried to feel calm in the hold of his gaze.

The elevator opened at eleven. Their steps were soundless on the gray carpeting. She took out her key. Her hand stopped at the sound of men's voices on the other side of the door.

She caught Mark's warning glance. He gave the door a push and it swung inward.

There was only a split second to glimpse the figure crouched in the living room, holding a flash camera. An explosion of light blinded her.

As the afterimage cleared, she saw a uniformed woman officer standing with a steno pad in her hands.

"I'm Mrs. Bingham's attorney," Mark said. "What are these people doing in my client's home?"

The policewoman looked at Anne carefully, as if searching for a typo in a line of fine print. "Would you come this way, please."

They followed her into the living room. A man wearing plastic surgical gloves was scattering crystals from a blue glass jar. The air had a heavy smell of artificial violets, masking a heavier, more disturbing smell. A lamp had been knocked over and boxes and plants had been spilled. A long black bag shaped like a sofa bolster lay in the center of the room.

A dozen men and women were crouching, crawling, measuring, marking, dusting, photographing. The policewoman led Anne and Mark around the outskirts of activity.

"Lieutenant," she said, "the owner of the apartment is here."

Anne recognized the police detective who had rescued her from the picketer and testified at the trial.

"*You're* Anne Bingham?" His expression was startled, almost incredulous.

"Yes, I am."

"I'm Lieutenant Vince Cardozo, Twenty-second Precinct." He kept staring at her. "Tell me, Mrs. Bingham—when were you last in this apartment?"

"Wednesday morning last week."

"Lieutenant," Mark interrupted. "I'm Mrs. Bingham's attorney. Could I ask what's happening here?"

"A neighbor reported smelling a gas leak in this apartment. Mrs. Bingham couldn't be contacted. Con Ed came in and found a dead woman in the bathtub."

At that moment Anne had a helium balloon for a heart.

"I wonder if Mrs. Bingham would be willing to identify her?"

Mark took Anne's left hand, protecting her. Her right hand went to her neck and touched Kyra's locket.

The detective crouched by the black bag. She could see the curves of a body. A zipper squeaked.

She stared down into lifeless green eyes. Recognition hit like a boot in the skull. "My God—Kyra—no! Oh, my God—my God!"

Cardozo spoke gently. "I'm very sorry."

Mark slipped his arms around her and held her close.

"The man who kidnapped Toby," Cardozo said, "had a letter. Kyra Talbot wrote that letter on stationery from this apartment. Which makes him the prime suspect in her murder. If you don't mind, Mrs. Bingham, I'm afraid I have to ask you a few questions."

"You're not going to ask Mrs. Bingham anything now." Mark spoke in flat refusal mode. "She's in no condition." He pressed a glass of water into her hand. "Take some. You'll feel better."

She sipped. His hand helped the glass up. A finger of fire stung her throat. It was brandy, not water. She pushed the glass away. "I'm fine. I'm all right."

She burst into body-racking sobs.

"Vince?" Tess diAngeli on the line now, something skittery in her voice. "You were right. They conned me."

Cardozo had to put a finger to one ear to shut out all the crime-scene ruckus. "What? Who? How?"

"In exchange for testimony, the Justice Department promised Mickey no prosecution for *any* previous crimes—and *no surveillance.*"

Cardozo's stomach felt as if he were trapped in a free-falling elevator. "Then what about those guards?"

"They lied to me. They were running passive surveillance. Mickey phoned in three times a day." In a tired voice, she reeled off the flat details. "It was a ruse to pacify me and a few other New York types who worried about Mickey being a danger to society. Vince—you were right and I was wrong and I'm sorry."

"I'm sorry too." Cardozo's tone held no criticism; he himself had been burned in more than one Justice Department power play. But this was obviously Tess's maiden voyage. "Don't brood and don't take it personally. It's not the first double-cross they've pulled. It certainly won't be the last."

As he hung up the receiver, Greg Monteleone shoved his way into the apartment. "Hey, Vince, what the hell's wrong with Bingham's phone? I've been trying to call you for half an hour."

"There weren't any rings here."

"Sometimes the line was busy, and sometimes I got a recorded Ding-a-ling spiel and a dozen beeps."

Cardozo glanced down at the phone and realized what had happened. "The machine's set to pick up, but the answering tape's full. Why didn't you beep me?"

"I did."

Cardozo pulled the pager off his belt and saw he'd forgotten to reset it after Tess's beep. "My fault. What's up?"

"More activity on Catch Talbot's MasterCard. The Organic Gourmet in Scotsville just attempted to post a charge."

Cardozo lifted the receiver and jiggled the cradle till Nynex finally yielded up a tone. He dialed northern

New Jersey information and asked for the Organic Gourmet in Scotsville.

"Organic Gourmet, may I help you?"

Cardozo identified himself. "I understand you just posted an order from Catch Talbot?"

"Last Saturday, the twenty-first, Mr. Talbot placed an order for organic venison. It came in today, and now we learn that he's stopped his card."

"Was that order a delivery?"

"Yes, it was—72 Turkey Lane, Scotsville. Is this man a criminal?"

"A criminal's been using his card."

"Who's going to pay for the venison?"

"It'll be taken care of." Cardozo broke the connection and dialed Bill Benton at the Scotsville precinct. They had a thirty-second discussion. As he hung up the receiver, he realized Mark Wells was blocking his way.

"Did I hear you just mention Toby Talbot?"

"That's right."

"Mrs. Bingham and I are coming with you."

Cardozo shook his head. "Mrs. Bingham's had a severe shock. You yourself said—"

"Lieutenant," Anne Bingham interrupted. "I've just lost a sister. That leaves me two living relatives left in the world—my father and my nephew. I'm coming with you."

FORTY-TWO

2:55 P.M.

The stenciled letters on the mailbox spelled *72 Turkey Lane, Sanderson.* Cardozo slowed the car, reached through the driver's window, and opened the mailbox.

"The Sandersons have been renting through an agent," Bill Benton said. "The name on the lease is Talbot. He signed Monday the sixteenth—paid cash."

"Figures." Cardozo pulled out an ad for a rug-shampooing service, addressed to occupant. He put the flyer back and eased the car into low gear. The driveway needed weeding. The shrubs on either side needed cutting back. They rounded a bend, and there was the house—your basic two-story suburban white clapboard box. Strategically placed green trim and shutters gave an impression of asymmetry.

Cardozo pulled to a stop. He got out and crossed the unmowed lawn. There was a flicker in one of the ground-story windows, and then another in one of the dormers. A shadow approached them in the panes of the door.

"There's someone home," Bill Benton said.

"He's covered the windows in Mylar." Cardozo pressed the doorbell. "It's a reflection."

Something electronic went dingdong inside the house.

They waited. No footsteps, no dog barking.

Cardozo could sense Benton's nervousness about trespassing. But they weren't trespassing—yet. It could be an honest mistake, turning into the wrong drive, asking for directions.

He dingdonged again. Silence.

He slipped on a pair of plastic gloves and tried the door handle. Locked.

He walked to the side of the house, shaded his eyes, and peered through the garage window. "No car. Guess no one's home."

He went back to the house and hunkered down by a rear cellar window.

"No Mylar," Benton observed.

"From this point on, we're in violation." Cardozo unhooked the flashlight from his belt and rapped the glass sharply with the battery end. The pane shattered.

There was no alarm.

He lifted out the shards. The window was double-hung and there was a second pane of insulating glass. He reached past the weather stripping and rapped again with the flashlight. Glass tinkled to the cellar floor.

He cleared the shards, reached inside, and released the latch. He lifted the window, then lowered himself in feetfirst. "Be right back."

His feet touched down on concrete. He snapped the flashlight on. The beam swung past the furnace and waer heater to a steep, narrow stairway. Wooden steps reaked beneath him.

The Mylar certainly worked. Not a ray of light came hrough the first-story windows. The flashlight picked out Audubon prints on the hallway wall. The beam ound a switch on the wall. He clicked it. A light came on.

To the right of the hallway was a small living room vith old-fashioned sofas and armchairs in heavy brocade. The tables were laden with beaded lamps, statuettes, marble eggs—each one upright on its own wooden stand.

He went to the front door and slipped the two leadbolts. Mark Wells's Mercedes had pulled up in the drive and Wells and Bingham were hurrying across the awn. He waved them inside.

"Don't touch anything," Benton reminded them.

Cardozo led the way up a groaning flight of stairs to the second floor. He opened a door. A narrow bed was tucked into the dormer. A beat-up–looking computer game cassette had been tossed onto the thin white bedspread.

He picked it up. *Spider Man Scrabble.*

"One of Toby's favorite video games," Anne Bingham said.

Cardozo lifted the bedspread. "Bed's been slept in."

He led the way through a tiled bathroom into a room with a canopied double bed, chaise longue, huge Trinitron TV. The spread had been pulled over the bed without being straightened.

"A man's been keeping house," Anne Bingham said.

Cardozo studied the answering machine on the bedside table. He pressed the *replay* button. There were clicks, whirs, a beep. And no message.

He pressed the outgoing message button.

"You have reached area code 201-555-6789." The woman's voice had a vaguely Germanic accent. "No one is home at present, but if you wish to leave a message at the sound of the beep, your call will be returned."

Beep.

"That's Juliana," Anne Bingham said. "Kyra's au pair."

Anne took a left turn into the kitchen. At the flick of a wall switch a fluorescent ring sputtered and lit. The dishwasher had been left open. It held dinner service for three, caked with food particles.

Ripping a paper towel from the roll over the sink, she crossed to the fridge, gripped the handle with the towel, and opened it. The shelves held vitamins, mustard, yogurt, celery, bottled water.

As she was closing the door, she dislodged a magnet. A half-dozen pieces of paper glided like a flock of butterflies to the linoleum. She stooped and collected them. They were mostly receipts, but one was a note: *If you come back, we need some rug deodorizer, can buy it myself or you can get it—let me know—tel # 212-555-3037.* The seven was crossed, in the European manner, and the note was signed *Juliana.*

"Lieutenant Cardozo," she called.

Cardozo lifted the kitchen phone and tapped in the New York area code and the number. He held the earpiece so Anne could hear.

There were three rings and then a pickup. "Condom Nation, Henk speaking." The man spoke the flawless and slightly aristocratic English that they teach nowhere but in the state-funded grade schools of northern Europe. "May I help you?"

"May I speak with Juliana, please?"

"Juliana's not here, but I can take a message for her."

"Is there any way I could reach her?"

"You can leave a message."

"Would you tell her that Catch called—and I have the rug shampoo she wanted?"

"*Rug* shampoo? What is that, code?"

"Just tell her it's rug shampoo. She'll understand."

"Okay. I could tell her that. And how could she contact you, Catch?"

"I'll be downtown today—I could bring it by your store and maybe you could give it to her."

"I could do that."

"What's your address again?"

The sparkling showcases of the little store on Bleecker Street displayed hundreds of candy-colored designer condoms. Cardozo waited while a customer tried to make up her mind. She had narrowed her options to a salmon mousse–tinted sheath with spearmint-green stripes and a straightforward black latex model.

"Or if you're in the mood for something minimalist . . ." The clerk brought out a jeweler's tray of what seemed to be shower caps for elves. "These require an acetyline adhesive, which we sell." A tall man with a wedge-shape face, he wore a tricolor ponytail and granny glasses with tinted rose lenses. "The adhesive comes in cinnamon, lemon, and hot ginger." He winked. "I wouldn't recommend hot ginger for beginners."

The woman turned to stare at a shelf of polka-dot dental dams. "Do you ship to Australia?"

"We ship anywhere in the world. Why don't you take a moment and think about it?" The clerk turned his tanned face toward Cardozo. "Yes, sir?"

"I have a package for Juliana. I phoned."

"Oh, yes. I'm Henk." The clerk glided to the end of the counter. He lowered his voice. "Are you sure Juliana is expecting this?"

"She certainly is." Cardozo slid the package across the countertop. "Urgent."

Henk looked at his Mickey Mouse watch. "I'll see she gets it within the hour."

"Tall guy with granny glasses," Cardozo said, "and a red-white-and-blue ponytail. Said he'd deliver it within an hour."

Anne glanced at her watch. It was seven-fifteen and the evening light had faded on the windows of Bleecker Street's boutiques.

The waitress brought their cappuccinos.

"Have you got a phone?" Cardozo asked.

"There's one in back."

"Excuse me." He pushed himself up from the table. "Have to check my messages."

Anne ripped open a packet of sugar and stirred it into her coffee.

"No granny glasses . . ." Mark's head tipped up and nodded. "But that's got to be him."

Anne glanced out the window. Across the street, a tall man with a red-white-and-blue ponytail and a grim face was stepping out of the doorway of Condom Nation. He wore jeans with prefab rips and a maroon *Annie Get*

Your Gun national tour T-shirt, and he was carrying the wrapped package of rug cleaner tucked under his left arm.

Anne felt cheated. After a week of courthouse and hotel coffee, she had been looking forward to her cappuccino. "You said an hour."

"Lieutenant Cardozo said an hour."

The man looked west through traffic stalled along Bleecker. He grimaced and began walking briskly east.

Anne gulped a mouthful of coffee and grabbed her purse. "I'm going to follow him. You wait for Cardozo. I'll contact you at your place." She was up in a single bound, hurrying onto the sidewalk.

The ponytail was already half a block ahead of her, bobbing above a sea of pedestrians. It turned left on 10th Street.

She reached Seventh Avenue just in time to see it duck into a taxicab.

Anne's hand went up. "Taxi!"

It was one minute after seven-thirty when Anne's taxi braked to a stop on East 59th Street, under the grimy shadow of the Queensboro Bridge. She caught a glimpse of the ponytail bobbing into the service entrance of a restaurant called Hot Sushi. She thrust a twenty at the driver and didn't wait for change.

A sumo wrestler in a chef's hat stopped her at the door. She pointed beyond him at the ponytail cantering past a row of steaming vats and woks. "I'm with him."

He let her pass.

The kitchen was drenched in smells of ginger and garlic and curry. Juliana stood with a stack of bowls at the salad bar, frowning at a four-ounce container of I Love My Carpet potpourri-scented rug cleaner.

"That's a present from me," Anne said.

Juliana's eyes came around, startled. "I don't get it."

Anne opened her purse and took out the note from the refrigerator. "What does this message mean?"

Juliana slipped on a pair of glasses. "It means exactly what it says. I was working for Catch Talbot."

"How did that happen?"

"That doesn't concern you."

"You're working without a green card. I could phone Immigration."

Juliana motioned Anne to follow her into a murky storage room. She closed the door. "Catch phoned last week and asked to meet in a coffee shop. He offered me three thousand dollars to leave Kyra and bring Toby to him after school last Friday. But Kyra fired me and told the school I wasn't to pick Toby up, so Catch had to pick him up himself."

"And how did Catch manage that?"

"I have no idea. But when I phoned, he asked me to act as a transitional nanny until he got Toby out of the country."

"Can you describe him?"

Juliana described him. Ultra crew-cut hair. Stocky build. Brown eyes.

"That wasn't Toby's father. Catch has blue eyes."

"How was I supposed to know? I'd never met him before. Kyra never had photos of him. Besides, he showed me plenty of I.D.—with photos."

"But you knew Kyra had custody."

"No one's ever shown *me* any custody papers. And you may not be aware of it, but Kyra's a pretty casual mother. I told Catch if it meant a decent home for

Toby—I'd be glad to help. But I wouldn't do anything illegal. Catch said it was only going to be for four days. Till the passports came."

"He was planning to take Toby out of the country?"

"Look, I love that kid like my own little brother, but I can't get mixed up in this."

"But you *are* mixed up in it, Juliana."

"All he told me was—plans had changed—he wouldn't be needing me. He gave me a hundred dollars and that was that."

"Back up a moment. When did you last see Toby?"

Juliana screwed up her face, remembering. "Sunday. He was getting antsy. He was tired of reading and tired of his games; and he and his dad weren't getting along."

"Don't call that man his dad. He isn't."

Juliana shrugged. "Toby was playing with his modem—he was calling your computer. But Catch said they had to go to the supermarket. Four hours later Catch came back in a taxi, alone."

"Did he say where Toby was?"

"He wasn't making sense. He seemed disoriented—he was saying stupid stuff."

"Stupid stuff like what?"

"He said Toby talked back to him and he had to hand him over to the authorities."

"What authorities?"

"I don't know." Juliana began crying. "Catch was screaming and there was blood on his clothes. He asked me to phone a doctor to come pick him up."

"What doctor?"

"He had a name like a bottle of gin." She sniffled and blotted her eyes with the back of her hand. "Gordon something."

"Can you describe him?"

"He was driving a terrific Porsche 928. The license plate spelled *Bullion.*"

"Where's Catch now?"

"I don't know. He never contacted me. After two days I said to hell with this."

"So you just left a note on the refrigerator and walked away from it?"

"I'm not a legal resident. I can't save the world."

There was a knock on the door. A man with an angry face peered in. "Juliana—table eighteen."

"Excuse me. I have a living to earn."

FORTY-THREE

8:30 P.M.

They met at a quiet little Szechuan restaurant on Third Avenue.

"A doctor came in a Porsche and picked him up." Anne sipped at a bowl of clear vegetable broth. She had butterflies in her stomach and she knew she couldn't keep down anything heavier. "The doctor's name sounded like a bottle of gin."

"Gilbey's?" Mark suggested.

"Or Gordon's?" Cardozo said.

"Gordon. That was it."

Cardozo's chopsticks, clasping a ginger scallop, stopped in midair. "Gordon Gibbs?"

"Juliana didn't remember the last name."

"Gibbs does sound kind of like Gilbey's," Mark said. "Who is he?"

"Runs a clinic," Cardozo said. "He's a specialist in spleen viruses. And chairman of a self-help group for divorced fathers. Thursday the nineteenth, while Catch

Talbot was in Seattle, he had dinner in the Oak Room with a man *calling* himself Catch Talbot. The man claimed to need moral support in a custody battle with his ex-wife."

Mark spooned pork fried rice onto his cashew chicken. "You know what amazes me? How come the false Catch knows so damned much about the real Catch?"

"He could have got hold of the voir dire. Kyra gave the court a pretty complete rundown of her life and problems."

"Dotson Elihu mentioned something strange in court," Anne recalled. "He said the feds were hiding Mickey Williams in a clinic."

Cardozo glanced at her. "Which clinic?"

"DiAngeli objected before he could say."

"Gibbs runs a clinic."

"Hold it." Mark raised a hand. "If Gibbs is hiding a man who's killed three people, he's not going to talk to the police—not voluntarily."

"How do you figure three?" Anne said. "Kyra and the policewoman and who else?"

"Toby."

"No one's found his body," she stated flatly.

"But according to Juliana—"

She cut him off. "According to Juliana there was blood on a man's clothing. Period. We don't even know if the blood was Toby's. And we know Toby escaped from the Scottsboro station house."

"And no one's seen him since."

Anger flared in her. *"Toby is alive."*

"Okay. He's alive and Dr. Gibbs is going to hand over the fake Catch and the fake Catch is going to hand over Toby." Mark reached into his jacket and pulled out his cellular phone. "Be my guest."

"Mark has a point," Cardozo said. "Gibbs isn't going to want to talk to the police."

"Then he'll talk to me." Anne grabbed the phone and tapped in the code for directory assistance. "Do you have a number listed for a Dr. Gordon Gibbs?"

"We show a Gordon Gibbs, M.D., on East Sixty-second."

She glanced at her watch. It was almost nine o'clock—well past any Manhattan M.D.'s office hours—but most doctors were in touch with their answering services in case of emergency. She pressed disconnect and tapped Gibbs's number into the keypad. She waited through eight interminably sluggish rings.

"Doctor's office." The voice was female and curt.

"Dr. Gibbs, please."

"The doctor's office hours are Tuesday and Thursday, ten to four."

"This is an emergency."

"Your name and number, please?"

"Anne Bingham." She read the number off the headset.

"Are you a patient?"

"The doctor treats my family. Tell him I'm Toby Talbot's aunt."

Eight minutes later the phone rang.

"Ms. Bingham?" The voice was male and jocular and ever so slightly harried. "Gordon Gibbs. What's the emergency?"

"The emergency is my eleven-year-old nephew, Toby Talbot."

No reaction.

"Doctor, I want to find my nephew and I believe you can help me."

"How did you get my name?"

"From Lieutenant Vincent Cardozo of the New York City police."

"You said Toby Talbot?"

"Toby. As in Catch Talbot. As in Mickey Williams."

"I'm on my cellular phone and this is a rotten connection. Could you meet me in my office in fifteen minutes?"

Even at nine-thirty in the evening, dozens of people hurried through the marbled lobby of the granite building on 62nd Street and Second Avenue. Footsteps clattered across black and white checkerboard tile.

The night guard at the security desk stopped them and Anne explained that Dr. Gordon Gibbs was expecting them.

"Third floor." He motioned toward the first bank of elevators.

The directory on the third floor pointed them left, down a long gray corridor. A tall, full-faced man with a neatly trimmed white beard stood in the doorway of a consulting room. He was wearing yellow jogging shoes and green nylon warm-ups and a *Crain's Business News* sweatshirt. "Ms. Bingham?"

"Dr. Gibbs?" She introduced Mark. "My lawyer." And Cardozo. "And Lieutenant Vince Cardozo of the New York police."

"I keep running into you, Lieutenant." Dr. Gibbs held out a hand. "Won't you please come in."

Gibbs was one of those New York professionals who

had it all—the leather-and-mahogany office, the signed Jasper Johns lithos, the Harvard Med and Johns Hopkins diplomas on the wall.

They sat in brass-studded armchairs.

"We should get a few things straight." Gibbs had a voice that went fluty under pressure, like an adolescent's. It clashed with his heavy build and beard. "I specialize in viral diseases of the spleen. I'm chiefly a researcher. I don't discuss my patients, but I can tell you without violating medical ethics that I have never had any patients by the name of Catch Talbot or Mickey Williams. In fact, my patients are all women." He smiled a friendly smile, sorry to disappoint. But his fingertips were jittering on the armrest like strung-out junkies. "I've heard the name Toby Talbot, but contrary to your beliefs, I have no idea where he is."

Cardozo wasn't buying the smile. Or anything else. "Where did you hear Toby Talbot's name?"

"I've told you all this before."

"My friends haven't heard."

"I'm president of the New York chapter of P-Wok—Pops Without Kids. When Catch—when Mr. Talbot came to town he gave me a call. We had dinner. He believed his ex-wife had a scheme to seize sole custody at the next hearing. He was furious with her."

"Furious enough to want to harm her?"

"There's no way I can make that judgment."

"Tell me, Doctor. What sort of assistance were you giving the man you call Catch Talbot?"

"I've given him no assistance." Gibbs's eyes, glaring above his half-moon glasses, met Cardozo's unwaveringly. As though the ability to stare a cop in the face was proof of candor.

"In case your friend hasn't told you yet—he's using the real Catch Talbot's name and credit cards. Felony if he's charged over five thousand. He's murdered one of my policewomen. Felony. He's murdered the real Catch Talbot's ex-wife. Felony. And he's kidnapped Toby Talbot. Felony."

"I'm very sorry to hear it. But he's not my patient, so how does any of that involve me?"

"He's been using you to divert suspicion to the real Catch Talbot. Which means, like it or not, you're very much involved."

"As an accessory," Mark Wells said. "And since you say he's not a patient, I'd be very surprised if the law would consider medical ethics a defense."

"In that case . . ." The doctor stood up. "I have a right to speak to a lawyer."

"You're speaking to one." Mark Wells smiled. "Me."

"Now, look here—either you people leave my office right now, or I call *my* lawyer."

"I'd like to speak to your lawyer," Cardozo said.

Behind Gibbs, a grandfather clock ticked sonorously, unhurriedly.

Gibbs crumpled back into the chair. "Look—can't we straighten this out amicably? Can't you people see I know nothing about this man or his crimes?"

"Then why did you return my call?" Anne said. "And agree to meet me?"

"I was only trying to be helpful to a lady who sounded confused and distressed."

"Try a little harder," Cardozo suggested, "and you might wind up helping yourself."

"All right." Gibbs exhaled a surrendering sigh. "Here's the situation. Four or five days after our dinner

. . . Mr. Talbot was having emotional trouble. He contacted me."

"And?"

Gibbs studied Cardozo with calibrating eyes. "I came to realize he had obsessive resentments—but I swear I had no idea he was capable of acting on them violently."

"It's a crime," Cardozo reminded the doctor, "to withhold information in a murder investigation."

"Can't you grasp the fact that I *have* no information? Catch—or whatever his name is—never confided in me. He's not my patient." Gibbs's eyes dropped. "He's being treated by Dr. Lederer."

"And who's Dr. Lederer?"

It was a long moment before Gibbs answered. "Hillary Lederer, one of our best psychiatrists. He and Catch had a few consultations. I arranged for Catch to move into one of the spare rooms upstairs. I had no idea he was even suspected of a felony. I had no intention of abetting any crime."

"And is he upstairs now?" Cardozo asked.

"There's one way to find out." Gibbs reached across the desk for the phone.

"Let's save the phone call," Cardozo suggested, "and surprise him."

Dr. Gordon Gibbs rapped on the gray door at the end of the seventh-story corridor. "Catch—are you there?"

No one answered. He rapped louder.

And still no answer.

"Why don't you just let us in?" Cardozo suggested.

"Look, I want to be helpful, but I'm not sure I have the right."

"Under New York State law," Mark Wells assured him, "you have the right."

Gibbs searched his key chain. "I'm not sure I have the passkey."

Cardozo pointed to the Medeco skeleton key. "That one should do the trick."

With fumbling hands, Gibbs tried the key. It turned. The door opened on darkness. A faint scent of soap drifted out.

"Catch? It's just me—Gordon Gibbs." He flicked the electric switch. Light came up on a comfortable room with mocha walls and bleached-pine furniture. And no occupant.

Cardozo's eye inventoried: two walls of bookshelves. A daybed with leather bolsters. A 1950s Danish-modern desk with a phone and answering machine. A five-spring cable exerciser lay across the back of a chair; two twenty-four-pound dumbbells sat on the floor.

"Mr. Talbot seems to travel with a small gym."

"He says he enjoys working out," Gibbs said.

Cardozo crossed to the closet. Empty. The bathroom. A toothbrush and a Trac-II razor sitting in a Hilton Hotel tumbler.

"Don't you have to show me a search warrant?" Gibbs said.

"Not so long as you consent." Cardozo drew back the green metal swivel chair and sat at the desk. He slipped on a pair of evidence gloves and tried the drawer. Locked. "Do you have a key to the desk?"

"I do not."

Cardozo took out his penknife, snapped the lock, and pulled the drawer open. Inside were two leather cases, a man's medium-length brown wig, a simple clip-on gold earring, and a contact lens kit. The kit contained a pair of dark brown soft plastic lenses floating in clear solution.

The smaller leather case held a hypodermic syringe and eight replacement needles. The larger contained nineteen glass ampoules of a clear liquid. Cardozo held one up to read the label: *Somanabol (somatotropin) Human Growth Hormone (Synthesized).* "Tell me, Doctor, is this the anabolic steroid you refused to get for him?"

Gibbs stiffened. "I have no idea where he got that."

"How long would he have to inject this stuff before it altered his behavior?"

"If he injected two of those a day for eight weeks, you'd see some problems with rage."

"And violence?"

Gibbs nodded.

Cardozo turned his attention to the answering machine. A zero glowed solid in the read-out window, indicating there'd been no messages. He pressed *replay* just in case an old message hadn't been erased.

There was a click followed by silence.

He raised the lid and saw that the incoming message tape had been removed. But not the outgoing. He punched the *test-outgoing-message* button. The tape whirred past the sound head, blank.

But in a moment a rapid series of electronic blips sounded and then a second phone was ringing.

"He's forwarding his calls automatically." After eight rings, it was clear no one was going to pick up. Cardozo took out his notebook and jotted down the number on the telephone. "When did you last see the man you call Catch Talbot?"

"I don't recall," Gibbs said. "He can come and go as he likes. He's not a prisoner."

"Not yet."

Riding down in the elevator, Mark adjusted a necktie that needed no adjusting. "At least we've established one thing. He's not hiding Toby in his room."

"Then where has he put him?" Anne said.

"I'll contact the phone company," Cardozo said. "They'll trace where he's forwarding his calls. In the meantime, I wouldn't worry. Toby was a negotiating chip for the trial. There's no reason to harm him now."

Anne couldn't be that calm about it. "There was no reason to kill Kyra either, was there?"

"He couldn't risk leaving her alive after he had the note. She would have phoned the school. Killing her was a rational choice."

"He's *not* rational." Anne shook her head. "Juliana said he was a madman. She said he and Toby were fighting."

"Over what?"

She tried to recall Juliana's exact words. "She said Toby was playing with his modem and going stir-crazy, and—" She broke off.

"And what?" Cardozo said.

"She said Toby left a message on my computer."

The police had placed a strip of yellow crime-scene tape over the lock and across the crack between the door and door frame. Using the edge of his MasterCard, Cardozo cut through the tape and pulled it off the lock.

Anne took out her key. "Why do I feel like a housebreaker?"

Cardozo rolled the tape into a tight yellow ball. "It's your own home. Go on."

She turned the key. The door swung inward. She

flicked the light switch. As she crossed the room, her leg struck a stool that had no business being there. Pain jolted a nerve in her knee.

She sat down at the worktable. The surface had a changed, scattered feel. The cup of markers and the paper cutters and the ruler all lay in wrong places.

"Your people have been searching. Don't they need a warrant?"

Cardozo shook his head. "Not at a crime scene."

My home—a crime scene. Kyra's dead.

An image of Kyra flashed through her mind—a serious, curly-haired girl four years of age serving tea to her dolls. Miniature steel cups, real tea, real cookies broken into quarters. And she'd refused to invite Anne to the party.

She pushed the thought away and booted the computer. It kicked into life, sending out a humming beat like an overadrenalized heart. An amber glow came up on the monitor.

Her fingers positioned themselves over the keyboard and typed in the command to retrieve electronic mail. She hit a wrong key. The computer gave an electronic yelp. She canceled and tried again.

A message came up.

Sunday, September 22. Hi, Aunt Anne! Could you do me a favor and be sure Mom knows I'm okay? Sorry I can't say more. Thanks. Love, Toby.

And that was all.

She could feel Mark leaning close, his breath warm on her neck. "Does that blinking line mean there's more?"

"You're right." She entered the command to go to the next e-mail. A second message came up. Her eye dove to the signature. *Love, Toby.* Then back to the date: *Tuesday, September 24.* "Toby's alive!"

"He was alive Tuesday," Mark corrected.

"Don't," she said. "Don't be a lawyer."

Hi, Aunt Anne! I'm at Grandpa's—lots of adventures—a real horror movie. Remember to ask me about my night in jail. Where's Mom? Haven't been able to get hold of her. Please tell her I'm okay and give me a ring when you get in.

She grabbed the phone and dialed Leon's number. Four rings. And then Tim Alvarez's voice: "Brandsetter residence."

"Tim—it's Anne."

"Well, hello."

"Is Toby there?"

"Since Monday. He's probably asleep now, but if you want to talk to him—"

"No. Let him sleep. I just wanted to be sure he's okay."

"Very much okay. He's having the time of his life playing Robinson Crusoe in the cabin. We tried to phone you, but something's wrong with your answering machine. It does a lot of beeping and hangs up."

"I forgot to rewind the tape."

"You should come on up. Anytime. We'll all be here."

"I'll be up as soon as I can." She laid the receiver back in the cradle. It was the first time in seven days that she'd been able to draw a full breath. "Toby's there and he's all right."

"Thank God," Mark said.

"I want to talk to that boy," Cardozo said. "Tonight."

FORTY-FOUR

11:10 P.M.

After six pushes on the buzzer, something flashed behind the darkened bubble-glass window and Tim Alvarez opened the front door.

"Anne." He was wearing a crimson Harvard sweatshirt. When Anne introduced Mark and Lieutenant Cardozo, his face registered surprise, quickly covered. "What a great treat for your dad—he loves unexpected visitors." He led them into the house. "Leon's relaxing with his hot milk. He thinks it helps him sleep. The doctor says it doesn't do him any harm."

Leon was in the study, watching a *Court TV* rerun. Toby was sitting on the sofa beside him, pushing keys on a laptop computer.

"Aunt Anne!" Toby bounded up. "Did you get my message?"

"I got them both. And I was so happy. And so relieved." Anne hugged him and whirled him around.

"But I thought you were in bed. Isn't it late for you to be up?"

"Stop being a mother," Leon said. "You're his aunt. Aunts are supposed to be fun."

Anne deposited a kiss on her father's forehead. "You remember Mark Wells."

"Sure I remember Mark—your old beau." Leon held out a hand, half-rising. "The stockbroker, right?"

"I'm afraid I'm just a lawyer, sir."

"Glad you're back in her life, Mark."

"Mark gave Lieutenant Cardozo and me a lift." Anne turned to make the introduction. "Leon, this is Lieutenant Vincent Cardozo, from our local precinct in New York."

Leon tilted his head. "I take it you're Annie's police protection?"

"Come on, Leon, I don't need police protection."

"Oh, no? Haven't you been watching the evening news?"

"No. What's happened?"

"Norton Stanley announced that you're going to write a tell-all about sneaking onto that jury. When Judge Bernheim heard that, she went on the warpath and revoked your bail. She's been phoning all night, asking if I've seen you."

"Lord, does that make me a fugitive?"

Leon shrugged. "Don't worry, I'm not going to squeal. I've had it with Gina." His eyes came around to Cardozo. "What about you, Lieutenant? Are you planning to arrest my little girl?"

"No, sir."

"Then you're kind of far from your beat, aren't you? What brings you all this way?"

"The lieutenant would like to ask Toby some questions," Anne said.

"Don't tell me this renegade has been breaking laws too." Leon's eyes glowed. He tousled Toby's hair. "That makes three generations of us felons under one roof."

"Why don't we go to the living room," Anne suggested, "so Leon can watch his show."

Anne hung back in the corridor with Lieutenant Cardozo. "Toby doesn't know his mother is dead. I don't want you to be the one to tell him."

Cardozo nodded. His eyes were grave. "I understand."

In the living room, Toby was jabbing a poker at the birch logs smoldering in the fireplace.

Cardozo squatted beside him. "When did you last see your mother?"

"Saturday morning."

"Where was that?"

"Aunt Anne's. We spent the night there."

"Why did you spend the night in your aunt's apartment?"

"Mom said we had to water the plants."

"Did your mom have any plans to take you on a trip last weekend?"

Toby shook his head.

"Toby—are you sure?"

"Are you going to tell Mom?"

"No."

"Well . . . she was planning a trip—but she made me swear not to tell anyone."

"Do you have any idea why she sent a stranger to Mademoiselle with a note?"

Toby was silent, wounded. "I guess something came up and she wasn't able to pick me up herself."

"Did you know the man she sent?"

"He was a stranger," Toby said quietly, resentfully.

"Do you have any idea how your mom happened to know him?"

Toby looked down at the floor. "Mom knows a lot of people."

"Toby, do you remember a policewoman who spoke to you a week ago last Wednesday at school?"

"Sure I remember."

"What did she speak to you about?"

"There was a man in a car. Watching the kids. Taking photographs. She wanted to know if I'd ever seen him before."

"And had you?"

"I told her I hadn't."

"Did you see the policewoman talk to him?"

Toby reflected for a moment. "I saw her go over to the car. I guess she was talking to him—but I couldn't exactly see."

"Did she leave with him?"

"I didn't see."

"Was it the same man who picked you up from school last Saturday?"

Toby hesitated. Almost shrewdly. "Did something happen to that policewoman?"

Cardozo glanced at Anne. "Someone hurt her."

"How badly?"

"Very badly."

Toby was silent a moment. "It was the same man."

Cardozo handed Toby the photograph from Britta's wallet. "Is this him?"

Toby frowned. "The hair's different. I can't be sure."

Cardozo showed him the sketch. "And this man?"

"Kind of, I guess."

"Did he tell you his name?"

"He told me to call him Dad."

"But you knew he wasn't your dad. Why did you go with him?"

"He showed Mademoiselle a note from Mom." Toby shrugged. "I figured, Mom wants me to go with him. He must be going to marry her. Maybe they've already married."

"Did your mother ever tell you she was planning to remarry?"

"She mentioned it sometimes. And last weekend I knew she was planning something secret and important."

"Did the man offer you anything? Promise you anything? Threaten you?"

"He said we'd go hiking. And then he took me to an old house in New Jersey with the windows covered up."

"Did he do anything to you? Hurt you?"

"Not till Sunday."

"What happened Sunday?"

"We had a fight. The cops took us in. They kept me overnight and I ran away Monday."

"Where's the man now?"

"I don't know."

"How would you feel about sheltering a fugitive from justice?" Anne said. "Can I stay up in the cabin?"

Leon's eyes went to Lieutenant Cardozo. "What's the point hiding up there if your lieutenant friend knows?"

"He says he's not going to tell."

"Is that the truth, Lieutenant? You're not going to spill the beans on my little girl?"

Cardozo shook his head. "Federal problems aren't my province, sir."

"The lieutenant strikes me as an honorable man. Sure, if you don't mind sharing with Toby, you can have the cabin." Leon stretched out his left leg and pulled up his trouser cuff. A three-inch steel band had been locked above his ankle. "With this gizmo on my leg, God knows I'm not using the place anymore."

Cardozo took a startled step forward. "Is that a transmitter?"

"They claim it's a transmitter. For all I know it's just another piece of overpriced Gulf War scrap."

Toby chose that moment to pipe up. "It has a two-mile range. It broadcasts down to the police station."

Cardozo frowned. "You're under house arrest?"

"House-and-garden arrest." Leon smiled. "It's part of my plea bargain. I'm allowed to go as far as the flowerbeds. But not one step beyond."

"They've put sensors in the roses," Toby said. "You want to go see, Aunt Anne?"

"Careful you don't set off any alarms," Leon said, "or I'll be in the hoosegow."

"If you don't mind my asking, sir," Cardozo said, "what was the alleged offense?"

"Nothing alleged about it." On the table beside Leon's chair, the telephone made a soft electronic cooing sound. "I broke some interstate telephone laws that needed breaking."

"Seems kind of a severe penalty," Cardozo said.

Leon lifted the receiver. "Hello?" He covered the mouthpiece. "For you, Lieutenant. A lady by the name of diAngeli."

"Is there a phone where I could speak without disturbing you?"

"I'll show you." Anne led him to the phone in the hallway.

He lifted the receiver. "Tess?"

"It would be a lot easier to reach you if the precinct would stop garbling area codes. What are you doing in Connecticut?"

"Long story. What's happening?"

"I finally got through to my contact at Justice. We've located Mickey—he's been staying with his girlfriend at her place on the Upper West Side."

"Maybe part of the time. But he's also been using Catch Talbot's name and hanging out in a room at the Gibbs Clinic over on East Sixty-second."

"He denies knowing anything about Toby Talbot."

"You spoke to him?"

"On the phone."

"Maybe a face-to-face meeting with Toby will jog his memory."

"You've found Toby?"

"An hour ago."

"Thank God. How is he?"

Cardozo had to wonder if her concern was for the boy or for her own career. "Upset. He's been through a lot. But he's safe now and he'll make a good witness."

"What are you planning?"

"I want to bring Mickey in for questioning in connection with the kidnapping and the murders of Britta Bailey and Kyra Talbot."

A shocked silence whooshed out of the phone. "Why would Mickey have killed Kyra Talbot?"

"It could be he thought she was Anne. She had the kid, he wanted the kid. Where is he now?"

"He's with his girlfriend. They're seeing a movie."

"Better keep an eye on him till I can get a warrant for his arrest."

Tess sighed. "How soon can you get the warrant?"

"Couple of hours. Are you going to bed?"

"I wish. I've got work to do. You won't be waking me."

"Okay. I'll be in touch."

Mark looked at his watch. "Way past my bedtime. What about yours, Lieutenant?"

"Mine too."

Anne walked with them to the front door and opened it. Cool, moist air floated into the house.

"Thanks for your hospitality," Cardozo said.

"You're welcome, but there was no hospitality."

"Yes, there was." Mark kissed her. "Will you be okay?"

"Of course I'll be okay. Toby will take care of me. Won't you, Toby?"

Toby nodded. "Absolutely."

The men's footsteps crunched across gravel. Mark turned at the door of the Mercedes and waved. He looked tired but very fit, very handsome, and very smart. The combination was not unusual but the *verys* were.

Two car doors slammed. Anne and Toby stood a moment, watching the taillights vanish around the turn at the end of the drive.

He took her hand. "Aunt Anne—are you in bad trouble with Judge Bernheim?"

"I'm afraid so."

"Is there any way I can help?"

"That's sweet, but you mustn't worry about it. It'll straighten itself out. If your grampa will help."

"What do you need from Grampa?"

"His client's name."

"Which client?"

"Mathis v. *Doe."*

Somewhere out on the thruway, an automobile horn sent a Dopplered moan through the night.

"Aunt Anne, what do you know about Doe?"

"I know that during the last two years she spent some weekends up in the cabin. She drinks diet Dr Pepper and she likes hot dogs. She made a lot of phone calls. And she's kind of crazy."

"I'm going to the cabin," Toby said. "Maybe she left a clue."

"I'll be right up. Soon as I have a word with your grampa."

Leon looked up from the TV as she came in. "Why so glum?"

"Kyra's been murdered."

He flinched. "You're joking."

"I wish I were."

He picked up the remote and muted the TV. Silence caved in.

"My God," he whispered. "How did it happen?"

"We don't know yet. She was found dead in my bathtub."

"*Your* tub?"

"I took her place on the jury and she borrowed my apartment."

His eyes darted up. "Judge Bernheim mentioned you'd taken Kyra's place. She's furious."

"And she's throwing the book at me—she's talking a twenty-year jail term. I'm in a jam, Leon. And you can help me out."

"Of course. Anything."

"You were phoning Robert MacLeod and Gina Bernheim *before* MacLeod reached a decision in *Mathis* v. *Doe.* Would you tell me why?"

His eyes came around, blinking. "Was I?"

"The calls are on your phone bills."

He made swirls in his cup. "Well, I suppose I did communicate with Bob and Gina a little. A man's entitled to chat with old friends now and then."

"But these were conference calls."

Nothing happened in Leon's face. Not a twitch.

"Tell me the truth, Leon. Did you broker a deal? Judge Bernheim agreed to let Doe testify against Corey Lyle, under immunity. Two weeks later Judge MacLeod decided *Mathis* v. *Doe* in favor of Doe. I think it was a deal, and I think you put it together."

He shrugged wearily. "And what if I did facilitate an . . . understanding between Gina and Bob?"

"If the media got hold of the story, it would kill Bernheim's chances of ever getting appointed to the Supreme Court."

Leon drew back in the chair, defensive now. "What is it you want from me?"

"Doe's identity."

His face froze. "Why?"

"With Doe's identity, and those phone records, I can persuade Bernheim to drop charges against me."

"That wouldn't be ethical."

"Was it ethical to fix *Mathis* v. *Doe*?"

He had a wonderfully baffled expression, a look that said, *What are you trying to do to me?* "That was a judicial compromise. It's perfectly standard practice nowadays. Controversial, perhaps, and easily misunderstood—which is why court papers were sealed and Doe's identity is secret. And if you think I'm going to turn around and betray a client—not to mention two judicial colleagues—"

"But you know your client's using you! You didn't make obscene phone calls to your associates' daughters. Doe made them. She purposely imitated your voice and put the blame on you. Which is why Bob MacLeod has moved heaven and earth to hush those phone calls up. He doesn't want trails leading to the deal any more than you or Bernheim do."

Leon looked at her curiously. "What makes you think my client was a she?"

"*Judicial Abstracts* said so."

"And how do you know they're not just being politically correct with their pronouns?"

"Gender isn't the point." She realized she was shouting; she lowered her voice. "The point is, why on earth are you protecting a person who doesn't hesitate to sacrifice you?"

"If you'll give me a chance to speak, I'll tell you." Leon sipped the last of his hot milk. "*Mathis* v. *Doe* was a landmark decision. I was privileged to play a part in it, and in exchange, I don't mind suffering a few minor misdemeanor charges. *Mathis* will stand in case law for the next century. It's given me posterity. A place in legal history. So you see, my client owes me nothing. It's I who owe my client everything."

Leon amazed her. There he sat with his world crashing down around him, still absolutely sure of himself.

"As for those famous phone bills—" He pointed.

"Let's have a look. They're over there in the desk. Middle drawer."

She brought the bills.

"See?" His finger tapped the long-distance pages. "The last phone call to MacLeod and Bernheim was made three months ago—and Doe was decided a year ago. You're barking up the wrong tree."

It was his tone that pushed her over the edge. "When Kyra and I were young, you were abusive and withholding. You haven't changed. You go to the ends of the earth for crooked judges and sleazy clients. But in three quarters of a century you've never lifted a finger to help your children. *Not once.*"

"You haven't known me three quarters of a century. And I doubt your sister would have shared your opinion of me."

He was right, and she felt a shaming sting of jealousy. "But Kyra's gone—and you and I are the only people Toby has left. You've got to help me so that I can help him."

"It's better if his father helps him. A boy needs his father."

"He needs us too."

Leon shook his head. "Toby's father recommended Doe to me as a client. So I'm certainly not going to toss Doe to the wolves. It wouldn't be in Toby's interest to alienate his father."

She saw that Leon had turned all her arguments against her and boxed her in. She had never in her life won a disagreement with her father.

"I'm sorry, Annie, but you brought up the issue of Toby's welfare. And you're right: we've got to put it first."

She felt six years old; and a fool; and worthless. A

desolating thought whispered: *If my own father doesn't love me, no one ever will.* "And what about *my* welfare?" she cried. "I'm your daughter! Your own flesh and blood! Doesn't that mean *anything* to you?"

Leon did wounded innocence very well. "Young lady, I care a great deal about my own flesh and blood, far more than you apparently do. I've just lost a daughter whom I loved deeply. The prospect of life without her is pretty damned sad and dreary. Tonight I'd have been glad for a little compassion or condolence; but forgive me if I'm in no mood for this manipulative, self-serving caterwauling."

Anne tried to push the pressure out of her lungs. A door had slammed in a wall that she'd never even known was there. "Good night, Leon." She shoved the phone bills into her purse.

He picked up the remote. "Good night."

FORTY-FIVE

Saturday, September 28
12:15 A.M.

The sky was starless as Anne climbed the hill behind the house. There was no moon to light the way, but the lamp in the cabin window, gleaming faintly through twisted branches, guided her.

She stopped. She thought she heard someone whistling.

And then the sound was gone.

I was imagining it.

The spring on the screen door gave a full-throated, two-note squeak as she pulled it open. Toby and Max the cat sat inside on the floor, in a circle of light. Toby had emptied the desk drawers onto the carpet.

"Toby—what on earth are you doing?"

The cat skittered under the bed.

"Searching." Toby's expression was innocent and shrewd at the same time. "If Grandpa's client stayed here . . . she must have left *some* clue, right?"

"I'm sure she did." Emotional exhaustion dropped on Anne like a rain-soaked blanket. "And we'll look in the morning, okay?"

She went around to the three windows and drew the curtains, so old they were as crisp to the touch as newspaper. Her nose detected the sweetish smell of mildew and Lysol. The Lysol was new since her last visit.

Springs twanged as Toby jumped up on the bed to examine the wall of photographs. "Who are these people, Aunt Anne?"

"They're very important lawyers."

"You and Mom aren't lawyers." He unhooked the Christmas photograph and handed it to her. The yellowed paper backing was ripped and curling at one edge. "Who's the lady?"

She gazed at the faces—still young, still alive. It was like gazing down a hallway into the past, into a moment smelling of fir branches and cinnamon, a moment when Kyra and she still had half their presents to open and all their lives ahead of them.

"That was my mother—your grandmother. She was a beautiful person." She placed the photo back on its nail.

Toby was pushing buttons on the phone, his face radiant in concentration. "Maybe Grampa's client called her friends. If their numbers are still programmed, they could help us find her." But after a moment his expression turned to disappointment. "There's no one programmed."

Anne was thoughtful. "But we *do* know someone she was calling." She took the phone bills out of her pocket. She ran her eyes up and down the columns of numbers. She found the 427 number in Manhattan that wasn't Judge Bernheim's or Judge MacLeod's. The number that the client had called over and over from the cabin.

She took a ballpoint and drew two lines under it. "Now, if we only had a phone directory for New York . . ."

"That would take too long. And anyway, twenty-eight percent of New York City numbers are unlisted. But the telephone company has a reverse directory."

"That doesn't help us."

"I could try to hack into it. Grandpa bought me a computer and modem." Toby bounded across the room and whisked the dust cover off a small Macintosh.

"No." Anne shook her head. "This family's broken enough laws. We don't need the feds chasing you too. Go to bed."

"I'm not sleepy."

"Go to bed anyway." Anne kissed him on the forehead. "I love you."

Toby pretended to be asleep. He heard Anne's footsteps squeak across the cabin floor and then the soft slam of the screen door. He took his flashlight from under his pillow, crept out of bed, and picked up the telephone receiver. He found the underlined number on the phone bill and dialed.

A machine answered on the second ring. "Hi there. I welcome your call." It was a woman's voice, spookily depersonalized. "No one is home at present—please leave your name, your number, the date and time of your call, and I will get back to you as soon as possible."

At the beep, Toby identified himself. "This is Leon Brandsetter's assistant. I'm sorry to bother you, but—"

There was a click and a pickup. "Hello?" A man's voice.

"I'm trying to locate a person who's been calling your number from Leon Brandsetter's phone in Connecticut.

I don't know who she is, but she phoned you four times last July, twice last January, four times in September the year before last. I was hoping you could help me."

"Why do you need to know?"

"Because Mr. Brandsetter is paying for the calls—and a lot of other calls she made too—and I don't think that's fair."

The voice seemed surprised. "Are you sure this person phoned *my* number?"

"Positive. I have the phone company's records right here."

"Okay, I'll look into it. Where can I reach you?"

Toby shined the flashlight at the dial. "I'm at 203-555-1358."

"All right, I'll be in touch."

The man clicked off, and Toby realized he had forgotten to ask his name.

"Toby's not telling everything." Cardozo sat back in the passenger seat, hands laced behind his head, inhaling the luxurious smell of new leather. "It's almost as though he's trying to protect Mickey."

"I'm not surprised." Mark Wells handled the steering wheel almost absentmindedly, a driver with more important things on his mind than staying alive. "Kyra—God rest her soul—made a huge tactical mistake. She was determined to drive a wedge between Toby and his father. And except for two weeks a year when Catch has custody, she pretty well succeeded. The upshot is, Toby developed a hunger for father figures. Which is why he and I get along."

Cardozo looked over at Mark Wells. He didn't see a father figure. He saw an aging boy who could probably use a father of his own. "How's Anne going to handle all this?"

"That depends on what plans you have for her."

"I'm not a federal enforcer. The only thing I wanted from her was five minutes with Toby."

"Anne's handled impossibilities all her life. That father, that sister, that career. She had a disastrous two-year marriage. And she came sailing through all of it."

A pair of taillights loomed out of the night. Mark leaned on the horn. He swerved left to whip past a Chevy Escort that must have been going sixty.

"Could I borrow your cell phone again?" Cardozo said. "My judge may be home by now."

"Go right ahead."

Cardozo reached into the backseat and retrieved the phone. He tapped in the Brooklyn area code and Judge Tom Levin's home number. Over the years he had done the judge a few favors, and as a quid pro quo, the judge was fairly obliging about issuing warrants.

"Tom Levin."

"Tom—Vince. You were out. Hope it was a good party."

"Democratic Party fund-raiser. The pits. What's up?"

"The usual. I need a favor."

"I used the last blank warrant in the house. But my office has a few signed blanks—why don't you call them tomorrow?"

"I was hoping I could get it a little faster than that."

"That's the best I can do. Sorry. Someone will be in the office at eight."

It was better than nothing. "I appreciate it, Tom. Thanks." Cardozo broke the connection. He glanced toward Mark Wells. "Mind if I make one more call?"

"Be my guest."

Cardozo tapped in the number Catch Talbot had given him.

"Hello?" A deep, dispirited voice.

"Catch—Vince Cardozo. How are you holding up?"

"Worried."

"You can stop worrying. Toby's safe with his grandfather and his aunt."

Suddenly the voice had spine. And spark. "When can I see him?"

"Before you do that, why don't I take you out for a drink and fill you in on some details you should know. Where are you?"

"At the Plaza. Room 1717."

"I'll be by in a half hour to pick you up."

"Lieutenant—I know I've been a nuisance—thanks for putting up with me."

Mark Wells brought the car around to the 59th Street entrance of the Plaza. A storm front was blowing in from the Atlantic, and the windshield wipers were fighting back the drizzle.

"Thanks for the lift." Cardozo stepped out onto the sidewalk.

"My pleasure, Lieutenant. Regards to Catch."

A street musician was playing "Tenderly" on an out-of-tune sax. Cardozo bounded up the steps into the hotel lobby.

Tourists flowed around him, speaking a babble of German and Spanish and languages he couldn't even guess at. There was a logjam of baggage and Japanese at the desk and he decided to skip the formality of ringing ahead. He took the elevator up to the seventeenth floor and knocked on the door of 1717.

He heard the sound of a TV laugh track and footsteps and a chain sliding back. The door swung open. "You can put it—" Green eyes registered expectation quickly replaced by perplexity. "You're not room service."

"Sorry. I'm looking for Catch Talbot."

"Who?" He was a short, balding man in his mid-forties with big ears, and a bath towel around his middle. "You've got the wrong room."

"My mistake." Cardozo went to the house phone.

"Help you?" a voice offered.

"Could you tell me which room Catch Talbot is in?" He spelled the name.

"I'm sorry, sir, we have no Catch Talbot registered."

"You're sure?"

"Our last Talbot checked out this afternoon. Veronica."

Cardozo consulted his notebook. There was no mistaking his own handwriting: *C.T. Plaza Hotel 1717.* He took the elevator back to the lobby, dropped a quarter into one of the pay phones and dialed Talbot's cell phone.

Three rings. "Hello?"

"Catch—Vince. You did say Plaza Hotel, didn't you?"

"That's right. Seventeen-seventeen."

"Okay. There's been a slight delay. See you in a bit."

He hung up. He quickly flipped to the page in the notebook where he'd written another phone number: the room in Gibbs's clinic where the fake Catch Talbot had left his wig. And his answering machine rigged to forward calls.

Cardozo dropped another quarter into the slot and dialed. The call shunted through call-forwarding. There were three rings and then: "Hello?"

The voice was Catch Talbot's.

"Catch? Vince Cardozo again." And now, finally, he understood: the man pretending to be Catch Talbot *was* Catch Talbot. Not Mickey. Catch with his brown lenses in and his brown wig off to show his skin-cut. When he wanted to be his real self, he put the wig on, took the lenses out, and let himself be tailed to all the hospitals and precincts where a frantic father would be expected to go. "Sorry—my memory's Swiss cheese tonight. What did you say your room number is?"

"Seventeen-seventeen, Plaza Hotel. Where are you? Sounds noisy."

"Pay phone at Sixty-second. See you in a bit." Cardozo broke the connection.

Damn—I told him where Toby is!

He dialed Fairfield County directory assistance. They had a listing for Leon Brandsetter, but only the main house.

A man answered groggily on the seventh ring. "Hello?"

"Mr. Brandsetter? It's Vince Cardozo again. Are your daughter and grandson alone in that cabin?"

"Lieutenant, you're very hard to understand. Catch your breath and please speak clearly."

"Are your daughter and grandson alone in that cabin?"

"I should hope so."

"Get them out. They're in danger."

"Come now, there's no danger now that Corey's dead."

"It has nothing to do with Corey. It never did. It's Toby he wants. *Get them out of that cabin.*"

"Who are you talking about?"

"Catch Talbot is on his way. He's already killed two people—he'll kill more if he has to."

"Catch *Talbot*? You've been drinking."

"There isn't time to explain. He—"

The phone slammed down.

Cardozo redialed. Brandsetter didn't pick up. He tried Connecticut directory assistance, but they refused to give him the number of the cabin phone. "We can only honor state or federal authorization."

Cardozo saw that he had no choice. A woman in a gold evening dress jumped out of the way as he dashed toward the street.

FORTY-SIX

2:40 A.M.

Deep within the well of sleep, a synapse fired, triggering a chemical shudder along a nerve. Anne shot to the surface, bolt upright in a strange bed. Her senses groped for bearings in the unfamiliar silence.

Evergreen faintly scented the air. A breeze hissed silkily through pine branches. Somewhere nearby, a night creature rustled dead leaves. A twig snapped.

Closer, she heard Toby, asleep on his cot, breathing deeply and regularly. And closest of all, the thudding drum of her own heart, warning her: *do . . . not . . . relax . . .*

Something had signaled the sentinel in her. She reached back with her memory, trying to trap the echo of that warning. It had already become immeasurably faint.

Her eyes adjusted. She could make out the faint outline of windows with ringed curtains hanging from not-quite-level rods. The door with its pane of glass and its own tilting curtain.

She went to a window door and peered out. The sky had a dark, swirling look, like coffee that needed a stir. An owl hooted. A twig snapped, startling as the break of a bone.

Something flashed. She squinted. Sarabands of fireflies flickered in the trees.

She heard a sound that could have been a deer's footstep on dry brush. She opened the door a crack. Silence and pine-scented coolness flowed in. And then a branch twanged like a bowstring. Her heart jumped into her throat.

No more than fifteen feet away, under the branch of a yew tree beside the path, a sharp-edged light glinted.

Taking a carving knife from the sink drawer, she pushed open the door and the screen, slowly so they wouldn't squeak. She stepped into the woods and tiptoed down the slope.

A breeze stirred. A rush of tiny movements slapped the air. Something metallic clanked above her head. She peered up into the tangled branches and made out the silhouette of a bird feeder. A gleaming metal witch's hat of a roof capped the swaying cylinder.

A bird, she thought. *Only a night bird feeding.*

Smiling with relief at her own nervousness, she turned back toward the cabin.

A low, almost smoky male voice pronounced her name. "Anne."

She froze.

"Where's Toby?" A man stepped out of the shadow of the yew. His eyes were dark and his hair was shaved to the skull.

Instinctively, she blocked the path. "Who are you? What do you want with Toby?"

"Hasn't a man got a right to see his own son?"

"Catch?" She squinted. "Is that really you?"

"In person."

She recognized the voice. Gradually she recognized the planes and angles of her brother-in-law's face. But something had changed. More than the shaved head and the weight he'd put on. A vibration rippled off him, cold and alien and untrustworthy.

"Where's my son?"

"He's not here, Catch!" She raised her voice, calling now, warning Toby.

A forearm swung out and smashed her across the chest. The blow toppled her back into crackling rhododendron. His foot came down on her left hand.

With a slashing right-handed movement, she drove the knife at his leg.

He kicked the blade away, contemptuously. "Don't lie, or you'll get what Kyra got."

He jerked her up to her feet and pushed her forward. He yanked the screen door open. "Hey, Toby—Dad's here." Floorboards groaned under his weight. His eyes made a sweep of the cabin—the empty bed, the desk, the empty cot, the two chairs. "Come on, Tobester—hide-and-seek's over—allie-allie-in-free!"

Silence.

Catch peered into the shadow behind the refrigerator. Squinting, he had a face like a squeezed football. His hand flew out, big as a rat-trap, and caught the knob of the bathroom door. The door dissolved in a blizzard of splinters.

"What have you done with him?" He shattered a

glass shelf in the shower stall. *"What have you done with my son?"*

He turned, eyes narrowed to slits. He was holding a blue canister in his left hand, a handkerchief in his right. The two hands came together and a chemical stench ripped the air.

Anne wrenched to the side, but the damp rag caught her like a slap on the side of her face. A burning seared her eyes and sinuses. Her stomach contracted and she crumpled to one knee. Her good hand clawed at the edge of the desk for support.

"Leave her alone!" Toby shot out from the curtain beneath the stove. He was holding a narrow, three-foot shelf in both hands, baseball-bat style. Jars and cans avalanched to the floor. The cat flew across the room. "Don't touch her!"

"Easy there, kiddo." Catch backed off, but his hands were busy working the bottle into the cloth.

Toby swung. The shelf connected with the blue bottle, hurling it against the wall. A chemical wave pitched back and rocked the cabin.

Catch balled the handkerchief in his right fist. "Come on, Tobester—we're outta here."

"I'm not going with you! Not ever again!" Toby darted to the other side of the desk. "You're not my father anymore! You've turned into someone else!"

Catch vaulted the desk. Anne grabbed for his shoes. He slammed down and rolled to the floor, taking the desk lamp with him in an explosion of sparks. He lay unmoving.

Now there was only the light from the sixty-watt bulb in the bathroom.

Toby stepped back, chest heaving.

Catch pulled himself to his knees and slowly to standing. His eyes seemed dazed, unfocused. He let out a moan and raised the handkerchief high in his open hand and dove full-length at the boy, mashing the cloth into his face.

Toby sank his teeth into his father's hand.

Catch cried out and rocked backward, his neck corded with rage.

Toby swung. Catch grabbed the bat. His arm hooked the boy. Floorboards whined as weight seesawed across them. A chair went over and down.

Catch shoved the cloth into the boy's mouth. He booted the screen door open, dragging Toby with him.

Suddenly, as though he had come up against a glass wall, he stopped dead in his tracks.

A second man stood half-shadowed in the doorway. "Give me that kid."

Shielding Toby, Catch took a lurching step backward. The cat let out an ear-scorching get-off-my-tail screech.

"I want that kid." The light caught the man's shaven head. With a start, Anne recognized Mickey Williams. He was holding a narrow steel-bladed knife.

"No way." Catch pushed Toby behind him.

Mickey thrust the blade into Catch's throat. The force of the blow spun Catch around. He staggered two steps, sank to his knees, and pitched face-first to the straw mat.

Mickey lunged for Toby and clamped a hand over the boy's face.

"Leave him alone!" Anne cried.

"Sorry, lady. He knows all about me."

A stencil of light shot through the shattered screen door.

"What's all this ruckus?" It was Leon's voice, bad-tempered. "Tim and I could hear it clear down at the house."

The flashlight picked out two shapes—the boy twisting to free himself, the man holding him with bloodied hands.

"Mickey," Leon commanded, "let my grandson go."

But Mickey didn't let Toby go. "Damn it, Leon—why did you have to stick your nose in?"

The beam picked out the body on the floor. "What have we got here?" Leon took a step toward Catch.

"Hold it, Leon," Mickey commanded. "Right there. Nobody move."

"This man needs help."

"His own fault for being here. Everyone here has got to die. You too, Leon. This kid *knows.* I have to kill him and I can't leave witnesses."

"He *doesn't* know."

"You're wrong, Leon. The kid phoned me. He was asking about those calls. He *knows*!"

"Now, Mickey. Just listen to me." Leon's voice eased into crisis-management mode. "You're in the clear. I'm speaking as your attorney. *No one knows.*"

Anne was baffled. "If *Mickey's* your client—why did the abstract call him 'she'?"

"Who called me *what*?" Mickey shouted.

"Don't get your manhood in an uproar," Leon said. "It's a game the p.c. crowd plays with pronouns."

At that instant Anne understood: "You knew he was a murderer and you represented him *anyway*!"

"It wasn't murder!" Mickey screamed. "It was self-defense! I never harmed anyone! Those kids needed love—they wanted it! But Johnny saw me with a twelve-year-old girl and he said it was on his conscience. He wanted to confess so he could get to heaven. Fine,

Johnny Briar gets to heaven, and Mickey Williams is supposed to go back to jail and get castrated? No way, José."

"And Amalia?" Anne said. "Was that self-defense too?"

"That old bag died in her sleep. I didn't touch her."

"I knew it." Anne whirled to face her father. "You put together a deal and got him off."

"The government put the deal together," Leon said, "not me. They wanted Corey. They never wanted Mickey. Not then and not now."

"And meanwhile, Mickey was sitting here picking up messages from his answering machine." Anne saw it all now. "And then he saw those little girls in those photos on the wall and he just couldn't resist."

"You hear her, Leon? She knows!" Mickey's voice rose to a high, childish whine. Anne could see that you might mistake it over the phone for a woman's. "The kid and her both know!"

"It doesn't matter," Leon said. "No one can hurt you. I've taken the blame."

"Why, Leon?" Anne said. "Because Mickey threatened to expose the deal with MacLeod and Bernheim?"

"Don't you hear her, Leon? She knows *everything*!"

"She won't tell. Give him your word, Anne. You too, Toby."

"I can't take anyone's word, Leon—not even yours—we're talking about my *balls*!"

Anne's thoughts were racing. "Listen to me, Mickey. Those photographs on the wall are twenty years old." *God,* she prayed, *let him believe me!* "They're not girls anymore. You weren't committing an offense against minors."

"I was phoning grown women?" Mickey digested the

information. His eyes went hopefully to Leon. "Is that the truth? Am I in the clear?"

Anne flew at Mickey and slammed her knee up into his groin. He doubled over.

She pulled Toby free and ran. Tried to run. Mickey's hand caught her foot. His blade tore into her side. She slammed down onto one burning knee.

She saw her father's face, an ashen O of shock.

Toby dove at Mickey, clawing and screaming. Mickey's arm sideswiped the boy, lifting him like a newspaper, floating him back onto the bed.

Anne crawled toward the desk, scrabbling for cover. She had no strength to push Mickey away. He was on top of her now.

"Let her go!" Toby was hammering on Mickey's back. *"Let her go!"*

"Okay, Mr. Brandsetter." A state trooper stood in the open doorway. "You and your ankle radio are about two hundred yards off-base." He stepped into the cabin. "Say, what the hell's going on here?" His hand went to his semiautomatic. "Get up and drop that knife, fella."

Mickey raised the knife and charged.

FORTY-SEVEN

3:20 A.M.

Cardozo slammed his Honda to a stop in front of Leon Brandsetter's Connecticut home. The lights in the house were blazing. A state police car and a blue Pontiac with a federal license were parked in the driveway, and a Porsche was crazily angled on the lawn. Its New York State vanity license spelled BULLION, and its radial tires had chewed up two yards of Leon Brandsetter's carefully nurtured sod.

He heard voices. Screams. He ran around the side of the house. A voice called from the woods, shouting the name *Mickey.* Movement rippled the rhododendron leaves, and a knife-waving figure exploded through.

"Mickey," Cardozo said. "Mickey Williams."

Mickey jerked to a standstill. He gave Cardozo a puzzled, fumbling look.

"Why don't you drop the knife."

Mickey squinted. "Is that Vince?"

"Long time, hey? Drop the knife."

The knife arm stayed above Mickey's head, swaying like a branch in a slow wind. "If I drop the knife, you'll kill me."

"No one's going to kill you, Mickey."

"You're lying."

"I've never lied to you, Mickey. I'm not going to start now. Drop the knife."

"Oh, Christ," Mickey cried out. "Every chance I ever had I screwed up."

"We all screw up, Mickey. It's okay. Drop the knife."

One by one, the fingers of Mickey's right hand opened. The knife dropped like a spark through the night air. His left hand caught it and he made a fast, low dive.

The crown of his shaved head smashed into Cardozo's shoulder. They pitched over and hit the ground and tumbled and rolled. Mickey managed to thrust himself on top. He swung the knife up and slashed down.

Cardozo wrenched to the side. The blade missed his eye by a millimeter, then gouged a chunk out of his temple and dug into the lawn.

Cardozo freed his arm and scrambled a hand for his shoulder holster. He jerked the gun loose and thumbed the safety off. As the blade crunched into his upper arm, he twisted to the side and jammed the gun barrel against Mickey's ribs.

"Drop the knife."

The blade came arcing down. Cardozo pulled the trigger.

The force of the bullet kicked Mickey backward, eyes wide, mouth shaping a liquid red scream.

Two state troopers came crashing through the branches, guns drawn. Mickey lurched to his feet, took a staggering step toward them, and toppled forward onto the grass.

In the emergency room of the Bridgeport hospital, a male intern sewed ten stitches into Anne Bingham's side, and six into Cardozo's shoulder and three into his temple. He asked if they planned to be going far. "I wouldn't drive. You've both lost a little blood and you'll feel woozy."

Anne nodded, and Cardozo had the impression of a shocked and decent and deeply befuddled woman trying to make sense of events that were coming too fast and crazy to make any sense at all.

"We won't drive," Cardozo promised. He held the door to the waiting room.

"Drink liquids!" the intern shouted.

Anne bought two cups of Pepsi from a machine. She handed one to Cardozo. They sat there for a moment and then the moment was a minute.

"I keep trying to understand what happened," she said, "and why."

"Two of the oldest reasons in the world." Cardozo cracked his knuckles. "For Mickey, it was sex. For your sister and Catch, it was money."

"I never knew they were having money problems."

"They were, and they both saw Toby and the trust fund as the solution."

"But how could either of them have gotten hold of the money if they sneaked Toby out of the country?"

"Nowadays, New York allows divorced parents with custody to take their children out of state—even if the ex-spouse has visitation rights. Toby was free at age twelve to choose to live with either parent, so whoever had the boy got the money, no matter where they went. When Kyra got her jury summons, she decided the trial made a good cover to get Toby out of the country. She phoned Catch on the thirteenth, as soon as she was selected, and told him the custody hearing had to be postponed. Then she finagled you into taking her place on the jury."

"But Mark phoned on the seventeenth and told Catch the same thing."

"And by then, Catch was already in New York. Kyra's call had made him suspicious, and Mark's call made him more so. He'd come up with a plan of his own. He knew Mickey, and he knew the male Coreyite grooming code. Thanks to nine months of weight lifting and steroids, he was starting to bulk up. After Kyra's postponement, he shaved his head and bought brown contact lenses. In a generic way he looked like a Coreyite *trying* to look like Catch. In fact, verbally described, he looked like *Mickey* trying to look like Catch. Of course in person, with or without his wig, Catch was still recognizably Catch. Toby was probably surprised at the hair and the eyes and the weight, and he probably asked questions, but he still recognized his father. Which is why he went with him."

"Devious."

"Very. When Catch came to New York on the fourteenth, he had his secretary forward Seattle calls to his cell phone; he made phone charges at Seattle shops, so it seemed he was still in Seattle. The idea was to snatch Toby and make it seem the Coreyites had done it to hang the jury."

"That's why he phoned the threat to Kyra."

Cardozo nodded. "But he knew it was you on the phone. He'd already killed Kyra. The call was camouflage. It had nothing to do with the Coreyites except to throw suspicion on them."

Anne's eyes held a musing wonder. "My father said Catch recommended Mickey to him as a client."

Cardozo nodded. "A little over two years ago, when Mickey was living in Seattle, Catch represented him in a welfare suit, pro bono."

"But when did Mickey get involved with my father?"

"When Mickey's old cult buddy John Briar was dying. The Coreyites flew Mickey back East to keep vigil by the bedside. I don't know why Mickey killed Briar, but I don't buy that Corey Lyle hypnotized him."

"Tonight Mickey said he was afraid John Briar's dying words would implicate him in child molestation. That's why he killed him."

"Children." Cardozo sighed. "Mickey's addiction and nemesis. He'd already been found guilty of child abuse in Texas and he'd broken parole. When the Briar case hit the evening news, Texas sued New York for extradition. Catch put Mickey in touch with your father. By then the BATF was trying to hang the Briar killings on Corey Lyle. Leon put together a secret deal that gave Mickey a free hand."

Anne shook her head. There was enormous sadness in her eyes. "And then Mickey was caught making dirty phone calls from the cabin. He forced Leon to take the blame by threatening to expose the deal."

"What a tangle, hey?"

Anne gazed at Cardozo with an uncomplicated desire to understand. "But why did Mickey and Catch have to *kill*?"

"In Mickey's case it was fear. He got scared that the calls would be tied to him. He didn't want to be sent back to Texas."

"And what was Catch's reason?"

"Greed plus steroids triggering murderous rage. Sergeant Bailey saw him watching Toby at school. He couldn't risk her identifying him later. Same thing with your sister. After he forced her to write that note, she was a dead woman."

Anne was somber. "What about the evidence in the trial?"

"I wouldn't have too much confidence in it. The BATF tried for a decade to jail Corey Lyle, and they'd stopped caring how. I think they saw their chance two years ago, when Yolanda Lopez phoned to report that Mickey Williams had murdered John Briar. In twenty-four hours, the whiz kids at BATF worked out a scenario to nail Corey. They got Mickey to confess to two murders and claim Corey had put him up to it."

"But Mickey didn't kill Amalia."

Cardozo shook his head. "Amalia died a natural death six hours before her husband. The autopsy was suppressed."

"Then Yolanda was lying? Those tapes and those phone calls were fakes?"

"Let's just say someone fiddled with the evidence. Yolanda was doing her job, and it happened to involve a lot of phoning and a fair amount of lying."

"You believe that?"

Cardozo shrugged. "I'll lay you odds she doesn't serve a day in jail."

"But a federal agency wouldn't—"

"They might if they thought their budget was about to be cut."

"If only people didn't get so scared and greedy."

"The world would be a better place, and I'd be out of a job." Cardozo crushed his paper cup and dropped it into the trash basket. "Come on. We should get you back to your father's."

As they came out of the hospital, the headlights of early morning traffic were moving thinly down the street.

"Anne!" A solitary figure stood waving on the curb beside a Connecticut state trooper's car. "Lieutenant!"

Anne squinted. "It's my father." She broke into a run.

"Anne." Leon's eyes were frightened. "Are you all right?"

"All patched up."

"Thank God."

They embraced.

"Lieutenant." Leon leveled a rueful smile of greeting and held the car door. "Why don't you come with us and get some sleep? We have two guest rooms."

"Thanks, but I should be getting back to New York."

"Lieutenant," Anne said, "how can I ever thank you?"

"You just did."

She darted a kiss onto his cheek, then slid into the backseat.

Leon slid in beside her. "You're sure you're all right?"

"I'm sure."

The car moved slowly down the street.

"I've said some pretty inexcusable things to you." Leon placed his hand on hers. "I hope you know I didn't mean them."

"I know you didn't. And I've said some inexcusable things myself. Let's forgive each other and forget it."

"Agreed." His hand squeezed hers, then withdrew. "What's next on your agenda?"

"A little sleep—and then the big job. I have to make a home for Toby."

"You'll be a good mother."

"I hope."

"But a boy needs a father too." Leon's gaze came around slowly. "Mark Wells has been phoning. He's phoned three times since you went into emergency."

"Really?"

"Can't blame him. He's worried about you. You should call him back."

She nodded. "I will."

"You know, Anne, of all the men in your life—"

"Come on, there haven't been that many."

"But of them all, I think I've always liked Mark the most."

She was thoughtful. "So have I."

On Christmas morning fifteen months later, a Maine spruce tree glowed in the living room of a Murray Hill town house. Anne sat on the sofa, peeling the green-and-gold wrapping off a flat package the size of a framed photograph.

She peered at the beautifully penned lettering. " '*Whereas Mr. and Mrs. Mark Wells, hereinafter referred to as the parties of the first part. . . .*' What in the world is this?"

"It looks like a contract." Mark slipped on his glasses and studied it. "A five-year-renewal with option to extend."

"Renewal of what?"

"Of our family." Toby dropped onto the sofa between them. "To make sure we stay together." He tipped back his French Culinary Institute baseball cap. "I've already signed, see?"

"I'll sign on." Mark scrawled a signature above Toby's and passed his ballpoint to Anne.

"I don't know." She smiled. "Shouldn't I consult a lawyer?"

"Your lawyer," Mark said, "advises you to grab a good deal while you have the chance."

Anne signed.

Toby hugged them both, then went back to the tree and began searching among the presents.

"Look at that kid," Mark said softly. "Who'd ever guess what he lived through a year ago?"

"He's got guts," Anne said. "And a lot of sense."

"And you've done a great job."

"No. We've all done a great job."

"Hey—Aunt Anne—Uncle Mark—look what Lieutenant Cardozo gave me!" Toby came running across the room, waving a small black book with silver lettering: "A police officer's handbook! And he signed it!"